Leave It to the March Sisters

ALSO BY ANNIE SERENO

Blame It on the Brontës

Leave It to the March Sisters

ANNIE SERENO

FOREVER

New York Boston

Copyright © 2023 by Annie Sereno

Cover design and illustration by Sarah Congdon
Cover copyright © 2023 by Hachette Book Group, Inc.

Forever
Hachette Book Group
1290 Avenue of the Americas, New York, NY 10104
read-forever.com
twitter.com/readforeverpub

First Edition: May 2023

Forever is an imprint of Grand Central Publishing. The Forever name and logo are trademarks of Hachette Book Group, Inc.

The publisher is not responsible for websites (or their content) that are not owned by the publisher.

The Hachette Speakers Bureau provides a wide range of authors for speaking events. To find out more, go to www.hachettespeakersbureau.com or call (866) 376-6591.

Epigraphs on pages 65, 75, 116, 136, 175, 304, and 365 are from the 2019 film *Little Women*, screen adaptation by Greta Gerwig and Sarah Polley.

Library of Congress Cataloging-in-Publication Data

Names: Sereno, Annie, author.
Title: Leave it to the March sisters / Annie Sereno.
Description: First Edition. | New York ; Boston : Forever, 2023.
Identifiers: LCCN 2022057831 | ISBN 9781538721469 (trade paperback) |
    ISBN 9781538721445 (ebook)
Subjects: LCGFT: Romance fiction.
Classification: LCC PS3619.E743 L43 2023 | DDC 813/.6--dc23/eng/20221208
LC record available at https://lccn.loc.gov/2022057831

ISBN: 978-1-5387-2146-9 (trade paperback); 978-1-5387-2144-5 (ebook)

Printed in the United States of America

LSC-C

Printing 1, 2023

To my family, with love and appreciation

I'm not afraid of storms, for I'm learning how to sail my ship.
—AMY MARCH, *LITTLE WOMEN*

CHAPTER ONE

*I'm so sick of people saying that love
is all a woman is fit for.*
—JO MARCH, *LITTLE WOMEN*

*L*ooking backward and forward and every which way, Amy had to admit that dating Banana Brad had marked a new low in her love life. Still, she wouldn't trade her brief relationship with the guy who wore humongous fruit costumes in public for someone less...memorable. Because now she was ready for anything. Like Derek, her latest boyfriend, greeting her at the door of their apartment dressed in nothing but tighty-whities. And a sliver of pepperoni stuck to his right knee. All right. No biggie. After a long day of faculty meetings and budget reviews, she was up for a few laughs.

"How's it going?" she asked him.

"I've met someone," he said as eagerly as if he'd spent the last eight hours without human contact. Which was usually the case. Seriously, it was like coming home to a lonesome puppy. Yesterday, he had babbled on and on about Manet and his water lily paintings before she'd even pulled the key out of the lock. Monet, *not Manet*, she'd mumbled under her breath. Monet *is the artist who painted water lilies.*

"Hope you're hungry," she said. "I've got takeout."

He popped the pepperoni from his knee into his mouth. "You're not listening."

"Sure I am."

Amy breezed by him and dropped the China Castle bag onto the kitchen counter. Spending an hour in the Honda service station, only to be told that her Civic was "a goner," required an immediate infusion of wine. She looked in the refrigerator, its shelves crowded with cartons of restaurant leftovers. "Where's the bottle of merlot?"

Derek leaned against the doorway, arms folded across his bare chest. "We drank it."

"We did?" *One glass, flat on her ass,* described her tolerance for alcohol. "I don't remember. Though I guess oblivion is the price of inebriation."

"Another famous quote I'm supposed to know, professor?"

"What? No. No biggie. I was just—"

"Nothing's a big deal to you, is it?"

"Let's see," she said, closing the refrigerator. "Unreliable cars. The slow, agonizing death of print journalism. The gunky glue on labels that sticks to things forever."

"Haha. Very funny."

She was going to tell him to keep his shirt on, but he wasn't wearing one. "I'll open the chardonnay. Want some?"

"It's all yours."

His undies were in a bunch about something, but where the heck was the corkscrew? Amy checked under the dirty dishes in the sink and peeked into a box with a half-eaten pepperoni pizza inside. Derek routinely left things in odd places to, as he put it, exercise his creativity. The only items in the recycling bin were a cream-of-mushroom-soup can and the empty bottle of merlot they had presumably drunk. Finally, she found the corkscrew beneath yesterday's pile of mail. A copy of the literary journal *The Rustic Review,* addressed to Dr. Amy Marsden, was on top of it. She'd been a subscriber ever since they published one of her sister's short stories last year.

She opened the journal and read aloud from the table of contents. "'Escarpment' by Jo Marsden."

Derek grumbled a comment and snapped the waistband of his briefs.

"It's not my fault if you ran out of clothes," she said. "It was your turn to do laundry."

"Don't change the subject."

"There's a subject?"

She rubbed her forehead. The apartment always reeked of varnish and wet rags, giving her a perpetual headache. Like his idol, Jackson Pollock, Derek dripped paint onto huge canvases—but from interesting angles, he had assured her when he showed her his work for the first time. All of them were untitled, a lack of commitment she applauded, if not necessarily the paintings themselves. You either *got* Pollock—and Derek—or you didn't, she supposed.

"Yeah, there's a subject," he said. "See? I told you you weren't listening."

Wine would have to wait. He obviously needed her un-inebriated attention. If that was an actual word. Though it should be. And why were boyfriends so fricking high-maintenance?

Derek turned on his heel and walked out of the kitchen. Crouching over *Untitled No. 9* in the middle of the living room floor, he slowly poured a stream of tomato-red paint in the upper left-hand corner. Lifting heavy cans had done wonders for his muscles. What his labors had done for the art world had yet to be revealed.

Amy grabbed a fork and a carton from the China Castle bag, and followed him to the living room to check out his latest creation. Blue violet was her favorite color, but she had yet to see him use it. She rummaged through her mind for a constructive criticism. "The streak of green on the bottom balances the composition," she offered.

"I've met someone."

The words sounded familiar. Had he said this already?

"How'd you meet anyone? You never leave the apartment."

"She comes here." Derek straightened up and regarded the canvas. "I think I'll call this one *Jaycee*."

"The first painting you ever title and it's the name of our pizza-delivery girl?"

"You're the chair of an entire history department. You figure it out."

"*English* department," she said, correcting him. "Figure what out?"

He fixed her with his dark, hooded eyes as she shoved forkfuls of lo mein into her mouth—and spit them right back into the carton.

Jaycee Chambers, whose hair was cut to within an inch of its life, like Derek's. Whose compact, sturdy body in its Marconi's Pizza uniform was a perfect match for his.

Derek threw globs of yellow paint onto the canvas and whistled. In the six months of their relationship, Amy had never heard him whistle. What kind of name was Derek Demerest, anyway? It was what a character in a porn movie would be called. Or a soap opera. Which this day was starting to feel like.

"I should have guessed," she said, closing the flaps of the lo mein carton. "Your stuff has been looking like pizzas lately." Not to mention that they were down to having sex about every two weeks.

"My work is art, not *stuff*," he said with a sniff.

"How long has it been going on between you two?"

He shrugged. Since he never left the house, she assumed his days bled into one another like the paint on his canvases.

"Do you have sex with her here?" she asked.

"Between deliveries."

As recently as the pepperoni pizza in the box on the kitchen counter. And the empty bottle of merlot.

"On our bed?"

"*My* bed," Derek reminded her.

His bed in his apartment.

Amy had agreed to move into his place when her apartment building was sold and reconfigured into a mental health clinic. The boyfriend's turf—never a good idea. But she didn't have to sign a lease. She could pick up and leave whenever she wanted. And it was ideal. Affordable, conveniently located near Laurel's shops and restaurants, and a short commute to her job at Southern Illinois College.

"This is the worst time for me to move, Derek. The fall semester begins in two weeks." Her budding headache was in full bloom.

He poured a wide white stripe across the top of the canvas in reply.

"Any chance *you* can move?" she asked.

"No way. I need these big windows for the light."

So do I, she would have said—if she wanted to hear his

spiel about how he was the professional artist and she a mere amateur.

"Finding an apartment in August is impossible." Students would have snatched up everything in Rosewood, the college town, already. And Laurel, for all its recent gentrification, had few rental options. "I'll pay you double for the room where we keep our art supplies. I'll sleep on the futon."

"No can do. Jaycee's lease ends soon, and she'll be moving in."

"Gee. You guys didn't waste any time."

Tears formed in her eyes from the paint fumes. Amy Marsden did *not* cry over breakups. Ever. On the bright side, *Untitled No. 9—Jaycee*—looked much better blurry. "You might have told me sooner."

"Yeah. S'pose so."

"Well? Why didn't you?"

Derek looked down at his body as if trying to remember where he'd left his clothes. All over the bedroom floor. Where he'd flung them in horny haste to screw Jaycee before Amy came home. "Sooner. Later. What difference does it make?" he said. "Nothing lasts forever."

Amy opened her mouth but no words came out. Her mind went blank. She was acutely aware, however, that her long, blond curls were spiraling from the August humidity. Her chest was flattened unflatteringly by the Jil Sander suit she had splurged on when she was promoted to chair. Derek squinted at her, probably wondering, as she was, what had brought a painter and a professor together in the first place.

A shrill laugh nearly escaped her. Two people sharing their passion for art! They'd be both muse and mentor to each other!

"The way I see it," he said, "you act like you can take me or leave me. So I took Jaycee."

Right about now, when a relationship was heading due south, Amy would let loose a zinger or two. Witty repartee was her specialty, sharpened by years of growing up with her sister, Jo, and perfected by years of ending relationships. She clutched at her throat with one hand but couldn't pull even a syllable out— or dump the lo mein onto the painting with the other hand.

"Anyway, no biggie," Derek said, swirling an orange *J* in the middle of the canvas. "And you can have the coffeemaker. Jaycee's got a brand-new one."

And stop obsessing over her speechless, zinger-free reaction earlier.

She reviewed the syllabi for her fall semester courses—Canadian Short Fiction, Masters of the Russian Short Story, and Microfiction. Because of her innovative curriculum, her classes typically had waiting lists. But Athena Murphy-Kent, the latest addition to the English Department, was the star teacher of the faculty.

Amy wished that she had Athena's theatrical talent to make fictional characters come alive for her students. And—she had to hand it to him—the chutzpah of her pre-Derek boyfriend, Banana Brad. An aspiring actor, he had decided that dressing as various giant fruits was his *brand*. In a competitive job market, he needed to stand out from the crowd, he'd explained. In the short time they were together, he'd landed a few gigs at food fairs and supermarkets, a couple of children's plays, and—go figure—a banking executive's retirement party. (But alas, no Fruit of the Loom commercials.) He attracted a loyal, if small, following to his YouTube videos in which he hectored grocery shoppers to *pump up* their potassium. Even after an irate senior citizen assaulted the stem of his apple, Brad soldiered on.

Originality, ambition, and courage in the face of a swinging handbag—what wasn't to like? Until one night, he writhed on Amy's bed, in full banana mode, moaning, "Peel me, babe. Peel me raw."

"It's time you took the show on the road, Brad."

"Haven't you heard of method acting?"

"Haven't you heard of therapy?"

"I'm committed."

Since Derek monopolized the living room most of the day, Amy stayed in her campus office till early evening. They exchanged grunts when they passed each other on the way to their bedrooms or the bathroom. But she refused to eat in a kitchen where a growing stack of empty Marconi's Pizza cartons on the counter advertised Jaycee's presence.

One a day. Like vitamins. She kept count.

"Thorne wondered why you've been eating here all week," Athena said over lunch in As You Like It Café, Laurel's most popular restaurant. With its beamed ceiling, pendant lamps hanging from ropes, and brick walls lined with antique hutches, the café was reminiscent of Tudor England. On winter days, the oak tables around the central stone hearth were coveted spots. "What should I tell my hubster?"

"That I got kicked to the curb." Amy moaned with pleasure as she bit into a panini stuffed with grilled portobello mushrooms and roasted red peppers and eggplant. "And that he makes the best sandwiches in the universe."

"I won't mention the pizza-delivery girl; otherwise, he'll give Derek a hard time. You know Thorne. Café proprietor and knight in shining armor rolled into one." Athena licked mayonnaise off her thumb. "And, I might add, a gorgeous specimen of manhood."

If Amy didn't like Athena so much, she might envy her happiness with her knight, the only person in the world she let call her *Thena*. "Thorne's all right. In a tall, athletic, wheat-gold-hair kind of way," Amy teased her.

"And don't forget bone structure to die for."

"Your looks are to die for, too."

Tall and voluptuous, with dark curls cascading around her face, Athena was both girlishly cute and womanly sensual.

"We do make a handsome pair if I don't say so myself," Athena said. "No offense, but you and Derek were a classic case of beauty and the beast."

"He might have looked furtive, like he'd stolen your money, but he had sex appeal."

"Was sex the main attraction?"

"Yeah. And my fantasy that we'd inspire each other's art."

They looked at each other for a few seconds and then cracked up. The other café patrons smiled, familiar with Athena's hearty laugh.

"Come to think of it," Athena said, "it's Thorne's fault you were living in Derek's place to begin with. He campaigned really hard for a mental health clinic in Laurel. Your apartment building was reconstructed because there weren't sufficient funds to build a new one."

"An admirable cause worth sacrificing for." Amy reached across the table to clasp Athena's hand. "How do you two manage, living with his half brother?"

"Just fine. We converted the greenhouse in the backyard into a cottage so Robin has privacy. And so do we."

"Is he responding well to the new schizophrenia medication?"

"Remarkably well."

As Amy polished off the panini, Athena watched, wide-eyed. She pointed to a table where stout guys in overalls and John Deere caps were devouring enormous cinnamon buns. "Your appetite gives the bachelor farmers a run for their money."

"They are so adorable. All shy and awkward like teenage boys."

"Rock their world and date one of them."

"No way. I'm going dateless for the foreseeable future. And the unforeseeable."

"Word around town is they're good marriage material," Athena said with a playful wink.

"Farmer's wife." Amy stared at the ceiling, trying the notion on for size. "Nah. Don't see that happening."

"Ever wish you were back in Chicago?"

"Only when I can't get takeout in the middle of the night. Or have to drive all the way to St. Louis to visit the art museum."

"*How* long did you live there?"

"From BA to PhD at the University of Chicago."

Twelve years of benefitting from all the social, educational, and cultural riches the city offered. Four *more* years of enjoying a rewarding academic position and a healthy bank account. Advantages Jo had *not* had the benefit of. Thanks to Amy. She had every intention of making it up to her sister. She just hadn't figured out how yet.

Slightly nauseous, Amy pushed her plate away. "I'm really in a jam, Athena. Classes start soon. If I don't get an apartment, like, yesterday, I'll be sleeping in my office and showering at the gym."

"I told you, come live with us. We've got extra rooms. You can use one as an art studio."

"Tempting, but strictly speaking, I'm your boss. The other professors already think I give you preferential treatment as my friend. If I moved in with you..."

Athena grinned. "I *am* the chair's pet. But I have an idea. Remember I told you my mother is a real estate agent? If Lydia can't find you a place, nobody can."

Amy read the business card that Athena handed to her. "Your mother's last name is Moretti?"

"She and her partner, Ricki, traded names when they got married. And here Thorne and I thought we were cutting-edge when we hyphenated ours."

The Gallaghers, the Murphy-Kents, the Moretti-Murphys—everywhere Amy looked, couples found solutions. Even Derek and Jaycee had solved the problem of a surplus coffeemaker.

Amy Marsden and Theo Sinclair were never a couple. Solving *their* problem should have been possible. But when a friendship is tested to the limit...

Nothing lasts forever.

Except gunky glue on labels.

Amy gathered her satchel and bike helmet. With the Civic officially dead and on its way to the boneyard—where her last two cars had gone to meet their Maker—she'd decided to try cycling as a means of transportation.

"Wanna ride on my handlebars and pretend you're ten years old again?" she asked Athena. Her adult tricycle was squat with thick tires and a basket in back to hold her belongings and groceries. Safe. Practical. Something a ten-year-old wouldn't be caught dead on.

"Sounds like fun, but I'll take a rain check. I need a refill."

"Of iced tea?"

Athena waved to Thorne, pouring coffee for a table of middle-aged couples across the room. "Of my handsome hunk of a husband."

CHAPTER THREE

I am lonely sometimes, but I dare say
it's good for me.
—JO MARCH, *LITTLE WOMEN*

Thanks to Lydia's no-nonsense professionalism, Amy saw every available rental in Laurel and Rosewood. But the apartments were either unfurnished, too shabby, or located on a noisy street. The few houses she considered were newly renovated and worth investing in furniture for, but she had neither the time nor inclination to maintain an entire property.

The search was exhaustive, exhausting, and futile. With one day left before Jaycee was to move in, and with Amy's stress peaking, Lydia texted her.

New Laurel listing. Immediate occupancy. Second floor of house, no upkeep required. Interested?

Yes!

Can you meet me there now?

I'm on my way, Amy replied, adding the address Lydia had texted to her contact info.

"I should have asked if you were allergic to cats," Lydia said when they met on the porch of the Craftsman-style house.

Thankfully, Amy wasn't, because a half dozen cats had

colonized the first floor where the owner lived. They draped their languorous bodies over the backs of the sofa and armchairs, huddled beneath end tables, and posed proudly on the rippled hill of toilet paper below the empty roll in the powder room.

"A pet sitter is taking care of them while the owner is traveling," Lydia said. "And there's a dog being boarded, I believe. Do you mind living with so many animals?"

"Not at all. And this is too nice to pass up."

The entire second floor would be Amy's, but she had to share the kitchen, a minor inconvenience since she rarely cooked. The house was located a comfortable biking distance from town and the college, making *any* inconvenience worth it.

"I may be able to negotiate a month-to-month rental," Lydia said.

"Thanks, but I prefer the security of a year's lease."

"Let's get the papers signed, then," Lydia said, handing her keys to the private entrance accessed by stairs at the back of the house.

As soon as Amy returned to Derek's apartment, she arranged for a U-Haul van rental and started packing her belongings. She carefully placed her collection of ferns in the plastic crates she'd moved them in with.

"The fuzzy one isn't looking too good," Derek said from the doorway of the spare room. The first words he'd spoken to her in days. The first time he'd commented on her plants, ever. "I kinda like it, though."

"Want it?"

"Sure. I'll make it the subject of my next painting."

The ailing squirrel's foot fern seemed to shrink in its pot. And since when did his paintings have subjects?

"Hey, you know what?" he said. "Jaycee's moving in tomorrow. Once she unloads her things from the pizza-delivery van, you can fill it with yours. Save you bucks on the U-Haul."

Like relays. Girlfriend out, girlfriend in.

"You think she'd mind?" Amy had enough trouble keeping cars alive. No use risking a U-Haul van's life if she didn't have to.

Derek's fingers flew over the phone as he texted Jaycee. "She's cool. But she has to drive you to your new place 'cause she's responsible for the vehicle."

"Fine with me."

The next morning, she and Derek helped Jaycee bring in her suitcases, guitar, and two boxes marked CRAP I DON'T NEED, BUT YOU NEVER KNOW. Jaycee walked over to the pile of Amy's belongings and picked up a canvas. "Shit. I didn't know you painted too."

Still Life With ? Amy called the unfinished painting. She'd fill in the rest of the title once she decided what else to add to the basket of pansies and three lemons on a wooden table.

"A college professor. And an artist. Wow." Jaycee punctuated each phrase with a crack of her gum.

Amy started to modestly protest that she didn't *quite* consider herself an artist yet. Her formal training had been inconsistent, her career took priority, there were only so many hours in a day, and—

"It's not art," Derek said. "It's like the stuff hanging in hotel rooms."

And this from the guy who, unlike Amy, hadn't exhibited a single painting in a single art show in his life. Who'd had no formal training whatsoever.

"*I* think it's pretty," Jaycee said.

"Exactly," he said. "*Pretty.*"

Amy worked her jaw as if *she* were chewing gum, biting back all the Jo-worthy things she wanted to say. But she was thirty-four years old and a serious professional woman. Soon enough, Derek and his "raw genius paintings"—his assessment, not anybody else's—would be in the rearview mirror.

In no time at all, the three of them had loaded Amy's possessions, including her bike, onto the Marconi's Pizza van. Derek had the compunction to look sheepish, twirling the end of one of Amy's long curls. A yellow splotch on his thumb gave her the teensiest twinge. His hands were good for something besides smearing paint on a canvas.

"Guess this is it," he said, looking off into the distance as if he'd lost something but couldn't remember what. Like the past six months.

"Guess so," Amy said.

"Guess I'll see you around."

Not if there's a God in heaven.

"Sure you don't need my help moving in?" he asked. Considering he rarely left the apartment, this was contrition indeed.

"Positive," she said, feeling a tad guilty for drawing mustaches on the mannequin heads with a black Magic Marker last night. But only a tad.

"Guess we oughta go," Jaycee said, jingling the van keys.

The ride would be mercifully brief. Amy was moving to Laurel's oldest neighborhood, a couple of miles from the center of town. The avenues were lined with charming Queen Anne and Victorian homes beneath mature oaks and sycamores. Athena and Thorne living nearby was an added attraction. When all was said and done, this split from Derek was long overdue. Six months was a relationship record she was glad to break.

After weeks of overcast skies and oppressive humidity, the day was refreshingly cool and the sky bright blue and cloudless. "Nice weather for a change," Amy said.

"Sure is," Jaycee said.

"Thanks for helping me move."

"S'okay. How come you don't have a car?"

"It died. I don't mind cycling, though. It's great exercise, and it reduces my carbon footprint."

Jaycee cracked her gum with a frown. "Carbon what?"

"Gaseous emissions? The eroding ozone layer?"

"Global warming shit. I hear ya."

Buzz cut aside, Jaycee's lush lashes, delicate nose and chin, and enticingly curved lips lent her a piquant beauty. If Amy still painted portraits, she'd paint hers.

"I don't have any hard feelings about this, Jaycee. I really don't."

"I wanted Derek to tell you when we first started...you know. Doing it. But he's a total chickenshit."

Amy swallowed a laugh. *Chickenshit No. 9.* Now *that* would be a good title for his latest painting.

"I'm moving in with him to save money," Jaycee said, yielding to a truck filled with hay bales. "It's not like we're serious. He's a lot older than me, and he paints, I mean, *all* the time."

"Nice work if you can get it," Amy murmured. Thanks to a trust fund, the amount of which he'd never disclosed to her, Derek had never held a job in his life.

"I'm not committing to *anyone* until I get my shit together," Jaycee said.

Talking about Derek had launched another gum-cracking spree. Amy spoke above the noise to give directions to her new address—and had a delicious image of Derek pouring paint onto the canvas of *Chickenshit No. 9*, only to have his concentration interrupted by the sound of gum popping.

The two graceful river birches framing the house seemed to nod their welcome in the light breeze as Jaycee pulled up to the curb. They unloaded the van, carrying everything up the brick pathway on the side of the house. The stairs to the private back entrance were narrow, but the door opened to a wide hallway where they stacked Amy's things. The bike fit inside the back-yard shed with plenty of room to spare. The owner shouldn't mind her parking it there.

"I can help unpack your stuff," Jaycee offered.

"No thanks. You've done more than enough already."

The double meaning of her words was lost on Jaycee, who cracked her gum with every step down the pathway to the street.

"Can I take a peek inside before I go?" Jaycee said.

"Sure."

They climbed the porch steps and peered into the large front window. A marmalade cat stared at them from its perch on the windowsill. Amy stuck her tongue out like a brat. It blinked one eye, as if it were winking at her.

"What's the deal with all the cats?" Jaycee asked.

Amy grinned. "Squatters."

"Wonder who the owner is."

"No idea. I haven't met them yet."

Jaycee's phone chimed and she checked the text message. "My boss, Lando, says I've got to get the van back soon."

"Sorry if I held you up."

Apologizing. To the girl who, you know, *did it* with Derek.

Jaycee pulled a slip of paper from her jeans pocket and handed it to her. "Here. Maybe you can use this."

"A Marconi's Pizza coupon?"

"You always tipped me well. I owe you one."

~⌒◯

The first clue Amy had that the owner of the house might be un-usual was the behavior of the cats. They formed a line at the bottom of the stairs whenever she went back and forth to the kitchen, though they never ventured to the second floor themselves. Their heads moved in unison as she ate, following the path of food to her mouth or a cup to her lips. The pet sitter managed to show up whenever Amy ran errands or dropped in at her college office, so she hadn't had a chance to ask how freaked out she should be.

Oddly too, there were no photographs or personal effects in the living room, nothing stuck on the refrigerator with a magnet. She preferred the cozy shabbiness of the mismatched furniture in her rooms to the spare décor of the first floor, courtesy mostly of IKEA. If she had the nerve—or rudeness—to snoop in closed rooms and closets, she might have had a shot at guessing the owner's gender or age.

"Health foodie, huh?" she asked the marmalade cat, looking at containers of nuts, dried beans, and grains in the pantry.

It blinked its one good eye. She felt like a douche for having stuck her tongue out at a half-blind cat the day she moved in. "Any idea when my landlord or landlady is coming back?"

The cat shrugged and sauntered away.

"Just checking," she called out. "It's not like I'm lonesome or anything."

With a spacious bedroom, large bathroom, and a spare room to use as a study and art studio, Amy had as much living space as she needed. By the time Sunday rolled around, she was organized and ready for anything the new semester, beginning tomorrow, would throw at her.

And not a moment too soon. She had initiated enough conversations with the cats that they were on the verge of talking back. Athena was *busier than stink* herself, preparing for classes, and getting ahold of Jo had been hard lately since she'd gone camping with friends.

Settled in my new place, Amy texted her.

Took you long enough to dump a-hole Derek, Jo answered three hours later, unenlightened about who dumped whom.

House is great but cats everywhere. Reminds me of Theo's menagerie.

Oh yeah. The Ladue Zoo we called it.

Amy was eleven and Jo thirteen when their father died. Two years later, their mother remarried a wealthy lawyer, and they moved from their mobile home in Normal, Illinois, to a stately manor in Ladue, an exclusive St. Louis suburb. The Sinclairs were their closest neighbors—*next door* having a different meaning when a house was nestled in acreage—and only-child Theo had grown up accustomed to the finest in everything.

It took a while for Amy and Jo to adjust, particularly in the private school where their first names, thanks to their mother's fondness for Louisa May Alcott's novel *Little Women*, drew unwanted attention. *Want to buy some limes, Amy?* the other students would tease. *Have you burned your dress and sister's hair yet, Jo?* They'd protest that their last name was Marsden, not March, to no avail. Luckily, none of their classmates made the connection between Theo Sinclair and the character of Theodore Laurence—Laurie—in the book.

Heard from him lately? Amy texted Jo.

Who?

Theo. Who else?

Nope.

Ever going to tell me what you guys fought about?

Never ever.

Sounds passionate enough to be a lovers' quarrel. Amy added a laughing-face emoji to her comment.

Yuck. As if. Don't even. Jo taught high school English in Seattle and occasionally slipped into teenage-speak.

The sisters had been best friends with Theo since their early teens. Tomboy Jo used to joke that she was the brother he never had. The trio had squabbled and made up too many times to count. But an argument last year between Jo and Theo had sent them to opposite sides of the boxing ring—and kept them there. As for Amy and Theo...there wasn't a referee in the world who could resolve their differences. Sporadic FaceTime calls with Jo, texts, emails, and one random encounter had been the extent of their contact the past five years.

Amy clicked on her laptop picture file and opened her favorite photo of Theo. He was wearing shorts and a one-size-too-small T-shirt, printed with a picture of the Harbour Bridge in Sydney, Australia. His wavy hair—raw umber was the best description of its rich brown color—grazed his shoulders. His beard was just this side of scruffy, his legs just this side of tree trunks. Amy zoomed in on his smile bracketed by deep dimples, zooming out as she exhaled.

Bet Theo's traveling again, she texted.

Who gives a hoot? Jo replied, adding a rolling-eyes emoji.

Just wondering.

Leave it to Amy to moon over a high-school crush.

Jo, looking in Amy's closet for a sweater one day, had found her stash of drawings that chronicled her secret love. Theo rowing in a lake. Theo bent in concentration over a model airplane. Theo laughing at Jo's antics. The dimpled smile. Eyes like no one else's eyes. Jo had never taken what she called Amy's "puppy love" for Theo very seriously—to Amy's enormous relief.

Leave it to Jo to jump to conclusions, Amy wrote back.

Leave it to was the sisters' affectionate shorthand for expressing everything from sympathy to disapproval.

What do you think of my latest story? Jo texted.

Loved it. Might add it to my syllabus next semester.

If you mainstream me, I'll thwack you on the head like Bob Ross thwacked paintbrushes on trash cans.

Haha!

That was Jo in a nutshell—upstream all the way. Hiding her pride with bluster. Making her way in the literary world against all odds. With a little help from her little sister.

Btw, did you get the check for your car payment? Amy wrote.

Came yesterday. I owe ya.

No rush. Miss your face.

Miss yours too.

Jo signed off with a GIF of Bob Ross feeding a baby squirrel. With the prospect of a busy day tomorrow, Amy went to bed early and fell immediately into a deep sleep—until noises dragged her from a dream of Jo galloping across a prairie on a horse with a mane of raw umber. Holding her breath, Amy listened intently as the microwave door banged shut, water gushed, and cats meowed in chorus.

She tiptoed to the hallway and, grabbing a palette knife from the study, crept down the dark stairs. More noises—an ominous thunk, a grunt, a cat hissing—were coming from the kitchen. Had the owner of the house returned at the ungodly hour of one a.m.? Or had an ungodly burglar decided to make himself at home?

She could run back upstairs and hide under the covers like she used to when Jo told her scary stories. Or she could stop being the girly girl her sister always complained she was and take charge of the situation.

She stepped boldly into the kitchen, its bright lights illuminating a buck-naked male body standing in profile at the refrigerator.

Chest broad.

Arm muscled.

Butt just this side of spectacular.

And Amy just this side of drooling.

But when he let the top freezer door swing open, it hit her right smack-dab on the forehead. And as she fell down, down onto the floor, her last coherent thought was, *Whaddya know? Theo has dimples on* those *cheeks too.*

CHAPTER FOUR

If we are all alive ten years hence, let's meet,
and see how many of us have got our wishes,
or how much nearer we are then than now.
—JO MARCH, *LITTLE WOMEN*

*H*ey, are you okay, Amy?"

Amy's eyes fluttered open, and there was Theo Sinclair, bending over her. Somehow, between his derrière-dimple reveal and her return to consciousness, he'd dressed in grubby jeans and a wrinkled black T-shirt. The big gray cat, who always looked keen for a philosophical discussion, climbed onto her stomach and settled down as if for a long chat.

"I am really sorry," Theo said. "I didn't even see you."

Questions rat-a-tatted through her mind. *Theo in the nude? Theo in this house? Which apparently was* his *house?*

WTF?

"When it comes to refrigerators," she said, "I prefer a bottom-load freezer."

His face relaxed into a smile. "It came with the kitchen. Are you all right?"

"I'm fine. While we're on the subject, an automatic ice dispenser would be nice too."

"I agree."

"Have you considered dimmer switches for the light fixtures?"

"I will now since...uh...apologies for...uh...no clothes. I didn't realize the new tenant had moved in."

Amy extended her hand. "Let me introduce myself. I'm the new tenant."

"So I've gathered. When did you arrive?"

"Couple of days ago."

"Can I help you up?"

"Not yet."

Theo sat cross-legged and rubbed his chin. Except for a ridge on his once-perfect nose, his looks hadn't changed since they'd met by chance two years ago. Longish hair, beard scruff, eyes as pensive as ever.

There really should be a paint color called Aegean Sea. Deep blue with a hint of green.

The tortoiseshell cat padded over and licked her cheek, and the marmalade tugged on a few strands of her hair. Flat on her back like this, Amy could imagine she, Jo, and Theo were teenagers again, lazing on a summer lawn and sharing what they wanted to be when they grew up.

Lying on the floor like this, she could remember the time that she and Theo...

"So, what's the deal?" she asked him.

"Deal?"

"With you suddenly appearing in the kitchen at one in the morning." *In the buff. Naked as a jaybird.*

"I just got in from an overseas flight. I was starving and had no clean clothes, so I threw some in the washer and raided the fridge."

"Multitasking." *In his birthday suit.*

"Sorry if I scared you. What's the deal with the palette knife?"

"Multipurpose tool." She waved it in the air. "I'm ready for anything."

"You always were." *Perpetually Prepared Amy* he and Jo used to call her.

"But not ready to run into you. In the flesh. Which I haven't done for a while. *See* you, I mean. In the...Can you help me up now?" Rising would explain the rush of blood to her face at the mention of all the naked flesh she was thinking of.

Theo scooted the cats away and, extending his hand, pulled her to a standing position. Perpetually Prepared Amy believed firmly in lovely lingerie—in case she died in her sleep—and was wearing a pretty pink pajama set made out of seersucker, a fabric that breathed. Even if the wearer of said seersucker could not herself breathe.

Because all at once she was fourteen years old again, and Theo, the boy next door she was crushing on, was inches away from her. His familiar sandalwood scent made her nostrils twitch.

"You look like you're going to sneeze," he remarked.

"Cat hair." She tossed the palette knife onto the table. "Or something."

Theo picked up the gray cat twining itself around his ankles. "Whaddya say, Coltrane? Did you miss me?"

"Let me guess. John Coltrane, the jazz musician."

"The very same."

"You always did like jazz. And animals. Why so many cats, though?"

"I foster all kinds of animals who were abandoned or whose owners died. I coordinate with the local vet to place them in permanent homes."

The washing machine in the utility room shuddered in the final throes of the spin cycle, making the ceiling lights flicker. "Gotta put the laundry in the dryer," he said.

"If you're not too tired, can we talk? About this situation?"

He arched one eyebrow. "That's what we're calling it?"

"For lack of a better word." Like *disaster*.

"All right. Meet me in the living room. Watch you don't trip on anybody."

Amy made it from the kitchen to the living room without stepping on any tails, and sat in one of the armchairs with a slight shiver. The bare-bones décor chilled her to the bone. There wasn't even a television. Something shrank or swelled inside her—she wasn't sure which—remembering how she and Theo would watch TV together after school, just the two of them.

From the kitchen, she heard a cat or two thump against a wall and the whine of a blender. Theo appeared in the doorway and raised a glass of creamy liquid. "Protein smoothie," he said. "Want one?"

"No, thank you."

He crossed the living room and dropped onto the sofa in front of the stone fireplace. When he slid a glance along the length of her legs in the shortie pajamas, she tucked them beneath her body. "Cold in here," she mumbled.

"The AC must be set too low."

The careful way Theo put the glass on the coffee table suggested his own personal thermostat had lowered from casual to caution. Coltrane leaped to the sofa and moseyed over to his lap. "How long's it been since we last saw each other?" he asked. "In the flesh?"

She didn't bat an eye at his choice of words. "Two years or so, remember? Jo and I ran into you at that bar in St. Louis."

"That's right. I was getting ready to start grad school in counseling."

"And Jo had flown in from Seattle to celebrate my promotion to chair of the English Department."

Amy had begun the evening in a celebratory mood, but Theo's chilly politeness put a damper on it. *His shoulder was colder than the beer*, Jo had joked.

Sometimes Jo and her clever quips really got on Amy's nerves.

"Academia treating you well?" Theo asked, gently massaging Coltrane's head while the cat purred loudly.

"Yes. Four years and counting at the college here. Did you get your master's degree?"

"Graduated in May and moved to Laurel right after."

"Congratulations. You didn't want to stay in Syracuse?"

"Nope." He pronounced the word with a hard *p* like Jo. "Laurel is close to St. Louis, and my best friend lives here. He'd been bugging me to invest in the area because it has a lot of potential, so I bought a few houses to rent out last year, including this one."

"I must have seen some of them when I was apartment hunting."

"Probably. A management company has been handling anything I couldn't do long-distance."

"It makes sense for you to move here since you're from St. Louis." Knowing Amy lived in Laurel was neither here nor there in the Theo universe. "You might have ... um ... let me know you were in town. Or Jo."

"The hell with Jo." He pressed his lips together as if to keep another remark about her sister from escaping.

"Guess you've been busy," she murmured.

"The past few months have been a whirlwind—settling in, renovating the properties, and starting a job. I'm working toward my clinical hours for licensure as a counselor."

Theo Sinclair, dysfunctional family survivor helping other families survive. His parents' miserable marriage a cautionary tale for other marriages.

"Do you prefer counseling to—"

"To being a doctor? In a heartbeat."

Theo Sinclair, dutiful son who'd followed his parents into their profession.

He leaned forward and steepled his hands. "Okay. We're up to speed on our lives. Let's get to the point and talk about our living arrangement." He spoke in what Amy supposed was his counselor voice—borderline stern with a hint of giving a shit.

If she had a lick of sense, she'd say, *Let's not*, go upstairs, repack her things, and ask Athena tomorrow if her offer to stay at her house was still open.

But she'd signed a year's lease. And living with newly-weds, whose household already included Thorne's half brother, would be an imposition. As for her, envy of the Murphy-Kents' happiness might rear its nasty head, jeopardizing her one good friendship in Laurel.

"Just for the record, I auto-signed the lease when Lydia emailed it to me," Theo said. "I didn't bother checking the renter's name."

Yeah. She got it. He wouldn't have signed if he'd known the tenant was her.

"I was in a hurry and didn't notice your name either," Amy said.

She wouldn't have signed if she'd known the landlord was Theo. She didn't think.

"A hurry?" Theo asked.

"I had a housing emergency." And evidently still had one.

"My properties are listed under Lincoln Enterprises. You wouldn't have known I was the owner."

"Lincoln...That was your mother's maiden name, wasn't it?"

"Yeah. She reverted to it after my parents divorced."

Great. A half hour in each other's presence, and she and Theo had already fallen into the conversational cauldron that was his family life. The one she'd lit the flame beneath.

"Any chance we can switch to a month-to-month lease until I find something else?" Amy asked.

He shook his head. "Rent money covers most of the properties' expenses. And finding responsible tenants is a major pain. The previous one who lived here split for Paris without paying two months' rent."

"The City of Lights. How..." She was going to say *romantic* but thought better of it. "How adventurous."

"He wishes. Paris, *Texas*."

"With all the students in the area, though..."

"The management company strongly advised against renting to them. The property damage and complaints from neighbors aren't worth it."

Another option occurred to her—suck up the loss on the lease and move into one of the apartments she'd seen. Owning her own furniture wasn't the worst idea. And she could buy another car if the commute was too far. Earplugs if the street was noisy.

But she didn't have time to scratch her head, much less move again. The English Department budget needed a major overhaul, and next semester's curriculum had to be discussed and finalized with the dean. There were hissy fits to deal with (the faculty's) and what the administration called "grievances" (the students'). And it was up to her as chair to handle it all.

"You and me living together is pretty weird, Theo. To say the least."

"True. But the house is big enough to keep out of each other's way. And I can put up with anything for rent money. You know what they say: *Beggars can't be choosers*."

Amy being "anything."

"I suppose we'll manage," she said.

"I suppose we will."

Truce? she almost said. But hostilities hadn't been openly declared.

"Is it okay that I parked my bike in the shed?" she asked. "It's my main means of transportation, and I don't want it to rust or get stolen."

"Sure." He flashed a smile. "Finally taking mercy on cars?"

"How do you know about—" That's right. It was Theo who had helped her negotiate with mechanics and insurance agents after the car catastrophes of her teens and twenties. "Actually, the cars have started dying of their own accord."

"Can't blame them." He rose, gathering Coltrane in his arms. "I've got to get to sleep or I'll be worthless tomorrow. My supervisor barely approved of my taking a week off."

"Where'd you go this time?"

"The Czech Republic. Let's discuss sharing the kitchen and cleaning chores tomorrow."

"I rarely cook. And I make a point of never leaving anything behind."

Theo arched an eyebrow again, as if she meant more than spilled sugar on the counter or unwashed pots in the sink. She probably did. One conversation with a counselor and she was Freudian-slipping all over the place.

"G'night," he said over his shoulder as he walked to his bedroom, followed by a troop of cats.

Bolting upstairs two steps at a time, Amy threw herself on the bed and muffled her groans in the pillow. Cursed the crap month of August, the town of Laurel, and Honda Civics while she was at it. Added variations to Derek's last name. Doofus. Dingbat. Dickhead. Bemoaned her bad luck. "This isn't happening," she wailed.

Thump. Thump-thump. Thump.

"Opportunity knocking?" she called out as the low rhythm of knocks was repeated.

"Is my cat in there?" Theo asked.

"You have six," she reminded him.

"The Russian Blue. Silvery coat. Her name is Nina."

Amy got up to check inside the closet and behind the trash can and knelt to look under the bed. A pair of almond-shaped emerald eyes blinked back at her. "When did you sneak in here?"

Nina twitched the ear covered in a cobweb.

Theo's arms were braced against the doorframe when she opened it. PRAGUE, she just noticed, was printed in small gold letters on the pocket of his T-shirt. "Did you find her?" he asked. "Or is she in your other room?"

"She's under the bed, stalking dust bunnies."

Amy stepped aside to let him in, and he slipped by her, coaxing in a low voice. "Come on out, girl. Let me see you. Come on, Nina."

"Nina Simone?"

He nodded and, dropping to the floor, reached beneath the bed. "She's shy and needs a break from them all once in a while."

"I didn't think the cats ever came upstairs," Amy said, focusing on the tiny red LEVI'S label on his jeans pocket. So much to read on Theo Sinclair. Except his face.

"First time. Unless they sneak up here when I'm gone."

"They haven't since I moved in. How *do* you get them to stay downstairs?"

He got up and brushed dust off his arms. "I tell them to. They listen when it pleases them."

"Theo the Cat Whisperer."

"The Newfie who's been boarded all week is really the one who keeps them in line."

Nina peeked out from beneath the bed. For reasons she'd be hard-pressed to explain, Amy didn't tell him.

Theo peered at her forehead. "You may want to put ice on that or you'll get a lump. There's a bag in the freezer."

She rubbed the bruise. "Jo will laugh her head off when she hears about all this." The freezer door. The jazz-named cats. Theo, in the flesh. Their *living arrangement*.

"Nina?" he called out again, ignoring her reference to Jo.

"I don't mind if she stays."

"You sure?"

"I'm sure."

"Okay, thanks," he said, stepping out of the room and closing the door behind him with a quiet click.

Amy went to the window, pushed it wide open, and drew in one deep breath as if she were emerging from a plunge into freezing water. This situation sucked, and there wasn't a whole lot she could do about it. It was a biggie. Stay in this house or go, she and Theo were living in the same small town. Not running into each other these past few months had been a matter of sheer luck.

Lucky. To avoid Theo.

Amy could never have imagined such an idea when he was her secret love. The years when she believed that, however long it took, however many other people they dated, they would be together. She had a special claim on his heart for their shared history. For being the one he went to whenever his home became a battleground. For how they understood—without words and without question—that they could rely on each other, no matter what.

Nina rubbed against her ankles, and she bent to pick her up.

"We almost made it," she whispered, burying her face in the cat's silky fur. She and Theo *were* getting closer, finally, with trips back and forth between Chicago, where she was a PhD candidate, and St. Louis, where he was an internal medicine resident. They were taking those first steps into the couple zone, inch by delightful inch.

Until her fateful decision to enter four of her paintings into the *Scenes from a Marriage* exhibit in Chicago. Blistering, unsparing portraits of Theo's parents engaged in the violent arguments she'd witnessed. To her joy and amazement, she won first prize and her work was featured in art articles.

To her horror, Theodore and Marlene Sinclair, in all their fury, were identified as the subjects of the portraits to the St. Louis press. Shamed by the scandal, the Sinclairs divorced and resigned from their medical school faculty positions. Theo dropped out of his residency program and, despite Amy's tearful apologies, dropped her from his life with three simple words: *Nothing lasts forever.*

Art did not offer its usual consolation. Like a writer, she was blocked, unable to even draw for nearly two years. Though to this day, she couldn't bring herself to paint a portrait. Or to stop wondering who had revealed the Sinclairs' identity.

Six years ago—but it felt like yesterday when her dream was shattered. And though she and Theo had resumed contact, if only intermittently, there was no escaping the painful truth that she would never have a special claim on his heart again.

As Nina wriggled out of Amy's arms, her phone lit with a text from Jo.

Almost midnight here and I'm going crazy for some Ted Drewes frozen custard. Quickly followed by a close-up of a pimple on her chin. Hamlet dilemma. To pop or not to pop? And then a photo of the arm she broke last year when she fell playing pickleball, covered with stickers of barn animals.

Random, screwball texts from the sister she adored and who could make her laugh till her sides ached. Proud, bristly Jo, who'd never admit how badly she was hurting from her estrangement from Theo, her *Teddy*, her *Broody Bear*. Any more than Theo would admit he missed Jo.

"Not much longer." Amy reached up to close the window,

and the prickly fronds of the asparagus fern on the windowsill scratched her thigh. "Not if I have anything to do about it."

If she was stuck living in this house, she'd make the pain-in-the-ass of it worth her while by reconciling Jo and Theo. She owed it to them both. And maybe, just maybe, the Amy-Jo-Theo friendship of their early years would shine again. And then gradually, perhaps, she and Theo...

Amy threw back the covers on the bed and punched the pillow hard, twice. No way, no how. She was *not* going there again. Not returning to the time when she believed that she and Theo would share a forever love.

She lay down and curved like a comma on the bed, and Nina nestled into the crook of her body. She'd fill Jo in tomorrow. Or as soon as she stopped wanting to cry. Or scream. Or both. Shutting her eyes, Amy willed herself to sleep. But sleep didn't come until the first wash of gray lightened the sky, just as she was thinking that there really should be a color called Dismal Dawn.

CHAPTER FIVE

*Go on with your work as usual, for
work is a blessed solace.*
—MARMEE MARCH, *LITTLE WOMEN*

𝒰nless Theo wanted to endure a week of stink eyes and strategically placed piles of vomit, keeping the cats out of his bedroom after an absence was not an option. He woke at seven to Coltrane kneading his head and the marmalade, Ray Charles, nibbling on a toe.

"Guys, give me a break, will ya?" he grumbled.

Bessie Smith dropped her heavy tortoiseshell body onto his stomach and meowed her protest.

"No need to get righteous on me, Big B."

He didn't have to be at the counseling clinic until ten, but sleep was impossible in a room full of hungry, restless cats. Shrugging off Bessie, he motioned them to follow him. After filling their food and water bowls in the kitchen, he shuffled back to the bedroom and tried to empty his mind so he'd fall asleep again.

Except he couldn't. Not when it was overflowing with thoughts of Amy. Those forever legs and corn silk hair. That freckle below her left eye like a teardrop. As pretty and as quirky as ever. So calm and composed as she lay on the floor talking to him. After being knocked out and swarmed by cats, no less. While he, *faking* calm and composure, calculated the odds that she would be back in his life—less than zero.

Theo thumped the mattress at his side. *Beggars can't be choosers.* What a mean thing to say. There was no excuse for being so damn rude. None.

Except fear of whatever other emotion he might express.

"Insight," he muttered. "The counselor's curse."

Bounding from the bed, he took one look at himself in the mirror above the dresser and headed for the bathroom. His eyes burned and his beard itched. He stank after nearly a day in transit and falling into a deep sleep without even washing his face. Grabbing a pair of scissors, he trimmed his hair, shaved, showered, and dressed.

As he reviewed case notes for the morning's clients in his study, his phone chimed.

Back home in one piece? Lando texted.

One hungry piece.

Get your ass over here and I'll feed ya.

Within the hour, Theo texted back.

His friend Lando owned Marconi's Pizza, a convenient place to grab a meal—and avoid a housemate. He'd considered adding a kitchenette on the second floor when the previous tenant fried fish at two in the morning, sending the cats into a frenzy. Amy's inconvenient presence might make the addition worth the trouble and expense.

From the kitchen, Theo heard running water, footsteps on the tiled floor, and the back door closing. Through the slats of the blinds, he watched Amy walk her bike up the pathway along the side of the house. The gray suit she wore tried, and failed, to sabotage her curves. In the sunlight, her curls shone around her head like a halo. He'd always measured his time with and without the Marsden sisters in years. Now, living with Amy, it would be days.

Hours.

Minutes.

～◯

Theo parked his burgundy '57 Chevy Bel Air outside Marconi's Pizza. The slogan on the awning cracked him up every time—PIZZA DELIVERED FASTER THAN A TELEGRAPH. He and Lando had been best buds ever since they tended the same bar in St. Louis four years ago.

"Dora the Explorer, home from his world travels," Lando said from behind the counter when Theo entered.

"Bite me, Signore Salami Breath."

"What's with the dorky blazer?"

"Headed to work. And I'm not the one wearing a hairnet and apron."

Lando pointed to the Chevy. "When are you going to get rid of that clunker, Theodore?"

"It's a classic muscle car. When are you going to stop breaking my balls, Orlando?"

"When you grow a pair."

A couple of college students, wolfing down pizza at the counter, laughed and gave Lando a thumbs-up.

It had been a stroke of genius opening the restaurant near Southern Illinois College in Rosewood, the town next to Laurel. The students' erratic schedules and ravenous appetites guaranteed business nearly every hour of the sixteen it was open. *They're paying for my future Maserati, one slice at a time*, Lando boasted. His short, wiry frame was in constant motion so he looked like he was tossing dough even when he wasn't.

"Where's this pizza you promised me?" Theo asked. "I have to leave by nine thirty."

Lando pulled a pan out of the brick oven. "I call it 'The All-Nighter.' It's topped with pepperoni, sausage, three kinds of cheese, and peppers."

"And anyone who eats it is up all night with heartburn."

"This is the thanks I get for substituting the meat with extra peppers for you?" Lando expertly divided the pizza with the mezzaluna and put two slices on a plate. "Here. Knock yourself out."

Theo blew on one and took a bite. Then two more. "Thanks. From the bottom of my empty stomach."

"Let's go to a table and shoot the breeze," Lando said when the student who worked the morning shift arrived.

The pizza parlor was long and narrow with a single row of wooden booths. Photographs of Italy hung in antique frames on the brick walls. Lando pointed to the picture, hanging above their table, of a yacht off the Amalfi Coast at sunset. "I want to take Stella on a romantic trip to Italy one of these days. What's your favorite city there?" He and Stella Amoroso had been a couple for two years and had recently moved in together.

"Florence. Everywhere you look you see something beautiful. And the food, of course, is *delizioso*." Theo had spent hours in the Uffizi Gallery, entranced by its treasures. Amy had sparked his interest in art when they were in high school. It was she who told him that *Theo* was the name of Vincent van Gogh's younger brother and *Jo* the name of Theo van Gogh's wife. He had laughed, but for some reason, the coincidence of names hadn't amused her.

"Whenever I mention Italy," Lando said, "Stella says we should move out of Rosewood first and then talk about traveling. I love it here, but she's always complaining about this town. The entire state of Illinois, for that matter."

"Where does she want to live instead?"

"Colorado, where everybody's as crazy about cycling as she is." He stared at the ceiling. "I can see it now: me pushing her around in a wheelchair after she breaks a leg in a race, and her cursing me blind."

"Yo, who asked you to push me?" Stella said. "I'll get a motorized one."

She grinned down at them, gripping the posts of the booth. She wore cycling gloves, bike shorts, and a neon green shirt with SPIN CYCLE and the logos of corporate sponsors printed on it. Wisps of light brown hair that matched her eyes poked through the openings of her helmet.

"Hello, my star," Lando said, referring to the English translation of her name.

"Hello, my general." She'd shortened Orlando to Lando after the character of General Calrissian in *Star Wars*, and the name had stuck ever since. "Forget to shave?" she asked, leaning over to kiss him.

"I have a perpetual five-o'clock shadow."

Her elfin face lit with a grin. "That's not all that's perpetual."

Stella was so petite that Theo thought it likely their bedroom gymnastics included Lando tossing her into the air like one of his pizzas.

"Sit down, babe," Lando said. "Have a slice."

"Can't. I just came in for the kiss and to tell you I'll be working late at Spin Cycle. Big end-of-summer sale." She turned to Theo. "Long time no see. Geez, you look like something the cat dragged in."

"What the hell, Stella?" Lando said.

"Gee, thanks, Stella," Theo said, laughing.

"You do look like shit," Lando said. "Problem is, my mom always uses that expression to describe my dad. It's freaky hearing my mother's words come out of my girlfriend's lips."

"No shit," Stella said. "If we turn into your parents, we're in big trouble."

Theo wiped his mouth with a napkin to hide a smile. He'd been hearing the bickering voices of Lou and Rose Marconi when Lando and Stella talked ever since they'd met.

"C'mon, Stella," Lando said. "You can sit for five minutes."

"Me? Sit? That'll be the day. Yo, Theo, we'll catch up later." The clips on her bike shoes clicked like tap shoes as she walked out of the restaurant.

"So, how's it feel to be back?" Lando asked Theo.

"Can't tell yet. Still jet-lagged. Which sucks because I've got a lot of clients to see today." He added *Pick up Moose from Caring Kennels* to the Reminders app on his phone. "And then I have to lug a one-hundred-and-fifty-pound Newfoundland into my car. The big baby hates getting into it."

"Moose!" Lando exclaimed. "I love that dog."

"Me too. Though the house feels a lot bigger when he's not home."

At the crash of a plate onto the tiled floor, Theo sat back in the booth with a jolt.

"Sorry," the student working at the counter called out.

"Relax, Theodore," Lando said. "It's just a dish."

"I'm a bit jumpy. Not enough sleep," Theo mumbled. He plucked a burnt pepper off the second slice of pizza. "A new tenant moved into the house while I was gone."

"Make sure you get a deposit so he doesn't screw you on the rent like the other tool."

"A professor wouldn't be so irresponsible."

"That's what you said about the optometrist the management company evicted. The guy who punched a hole in a wall and trashed the furniture with cigarette burns."

"A woman isn't likely to wreck the place," Theo said.

"A female tenant? What's her name?"

Theo licked cheese off his thumb. "Amy Marsden."

"Hmm. The name sounds familiar."

"Amy and her sister, Jo, were my neighbors growing up. I told you about them."

Lando snapped his fingers. "That's it. And you were all good friends too, right? Weird I've never met them."

"Jo's lived in Seattle for years. And I haven't seen Amy in ages. We were both surprised by this…uh…this situation."

Lando sat back in the booth with a grin. "This I have to hear."

"Hear what?"

"Every time you say *Amy*, you frown. C'mon, what's the story?"

"There isn't one."

"Don't bullshit a bullshitter."

Theo shrugged. "We were close friends once. We're not anymore. End of story."

"She teaches at Southern Illinois College?" Lando asked, typing into his phone.

"English Department."

Lando let out a low whistle. "Found her photo on the school website. What a beauty. And, may I add, you lucky dog, you."

"Not going there. She was always like a sister or a friend to me." Or a combination of the two. *Frister and frother*, Amy had jokingly labeled them.

And yet...

When she was a sophomore in high school, she asked him to teach her how to kiss so she wouldn't be inexperienced when she dated. Perpetually Prepared Amy. So Theo had obliged her. He drew close, looked into those blue-gray eyes, waited for her to stop giggling, touched his lips to her soft, full mouth—and Amy bloomed into someone else. Someone open to other possibilities besides *frister*. Possibilities that nearly became reality.

"Dunno, Theodore. I sense *amore* in the air."

"Love? I think the hairnet has squeezed your brain cells to death. And have you forgotten about Brittany?"

"Dating a woman longer than a month is a Sinclair record."

Theo pushed his half-eaten pizza slice aside. "When you start dissing my love life, it's time for me to hit the road."

"Show me pics from your trip, *then* hit it."

Theo scrolled through row after row of photographs on his phone, looking for the shots of Prague Castle and Wenceslas Square. He was due for another album purge. Why did he keep pictures of animals who'd already found homes? Delete. Or of the shepherd's pie he'd eaten in London? Delete.

And the portraits of his parents that Amy had painted and exhibited, closing those other possibilities between them.

His finger hovered above the trash can icon. But he did not delete.

CHAPTER SIX

Ambitious girls have a hard time.
—AMY MARCH, *LITTLE WOMEN*

*Y*our spring curriculum plan is grand. Simply grand." Dean Fiona Reilly closed the computer screen and swiveled in her chair to face Amy. "Topics in Global Literature, Postcolonial Literature and Criticism, and Multicultural Voices. Precisely the direction I want to take the School of Arts and Sciences. Well done, you."

Amy murmured her thanks and clenched her toes in the black pumps to keep from dozing off. Twenty minutes into the meeting, and she had fallen into what she and Athena called the Fiona Trance. The sweet scent of fresh flowers on the desk, dim lighting, and the dean's Irish brogue, as soothing as a lullaby, all conspired to lull her into a stupor.

"I do have a wee criticism," Fiona said, glancing at the framed photo of her partner, who she called "my bonny Brigid." Amy had never actually seen her and was curious just how *bonny* Brigid was.

She tugged a few curls across her forehead to hide the freezer door lump. "Yes?"

"Gary has taught the same course on the Scandinavian noir novel for three semesters. I think you should persuade him to expand his focus."

"I'll try. His classes *are* popular, though. Maybe next fall?"

Ideally, never. Amy was scared shitless of Dr. Gary Ericson. She had a morbid conviction that blunt force trauma was the only persuasion he'd respond to. He skulked campus like a character out of a Jo Nesbø crime novel and glowered during faculty meetings as if he were about to detonate a bomb. Her best bet would be to encourage a sabbatical. To Norway. During which he'd write his own version of Karl Ove Knausgaard's *My Struggle*. All six volumes.

She cleared her throat. "I hope you're satisfied with the other faculty members' schedules and course assignments."

"I see you've sent the junior faculty to the gulag of introductory and composition courses." Fiona flashed a toothy smile. "*Your* time in the gulag was brief, fast burner that you are. It's not everyone who makes tenure at thirty-three and is promoted to department chair at thirty-four."

"The position fell into my lap last year. I got lucky."

An unfortunate choice of words since the previous chair had pulled female students onto *his* lap, resulting in his immediate dismissal.

"A word of professional advice, Amy. Never make excuses for your success. And never apologize unless it's absolutely necessary."

"Thank you, Fiona. Your mentorship has been invaluable."

The truth was, for all her academic achievements, Dr. Amy Marsden suffered from impostor syndrome. She still couldn't believe that she'd made it this far this soon. Ever since her stepfather, Ben Cooper, had financed her undergraduate education at the University of Chicago on the stipulation that she go to law school, years of lucky breaks, dedicated mentoring, and promises that no glass ceiling would impede her progress had propelled her career.

Oh, she had relinquished her dream of going to art school to meet Ben's conditions—and her dream job of professional painter. She'd had to change course when he died suddenly her senior year, and law school was no longer an obligation to fulfill or an option she could afford. But then the English Department welcomed "A-student Amy who is always so pleasant and writes such elegant essays" into its MA-PhD program with a generous financial package. She snagged an assistant professor position on the first try, secured tenure, and made chair in the blink of an eye. And whenever she looked back wistfully at her original goal to get a fine arts degree and make a living as a painter, she consoled herself that artists didn't make much of a living unless they were extraordinary.

Only problem was, Amy believed she *would* have been an extraordinary artist. Okay, semi-extraordinary. Or remarkably talented, at the very least. In any case, she should have ignored Practical Amy, who wanted the security of a career and paycheck, and risked it all to find out. Even if it meant starting over again and enrolling in art school.

Screw Ben's money and his demands, Theo had advised her. *Follow your dream.*

To which she'd retorted, *You should talk. You're only going to med school to please your parents.* He was being supportive, in his way, otherwise she'd also have pointed out that he grew up rich so who was he to say.

"I must address one area in which you have been remiss," Fiona was saying in a lilting voice.

Amy fluttered her eyelids to keep them from drooping and braced for another "wee criticism."

"As you know, one of your responsibilities as chair is to actively recruit faculty and encourage innovation. I'm sorry to say you haven't demonstrated any progress in this regard."

"Yes, I'm aware of my..." Amy swallowed the word *deficiency*. *Never describe yourself in negative terms* was another pearl of Fiona wisdom. "My lack of progress. I'll make more of an effort."

"See that you do. After all, you do want to be a dean someday, don't you?"

Amy nodded, though ambition in academia was another area in which she was *remiss*.

"I must ask," Fiona said, perching her reading glasses atop her black hair.

Amy straightened her spine in the chair. *I must ask* was the dean's usual preface to an unpleasant subject.

"Have you made any progress on your next book, Amy?"

Amy had fulfilled the publishing requirement for tenure with her book, *King Arthur: Man, Myth, Legend*. While the title had humorous T-shirt possibilities, the text itself drew heavily on her dissertation on the Arthurian legends through history—and was as dull to read. Since then, Fiona had been encouraging her to write another.

"I'm currently reading a biography of Alfred Tennyson," Amy said. "It's critical to my analysis of his *Idylls of the King*, which is the subject of my book."

"I'm not convinced that there will be much interest in... how shall I describe it? A dusty epic poem." Fiona's specialty was

Irish literature. Before her ascension to dean, she had been the one faculty member fearless enough to take on the mighty James Joyce.

"My goal is to make Tennyson's stories of King Arthur's court come alive for the contemporary reader."

A tall order. For while Amy adored medieval literature with its poems and tales of the burning flames of courtly love, she realized that, to many people, the Middle Ages might have been the Dark Ages, not a glowing ember in sight.

"The administration is encouraging faculty to publish books with commercial potential. Something with both academic *and* popular appeal." Fiona tapped her fingers on the edge of the desk. "Perhaps you should write about a beloved American classic. A novel nearly everyone is familiar with."

"*Little Women*," Amy mumbled. She wasn't just familiar with it. She'd practically memorized it.

"Why, yes! I just read that there's another movie adaptation of it in the works. You can take a fresh approach to its sisterhood dynamics. Or examine female ambition at a time when women were not empowered to achieve their dreams."

Amy could write volumes on ambition—especially the price it exacted—without referencing the favorite book of her childhood.

"With all due respect, Fiona, medieval literature is my specialty."

"Needs must, Amy. Needs must. See that you turn your attention to a relevant topic, aye?"

"Aye," Amy replied without thinking.

Fiona continued to talk murmurously about the budget and upcoming conferences as Amy got drowsier and drowsier. She had to get out of there before she fell asleep and slid out of the chair onto the floor.

"Has the administration made any decisions regarding benefits for the adjunct professors?" she asked. The dean's least favorite topic was sure to cut the meeting short.

"Administrative issues have their own timetable." Fiona removed the reading glasses from her head and cleaned the lenses with the hem of her blouse, her signal of dismissal. "We're off to a good start this semester. Let's keep the momentum going."

Amy kept the momentum going through her lectures on Chekhov and Cheever and during a long meeting with Ian Prescott, who taught all the poetry courses. A minor miracle since she'd barely slept after her encounter with the freezer door and Theo in the flesh.

She managed to get Jo on the phone before lunch to fill her in on this latest turn of events.

"Leave it to Amy to go from the frying pan into the fire," Jo said, laughing.

"Leave it to Jo to get the Supportive Sister of the Year Award."

"How's this for support? If you get Theo-moony again, I'll fly out there and scold some sense into you."

"I *want* you to come here. We have so much to catch up on." And Jo's visit would set her plan to reconcile Jo and Theo in motion.

"Too busy."

"But I miss you."

"We talk or text all the time, for Pete's sake," Jo grumbled.

"It's not the same."

"August in Illinois is too fricking hot and humid. You come out here."

"You know I have a ton of responsibilities now that I'm department chair."

"Oh, and my job isn't as important?"

"That's not what I meant. C'mon, Jo. Pretty please?"

"I'll think about it, Amy Mamy."

"Think about it really hard, Josyphine," Amy said, using the name Aunt March called Jo in *Little Women*.

"That's so funny I forgot to laugh."

"Get out here, and you'll remember how."

"When'd you get so pushy?"

"Since I grew up with you."

"Love you too."

"Love you back."

The rest of the day, Amy organized her files, replied to student emails, and reviewed an article on Alice Munro. By six thirty, she was tired, hungry, and ready to murder her high-heeled shoes. Changing into sneakers, she unlocked her bike from the rack and headed home.

"Shit!" she cursed as the sky released a downpour a half mile from campus. Biking everywhere was great until she was drenched to the skin and skidding on wet asphalt. A car sped by, spraying a sheet of cold water onto her stockinged legs—and the cold, hard fact on her conscience that she'd been beating back since Fiona's reference to "sisterhood dynamics" and "female ambition." The grim truth that, on the way to sacrificing her dream of becoming a painter, she'd derailed her sister's dream of becoming a writer.

It had taken Jo ages to break into fiction, but she'd finally done it—and with resounding success. She had recently published "Strata" to great reviews, and another short story was due out in two months. The only thing *Amy* had created lately was a four-page requisition list for the English Department. And paintings Derek had pronounced "pretty." Was it worth what she'd done to Jo so long ago to come to this?

Amy pedaled into the driveway where a Toyota Camry was parked next to Theo's car. The front door of the house opened and a young woman emerged, wearing a floppy straw hat, a tie-dyed blouse, and white pants. She ran through puddles to the Camry, squealing with laughter.

"Be careful, Brittany," Theo called out. "The roads will be slippery. Give yourself enough room to brake."

He leaned against the pillar of the porch, barefoot, bare chested, a barely concealed postcoital grin from ear to ear. Amy could swear steam was coming off his skin—and coming off hers too as she fell, momentarily, into a Theo Trance.

CHAPTER SEVEN

I'd rather take coffee than
compliments just now.
—AMY MARCH, *LITTLE WOMEN*

*L*iving with Theo was like having a college roommate all over again. One you wish would spend more time at the apartment of their significant other. Assuming Brittany wasn't just a booty call. As big as the house was, and for all his assurances otherwise, Amy and Theo couldn't seem to keep out of each other's way.

Mornings were a particular pain in her patootie. If she weren't a caffeine addict, she'd shower, dress, and drop in at the Starbucks near campus. But no. She was weak. She needed a fix the minute she woke up. Dressed in pajamas, disheveled, discombobulated, and in full view of Theo. She had no problem with him being one of those guys who liked to cook and knew their way around the kitchen. He just never seemed to find his way *out* of the kitchen.

She'd snuck downstairs a few times, an hour or so before she had to leave for work, hoping the coast was clear. Nope. There he was, mixing a protein smoothie or chopping kale. Kale for breakfast? The Theo she'd grown up with reduced boxes of Froot Loops to dust in one sitting.

After nearly two weeks, Amy gave up. Thursday morning,

she stumbled down the stairs in her favorite pajamas, sky blue with puffy clouds all over them, her hair as straggly as seaweed. Nina was at her heels, tail in the air. They were roomies by unspoken agreement, and Nina lorded her special status over her fellows.

"Morning," Amy mumbled to Theo, who sat at the kitchen table, the toaster and an array of tools spread in front of him.

"Morning," he replied.

She tiptoed between Ray and Bessie lounging on the floor. Two of the cats had been placed in homes, so only four remained. She filled and turned on the coffeemaker, her daily reminder of Derek—and of the amusement on Theo's face when she gave him the microfiction version of their breakup.

Another oddball boyfriend, his dimples said. And in a flash, she was sixteen years old again, waiting for Theo to pick her up at a gas station. She'd gone into the mini-mart to buy potato chips while her date filled the tank of his mom's van, and he'd absent-mindedly driven off without her.

"Clinic today?" she asked Theo.

"Not till the afternoon." He peered into the toaster, screwdriver in hand. "Looks like the heating element's broken."

Since she didn't know heating elements from Shinola, a sympathetic grunt would have to do.

"Law of entropy," he said. "Sooner or later, everything breaks down."

"Law of Theo—sooner or later, you'll figure out how to fix it." When their computers crashed or bicycle chains broke, she and Jo went straight to him.

And he went straight to her—Amy—when *he* crashed.

"It's not hard," he said. "Machines have a logic."

"Know anything about the logic of Honda Accords? I just bought a used one." Cycling in the cold rain had sent her back to the dealership. The salesman had grinned when she walked in, bike helmet in hand.

"What's wrong with it?" he asked.

"It's making strange noises like *ka-ching, ka-chong*. Oh, and *groosh*."

Theo banged the bottom of the toaster, the dimples on his cheeks appearing and disappearing as if he were fighting back a smile. "I'll take a look at the engine."

Amy poured coffee into her SERIOUS GOURMET SHIT mug, a gift from Jo, and spread margarine on a roll. Her first class wasn't until eleven, giving her plenty of time to restore herself to humanity. Coltrane, curled up on a chair, blinked at her a few times before closing his eyes with a grimace.

"Want a cup?" she offered Theo.

"No thanks. I don't drink coffee anymore."

"Since when?"

"I got tired of it. I prefer tea since my last trip to England."

Theo didn't look at her when she sat across from him, possibly out of repulsion like Coltrane. Or plain old good manners. Whatever the heck, it freed her to check him out as she ate the roll and sipped the coffee. TORONTO had faded to TONTO on his T-shirt. Sweatpants and bare feet completed his just-rolled-out-of-bed ensemble. How someone who rarely ran a comb through his hair, who threw on any old thing, always managed to look so...so...

Moose, the Newfie, bounded into the room, his black fur undulating with every step. Ray and Bessie immediately sat up at attention.

"Get over here, you big lug," Amy crooned. The cuddly bear of a dog was a welcome distraction from her thoughts meandering in the direction of Theo-as-hottie. Being semicomatose might have had something to do with it.

"His eyes just kill me," she said, drinking the coffee with Moose's head in her lap. "Like he's a wise, old man who knows the secrets of the universe."

"If the universe were his food bowl," Theo said. "Believe it or not, he's just a puppy. His former owners turned him over to the vet when he got bigger than they could handle."

"People do that?"

"People do that. I didn't have the heart to call him Charlie Parker or something."

"But you don't have a problem changing the cats' names?"

Theo grinned. "They never pay attention to what they're called anyway."

"Hmm. Maybe I'll change Nina to Billie Holiday, one of my favorite singers."

Whose recording of "Lover Man" was playing while Amy and Theo nearly kissed themselves out of the friend zone and into the couple zone.

She peeked at him over the rim of her mug, but his look of concentration probably only concerned the toaster. Not a thought at all in his head about the weekend she'd come down from Chicago to get a break from her PhD studies and met up with him in St. Louis.

That unforgettable weekend.

Her dissertation on the Arthurian legends through history had hit a few snags and revisions weren't going well. The source materials in Welsh had driven her batty. Couldn't the good people of Wales have sprung for a few more vowels besides *y*? A change of scenery was just what she needed, and Theo had time off from his internal medicine residency.

And they were both free of romantic entanglements.

They amused themselves conjugating that word. *I entangle. You'll entangle. We will have entangled.* Joking, teasing, pretending they'd just met. Fake flirting. Or not so fake, as an affectionate hug here, a playful smooch there, became an embrace, a deep kiss.

Which was how stressed-out, horny, friends-since-forever Amy and Theo wound up on the living room floor of his apartment, halfway out of their clothes, on the brink of having sex—until his roommate walked in. And they disentangled.

They were beyond embarrassed. They were laughing their heads off. And they were determined to pick up where they'd left off and conjugate—to pair and fuse—some more. Because it wasn't a friends-with-benefits moment. It was the beginning of AmyandTheo. One word.

But she'd entered the portraits in the *Scenes from a Marriage* exhibit weeks before, and when the day of the actual exhibition arrived...*Amy*...*and*...*Theo*.

"There. That should do it," Theo said, tightening the screws on the bottom of the toaster.

The roll was so dry that Amy could barely swallow it. She tossed a chunk to Moose, who scarfed it down in midair. "Good boy!"

"Don't encourage him."

"Like *you* can catch food in your mouth like that."

"Not a skill I aspire to."

"Speak for yourself." She tossed the rest of the roll in the air, her mouth open, but missed. Moose pounced on it with a grunt.

"If you feed him, he'll never leave you alone when you eat," Theo warned her.

She held Moose's huge head in her hands and kissed him on the snout. "I don't mind."

"He gobbles everything in sight. Which reminds me, you didn't happen to see a pair of feather earrings lying around, did you?"

"No. Why?"

"Brittany said she might have left them here, but I can't find them. She's always losing things."

Amy hadn't seen Brittany since the evening she'd run to her car in the rain. Presumably, the giggling coming from his bedroom was hers. If she bothered to presume.

"Maybe she leaves her belongings behind on purpose," she said. Sean, two boyfriends before Banana Brad, would hide his phone or laptop in her apartment, using them as an excuse to drop in at odd hours.

Theo rose and put the toaster on the counter. "Not likely. Brittany doesn't have a devious bone in her body."

Amy pushed her chair back to get up, but Moose dropped his head onto her lap again and she couldn't move.

"Back off, Moose," Theo said.

"Woof!" Moose barked, startling Amy, and scaring the cats to standing positions.

Grabbing Moose by the collar and dragging him away, Theo stumbled, bumping into Amy's shoulder and putting his hand on her thigh, for just a second, to catch his balance. She gripped the edge of the table, fully awake now, as his oh-so-swoony, preshower condensed scent went from her nose to her curled toes.

"Sorry," he mumbled.

"S'okay."

Or would have been if she hadn't just remembered his hands all *over* her body. All. Over. Till she was All. Wet.

Amy gulped the rest of the coffee and, going to the cabinet where she kept snacks, tore into one of the bags of Cheetos.

"For breakfast?" Theo said.

"I've always been a Cheetos freak. What else is new?"

"Yeah but...three bags?"

"One for everyday use. One for an emergency. And a third for backup."

He pointed to the bags of Fritos and potato chips in the cabinet. "No offense, but you eat a lot of crap. You didn't use to, Amy."

"And you didn't use to live like a monk," she said through a mouthful of Cheetos. "The house is so...bare. You don't even have a rug on the living room floor."

"Makes it easier to keep the place clean. And Moose needs a lot of room."

"Yeah. Well. Moose won't be here forever. And it's kind of weird. Like, Marie Kondo weird."

She'd been wanting to say this, but it never seemed the right time. Till now, when he was looking and smelling so...Theo.

"Who's Marie Kondo?" he asked.

"An organizing genius. She advises people to get rid of any- thing that doesn't spark joy."

Clearly, Amy wasn't sparking joy, judging by his scowl. And that's when she realized why Theo's spare décor, his pared-down life, bothered her so much. It reminded her that he'd pared *her* out of his life.

She reached for the bag of Fritos, and he rolled his eyes.

"Don't knock junk food," she said. "It's convenient." And the perfect comfort food. Because suddenly she needed a lot of comfort.

"Processed food is not nutritious."

"Food shaming is not attractive. At all. And excuse me if I'm not a vegan."

"Vegetarian, not vegan. There's a difference."

"I stand corrected. What's it to you anyway?"

"I saw firsthand the damage poor nutrition does to the body in med school."

The bubble of their just-like-old-times banter burst at his mention of the medical career he'd walked away from. All the cats except Ray slunk out of the kitchen as if a shadow had fallen over the room.

Sitting at the table again, Theo gathered the tools into a tidy pile. "Coronary disease is one consequence of a bad diet. Theo the First is proof."

Theo the First, his beloved grandfather, and one of Amy's favorite people, had died last year of a massive heart attack while air-guitaring Django Reinhardt's "Minor Swing." He had lost no occasion to enlighten his grandson and the Marsden sisters that B. B. King was his personal god, music after the sixties was shit, and fried food and whiskey made life worth living.

"He was an original," Amy said softly.

"That he was. During one of our last conversations, he said, *Float me down to the Delta when I'm gone, Theo the Third.* I spread his ashes over the Mississippi River, blasting B. B. King on his boom box." Theo ran a hand through his tangled hair. "He was always telling me to *eat the fucking bacon already*. He'd hit me upside the head if he knew I ate tofu."

"And that you'd KonMaried your life."

"I what? Oh, I get it. Yeah, no kidding. The man was a major pack rat. I donated everything to Goodwill like he wanted."

"Including the hula girl lamp he bought in Hawaii?"

"His last girlfriend took it."

Theo the First had promised to leave it to Amy since she enjoyed kitsch as much as he did. But the loss of his friendship was another fallout of the Sinclair family scandal.

"He left me a generous legacy, along with his 'fifty-seven Chevy. Enough money to invest in properties and work in a job that's low-paying but rewarding." Theo got up to tighten the sink faucet, though no water was dripping. "I miss him every day."

Of course he did. Why else had he surrounded himself with so many animals if not for consolation? Like the menagerie that had comforted his lonely childhood. When Theo the First died, he lost the one person in his life who'd always been there for him, besides Amy and Jo. But mostly Amy. Except it wasn't disastrous dates she'd rescued him from.

"I should have nagged him more," he said, shaking his head. "Worked out with him. Something."

"He preferred giving advice to taking it." Amy rose and, standing beside Theo at the sink, washed her mug. "Apologies again for not making it to his funeral. I was a keynote speaker at a conference and had to present a paper." Not that Theo or his parents would have welcomed her presence.

"The flowers you sent were nice."

"Jo couldn't make it either because ... well, you know."

Jo and Theo had been as mad as hornets at each other, having quarreled a month before his grandfather's death. On top of everything, Jo had broken her arm and was in a general state of aggravation.

"It didn't matter that she wasn't there." Theo rubbed the ridge of his nose. "It was just as well."

At the sound of retching, they watched Ray's back heave three times as he deposited a pile of puke on the floor. Sticking up out of the mound was a brown feather and two gold hoops.

"I doubt Brittany will want her earrings back now," Theo drawled as Moose plodded over to investigate.

Amy and Theo looked at each other. And in that place where tragedy meets comedy, they laughed. And kept laughing as the other cats straggled back to the kitchen to check what all the fuss was about.

She wrapped her arms around him. It had been ages since she'd hugged him, another lifetime. And yet—here were the same taut back muscles, that woodsy scent, the broad chest she'd rested her head against so many times. "I'm really sorry about Theo the First," she murmured. "I know how much he meant to you."

At the sharp intake of his breath, she stepped back and into his Aegean Sea eyes. This gaze too was familiar. It was Theo, once again, searching for a place to go when there was nowhere else he could be.

CHAPTER EIGHT

I think we are all hopelessly flawed.
—FRIEDRICH BHAER, *LITTLE WOMEN*
(2019 FILM)

$\mathscr{T}$uesdays at the Happy Haven counseling clinic were easy for Theo since only four clients, Warren and Cynthia Sprague and Eugene and Tildy Farragut, were scheduled. The Spragues were thirtysomething newlyweds. The Farraguts, married forty-four years, had reunited after a brief separation last year. Both couples seemed bewildered by the new emotional journey they had embarked on.

"Why doesn't anyone get that I need my personal space?" Cynthia complained, crossing her long, slender legs. Light brown hair draped over the right side of her face, concealing her pretty features.

"Work has been ridiculous lately," Warren said. "Everybody wants something for nothing." He was tall and stout, with an affable face beneath a thatch of black hair.

"The carpet guy can't make it to the house this week," she said.

"Three dollars for a cup of coffee," he griped.

After a few more remarks about carpets and coffee, Cynthia went on to talk about the career advice she'd given a friend while Warren described a traffic accident he'd witnessed. Theo interjected occasionally, attempting to steer their comments into a conversation about their marriage—but they steered themselves right out of one.

Since he began working at the clinic in May, he had made excellent progress with his clients. Paul was starting to take a stand against the junior-high bullies, and James, a retired florist, was making a serious effort to manage his obsessive-compulsive condition. Theo was a natural when it came to coaching families how to communicate better. *Listen with your eyes* never failed to elicit smiles and understanding nods. He was certain that, with more experience, he would match the impressive achievements of his Happy Haven colleagues.

As for his couples-counseling skills, he needed more than clinical experience. His instinct and intuition weren't cutting it. He didn't know whether to approach them as a unit or as individuals. Or how to get to the heart of their problem. The Spragues were particularly challenging. Their sentences to each other were parallel lines, rarely intersecting, their eyes barely making contact. Given enough time, they might talk right past each other and out of their marriage. And he had no idea how to stop them.

"I want to get a dog," Cynthia said as they left the office at the end of the session.

"The car needs an oil change," Warren said, lumbering behind her.

Theo jotted down *dog* and *car*, drawing a two-headed arrow between them. Nope. Zero connection as far as he could see.

Connection—that might be at the heart of *his* problem as a couples counselor. Maybe if he were married or had ever been in a loving, committed relationship, he'd be more in tune with the issues his clients faced.

Waiting for the Farraguts, Theo replenished the box of tissues on the end table and straightened the framed poster that went askew when the Spragues closed the door. The quotes printed on the posters in all the offices were corny, if popular. The clinic's sleek, ultramodern furniture managed to be both formal and comfortable. Large picture windows flooded the rooms with sunshine, though some people shrank from their revealing light, insisting that the blinds be closed.

Tildy's timid knock signaled the Farraguts' arrival. Of all the couples Theo counseled, they were his favorite.

"Good afternoon," he said once they'd settled in their seats. "Are we ready to begin?"

Tildy perched on the edge of her chair, plucking the handkerchief she always held. "We've had a tremendous breakthrough," she announced. "It's been wonderful!"

Theo glanced at Eugene, waiting for a comment or reaction. But exuberant adjectives and exclamation points weren't part of his emotional syntax. His range of expressions was as narrow as his face—from cranky to less cranky. "Is that a smile I see?" Theo asked, trying to draw him out.

Eugene lowered his head, revealing wet comb marks in his thin gray hair. "Reckon so."

"Tell me about your breakthrough, Tildy," Theo said.

"I told it to him straight, like you suggested," she said.

Theo had deduced early on that she was too shy to assert herself. A petite, birdlike woman with darting, bright blue eyes, the boldest act of her life had been walking out of her marriage and going back to Cleveland, her hometown. He'd gradually persuaded her, through gentle nudging, to speak her mind.

"Does this mean you're more comfortable expressing yourself?" he asked her.

"Yes, it does."

"You told Eugene what you want?"

"I most certainly did."

"Would you mind sharing what—"

"Sex," she chirped. "More of it."

Her husband shifted his gaunt, angular frame in the chair.

"And sex...uh..." Theo cleared his throat. "How did more of it affect—"

"He's not such a grumpy grouch since I got him between the sheets." Tildy's expression was triumphant, despite Eugene's disapproving grunt.

Theo clicked his ballpoint pen repeatedly, checked his fingernails, and looked up at the ceiling lights. Anything to keep from howling with inappropriate laughter.

"Can we keep coming, Theo?" she asked. "Even though we've made this big step?"

"By all means. My clients initially attend weekly sessions, then after a few months we discuss their progress. If you agree, you can come bimonthly after today. We'll reassess at a later date."

"Sounds good to me," Eugene said.

"Such a kind young man," Tildy said. "I hope *you're* happily married."

"Confirmed bachelor, thank you," he said with more confidence than he felt.

"Not married," Eugene said. "We weren't aware."

A frown furrowed Tildy's brow as she twisted the handkerchief. Anxious, perhaps, that her desire for sex was no longer valid. Like getting married by a cruise ship captain.

"Academic degrees are one thing," Eugene said, shaking his head. "Real life is another."

"Relationships are relationships, whether one is legally united or not," Theo said, guarding against any defensiveness in his voice. "I've certainly had my share of them. And I've observed many marriages. Some my whole life, like my parents'."

Tildy's face brightened. "They must have had a lovely marriage to produce a fine gentleman like you."

Theo wanted to howl again, but not with laughter. If he had learned anything from Theodore and Marlene Sinclair's disastrous union, it was that divorce was, in some cases, the only—the necessary—solution.

He caught up on case notes after the Farraguts left, waiting for his supervisor. His monthly "mini-eval," as Clifford Callaghan called it, was as welcome as a toothache.

Is everyone a happy camper? Clifford always asked in greeting. Today was no exception.

He sat across from Theo, dressed in his counselor uniform—tan polo shirt, green sweater vest, brown trousers, and beige Hush Puppies. When they met during Theo's interview, he said his initials stood for *Care and Communicate*—and he wasn't entirely joking.

"Everyone's a happy camper. The Farraguts are on the right track. Did you enjoy the Labor Day weekend?" Theo asked to turn the conversation away from the Spragues.

"Very much. Lots of fun. Terrific to spend quality time with the family."

Clifford had a habit of staring to convey sincerity—which had the unfortunate result of conveying *insincerity*. Theo guessed he was lying through his teeth about having fun. With six kids at home, he arranged his schedule to spend as little *quantity* time there as possible.

"I'm afraid you have a problem, Theo. Your success rate with couples is..." He lifted a hand and rocked it back and forth. "Two of them are headed to divorce court."

Beats criminal court after one of them kills the other, he'd reply if his supervisor had a sense of humor.

And if Theo himself didn't agree that he had a problem.

"I've had other positive results," Theo said. "My client with the eating disorder reported that she's gained eight pounds since our sessions. And she feels great about it."

"All well and good. But we strive at Happy Haven to heal sick *relationships* too, not just individuals. Diagnose. Find a cure and treat. Send couples back into the world as healthy as possible. Do you feel you are practicing your best medicine?" Knowing Theo's medical background, Clifford never failed to reference it.

"Yes. Yes, I do. *Honesty* is the best medicine. I encourage my clients to be frank with each other about their expectations." Since Theo was still feeling his way through couples counseling, this was the limit of his methodology.

"But are you exploring the *source* of their problems? Events in the past that contributed to their issues today?"

"I prefer concentrating on the present. If they get too bogged down in the past, they may not move forward."

Clifford frowned. "I'm not sure I agree with you. Relationship dynamics—"

"Repeat themselves. Yes. I know." From parent to child. One generation to the next. Theo knew it down to his bones. "I focus on optimism and the future with my clients. Offer them hope for happiness."

Clifford's eyebrows shot up. "Happiness?"

"Isn't that why the clinic is named Happy Haven?"

"I see. Yes, it is. Yes."

"If there is no chance for happiness, it follows that divorce is a valid option. Those two couples you mentioned—"

"I appreciate your insight, Theo. Thank you for sharing," Clifford said without blinking his eyes.

After more remarks about some couples needing Band-Aids and others needing major surgery, Clifford got up to leave, his Hush Puppies silent, the door shutting behind him any- thing but.

Theo closed the blinds and straightened the pillows on the sofa. Another day closer to his license. He was no whiner but . . . couldn't Clifford give him more credit for his successes?

He was made for this job—he was sure of it. Though his background in medicine had little to do with it. It was while traveling and working odd jobs that he'd discovered his voca- tion. He had a flair for offering a sympathetic ear, for listening closely to what people didn't say, watching what they didn't want anyone to see—a solid skill set for a counselor in his book. Living through his parents' marriage, surviving the Sinclair family's dirty secret—and wanting to save others from a similar calamity—further validated his career choice.

Theo paced the room as the shadows gathered around him. A dirty secret to everyone but him, Theo the First—and Amy and Jo. Unlike his other friends, they were in and out of his house so frequently that his parents barely registered their presence. It was inevitable they would witness the stress and alcohol-fueled furies that started as nasty verbal exchanges and escalated to physical violence. If his grandfather was there, he'd bring Theo to his apartment to *ride out the storm*. Otherwise, Theo hunkered down in his room, muffling the noise with headphones blaring jazz. When he saw the Marsden sisters' horrified faces the first time that they watched his parents yank each other's hair, he realized he had adapted too well to an unhealthy situation.

Don't worry, Teddy. Your secret's safe with us, Jo had assured him in her brusquely affectionate way. *Besides, I've seen worse.*

In her imagination. In her stories.

As for Amy...

Calm, composed Amy quietly retreated to her sketch pad after every display of Sinclair family dysfunction.

Only once, during a particularly vicious argument when he was fifteen, did Theo dare to intervene. *Please don't hurt Mom*, he pleaded with his father. *Please don't hurt Dad*, he begged his mother. When they ignored his entreaties, he called the police.

But the Sinclairs were, as Jo sarcastically put it, "pillars of the community." They contributed generously to fundraisers and attended every significant social event in the city. When they laughed off their son's call as "a big stink over nothing" and invited the cops in for coffee, the incident was swept under the rug. And from that day forward, they resented Theo for having *betrayed the family*.

Until Amy ended the nightmare, once and for all.

Theo stopped pacing in front of the poster. It was a picture of a couple embracing above the quote, *Love means you never have to say you're sorry.*

"If only love were that simple," he muttered, grabbing his car keys and letting the door slam behind him.

The burning seat of his hot car didn't improve his mood. He couldn't wait to sit in the shade of his porch with a cold beer. He'd watch the Shea twins across the street jump on their trampoline and listen to the Martinelli kid two houses down practice piano. Happy children from happy families.

As he must have appeared during the stretches of peace between his parents. His childhood hadn't been *all* bad. He remembered tossing a football with his dad and enjoying the oatmeal cookies his mom had baked just for him. They tolerated his menagerie with surprisingly good humor. Photo albums chronicled family trips to water parks and ski resorts and their annual search for the perfect Christmas tree.

Theo pulled out of the parking lot and into traffic, looking forward to the beer and to Amy coming home from work. She'd complain about the ominous sounds her car was still making, and he'd tinker with the engine again. They'd eat, together or alone. She'd go upstairs with Nina, and he'd read or listen to music in his room. The power of routine to smooth the sharp edges of life.

It had been five days since she'd comforted him for his loss of Theo the First. Her teardrop freckle beneath a real tear. Her arms reaching for him, her body warm against his. The years rewinding to a time when the last thing he wanted was distance between them.

It was Amy he'd gone to the day he'd infuriated his parents by calling the police. He huddled on the beanbag in her bedroom, hiding from everyone, even Jo, while she turned the pages of a Renaissance art book, showing him picture after picture of

Madonnas and angels and hills of cypress trees. Calming and consoling him with art. The first of many such solaces.

It was why, in his heart of hearts, he truly wanted to be a counselor. To offer understanding and sympathy as she had given to him. He might not have been able to do anything for his parents, but there was a hell of a lot he could do for other people.

As Theo waited for the red light to change to green, he scrolled through his phone photos of the portraits Amy had exhibited. Relived, yet again, the terrible moment of recognition he'd experienced confronting them for the first time: *This is your family. This is your life.*

The realization he had been unable to deny, remembering the awful day he'd flung a plate across a room, its shards flying everywhere like tiny knives when it hit a wall. One moment of anger that told him, like the portraits, *This is who you are.*

How brilliantly Amy had captured his parents' rage. Such power and raw emotion in every brushstroke. The chronicle unsuitable for the Sinclair family photo album. Their faces should be hung on the clinic walls, not the sentimental posters. But no. Hope for happiness was what he wanted for couples. Even if he had no chance for it himself.

CHAPTER NINE

*I intend to make my own way in
this world.*
—JO MARCH, *LITTLE WOMEN* (2019 FILM)

$\mathscr{B}$y mid-September, Amy welcomed relief from the summer heat as well as from the many adjustments of a new semester. Morning kitchen encounters with Theo had fallen into the pattern of her gradually reaching consciousness as he worked the blender into various smoothie concoctions. Her munchies and his monastic habits were the topics of comfortable banter. Uncomfortable subjects like the past, or Jo in the present, were as taboo as Amy asking Theo if he ever thought about the Almost-Sex Incident. As forbidden as her thinking for even a nanosecond that she and Theo would be anything other than housemates.

Who needed the distraction anyway? She had too much to do. Like finishing her painting, *Still Life With ?* Propped on the easel in her study, it had the dejected air of an abandoned building. The colors of the lemons and violet pansies were vibrant enough, but her brushwork lacked dash and verve. The weave of the basket deserved more detail. And the gaping area of white where *?* was to be filled in was downright depressing. Inspiration would come. It always had. Well, not in recent memory, but...

Amy mixed alizarin crimson and cobalt blue with the new palette knife Theo had given her as a joke *for the next time there's a naked guy in the kitchen*. Nina strolled in and hissed, hair on end, as she stared at the canvas. "Everybody's a critic," Amy snapped. *"Still Life with Purple Cat*. How do you like them apples, Miss Snootface?"

Nina narrowed her emerald-green eyes into slits and stomped out of the room before Amy could apologize, a feature of a relationship with a pet she hadn't anticipated, never having had one. Her phone rang, and *Marmee* lit the screen. She let it go to voicemail as she finished blending colors.

Of all the terms of affection for their mother, Amy and Jo would never have chosen the name of the saintly matriarch in *Little Women*. But their mother, who'd loved the book since childhood, believed that emulating the March family's triumph over genteel poverty would elevate their own lives. The Marsdens were poor, all right. But the ways that they were *not* like the Marches far exceeded the ways that they were.

Their father, Henry, kept losing jobs as an insurance claims adjuster because he was sympathetic to hard-luck stories. A far cry from the Civil War heroics of the March family patriarch. He did call their mother Meg, though, short for her first name, Margaret. Their mobile home could barely hold four people, much less the six Marches who lived comfortably in Orchard House. And Marmee Marsden's abysmal domestic skills would have inspired many a smarmy lecture from Marmee March.

Amy and Jo dearly loved their mother and went along with it—except her philosophy that marriage was the key to happiness. Marmee was currently on her fourth husband, each of whom had called her a different version of Margaret.

"Black Widow," Jo wickedly referred to her, since all her spouses bit the dust under tragicomical circumstances. Their own father died from stepping back on the roof to watch a flock of geese in formation. *Meg, come take a look at—* were his last words.

Wiping the palette knife clean, Amy listened to her mother's voicemail, panic rising at the crackle of static but nothing else. Jo had speculated that Marmee's latest husband's name, John Smith, was the alias of a black *widower*, and that their mother's life was in constant danger. Another of her sister's jokes that Amy didn't find particularly funny.

"Marmee? Are you okay?" she asked when she returned her mother's call.

"Right as rain. Why wouldn't I be?"

Out of the blue, Amy remembered that today marked her father's birthday, a day she, Jo, and Marmee had gradually stopped commemorating. As well as the day he died. "Your voicemail was just a lot of strange sounds," she said.

"Maybe because we're on speakerphone?"

"Could be." Amy closed her eyes, remembering the scent of pipe tobacco on her dad's tweed jacket, his ready smile. The way he'd say he was *right as rain*. "Where are you calling from this time?"

"We're on our way to Hillsboro, Ohio, to see the giant horseshoe crab. Eighty-eight feet long and twenty-four feet tall. Imagine that."

"I'd rather not. I'm still recovering from your photos of the world's biggest ball of paint in Indiana."

"Twenty-four thousand three hundred and fifty coats of paint on a baseball," John said. A wealthy retired physician, his idea of fun was to travel the country in a Minnie Winnie to see strange roadside attractions with Maggie, *his* name for his wife. He could cite the statistics of every one.

"John, tell Amy about the—" her mother began, but the roar of an airplane in the background swallowed the rest.

When the noise quieted, Amy heard them chatting to each other. They'd probably forgotten she was on the other end. "Did you call about...Marmee, did you want to talk about Dad?"

"Why would I...Oh, dearie me. My Henry's birthday. Thanks for reminding me, Amy. I'll say a little prayer."

"We'll say one together, Maggie," John said kindly.

"How was your visit with Great Aunt...Sophie, is it? Or did you say Sadie?" Amy asked. Marsden and Beauregard relatives were scattered all over the country, and she and Jo had met only a few of them.

"We just missed seeing my Aunt Sophie," Marmee said. "She died, poor thing. Just a bag of bones in the end, they told me. Her son, Byron, inherited the pig farm."

"So Jo and I have a second cousin named Byron. I wonder if he's 'mad, bad, and dangerous to know,'" Amy said, quoting Lady Caroline Lamb on the subject of Lord Byron, the Romantic poet.

"I doubt it. He does smell bad, though. Like pigs."

Amy could picture her mother crinkling her delicate nose. She had inherited her pale complexion, blue-gray eyes, and slim hips as well. Someday, her hair would be an indistinguishable color between blond and silver too.

"The world's largest pig hair ball is in Oregon," John said.

"I did not know that," Amy said, smothering a laugh. "Are you planning to go there?"

"Too far for this trip," he said. "Maybe next time."

"All settled in, sweetie?" Marmee asked her. "I imagine everything's working out splendidly in Theo's house." As far as Marmee knew, her daughters were still good friends with the boy next door who suited her idea of Laurie from *Little Women* to a tee. Theo had good-naturedly tolerated the comparison, being fond of "Mrs. M," but drew the line at actually reading the novel.

"Just like the good old days," Amy said. She and Jo had decided that their mother's life was complicated enough without burdening her with the details of their personal lives.

"And are you doing well in your job?"

"Yes. Very."

"The chair of an entire department," Marmee said rapturously. When Amy had shared the news of her promotion, she could practically hear her mother levitate.

"I was studying to be a French teacher, but had to quit college because my parents didn't have two cents to rub together," Marmee told her for the umpteenth time. "I might have accomplished something in this life if I'd finished my degree."

"But you did. You were a great mom, and your jobs kept the family finances afloat."

"Dead-end jobs." Her mother sighed. "I do wish Jo would aim higher in her career like you."

"She loves teaching high school English. It pays the bills and frees her time to write in the summer."

"That's true. She didn't have to go all the way to Seattle, though."

"Don't you remember? She visited a college friend there and

fell in love with the city." And loved it so much, apparently, she wouldn't leave it to see her own sister. Amy begged for her to visit at least three times a week—*You don't even have to* look *at Theo*—but Jo wouldn't budge. Her plan to reconcile Jo and Theo was going nowhere fast.

"Everything would have been different for her if she'd been nicer to Ben like we told her to be," Marmee said.

Amy put the cap back on the tube of alizarin crimson and picked up the cobalt blue. "You know Jo. Stubborn as a mule." Not only did Jo ignore their advice, but she had taken wicked delight in defying their stepfather every chance she got. Though, like Marmee, Jo thought Amy should grab any opportunity that was offered. She hadn't begrudged her arrangement with Ben one iota.

"She got into Washington University and could have gone there with Theo instead of the University of Missouri. All because she made fun of Ben and called him 'Buccaneer Ben,'" Marmee complained as John chuckled in the background.

"Jo had an absolute blast at Mizzou and was editor of the school newspaper. And the eye patch *was* fake," Amy said. She and Jo used to speculate whether he kept it on during sex or not. "He had two perfectly good eyes, Marmee." If not an effective choke reflex.

Husband number two, Ben Cooper, had been a successful personal injury lawyer. Billboards advertising his firm, including a photo of him wearing the eye patch, appeared every few miles along the interstate. Madge, *his* name for Marmee, did not find the transition to Ladue society at all smooth. To Amy and Jo's amusement, her parties were disasters, especially the last one.

Ben, exasperated by her habit of serving hors d'oeuvres garnished with toothpicks, declared, *This simply is not done, Madge*, chomped on a square of cheddar—and promptly choked to death on the toothpick. The kind with colorful frills at the end. Unfortunately, he hadn't gotten around to changing his will, and the bulk of his fortune went to his first wife and their son. And fortunately, they didn't sue Marmee for personal injury.

"If Jo had played her cards right, that eye patch would have paid for her dream graduate school too," Marmee went on.

"She publishes stories all the time. She didn't need to go to the Iowa Writers' Workshop." Amy got up and gazed out the window. The best light to paint by was fading. "Jo always said she intended to make her own way in the world."

Exactly what Amy told herself to justify not having helped her sister. Along with believing that Jo was a naturally gifted writer who would publish sooner or later. Though probably sooner with a degree and the contacts she would have made in grad school. Amy tightened her hand into a fist, sticky with cobalt-blue paint. She'd been squeezing the tube without realizing it.

"I hope you're still drawing and painting, Amy. I'd hate for you to let it go again."

"Don't worry. I am."

It was Marmee who'd told her that May Alcott, Louisa's younger sister and the basis for the character of Amy March in *Little Women*, had been a successful painter. May had exhibited in Europe for a decade and wrote a guidebook for women artists. On the first of many Marsden family trips to Orchard House in Concord, Massachusetts, Amy had been fascinated by her artwork. Nearly every room featured one of her watercolors, paintings, or drawings. The panel of calla lilies and nasturtiums at Louisa's writing desk was her favorite.

"...And faces," her mother was saying. "You did faces really well."

"It's called *portraiture*."

Like most aspiring artists, Amy had experimented with every medium, from pastels to acrylics, and every *ism*, from impressionism to abstract expressionism. And like Amy March, who plastered her foot attempting to sculpt, she'd had her share of mishaps. Watercolors that dripped or bled through the paper. Superglued fingers. And the pot on the potter's wheel that spun up, and away, and across the room. She eventually discovered her true talent lay in painting portraits.

"*Portraiture* sounds like a French word to me," Marmee said. "Now if only I had—"

John tooted the horn of the Minnie Winnie. "We're going to stop for dinner now, Amy."

"Okay, thanks for calling."

"Love you, Amy dear," Marmee said. "Au revoir."

"Love you too. Theo asked me to say 'Hi, Mrs. M' next time we talked."

"And 'Hello' to him."

Tossing the phone onto the desk, Amy wiped the paint off her hand and covered the palette. And uncovered a painful memory.

Feel Ben out for me, will ya? Jo had asked Amy when she was accepted to the Iowa Writers' Workshop. *See if he'll help me with tuition this time.*

You can ask him yourself.

He doesn't like me. And this is too important for me to mess up. I can't go without his financial support.

Though Amy doubted that their stepfather would ever change his mind regarding Jo, she promised to intercede. It was a chance to test her powers of persuasion, a necessary skill when she went to law school. She rehearsed her request, couching it in legal terms to appeal to lawyer Ben, and constructed a watertight, logical argument.

But when the rubber met the road, Amy worried that she would jeopardize her own tuition at the pricey University of Chicago. Why *should* Ben help Jo when all she'd ever done was disobey and ridicule him, no matter how many times Amy advised her to be diplomatic? Jo had gotten along perfectly fine without his help, hadn't she? She prided herself on her independence and would chafe under obligation to him. She was so gifted, going to graduate school for writing was superfluous.

And why should Jo go to her dream school when Amy couldn't go to art school and would spend her career spewing legalese, which she had discovered she loathed with a passion? Not to mention the fact that she didn't give a hoot about plaintiffs, defendants, and legal precedents.

However little their lives compared to those of the characters in *Little Women*, there were a few parallels. Amy's lie to Jo, that she had asked Ben to help her financially, but he refused, was like Amy March burning Jo's manuscript of stories.

She examined *Still Life With ?* again. Dull. Uninspired. *Pretty*. Pulling it off the easel, she placed it on the floor, front to the wall. So much for her aspiration of being an artist. *She* was an unfinished still life. Which, considering what she'd done to Jo, was exactly what she deserved.

Before she could talk herself out of it, Amy emailed Ralph Wilkinson, her art instructor when she lived in Chicago. If he agreed to meet with her, she'd bring the portfolio of her recent work for his appraisal. It was time to put herself out there again. Subject herself to the judgment of experts. Find out once and for all if she was extraordinary—or had any talent whatsoever.

"Let's do this thing," she said, hitting Send.

CHAPTER TEN

*I can't explain exactly, but I want to
be above the little meannesses and
follies and faults that spoil so
many women.*
—AMY MARCH, *LITTLE WOMEN*

Working late in her campus office, Amy laughed her way through the stories the students in her Microfiction class had turned in. Jo would love the one about the gymnast who somersaulted across a tennis court during a Wimbledon match. And the story written from the point of view of a chimpanzee in a zoo.

Her stomach growled loudly as she read, craving a veggie burger with homemade sweet potato fries. While she and Theo weren't "at war," the kitchen had briefly been a combat zone— her instant or defrosted meals on one side, his made-from-scratch on the other. She'd surrendered during what they now referred to as the Zucchini Bread Incident, during which she demolished half a loaf in the time it took to say *zucchini bread*. Defeated. By a squash.

At the sound of knocking, Amy froze in position so the chair wouldn't creak. If it was Athena, she would have called out, *Yoo-hoo, anyone home?* And with the exception of Fiona Reilly and Gary Ericson, faculty and staff rarely stayed on campus after six o'clock. Which meant either her boss or her bête noire was on the other side of the door.

The rapping continued. She waited as motionless as was humanly possible for her or him to give up and walk away.

"Amy? Are you in there?"

She let out a breath. It was Eileen Thomas, one of the adjunct professors. "Hi, Eileen," she said, getting up to open the door. "What can I do for you?"

"Sorry if I'm disturbing you. I saw the light under the crack."

Crap. So Gary knew she was hiding last week when he kept knocking and repeating, *A minute of your time*, like a robot.

Eileen entered, carrying books, a laptop, and a large thermos. She had the exhausted look of most of the adjuncts who trudged the hallways, coffee cups in hand, on their way to their next class. If they had one to teach. It wasn't fair how they labored without offices, job security, or benefits.

"I hope the semester's going well for you," Amy said, pulling out a chair for her. "How's Tommy?" She guessed that the circles under Eileen's eyes were from teaching Composition 101 and raising a very active thirteen-year-old boy.

Eileen blew a strand of auburn hair off her forehead. "Running me ragged. I'm hoping to catch up on sleep when his dad takes him this weekend."

"How can I help you?"

"I met my students in the main reading room of the library last week to go over their essays. The reference librarian got huffy when some of them talked above a whisper."

"Mrs. Fisher once scolded me for sneezing. How about the conference rooms?"

"Availability is hit-or-miss."

"Do you want to use my office for your meetings?"

Her sallow face brightened. "I was hoping you'd offer. I only need it a few hours each week."

"Email your schedule, and we'll make it happen."

"Thank you so much, Amy. You're a lifesaver."

"Glad to help. Anything else I can do for you?"

"Yes." Eileen balanced the pile of books on her lap. "The adjuncts have submitted a proposal to Dean Reilly for improved working conditions. She hasn't responded to our requests to discuss it."

"There are many demands on her time."

"Demands? I'm working three jobs to make ends meet."

"Patience is needed. Be assured the subject will be addressed," Amy said, retreating to the safe distance of the passive voice.

"Any chance you can mediate on our behalf?"

I'd be glad to was on the tip of Amy's conscience, if not her tongue. But it wouldn't do to aggravate Fiona, whose attitude toward the adjuncts was dismissive at best—and who might interpret Amy's intercession as disloyal to the administration.

"My advice is to let it play out a little longer, Eileen. An aggressive approach may backfire."

"Backfire. Right." Eileen waved the thermos as she rose from the chair. "I may start filling this with wine instead of coffee."

Amy drove home through the late-September dusk, seeing Eileen's hunched, defeated shoulders on the road before her. *Scaredy-cat*, she could hear Jo say. *Way to cop out, Amy Mamy.*

Back home, she slipped on a pink fleece top, leggings, and ballerina flats, her go-to outfit for when a day had gone to shit. Hearing giggling in the kitchen, presumably Brittany's since the Camry was parked in the driveway, she unwound her coiled bun and let her hair ripple down her back as she went downstairs.

The cats, supervised by Moose, were lined up behind Theo as he cooked at the stove. The sleeves of a Habitat for Humanity shirt were rolled up to his elbows, revealing forearms taut as wire. Flecks of sawdust dotted his dark hair and shoulders. A walking advertisement for alpha-meets-beta male if Amy ever saw one. Her mouth watered, a normal salivary response to the smell of sizzling bacon and sausage. And other sensations.

Brittany sat in Coltrane's favorite chair, wearing Theo's Eiffel Tower T-shirt. And nothing else but panties with butterflies on them. "You must be Amy!" she said, waving a sausage link at the end of her fork. "I'm Brittany."

"Nice to meet you, Brittany."

"This has got to be, like, the best dinner ever!"

Having never been irritated by a sausage link before, not to mention a whole fricking bowl of bacon, Amy was at a loss for words.

"Help yourself, Amy," Theo said over his shoulder.

"Isn't he the nicest guy?" Brittany gushed. "He worked at the clinic and helped rehab a house, and now he made all this meat just because I wanted it. And he's not even going to eat any."

There was such a thing as being *too* perky, no matter how many orgasms you'd had. Orgasm-less Amy wanted to retort, *Oh yeah? Well, I knew him first.* She sat and gnawed a bacon strip instead. Coltrane, dispossessed of his chair, glared hard enough at Brittany for them both.

"You work with the Habitat for Humanity crews?" Amy asked Theo. "Since when?"

"Started last week. Want some scrambled eggs?" he asked, heaping spoonfuls onto Brittany's plate.

"Sure but...breakfast food for dinner?"

"Why not? We used to eat waffles for supper and spaghetti for breakfast sometimes."

A blush overtook Amy's cheeks, remembering the two of them playfully sharing a strand of spaghetti like the dogs in *Lady and the Tramp*. Theo had bit down on it hard, one inch before their mouths met. "Fun times," she mumbled.

"Indeed, they were," he said, placing an empty plate in front of her and grazing her arm with his. Since the Zucchini Bread Incident, when he'd repeatedly nudged her shoulder, victor that he was, more accidental grazing incidents had occurred.

"Are you two, like, related or something?" Brittany asked, wide-eyed.

"Or something," Theo said, looking yet not looking at Amy as he cracked eggs in quick succession against a bowl.

Brittany's forehead puckered into a frown, but Amy saw no reason in the world to explain that she and Theo were reluctant housemates who had once been good friends. Who had nurtured their friendship with visits and steady streams of texts and calls as they pursued careers in different cities and commiserated over failed relationships. Who once were minutes away from their own romance.

Theo shot her a glance as he dropped oil into the pan and it sizzled loudly. Which she decided to interpret as him picturing them on the floor of his apartment, half-dressed. No—half-naked.

Amy helped herself to another strip of bacon and slipped one to Moose on the sly. "Are you a student?" she asked Brittany.

"No, I'm a dancer!" Brittany stretched out one long leg and arched her foot. "I did ballet for years, but I'm doing more tap lately because, I figure, when I open my dance studio, I'll attract more students."

"Dance studio. Impressive." Really. It was.

"It's been my dream since, like, forever. I have my eye on a building in Rosewood to rent, and I know all these women with little kids, and they want them to learn to dance, and I think it'll be great."

"So do I. Good for you."

"Do you have a dream too, Amy?"

If Theo hadn't slowly turned around and given Amy his deep-sea gaze, the one that used to read her thoughts, even the ones she wasn't consciously thinking, she might have expressed her artistic ambitions to Brittany. But she didn't feel like diving into the deep sea and its memories of Theo encouraging her, assuring her that she was a gifted artist and that anything was possible. And her believing him.

"My career is my priority. For now," Amy said. "Its challenges keep me on my toes."

Brittany giggled. "On your toes. Like a dancer."

"Eggs ready yet?" Amy asked Theo, spearing a sausage link with a fork.

"Eggs ready," he said, filling her plate and his own.

As they ate, Brittany chirped nonstop about how she could eat like a horse and never gain a pound. How her last boyfriend— no, wait, the one before—dared her to eat ten hot dogs in one sitting and she did, and she still got into her leotard a half hour later and danced her feet off and . . .

"My gosh!" she suddenly exclaimed.

Amy knew from Theo's startled expression when he looked up from his dish that he had stopped listening somewhere between Brittany's description of her gnarled big toe and her childhood collection of My Little Pony dolls. "What is it?" he asked.

"I just remembered I have to be home by seven thirty."

"Oh, okay. I'll see you out."

"No, no, don't bother. Finish your dinner before it gets cold."

No sooner had Brittany vacated the chair than Coltrane leaped onto it and settled into a legs-tucked-under lump.

"I hate to eat and run, but I've got to help my sister bake, like, tons of cupcakes for her daughter's Girl Scout troop," Brittany said, waving goodbye as she left the kitchen.

"Don't forget your pants," Theo called out.

"Got 'em," she replied from his bedroom.

"Don't forget to put them on," he said.

"Oh, you silly!"

At the sound of the front door closing, Amy stuffed a whole sausage link in her mouth. And promptly gagged and choked. Her eyes teared, and her life flashed before her eyes—including, mortifyingly, Banana Brad—while Theo patted her back. Nina meowed concern and Ray and Bessie stood at full attention, ready to do whatever they could. Coltrane looked disgusted at having to tolerate yet another demonstration of human absurdity. A chunk of meat slid down her throat; the rest she spit into a napkin. Moose thumped his tail, signaling he wanted it.

"Dude. No," she rasped.

"You okay?" Theo asked.

"Uh-huh. I do like a near-death experience now and again. Keeps me on my toes. Like a dancer." She looked down at the cats, ignoring Theo's grin. "They know CPR, don't they?"

"And the Heimlich maneuver."

"At least I didn't choke on a toothpick."

"Watch out for those frills."

He got up and filled a glass of water at the sink. One good thing about living with Theo, however reluctantly—she didn't have to explain every little thing.

"Here. Drink this," he said. "It'll soothe your throat."

"Thanks." Amy sipped the water, resisting the urge to brush sawdust from his shoulder. And hair. And anywhere else it might be. "Brittany's all right, by the way."

"Oh. Gee. Glad you approve."

"No need to be sarcastic. I mean it. She's sweet. How'd you two meet?"

"She got a flat tire on the county road. I changed it for her."

Of course he did.

"Think her dance studio will get off the ground?" she asked.

"With her ambition and talent, anything is possible."

Amy didn't know which was worse—that either he'd forgotten he'd once said the same thing to her or that he'd remembered.

"Been meaning to tell you, I have a three-day weekend coming up in two weeks, and I'm flying to Chicago." Ralph's reply to her email had been so cryptic—*Art. Yes. Art.*—she'd read it a few times to be sure he had agreed to meet her. Then decided it didn't matter since she was going either way.

What was up with the accidental grazing incidents anyway?

"Thanks for letting me know," Theo said.

"Can you bring in my mail and take care of Nina while I'm gone?"

"Glad to."

"And water the ferns in my study if they look droopy?"

"Will do."

Sir Theo the Do-Gooder, a name she and Jo used to tease him with.

When you're trained to please, he'd reply, referring to his impossible parents, *you have no choice but to do the right thing.*

The right thing.

Amy shivered as a chill autumn breeze wafted through the open window. Clearing the table, she put on kitchen gloves and rinsed the dishes at the sink. She hadn't always done the right thing by Jo and Theo. And she'd been telling herself that someday, somehow, she'd make it up to them. But who was she kidding? She'd just been offered a chance to support the adjunct professors, and she hadn't taken it.

"I should have helped a colleague today, but I held back," she blurted out.

"Uh-huh," Theo said.

She turned to face him. "I feel really crappy about it."

"Everybody has their bad days," he said, straightening the chairs. "Anyway, I've got to write case notes. Thanks for cleaning up."

Is that all you have to say? she wanted to ask.

But this wasn't the Theo she used to go to for advice—*Should I take Introduction to Economics? Which stereo speakers should I buy?* Or for sympathy. *I feel really crappy.* This was the Theo who told her that nothing lasted forever, including their friendship.

But sisterhood did.

Her hands were clammy inside the gloves. Amy tugged at them but they wouldn't come off. "We need to talk about you and Jo, Theo."

"No. We don't." His hair hung over his face so she couldn't read his expression.

"It's ridiculous that you two haven't mended fences by now."

"It's none of your business."

"Of course it is. She's my sister, and I—"

"Stay out of it, Amy."

"Is this how you advise clients to settle their differences?"

The ceramic salt and pepper shakers clicked loudly when he aligned them on the table. "I advise *you* to leave well enough alone," he said.

"There's nothing *well* about you and Jo. You're not making any sense." Why wouldn't the damn gloves come off?

"Makes perfect sense to me," he said sharply.

She was an idiot. Why hadn't she seen it before? Theo was glad, maybe even relieved, that the Marsden sisters were out of his life.

It made perfect sense to her.

"We've all gone our separate ways, Theo. But I'd like to think we can be family to each other again. Or friends. Or something," Amy added lamely.

In the hallway, Ray and Bessie were hissing loudly and swatting each other with rapid punches of their paws.

"Ray Charles, chill out," Theo said. "And Bessie Smith, quit bullying him, you hear me?"

They stalked off in opposite directions.

"Oh. Ray Charles because he's half-blind," Amy said, just figuring this out too.

"Could be worse," he said, walking out of the kitchen. "He could be completely blind like the actual Ray. And other people."

That look over his shoulder. A look that said, as far as Theo and Jo and Amy and the possibility of resuming their friendship were concerned, *she* was completely blind. And an idiot.

Yeah. Well. No biggie. She wasn't going to stop trying to make things right. Not by a long shot. No more fooling herself about *someday, somehow*. The opportunity to make up to Jo for the lie about their stepfather was right in front of her. Fiona wanted her to *actively recruit*, and recruit she would. She'd get Jo a position at the college, *by hook or by crook*, as Marmee liked to say. Not only would it boost Jo's career financially and every other way, but the job would bring her back to the Midwest, close to Amy and their mother. And Theo.

Is this part of a harebrained scheme to get me and Theo to make up? Jo had asked yesterday when she invited her to visit again.

Of course not, Amy had fibbed.

With one more tug, she removed the gloves. Thinking of her master plan, to get Jo the position *and* reconcile her and Theo, another Marmee expression came to mind—*killing two birds with one stone*. That's exactly what she'd be doing. Except for the killing part. And the dead birds. And the stone.

CHAPTER ELEVEN

I want to be great, or nothing.
—AMY MARCH, *LITTLE WOMEN*

Amy hadn't seen Ralph Wilkinson since she left Chicago four years ago, but they'd kept in touch with occasional emails. His small teaching studio in a converted garment factory had been a place of refuge from academic stress. Never robust—starving artist, penniless instructor, and all that—he now looked frail. As if a strong wind off Lake Michigan could knock him right over. When she hugged him, she couldn't help tearing up, feeling the sharpness of his bones against her body.

He sipped his wine, bringing the glass to his lips as gingerly as if he were stepping onto a patch of ice. To her disappointment, he'd insisted they meet in a bar instead of their favorite French restaurant where they'd engaged in lively debates over Rembrandt and Bosch (neither of whom she cared for), and Botticelli and the Pre-Raphaelite painters (whom she adored). Needing all her wits to keep him focused, she restricted herself to sparkling water since she became a blithering imbecile after one beer or glass of wine. An hour into the conversation, though, and he'd barely commented on the photos of her portfolio of drawings, watercolors, and paintings.

"In class, you always told us to draw the body as if we were sculpting it," Amy said to reel in his rambling discussion of chardonnay versus sauvignon blanc.

"Yes, I did," he said primly, signaling the waiter for another bottle of wine. That she was paying for. Ralph's enthusiasm for Dutch painters did not extend to going Dutch.

"What do you think of my hand studies? And the series of male backs?" Muscular backs strong enough to frame a house. "Do they look sculptural to you?"

"My sculpture *Armistice* won first prize in nineteen ninety-two," he replied. "The same year my painting *War Dogs* won a gold medal. How many artists can boast such an achievement?"

"Not many."

His work certainly warranted the acclaim it had received. Unfortunately, this recognition had not translated into significant critical or economic success. And did not alter her opinion that *Armistice* looked like a giant stainless-steel pretzel.

"*Cloud Gate* is a crime against humanity." He refused to refer to the sculpture in Millennium Park by its colloquial name, *The Bean*. "*My* work should be in the plaza."

Amy retrieved her phone from her handbag. Once Ralph embarked on his litany of slights, it would be impossible to return him to the subject at hand. "What do you think of this?" she asked, zooming in on her painting of a pond at dusk with herons.

"Can't afford one of those smartphones," he said, peering at it. "All my awards and I'm still a pauper."

"I'm sorry to hear it, Ralph. Now, about my painting. Do you—"

"I should have defected to academia like you." His watery blue eyes focused on her for the first time that evening. "What was the subject of your dissertation, Amanda?"

"The Arthurian legends through history." As she'd told him on many other occasions. "And I'm *Amy*. Amy Marsden."

"I loved King Arthur stories when I was a boy. I'd be rich too if I let literature inspire me instead of art."

She couldn't protest that she wasn't rich, not with a smartphone, a Jil Sander suit, and a healthy 401(k). Nor would she admit that her inspiration hadn't entirely been a lofty one. Her interest in Arthurian legends began when she saw the film *Camelot* in high school. She'd flail around her bedroom, pretending she was Guinevere lustily singing about the lusty month of May while pining for Lancelot. In her mind, the legendary Lancelot must have looked an awful lot like Theo.

"Shall I tell you what James Kenneth is doing these days?" Ralph said.

"Who?"

"Who?" he repeated. "Who, you ask?"

Amy had no fricking clue. Did Ralph have a partner? A son? A beloved pet to share his dotage?

"James Kenneth is my friend. He was one of the most promising artists on the Chicago art scene. They discarded him and he passes his days..." He shuddered slightly. "He does jigsaw puzzles. Of classical paintings."

"Maybe it relaxes him."

Ralph plucked at the buttons on his shirt as if trying to tear them off. "Will this be your callous response when you find out that I'm knitting ponchos? It *relaxes* me?"

The couple at the next table stopped texting long enough to look up at each other and mouth, *Ponchos?*

"Ralph, I can't imagine you would ever..." Amy's voice trailed off as the image of him bent over knitting needles loomed vividly in her sight.

"Callous and heartless," he harrumphed, "just like the rest of them."

The bubbles of her sparkling water evaporated, along with her hopes for advice and an appraisal of her work. She'd never have dreamed he'd be so hostile or compare her to the critics, art dealers, and galleries who had overlooked him.

"About my portfolio," she tried again. "Can you tell me if you think I—"

"You are a mediocrity, Amanda. As for encouraging you in any way, shape, or form, I'm not comfortable. Not comfortable at all."

As if he were discussing the purchase of a pair of shoes and not stomping on her dreams.

～◯

Amy stood on tiptoe and tilted her body at a forty-five-degree angle to see *The Bean* sculpture from her hotel window. "*Crime against humanity*, my butt," she muttered. "It's fricking awesome."

She rested her forehead against the glass. Stars studded the skies of Laurel, but city lights obscured them here. She caught patches of milky black between the skyscrapers. The sky, the day, Chicago were all dissolving, as was her relationship with the city. Ralph had dismissed her and her portfolio. Cassie, her best friend in college, had recently moved to Wisconsin. As

Amy wandered the city the past couple of days, it occurred to her that nearly everyone she had known there had relocated to pursue careers and raise families.

Dropping onto the bed, she picked up the phone to call Jo but realized she didn't want to be cheered up. Her expectations for this trip had blown up in her face, so she might as well let her remaining time go to pieces too. She'd had a glimpse of the dark side of her dream job—Ralph, James Kenneth, puzzles, ponchos—and she needed to take an unflinching look at other realities.

Like having convinced herself that Theo would be understanding when he saw his parents' portraits at the *Scenes from a Marriage* exhibit. After all, he'd always championed her art.

The reality? While she had wrestled between ambition and concern for his feelings, she knew deep in her heart that ambition would win out.

There Amy had stood with Theo in the gallery, a glass of champagne in her hand, flush with the unanimous praise for her work. Glorying in her first-place win. She'd done it. She'd kept her gift for painting alive despite the career compromises she'd made. And if Theo's reaction was more agitated than she'd expected, if he'd barely spoken to her before returning to St. Louis the same day when they'd planned a weekend together, their first since the night that they were locked in each other's arms on his living room floor...well, they'd work it out.

As the Sinclair scandal disastrously unfolded and Theo did not respond to her apologetic messages, she clung to the hope that their affection for each other would see them through the crisis. She hadn't meant to wreak such havoc. Certainly, he wouldn't imagine that she'd ever intentionally hurt him. She'd do everything she could to help him solve the mystery of who informed the press of his parents' identity.

Amy slid beneath the blanket and let it cover her completely. She shut her eyes and, in the absolute blackness, relived the days and weeks and months that had marched by without a word from Theo. Jo, who'd seen photos of the portraits and pronounced them first-rate, reproached her for exhibiting them. *Badly done, Amy Mamy*, she'd rebuked her. *Badly done.*

Unable to bear her unanswered messages any longer, Amy flew from Chicago and drove a rental car to Theo's apartment in St. Louis.

The last feeble cinder of her exhibit triumph flared into blazing regret at the sight of Theo standing in the doorway, his eyes as blank as a Roman statue.

"Can I come in?" she'd asked, shivering, though it was a warm summer evening.

"What for?" he said.

"To talk. So we can—"

"No."

"Why not?"

"I have nothing to say to you."

"But it's me. Amy. You have to—"

"I don't have to do anything."

His lips hardly moved. His body was as rigid as the doorframe. He'd come to her like this sometimes and gradually uncoil as he watched her sketch. Or they would go for a walk. Watch a movie. Or simply do nothing. She always knew what he needed. And right now, he needed an explanation.

"You have to believe me, Theo. I had no idea the press would ever—"

"I don't have to believe anything."

"For God's sake, will you let me finish a sentence?"

"What for?" he said again.

"To explain the portraits."

To confess that her ambition had burned through her qualms that Theo, seeing his parents publicly displayed in their worst moments, would be hurt and ashamed. Ambition had burned her scruples to charred earth. Which would be the landscape of her life if Theo didn't forgive her.

"Theo, I—"

"Don't bother explaining," he said sullenly.

"You're behaving like a child."

He turned from the doorway into the dark foyer. Panic rose like floodwater through her body. Amy reached out and grabbed his arm before he disappeared. A ghost. A phantom. Her Theo, gone, gone. "Please. I am so sorry, Theo. Please forgive me. We . . . we have something special. You know we do. That night in your apartment—"

He shook his arm free of her grasp. "You must be joking."

"But what about our friendship? All the years we—"

"Now, Amy."

"*Now, Amy* what?" she whispered, tears streaming down her cheeks.

"Nothing lasts forever." And with those devastating words, Theo retreated into the shadows and closed the door behind him.

Amy wriggled free of the blanket on the hotel bed and roughly wiped her teary eyes on the back of her hand. Here was yet another parallel in her life to *Little Women*. When Theo left her standing on the doorstep, it was as if she had fallen through the ice like Amy March—except neither Jo nor Laurie came to her rescue.

But she would come to Jo's and Theo's. She owed them both that much.

CHAPTER TWELVE

*I mean to make the most of every
chance that comes.*
—AMY MARCH, *LITTLE WOMEN*

Theo relaxed on the sofa while Nina paced the living room to the beat of the rain drumming the windows. He shifted slightly to make room for her, easing Bessie off his leg. "C'mere, girl. Come sit with me."

Her disdainful look was the same one she'd given him the day he took her in when her owner, an elderly woman, passed away. Pampered since she was a kitten, Nina comported herself as if she were the reincarnation of an Egyptian deity. Sometimes when she stared at him like a sphinx, he thought she might be.

"Stay chill," he told her. "Amy will be home today."

Nina stopped in her tracks and looked at the front door as if waiting for it to open.

"Not this exact minute. But soon. I think."

She emitted a low snarl and, tail pointed due north, made her dignified way upstairs.

What was Amy doing in Chicago anyway? No one ever came to the house to see her, and she rarely stayed out past ten. Visiting a friend, maybe. Or starting a long-distance relationship, putting the jerk she'd broken up with in the rearview mirror. Sometimes he gave the a-hole's coffeemaker the finger, just for the hell of it.

Theo rubbed his stubbled chin, picturing the boyfriend in Chicago. He was most likely someone she'd known for a while. A professor, like her, who submitted articles to obscure journals titled *Precambrian Interpretations: An Archaeology of Poetry*. Who went to Gregorian chant concerts and periodically left civilization to live in the wilderness. In a yurt. Built with his own two hands.

He pulled himself up to a sitting position. Whoa. *That* was pretty damn specific. And why was he thinking about Amy's dating life in the first place? Boredom, plain and simple. The house had been too quiet while she was gone. And in the second place...

Old habits did die hard. He was twentysomething Theo again, convincing himself he wasn't jealous of Amy's latest college boyfriend. That he didn't care there was another guy in her life free to call her at two a.m. with a case of the blues. Or that she only dated guys who *wouldn't* call her at two a.m. with a case of the Theo Sinclair blues.

His phone rang, eliciting a growl from Bessie, grumpy after her insulin shot. He pulled it out of his pocket and read *AM* on the screen. "Hi, Amy. What's up?"

"My car died, and I'm stuck at the airport."

"You do realize most Hondas live to a ripe old age."

"Mine never survive adolescence. Dying on me is their ultimate teenage rebellion."

Bessie glared at Theo when he let out a guffaw.

"Yeah. Hilarious," Amy said.

"I thought so."

"Here's something else to chortle about. I can't get a ride service to save my life."

"You do realize nobody ever actually *chortles*."

"Focus, please. No ride service."

"It's the torrential weather. The rain's pouring sideways."

"My friend, Athena, is in Florida with her husband to see his mother; otherwise, I would have called her. Oh, wait. I'll rent a car. I should have thought of it before bugging you."

"Don't bother. I'll come get you."

"It's too much trouble. I'll—"

"Sit tight. I need an excuse to get out of the house." Where his mind had strayed into the forbidden territory of her personal life. "I'll be there in thirty, forty minutes."

"Sure?"

"I'd wind up driving you back from a car rental office anyway."

"I hadn't thought of that."

"And we can't risk you killing another car."

"You'd definitely be an accessory to the crime."

"Would you rat me out?"

She laughed. "In a heartbeat."

Traffic into St. Louis was light, thanks to the storm. Theo spotted Amy at the airport's passenger pickup area and popped open the trunk after he parked. She put her carry-on suitcase in it and hurried into the car.

"It's raining cats and cats out there," she said, slipping out of her soaked jacket.

"Couldn't have said it better myself."

Her face was bare of makeup as usual, though her lips looked red against her pale skin. Kiss-rubbed lips and tired eyes.

Maybe her lover was an astronomy professor who called her his "heavenly body" while they burned up the sheets.

He should get his mind off other people's beds and flaming sheets. But hey, what guy wasn't thinking about sex every five minutes?

Astronomy geeks. Or professors who built yurts—that's who.

Theo turned onto Highway 70 and lowered the windshield wiper speed as the rain abated. "Good time in Chicago?"

"Not particularly. My latest car fiasco is a suitable ending to this weekend. Thanks for the rescue."

He almost said, *Want to talk about it?* but he was in helpful-housemate mode, not counselor mode. "You'll owe me one."

"You bet. I'll make you breakfast. Or your meal of choice."

"I can toast my own Pop-Tarts, thank you. And microwave a Hot Pocket."

"Everybody's a comedian. How's Nina doing?"

"Waiting impatiently for your return."

"Least *somebody* is," she mumbled.

He tuned the radio to his favorite jazz station and let theoretical boyfriends drift away on the crooning saxophone. Amy leaned against the headrest and turned to face the window, her less-than-wonderful Chicago trip hanging in the air. Along with the scent of her damp skin, citrusy yet sweet. He sniffed once, twice.

"Skin So Soft by Avon," she murmured. "In case you were wondering."

"Uh…yeah…smells nice," he said, swerving to avoid a gaping pothole, if not embarrassment.

"Supposedly, it repels mosquitos too. I'm nothing if not practical." She let out a long sigh. "Practical, practical, practical."

Theo was tempted again to ask what was troubling her, but he'd save his interview skills for tomorrow's counseling sessions. He was determined to get the Spragues on the same conversational track. Somehow. And make sure the Farraguts stayed on course and between the sheets.

Great. Thinking about sex again. When he should be more concerned about forming a lasting relationship with someone. He'd be a better man for it and, God knows, a better couples counselor.

"Anything you want to talk about?" he asked Amy. Counselor mode might get his mind going in the opposite direction of her fragrant presence. And of any thought that she could be that *someone*.

"I met with my former art instructor for an evaluation of my portfolio," she said.

Artist. Shit. He had a feeling *those* guys had sex on the brain every minute. "What did she say?" he asked.

"*He*. I won't be quitting my day job anytime soon." She crossed her eyes to make light of the verdict. "The crabby old fart could at least have said I showed promise."

Okay—male. But old and crabby. Good.

"Your art is *beyond* promise, and you know it," Theo said. "Show the world what you've got and prove him wrong."

"Goal number one hundred and twenty-three," she said, waving a finger in the air.

Theo glanced at her damp blouse, its clingy material defining the perfectly round contours of her breasts. Shifting in his seat, he gripped the steering wheel with both hands and stared straight ahead. The clouds in the eastern sky were clearing, a few tinged with gold from the late-morning sun. He'd call

Brittany when he got home and take her up on her sexting messages. Or not.

"Actually, Ralph did me a favor," Amy said.

"How so?"

"He helped me realize that if I'm going to accomplish anything in art, I should focus on my best talent and paint portraits again. I haven't painted one since . . . you know."

"That's too bad," he mumbled. The exhibit was like a stone creating an endless series of ripples in a pond.

"Just for the record, I slashed the portraits with an X-Acto knife. Every last one of them."

Theo turned to look at her. With her face in shadow, her eyes were more gray than blue, the teardrop freckle a tiny smudge.

"I'm just going to say this and get it over with," Amy said.

"Uh-oh. Should I pull over?"

"No. But quit staring at me and watch the road. I don't want to die before clearing the air."

He drove dutifully, waiting for the next stone in the pond. A few moments passed before she spoke again.

"What I want to say is—you never came right out and told me you forgive me, Theo."

"*Water under the bridge*, as Theo the First used to say."

"It's pretty fricking muddy water."

"No one goes through life without making mistakes."

"Great. Just what I wanted to hear," she said drily. "Counselor-speak."

"No, I'm not . . . Yeah, I am talking like a counselor. Sorry."

Amy plucked the seat belt from her chest and let it spring back with a snap. "I never meant for all those horrible things to happen."

"I know you didn't," Theo said.

"And you accept my apology? Excuse me—*apologies*? Plural?"

So many, but it was the last one he remembered most clearly. Shutting the door against her stricken, tearful face and pleading voice. Sliding down that closed door onto the floor.

"Of course I do," he said.

"So go on. Say it."

Their eyes met.

"I forgive you, Amy Marsden," he said solemnly. "And I accept your apologies."

"Thank you, Theo Sinclair," she replied.

"Sorry. I should have said it sooner." In his heart, he already had. He'd forgotten that Amy no longer *knew* his heart.

"Yeah. Well. Better late than never." She traced a meandering streak of rain on the window with one finger. "If your parents hadn't been identified...Boy, wouldn't I love to find out who did it and give them a piece of my mind."

"Yeah. Me too." Theo turned off the windshield wipers, hoping to turn the subject off as well. "Rain stopped. Should be nice the rest of the day."

"I do appreciate you taking the trouble to get me."

"No trouble at all. It occurred to me that I should have the contact info of the people you're meeting when you leave town. And where you'll be too, in case of an emergency."

Amy grinned. "Reminds me of how you'd wait up for me till I got home from my babysitting jobs, no matter how late."

"You never know what can happen, even in an affluent neighborhood. Or *especially* in one, with everyone sequestered behind their mansion walls."

"What was your rationale for grilling me about my dates?"

"Admit it. You always went out with the strangest guys."

"I prefer to think of them as creative, out-of-the-box thinkers."

"Your *spin* on them right now is certainly creative. And some of them had thrown the box away."

"Your dating track record wasn't so hot," Amy said. "If it weren't for me, you'd never have noticed that Sue Ellen was gaslighting you."

"*Suzanne.* And if it weren't for me, you'd have cried a lot longer over that jerk Stephen."

"*Stuart.* I'd never been dumped before," she said with a Nina-like look of disdain.

"Took you till you were twenty. I'd say you were overdue."

"Well, phooey to you too."

Amy had come home from college after the Stephen/Stuart jerk dumped her and cried on Theo's shoulder. Literally. He had welcomed the chance to comfort *her* for a change. Though mostly all he could think about was how soft her curls were and how her lips were so close to his.

The '57 Chevy's engine sputtered and he cursed under his breath. "This has been happening lately when it rains. I keep meaning to check it out."

"There's nothing wrong with Theo the First's baby," she said, patting the dashboard. "It's because She Who Kills Cars is with you. I'm cursed, like Jo. She Who Drives into Traffic Cones and Mailboxes."

Jo's car accidents had been a running joke for years. Since their argument, though, Theo doubted she'd laugh about one. "Kind of like her crash-and-burn relationships," he said.

"*Heart or art and nothing in between*," Amy said, imitating Jo's gruff voice. "If a guy distracts her from writing with the slightest demand, she sends him packing."

The car decelerated as Theo recklessly switched lanes. He swore out loud this time as another driver blared their horn.

"The Jo effect," Amy remarked.

"What are you talking about?"

"One mention of Jo and you're driving erratically and cursing." Amy wrapped her hair around her hand and tugged on it. "I called her this morning before my flight and asked her to visit for the hundredth time. You know, so I can get you guys in the same zip code area."

"Asking you to *stay out of it* obviously doesn't mean a thing to you," he said, repressing a few more choice expletives.

"You didn't ask. You snarled. So, no, it doesn't mean a thing."

Heart thumping, Theo pressed the accelerator to change lanes again as a Mack truck roared up behind them. Damn tailgating fool. "What'd Jo say?"

"I asked her to conduct a couple of writing workshops at the college. That was bait she couldn't resist. I'm kicking myself that I didn't think of it sooner."

"And?"

"She said she can spare some days in November. Any chance in heck you two can bury the hatchet before then? Or sometime this century?"

He smoothly maneuvered the steep curve of the Laurel exit. "Doesn't matter if we do," he muttered.

"It matters to *me*. And it's very simple—forgive Jo like you forgave me, Theo. Even if the argument was her fault."

Figuring out who was at fault was a rabbit hole he did not want to go down.

"I want to repair us," Amy went on. "Bring everybody together again."

"Pretty ambitious plan you've got going. Good luck."

Her eyes shot darts at him. "Oh, yeah? Well, I'm going to prove *you* wrong too. Not just Ralph. See if I don't."

"Suit yourself."

They rode in silence along the county road and through the subdivision of new homes, their backyards filled with toys and jungle gyms. Despite the recent rain, the high school's homecoming festivities were in full swing at the public park in the center of Laurel—food carts selling hot dogs and soft drinks, the band's instruments blaring from the stage, and families strolling across the expansive lawn.

Theo stole a glance at Amy. Fatigue had replaced anger in her eyes, and she slumped against the door. He ran his hands along the curve of the steering wheel, his fingers tingling. Sometimes at home, he just couldn't help nudging her or brushing against her. From habits of a long time ago. From desire. Weakness. She never reacted, but then she *had* mastered the art of nonchalance. And if she gave no hint that she remembered their feverish kisses, their bodies burning for each other, she was an even better actor than he was.

"Small-town America," Amy remarked, gazing out the window.

"Too small for you after Chicago?"

"No, I like it. It's peaceful, and the pace is less stressful."

"I agree. It's why I've invested in properties here. Finances have been a little tricky, but it's worth it." The two years Theo had lived in Syracuse pursuing his master's degree had been the loneliest of his life. Putting down roots in familiar territory, close to St. Louis and his friend Lando, had proved to be one of his better decisions. Knowing Amy taught at the local college had nothing to do with it. Or very little.

"Athena's mother, Lydia, has been sending me listings and encouraging me to buy a house," Amy said. "I have a good job, friends, and I like it here. But I can't help feeling...temporary. Like there's something else out there."

He saw her packing up, moving away—and it was a Syracuse winter all over again. "Take it from me. There isn't."

"This from the world traveler."

"I know of what I speak. Unless...Do you have friends in Chicago? Someone special you want to live near?"

"No. Nobody special."

Theo turned into the driveway. The harmonious proportions of the Craftsman architecture of his home and the lissome river birches framing it never failed to lift his spirits. Plus, Amy was home. And there was nobody special in Chicago.

They got out of the car and he retrieved her carry-on from the trunk. Passing it to her, he felt her hand tighten around his, holding on to him longer than was necessary.

"Mind if I follow you in?" she asked as they walked to the house. "I'm ravenous and need to make a beeline for the refrigerator."

"Sure. There's a pot of minestrone on the stove. Help yourself."

Moose and all the cats except Nina followed them into the kitchen. She remained behind, sitting on an armchair. Amy waited at the doorway, her arms opened wide. "Hey, girl," she said, "give me a hug."

Nina hissed and drew all four paws beneath her body.

"She doesn't mean it," Theo said. "She's just mad 'cause she missed you."

"Is that your professional opinion?" Amy asked, her eyes glistening with tears he sensed had nothing to do with Nina or the shit weekend in Chicago.

Theo nodded, though it was his personal I-want-to-hold-and-comfort-you opinion. Like she used to comfort him. A long time ago.

CHAPTER THIRTEEN

Why be ashamed of what you want?
—AMY MARCH, *LITTLE WOMEN*
(2019 FILM)

*E*ven on a chilly autumn day, the atmosphere of the dean's office reminded Amy of a hothouse full of tropical plants. The light-dimmer switch was set to low. Beads of moisture glistened on the petals of the flowers on Fiona's desk and windowsill. Their cloying fragrance suffused the room, making Amy "deep tranc'd," to quote Tennyson.

"Be with you in a moment," Fiona murmured in her musical brogue as she typed at her computer.

Amy had grabbed a cup of coffee before their meeting, but the caffeine was doing battle with the steady rhythm of Fiona's fingers on the keyboard and the song she was humming. One of those Celtic melodies in which a bonny lass laments her long-lost love, and he appears in a dream, and she doesn't want to wake up...

Fiona rapped the edge of her desk with a letter opener. "Amy? You had a matter of importance to discuss?"

"I'm sorry, I...um..."

"Mind's gone a-roving, has it?"

Into misty highlands. Onto the moors under a lowering sky.

But did Ireland *have* highlands? Or only Scotland? And where precisely *were* the moors located?

"Amy! Please. My time is valuable."

Amy concentrated on the tip of the letter opener Fiona was pointing at her until the misty highlands vanished. "We had talked about my responsibility as chair to be innovative," she said. "To that end, I'd like to propose the addition of a creative writing department. My students have expressed a serious interest in writing fiction and nonfiction with an eye to publication."

"Have they now?"

"Dr. Murphy-Kent's students as well. They told her they want to create content." An outright lie, but Athena had promised to back her up.

"I see," Fiona said.

Amy thought she heard ticking while she waited for the dean to say something else, but there weren't any clocks in the room.

"Your innovation is commendable," Fiona said finally. "But setting up an entirely new department is not a simple matter. It's a rather complicated one, in fact."

Amy was prepared for this objection. It fell right into her strategy—ask for something major, and something minor had a better chance of being approved. "Perhaps we should introduce creative writing courses into the existing curriculum, then? To test-drive my idea?"

The dean's toothy smile revealed canines sharp as fangs. She was on to her. But as Fiona herself had advised, *Never apologize unless it's absolutely necessary.* "And who will teach these classes?" Fiona asked.

"I've recruited my sister, Jo, to conduct writing workshops in November," Amy replied, emphasizing the word *recruit*. "Not only would the workshops help gauge student interest, but Jo may offer suggestions for the curriculum."

"Amy and Jo? Like the March sisters in *Little Women*?"

"My mother...um...she loved the book."

"More reason to make it the subject of yours, then."

All the reason not to.

Rather than debate her decision to write about *Idylls of the King* instead of *Little Women*, Amy planned to present the completed manuscript to Fiona. A fait accompli, as it were, not likely to be challenged.

"My sister is looking forward to meeting and working with the students," she said, turning the discussion away from the topic of her book.

"Two professors in one family. Impressive. My brother's greatest accomplishment is warming bar stools."

"Jo only has a BA, and she teaches high school in Seattle. But she is a published author. And she doesn't...uh...warm bar stools." Amy repressed a laugh, remembering the time Jo fell *off* one, her tolerance for alcohol being worse than hers or Marmee's.

"There may be objections to nepotism," Fiona said.

"Dr. Lowry in the Political Science Department hired her son as a lecturer," Amy reminded her.

"So she did."

Fiona swiveled her chair a full circle, got up, and flicked a wilted flower petal off the windowsill. A smidgen over five feet, she conveyed less authority standing.

"I applaud your initiative, Amy, but I must warn you that the administration could oppose it on financial grounds. The cost of hiring more faculty, et cetera, et cetera."

Amy was never quite sure who or what composed "the administration." In her mind, it was an invisible, mysterious entity with the uncanny ability to stop fresh ideas in their tracks. Unless funding for the ideas came from a source *outside* the administration.

"I'll write a proposal and make a case for the benefits of the courses to the student body," she said.

The "student body" was another entity, but it was highly visible, outspoken, and Amy liked it very much.

Fiona looked fondly at the framed photo of her partner on the desk. "My bonny Brigid writes stories. Total rubbish, though I'd never say so. She's bursting with creativity and could do with a course. Or three."

"Very interesting," Amy murmured.

"Are you prepared to assume full responsibility for setting up the classes?"

"Yes. Yes, I am. Yes."

Fiona arched her eyebrows at the repetition of *yeses*, as if to ask who Amy was trying to convince. Jo, for starters. She'd lured her for a visit with the workshops, but she hadn't figured out the rest. Like how to persuade Jo to move back to the Midwest and work at the college. To be best buddies with Theo again.

"You certainly have a lot on your plate," Fiona said.

More than you know.

"I'll make it all happen," Amy assured her.

"I must ask." Fiona perched her reading glasses on top of her head. "How *is* your book coming along?"

For a split second, Amy didn't know what she was talking about. "Oh. Yes. My book. Yes. It's a...a work in progress."

"Perhaps *you* could do with a writing class, too, aye?"

～◯

Amy slammed the laptop shut and stretched her arms to the ceiling of her study. A shaft of sunlight illuminated *Idylls of the King* on the desk, its cover faded and its spine creased. Calling the book she was writing a "work in progress" required a generous interpretation of the word *progress*. All morning she had tried to say something fresh and original about the "Merlin and Vivien" section in which Vivien, the evil sorceress, cast a spell on the magician, Merlin, enclosing him in a hollow oak tree. She'd make a case for female empowerment to impress Fiona—except for the small matter of Vivien's plan to destroy Camelot.

She leafed through Tennyson's epic poem again, pausing to make note of the descriptions of Vivien's wiles. She wasn't a *totally* unsympathetic character. Who wouldn't use the power of their charms to serve their own purposes? *She* had. Cooperative, pleasing Amy who, unlike Jo, never mocked her stepfather or gave him a moment's worry—leverage she'd applied in their deal to finance her tuition. And she'd gotten a great education and profession out of the deal. As for art school...

Amy tossed the book into the desk drawer. A bracing Saturday in October, a sapphire-blue sky, and the sound of whistling from the yard below—she simply could not concentrate under these circumstances. Or dwell on what-ifs.

A look out the window confirmed Theo was the whistler. He was raking leaves into mounds, his blue plaid flannel shirt rolled up to his biceps. In the autumn light, his dark brown hair shone with streaks of chestnut. "Need any help?" she called out the window.

He looked up, shading his eyes. "Sure."

She threw on an old sweater, ran a brush through her pony-tail, and bounded down the steps into the backyard. "Reporting for duty."

He nodded toward the tool shed. "You'll find an extra rake and gloves in there. Be sure to wear them so you don't get blisters."

She took the rake off the hook above her bike and rooted around the shed for the blister-proof gloves. *What does Theo nag Brittany about?* she wondered. *The perils of bacon? The danger of splinters from sitting bare-legged on a wooden chair?* Though Brittany hadn't been to the house lately. And he seemed to be home more, jazz pulsating from his bedroom all hours of the day and night.

They exchanged few words as she worked up a sweat and piles of red, yellow, and orange leaves. Squirrels rooted for acorns in the cleared grass beneath the oak tree. A blue jay pierced the air with raucous cries. She stopped to watch Theo fill a refuse bag, bend over, stand up, drop more leaves into the bag, wipe his brow, and bend over again, his movements smooth and steady.

And his mind preoccupied. *Broody Bear alert!* Jo would holler, enlisting Amy's help to snap him out of his funk. Making funny faces did the trick, or chasing him down the street for no good reason whatsoever. Snowball fights were her favorite, though he and Jo always pummeled her mercilessly. Without snow, leaves would have to do.

"Hey," Theo said, brushing the fistfuls she'd thrown at him off his shirt.

"Ready?" she asked.

"For what?"

Amy lifted the bag closest to her, stuffed with leaves. "Incoming."

He backed away but not quickly enough. She clutched the empty bag to her chest, ready for his next move.

"Somebody never grew up," he drawled, shaking leaves from his hair and body.

"Maturity is overrated."

"And your aim is as bad as ever."

"Says the man covered in leaves."

"First snowfall, you're on."

"Can hardly wait."

He pointed to the house behind her. "We have an audience. Check out the cats on the kitchen windowsill."

"Nice try. I'm not turning around so you can..."

Lift me in the air. Carry me to the nearest leaf pile. Lower me down, down...

"So I can what, Amy?"

How Theo managed to look both brooding and playful was a mystery even her advanced academic degrees could not solve. Degrees she should be stripped of for acting like a flirty teenager.

Stripped. As in denuded of clothes.

As in she'd better get a boyfriend lickety-split. Normalcy optional, as usual. Because Theo, the good sorcerer, and his Theo spell must be resisted.

"Well?" he said.

"So you can retaliate."

"No retaliation. But you still owe me for the ride from the airport. How about I finish up here while you cook dinner?"

Alas, there was to be no lifting or carrying or lowering.

"Cook," she repeated.

"Prepare food for consumption and enjoyment."

"Is this negotiable?"

"Not after an unprovoked leaf attack."

"How about just for consumption?"

"As long as it's for humans, not animals."

"Drat," she said, provoking a Theo dimple attack, *its* aim as good as ever.

"There's plenty of stuff in the fridge and a cookbook in the pantry," he said.

"By stuff, you mean—"

"Vegetables. Lots of them."

"Okey dokey, artichokey."

"But no artichokes."

Amy left the yard under the watchful eyes of the cat posse. They scattered in all directions when she entered the kitchen, as if they didn't want to witness an unspeakable crime. Moose, a giant ball of fur, was snoring on the floor.

She emptied the refrigerator of broccoli, eggplant, carrots, green beans, and a mysterious white tuber that might not have been edible. Marmee's admiration of the domestic skills of her *Little Women* namesake had not inspired imitation. Thanks to their sweet, patient dad, Amy and Jo learned how to prepare basic meals, clean house, and do laundry—though with as little enthusiasm as their mother.

How difficult can it be? Amy thought, thumbing through the cookbook. Peel, chop, steam or sauté, season. Simple enough— if the vegetables lined up on the counter didn't look like they were facing a firing squad. There was only one remedy for their distress—and for her zero interest in cooking them. Ripping open a bag of Cheetos, she munched on one, then three, then lost count.

"Hard at work, I see," Theo said.

Amy had been crunching so loudly she hadn't heard him enter the kitchen. "I'm waiting for inspiration."

"Hope it comes before the vegetables rot."

She pointed to the tuber. "What the heck is this?"

"Jicama."

"Why do I know less than I did before I asked?"

"There's a wild, wonderful world of food out yonder. You should learn about it."

"Is yonder where jicama comes from?"

"North of yonder, east of Jabip." He pointed to the bag of Cheetos. "What are your plans for those?"

"Appetizer." She held one out. "I dare you."

Theo sauntered over and, putting it between his lips, slipped it from her fingers and ate it.

"Crossing over to the dark side," she said in too high a voice.

"I can't resist a dare," he said, licking the salty orange dust from her two fingers that had held the Cheeto.

Quick-with-a-quip Amy would have joked that she was dessert, not an appetizer. Drooling Amy was unable to form a coherent thought. She washed her hands, got a knife from the drawer, and examined the eggplant. What the heck was she supposed to do with it? And with Theo, who thought he could just waltz over, lick her fingers, and then stand there plucking leaves from his shirt without a care in the world?

"Theo," she said firmly. Though she had no idea what she was going to say next.

"Another dare?" he asked, grinning. "What'll it be this time? Doritos?"

"The Flamin' Hot Nacho variety."

"I'm not afraid."

You should be, she nearly joked back.

Except that they'd had this exchange about daring and not being afraid before.

Right before they'd frantically torn at each other's clothes and kissed and licked and rubbed and—

"You have the weirdest look on your face," Theo said.

Moose lifted his head and grumbled agreement.

"About the Doritos dare," Amy said. "You *should* be afraid."

Theo just threw back his head and laughed. Forgetting. Not remembering. Or choosing not to remember how far they'd gone, how close they'd come. And she couldn't think of a single thing to say about it.

The eggplant, as it turned out, had the last word. As Amy was about to plunge the knife into its side, it rolled to safety—and the blade sliced her Cheeto-dust-free fingers.

CHAPTER FOURTEEN

*Love is the only thing we can carry
with us when we go.*
—BETH MARCH, *LITTLE WOMEN*

Theo remembered to duck going down the stairs to Benny's Bar but bumped into a guy in a Caterpillar cap making his way up, one unsteady foot at a time. Benny joked that leprechauns had built the narrow entrance. In every other way, Laurel's favorite watering hole was the quintessential Irish pub. It boasted a long mahogany bar that gleamed beneath fake Tiffany lamps, wood-paneled walls, comfortable leather chairs, tables with chessboards, and a piano stained with the rings of bottles and glasses. Shamrocks and signs written in Gaelic decorated the walls, while flags representing the counties of Ireland hung from the ceiling.

Theo slid into a booth across from Lando and Stella and gave his order to the waitress. Judging by the empty beer bottles and plates of chicken-wing bones in front of them, they were already deep into Friday's happy-hour special. Benny was a frequent patron of Marconi's Pizza, and Lando was glad to reciprocate.

"Yo, Theo," Stella said. "Where's Brittany?"

"Couldn't make it." Because he hadn't invited her. Hadn't followed up on her sexting messages either.

"What's with the *yo* all the time, Stella?" Lando said.

She lifted her small, pointy chin at him. "It's the way I talk. Got a problem with it?"

"No. But you said, *Yo, officer*, to the cop who stopped you for speeding last week."

"And, *Yo, thanks*, when I talked him out of the ticket."

Lando shook his head, grinning. "Piss and vinegar, twenty-four seven."

She kissed his cheek. "Shut up, my general. You love it."

"I love *you*, my star."

As many times as Theo heard his friend say this, it stung. Thirty-five years old and he'd never told a woman he loved her.

"Wanna hear the latest, Theo?" Stella said. "Lover boy over here made me a pizza with *Marry me* spelled out on top with black olives."

"What's the matter? You don't like olives?" Theo teased her.

"*Proposals*," she said, waggling a chicken wing in his face. "I don't like proposals."

The olive incident was but one in a series of Lando's failed pitches, most of them unintentionally comical. Like the anchovies that melted into the cheese, turning *Be Mine Forever* into *Be Mi Fever*. Lando maintained his matrimonial clock was ticking. Stella countered it was a bomb, not a clock, and she was staying out of the general vicinity.

Theo dove into the plate of jalapeño poppers the waitress brought as they started bickering about Stella's recent fall in a bike race. "Broken or sprained?" he asked, pointing to her bandaged left wrist.

"Sprained," she said. "Lando had a fit like I was in intensive care or something."

"You fell. Racing. Like, a hundred miles an hour," Lando said, his eyes wide with exasperation.

"Like, not even *close* to a hundred. And I keep telling you a sprain is no big deal."

"Yeah. Right. Anyway, about Brooklyn."

"Who the frick was talking about Brooklyn?" Stella said.

"Nobody. I'm changing the subject 'cause your racing gives me chest pains."

"Big baby," she muttered.

"As I was saying," Lando said. "My cousin Gina is coming down from Brooklyn to waitress at Marconi's Pizza for a while. She needs a break from the city and is going to stay with my parents."

"She's seen Lou and Rose in action," Stella said. "Is she out of her mind?"

"She's *available*. Theo, since you and Brittany are on the skids—"

"Who said I was breaking up with Brittany?"

"I assumed you were," Lando said. "You're about due."

Yeah. He was. Ill-timed giggling aside (After he came? Really?), Brittany's inability to keep track of her belongings was a major pain. Who loses their laptop, phone, *and* car keys all in the same day? Worse, she expected him to drop everything he was doing and help her look for them.

"Anyway, Theodore, I'm thinking you and Gina will hit it off," Lando said.

"Red alert," Stella said to Theo. "She has a short fuse."

"Thanks for the warning," Theo said, laughing.

"Gina flares up occasionally. So what?" Lando said. "With three older brothers, she's learned to stand her ground. But she doesn't *stay* mad."

"Like me? Is that what you're saying?" Stella said.

"You're *still* making a stink about the time we got lost on the way to Indianapolis."

"I believe in maps and asking for directions. Deal with it."

Lando grinned. "I can deal with anything you've got."

"Oh yeah?"

"Yeah."

"Show me."

Invigorated by their sparring, Lando and Stella locked lips until Theo thought they might pass out from lack of oxygen.

"Uh, guys, I'm still here," he said. "Don't you want to hear about my day?"

"Not necessarily," Lando said.

"Me neither," Stella said.

"Tough shit. I'm telling you anyway."

Stella sighed in mock resignation. "Oh, all right."

"One of the clients at the clinic had asked if he could try switching counselors—to me. I'd observed a couple of his sessions to learn, and he said I was 'a calming presence.'"

"You put *me* to sleep most of the time," Lando joked.

"Did it piss off the other counselor?" Stella asked.

"Not a bit. We work as a team. I'm lucky I get to learn from such amazing colleagues."

"So'd you meet with the guy yet?" Lando asked.

"Today. Which is why I'm telling you about it. Our session went very well and he's decided to stay with me." It was Theo's first time helping a combat veteran with post-traumatic stress disorder. Watching a grown man cry was one of the harder experiences of his professional life.

Stella fist-bumped him. "Way to go, Theo."

"Yeah, good job," Lando said. "The highlight of *my* day was deciding on the right balance of basil and oregano in the tomato sauce."

"My second highlight was that a nice retired couple adopted Duke," Theo said. "I dropped him off at the vet this morning." The photos in the veterinary clinic of animals available for adoption looked like wanted posters. In the case of half-blind Ray and diabetic Bessie, *un*wanted because of their special needs. He'd taken Nina's picture down since she'd found a home with Amy.

"Which one was Duke?" Lando asked.

"He was a dachshund. I only had him for a week." Dogs were adopted more quickly than cats, though Moose's size was a drawback. Theo wasn't ready to let the gentle giant go anyway.

"We should get a pet, Stella," Lando said.

"No way, no how," she said, tossing a chicken bone onto the plate.

"Why not?"

"Smelly house, hair everywhere, poopy surprises. Aren't I right, Theo?"

"You forgot kitty litter boxes to clean." And frequent visits to the vet, thanks to Bessie's diabetes.

"Whose side are you on?" Lando protested. "And I know what's up with you, Stella. You're afraid a pet is too much of a commitment."

"You got that right," Stella said. "By the way, Theo, we dropped by your house the other day, but you weren't in. We were hoping to meet your housemate since she's never there when we visit. All we got was Ray blinking his good eye at us through the window."

"I overhear college guys talking about her at the restaurant all the time," Lando said, grinning. "We're dying to see the 'brainy Botticelli beauty.'"

Stella rolled her eyes. "Who is this Botticelli anyway? An Italian designer?"

"Italian Renaissance painter," Theo said. "And call first before you visit next time. I'll let you know if she's around."

Though he wasn't all that eager for them to meet. Next thing he knew, they'd turn into a Theo-and-Amy, Lando-and-Stella social group. And he hadn't gotten his head around Theo and Amy yet. Licking her fingers that day in the kitchen—bad move. The same lack of impulse control he advised some of his clients about. He'd joked his way out of it, but Amy didn't look at all amused. Didn't even let him help bandage the fingers she cut with a knife.

Stella got up and wiped a spot of barbecue sauce off her jeans. "This has been tons of fun, but I have to get up early for a race tomorrow. I drove separately so you two can keep yapping."

Lando groaned. "Why don't you skip a race for a change?"

"Because it's what I love to do. And no one can stop me. Not even you, my general."

In a flash, Theo saw the spark of spirit and determination in Amy's eyes when she said she intended to prove the art instructor wrong. And reconcile him and Jo.

"Don't wake me if you get in late," Stella said, kissing Lando's cheek. "See you guys."

Theo was about to wish her luck but stopped as she made a gesture to him with her phone, mouthing the words *I'll call you* behind Lando's back. It would be a first. Not only had he and Stella never spoken on the phone, they'd never been alone without Lando.

Lando whistled softly, watching her walk out. "Is it sexist to say she's got the cutest tuchus east of the Mississippi?"

"Nah. I heard her say the same thing about yours."

"She's a *pain* in my tuchus, cycling like a maniac."

"Some people thrive on risk and excitement."

"But she won't risk marriage," Lando said. "I keep telling her we're not like my parents."

Across the room, a platter slipped out of a waiter's hands, and it clattered onto the floor, breaking into pieces. Theo's stomach lurched as the bar patrons whistled and the waiter bowed. One of these days he'd stop reacting to a shattered dish. The one he'd thrown in anger had long since turned to dust, if not his shame and regret along with it.

"Let me tell you about my master plan for my parents," Lando said.

"Uh-oh. Sounds serious."

"I want you to take them on as your patients."

"Sounds screwy. And we refer to them as clients, not patients."

"If you can help Lou and Rose, I don't care what you call them. Then Stella can't use them as an excuse anymore."

"Your parents don't seem like the sort of people who would welcome counseling."

"They would if I told them my marriage was on the line. They've been bugging me to 'get settled' since I was in high school."

"I don't think I've achieved the level of expertise they need," Theo said.

Once, at their home for dinner, he had watched Lando's parents argue for ten minutes over whether the pasta was al dente or not. The thick, throbbing veins in their temples were like the spaghetti getting decidedly *not* al dente as it—and the Marconis—continued to boil away. For all their intensity, though, he never detected the deep currents of rage that had coursed through his own parents.

"C'mon, man. I'm desperate here," Lando pleaded.

"All right. I'm game. If you can convince them to get counseling, have them set up an appointment on the Happy Haven website." With any luck, the Marconis wouldn't follow through.

"Thanks. Next few pizzas are on the house." Lando wiped his fingers on a napkin. "Personal question here. Do you ever wonder if your parents should have seen a counselor?"

Theo swigged his beer. Confiding in his friend had eased some of the pain of his dysfunctional family life. "Sure. But I don't think it would have made a damn bit of difference. Whatever their personal demons were, their incompatibility made them worse. And so much damage had already been done." Including to him.

"Being a counselor makes up for some shit, though, doesn't it?"

"It does." And would even more, once he was on firmer ground with couples counseling. "Amy thinks that I'm always repairing broken things for the same reason. She's not far off the mark."

Lando grabbed the last jalapeño popper on Theo's plate and ate it. "Okay, so, when *are* we going to meet her?"

"I don't know. Whenever."

"You realize the less you talk about her, the more our imaginations go into hyperdrive?"

"Dream away."

"I have another question. How come you don't back me up when I talk about me and Stella getting married?"

"I don't think I should get involved."

"Why the hell not? You're our friend."

"Okay. As your friend, I think you should hold your horses. What's the rush to get married?"

"If you have to ask, you haven't been paying attention. And what's your problem with never committing to a woman?"

"I don't think it *is* a problem," Theo said in his discussion-over voice. It had been a good day, and he didn't want to end it on a downbeat. Because it *was* a problem.

"If you say so." Lando pushed himself out of the booth with a scowl. "I can't hang out. I've got to get to the restaurant and supervise one of the new hires."

"We still on for racquetball Wednesday?"

"Yep." Lando slapped a few dollars on the table. "I'll make sure my parents sign up for an appointment. Try not to talk them into getting a divorce."

Theo added a five-dollar bill to the tip after finishing his beer and made his way up the stairway of Benny's Bar. The crisp, clean air was refreshing after the grease odors of the restaurant. He unlocked the door of the '57 Chevy but, instead of getting inside it, sat on a bench outside a gift shop and scrolled through his phone photos, searching for the picture of Amy.

The thing about Amy was, she was so casual about her beauty that you got used to it. And then it struck you like a thunderbolt if you hadn't seen her for a while. The night she lay on the kitchen floor, before he had a chance to register who she was, Theo's first wild thought had been that an angel had fallen to earth. The glow of pink-tinged skin. The full lips slightly parted. The blond curls spread behind her like wings.

Zipping past photos of his trip to Amsterdam last spring, he found the one he was looking for—his first sighting of Amy in Laurel. He'd just moved to town and was busy working at the clinic and renovating his properties. While at the hardware store, Nuts and Bolts, he turned into an aisle, and suddenly, there she was, examining the selection of light bulbs with her unique expression of concentration and confusion. Reflexively, he shot a photo without her noticing and hurried out.

One of these days, I'll get in touch with Amy, he'd promised himself. Better to make the first move than for her to catch him unawares. But then he'd see her walking swiftly across a street, her face animated as she talked on the phone, hair lit by sunshine—and he'd draw back into the shadows.

Theo lifted his face to the night firmament, its darkness softened by ghostly clouds. The kind of sky angels fall out of. All this time he was so sure he had put time and distance safely between them. Between what Amy meant to him and what she couldn't mean to him. But he was just fooling himself. Because the thing about Amy was, he never could get her out of his mind.

CHAPTER FIFTEEN

*You don't need scores of suitors. You
only need one if he's the right one.*
—AMY MARCH, *LITTLE WOMEN*
(2019 FILM)

After a week of grinding out the creative writing curriculum proposal for the administration and groaning while writing her book, Amy was looking forward to a Friday night out. Nothing as exciting as a date, not the way her social life was going. Just a quiet dinner with Athena at As You Like It Café to catch up on campus scuttlebutt.

Athena was sitting at a small oak table close to the central stone hearth. The café was originally open for breakfast and lunch only, but Thorne had recently extended the hours to include dinner on Friday and Saturday.

Amy warmed her hands in front of the fire, numb from cycling on the cold October evening. "Fire *is* man's best discovery, besides coffee."

"It's the first time Thorne's lit the fireplace since March." Athena lifted the teapot. "Are you okay with tea?"

"Anything hot will do."

Athena poured them each a cup. "How can you stand cycling in this weather?"

"I have a hate-hate relationship with automobiles. Getting my car towed from the airport was the last straw."

"Buying another one?"

"Not sure I want to tempt fate again." Amy leaned over to examine Athena's earrings. "How cool. They're wavy cloak ferns."

"They were a gift from the hubster. I'm an earring addict, and he's my enabler. Speak of the devil."

Amy turned to watch Thorne walk toward them, carrying a basket of rolls and a bowl of whipped butter. Athena bias aside, he *was* classically handsome, from his chiseled cheekbones to his broad shoulders and athletic stride.

"Hello, Amy." He brushed a lock of hair off his forehead. "How's life in the trenches of academia?"

"As long as I have my trusty Athena warrior by my side, I can handle anything."

"I couldn't get through a day without my feisty fighter." He leaned over to kiss his wife's upturned face, spilling the rolls onto the table. Amy tore into one of them like she was recovering from a hunger strike. How long *had* it been since she'd had sex? Too long if she couldn't remember.

"Have time to sit with us?" Athena asked Thorne.

"Sorry. The gang's coming soon and I've got prep work to finish."

"Are you talking about your dad and his friends?" Amy asked Athena.

"Uh-huh. I've started calling them the 'Leisure Geezers.' Some days they arrive for breakfast and don't leave till after lunch. I pity the waitresses."

"I remember you waitressed here when you were writing your book about C. L. Garland."

As was typical whenever Amy mentioned the author of the LitWit series of erotic novellas, whose secret identity was a perennial topic of speculation in the media, Athena and Thorne exchanged conspiratorial looks. One of those couples things, she assumed. Maybe they read excerpts from the books to warm themselves up for sex—though they were hot enough to write their own.

"I dropped the Garland project once you hired me," Athena told Amy. "I never did find out who she was."

"But she lives in Laurel, right?" Amy asked.

"So the rumor goes," Athena said, peering at the menu.

"Thena told me your sister's coming to visit from Seattle," Thorne said to Amy. "I practiced law there for years. Our friend Quentin still lives there."

"Unusual name," Amy remarked.

Athena grinned. "Quentin's one in a million. Bighearted with a hulking body to match."

"Like the bachelor farmers?"

"More like Shakespeare's character Falstaff," Thorne said. "Boisterous, in-your-face, and so persuasive you find yourself taking a road trip to wherever, whether you wanted to or not. It's partly why he's a successful criminal defense lawyer."

"Even if he's always one step ahead of the law himself," Athena joked.

"And I've been a few steps behind all day," Thorne said with a glance at the clock. "Back to the kitchen for me. I've got lamb to grill for the shish kebabs."

"Can we talk shop for a sec?" Athena asked Amy once he'd left.

"Sure."

"I've written a few chapters of my book for tenure on the Brontë family, but I think I need to narrow my scope."

"Let's brainstorm Monday. My schedule's free after four o'clock. And I could use your input on my book too."

"Tennyson troubles?"

"Meseems this damsel is perplex'd in mind. I haven't unlocked my central idea, a reason for the reader to care about *Idylls of the King* in the first place. It's like I can't find the key to the chastity belt." Which she might as well be wearing for all the sex she was having.

"Whenever I try to make a nineteenth-century novel come alive for my students," Athena said, "I act out a character so that they get emotionally invested in the story."

"Vivien the sorceress is too much of a stretch for me." Amy sipped her tea meditatively. Earl Grey, Theo's favorite. "If you had the power to beguile someone to fall in love with you, would you use it?"

"I already did," Athena said, wiggling the finger that sparkled with a wedding band and diamond engagement ring. "How about you?"

No, Amy realized, she wouldn't want to bewitch anyone. She wanted someone to love her all on his own. He'd wake up every morning thinking of her, happy to be with her, in her cloud pajamas, her hair tangled, and her mind a blur. In her worst moods. In her moments of exhilaration and doubt. No matter what she'd done.

The way she had believed Theo would love her.

Ivy Hagstrom, the waitress, came to their table, notepad, pen, and peeved expression at the ready.

"Everything okay?" Amy asked her.

"My boyfriend, Karl, is driving me crazy," Ivy complained. "But what else is new?"

"I was wondering if he was available for a few house projects," Athena said.

"Not sure. Hoglund Construction keeps him pretty busy."

"Will he be coming to the café later?"

"Probably not. Unless he wants to bring a letter confirming we're on a break." Ivy tossed her long ash-blond hair over her shoulder. "What is it with him? He writes notes all the time but refuses to text."

"Maybe he's old-fashioned," Amy suggested.

"If I wanted old-fashioned, I'd still be dating Bruce."

"One of the bachelor farmers," Athena explained to Amy.

"Karl left a note on the kitchen table. *Remember to pick up the new strings for your mandolin.* But he spelled it m-a-n-d-i-o-l-i-n first and crossed it out." A music major at the college, Ivy played Renaissance songs at the café occasionally. "And like I need to be told to carry an umbrella when it rains. Hello."

"Some guys are very protective," Amy said. Guys like Theo.

"And very annoying." Ivy let out a sigh so deep it might have originated in the fifteenth century. "Anyway, what can I get you?"

"The shish kebabs," Athena said.

"Same for me," Amy said. "But go easy on the peppers and onions. I'm on vegetable overload lately."

"I'm on Karl overload," Ivy muttered as she walked away.

Athena grinned. "Those two break up and make up so often it makes everybody's heads spin."

"Ivy reminds me of John William Waterhouse's painting *The Lady of Shalott*."

"Thanks to your crash courses in art history, I actually know what you're talking about. Thorne says Ivy reminds him of Ophelia from *Hamlet*."

Amy grimaced. "Yikes. Dead maidens floating down rivers. I think we should keep the comparisons to ourselves."

"Believe it or not, Thorne gets jealous when I compare Karl to a Viking. As for badass warriors, the faculty has given you a nickname after your latest budget cuts. 'Amy the Axe.'"

"Orders from the dean. I didn't have a choice."

"Really? I had the impression you and Fiona collaborated very well. And she is supporting your plan for the creative writing courses."

"Plus, she approved of my sister, Jo, conducting the workshops. But ultimately the administration will decide. As my mother always says, *There's many a slip betwixt the cup and the lip*."

Guilt pricked Amy's conscience. She had hurriedly changed direction in the hallway recently when she saw Eileen approaching to use her office. Fiona had informed the adjunct professors that their proposal was low on her agenda, and Eileen was bound to ask her to mediate again. With her plan for Jo in the works, Amy couldn't risk irritating the dean.

"*Gary's* the one who always gets his way," Amy said, refilling their teacups. "I initially denied his request for a new desk. Guess who's getting a new desk?"

Athena threw her head back to laugh. "This I have to hear."

"Have you seen the ratty backpack he's been carrying? Something inside it is making it bulge, and I'm not sure I want to know what that something is."

And then there was Turner Malcolm, whose requests Amy

never refused either. No one else in the academic universe willingly taught the eighteenth-century novel, so if he wanted something, he got it.

Except a night out with her. *I don't date anyone in the workplace*, she'd replied when he surprised her with an invitation to dinner and the symphony last week. Turner was reasonable, steady, and even-tempered. She doubted he ever wore strange costumes or needed to get in touch with his inner grape. She didn't tell Athena, since she'd make the same observation and encourage her to go out with him.

"Oh good, Robin's playing guitar tonight," Athena said, waving to the guy sitting on a stool by the front bay window. Thorne's half brother shared his height and chiseled facial bone structure, though Robin's hair and eyes were dark brown and his build was stocky.

"His new medication regimen is doing wonders," Athena said. "Or else it's Jaycee. They started performing together recently and have been doing gigs all over the county."

"Jaycee? *My* Jaycee?"

Athena's eyes widened. "*Your* Jaycee?"

Before she could explain, Jaycee entered the café, a guitar slung across her chest. Her hair had grown in, but her jaw was still working a stick of gum. She flashed a smile when she saw them and hurried over. "Hi, Athena. Amy! What are you doing here?"

"Having dinner with my friend and colleague."

"Right. You're both professors. Cool."

"I hear you've been performing with Robin."

"Yeah. We like the same songs from the old days. Bob Dylan. Joan Baez."

"They're old days to us too," Athena said drily.

"Robin's so talented and interesting." Jaycee bit her lip as she watched him strum his guitar. "It's like he sees stuff the rest of us don't."

"You've drawn him out of his shell," Athena said. "He used to be painfully shy."

"I told him a lot of great musicians had schizophrenia," Jaycee said.

"And artists too," Amy said.

"Hey, did you hear about Derek?" Jaycee asked her.

"What about him?"

"He sold two paintings for, like, megabucks. And got write-ups in badass art journals."

A sensation of searing heat and glacial cold shot through Amy's body as if she were being freeze-dried. *Two paintings? To whom? Megabucks?* "That's...uh...great news," she stammered. "You must be...uh...really glad."

And what fricking badass art journals?

Jaycee shrugged. "I don't give a shit. I moved out three weeks ago. The smell of paint got to me. But mostly Derek. He never left the apartment. I mean *never*."

Athena grinned as she connected the dots between Amy, Derek, and Jaycee, the pizza-delivery girl.

"I'm off guys for a while," Jaycee said with a crack of her gum.

"Still working at Marconi's Pizza?" Amy asked.

"I quit and got a job at the music store, Sharps & Flats. That's where I met Robin."

"Lots of changes in your life, Jaycee."

"And they're all for the better. I'm renting a room in a big, old house near campus with a bunch of students. It's dirt cheap, and everybody's my age." She gave a thumbs-up to Robin, who was beckoning her. "Show time. I better get over there."

"Tempted to pick up where you left off with Derek?" Athena asked when Jaycee joined Robin.

"Hunger is making you nonsensical, my friend." And envy at Derek's success was making Amy homicidal. Megabucks? For *Untitled No. Whatever*?

"Just checking if *your* hunger is enticing you into unwise relationships," Athena said. "And by *hunger*, I mean *horniness*."

Having Cheetos dust licked off one's fingers did render one susceptible. Momentarily.

"Not this girl," Amy said as Ivy placed their sizzling kebabs on the table. "I've had enough of oddballs. I'm off guys, like Jaycee." Her resist-Theo plan might sputter on occasion, but most days, she barely noticed the hair, that mouth. Those eyes.

"You sure can pick 'em, though," Athena said, chuckling.

"Or they pick me. Which may be worse," Amy said.

"Who *is* your ideal guy anyway?"

"Someone who will help me bury a body."

"Whoa! That rolled off your tongue pretty quickly."

"I've given it a lot of thought."

"Then I suggest you put Quentin's number on your contact list under *defense attorney*."

A commotion at the café door caught their attention. Athena ticked off the names of the Leisure Geezers coming in. "My dad, Charles, and his wife, Vivienne. Joe, Theresa, Dan, and Phyllis. The two that are dressed identically are Sam and June."

"And I recognize Geraldine and Pete Gallagher. Derek's apartment was next to theirs."

"Love nest is a more accurate description."

"You know about them?"

"As You Like It Café is a hotbed of news and romance. Sit here long enough, and you'll hear everything and fall in love in the bargain." Athena got up from her chair. "Excuse me for a minute while the kebabs cool off. I have to find out what the This Time Around Book Club is up to lately."

"I didn't know Laurel had a book club."

"My brainchild. But I have a sneaky suspicion all they read are dirty books."

"Like the LitWit series?"

Athena blushed and mumbled something unintelligible over her shoulder.

Amy looked around the crowded café, tapping her feet to the lively music. Jaycee and Robin had worked their guitars into a frenzy, playing a 1960s folk anthem. Athena was right. Couples in varying stages of their relationship filled the room. A pair of cute teenagers were sharing bites of each other's muffin. The dad of a fussy toddler jostled her on his knee as the mom hurriedly ate a bowl of soup. Amy guessed that the guy and girl glancing shyly at each other as they nibbled sandwiches were on their first date.

A man could walk into the café this very minute who was just right for Amy—intelligent, interesting, and with a built-in exit feature. Like the math professor who regularly got lost, including in his own neighborhood. One missed connection too many, and she had a valid excuse to break up. As for why she wanted exit features in the first place...

She knew why. Theo.

"All's well with the senior love fest," Athena said when she returned. "But if I don't hear the word *libido* for a year, I will be most grateful. What's wrong with you? You look green around the gills all of a sudden."

"Is this a good time to talk about something important?"

"It's always a good time for the baring of souls, girlfriend. Love or career?"

"Neither. My landlord."

"The vegetarian guy who fosters animals?"

Amy wondered what thumbnail sketch Theo might give people to describe *her*. *The junk-food girl who screwed up my life.*

"We were neighbors for years, growing up," she said. "Best friends all through college, including my sister, Jo. But the friendship broke apart. Between all of us. And it hasn't been pretty."

Athena's eyes widened. "Why've you been holding out on me?"

"Not sure. I guess I thought that if I didn't make a drama out of it, it wouldn't *be* a drama. And it's not. It's been awkward at times, but we get by. With Jo coming to town, I wanted you to be aware of the situation. In case she mentions him."

"I can't wait to meet her. Has she been to Laurel before?"

"She visited a couple of times when I first moved here, but I usually fly out to see her." Being the more financially solvent sister. "Or we meet up at my mother's house in St. Louis."

"What's your landlord's name anyway? I may have seen him around."

"Theo Sinclair."

"Hmm. Sounds familiar. Tall, dark, and handsome with a dreamy look like he's posing for a cologne ad?"

"I wouldn't put it that way, but yeah." Amy would specify a cologne that smelled like a forest after a spring rain. Dimples to die for. And, oh God, those eyes.

Athena snapped her fingers. "I know. He's eaten here occasionally. And at Marconi's Pizza. I've seen him there when I treat my seminar students to dinner."

"He's best friends with the owner. I almost asked Jaycee if she knew him, but she and I are complicated enough."

"Theo's always friendly and polite. He seems like one of the good guys. The kind you should be dating."

"Full disclosure—I used to have a crush on him." Crush. Such a harsh word for such tender emotions. Until those emotions crushed you. "We have a lot of history. Some of it good, some of it awful."

Amy pulled each chunk of lamb off the skewer as she gave Athena a short version of the *Scenes from a Marriage* exhibit and its consequences. But no version of how close she and Theo had nearly become.

Athena reached across to clasp her hand. "Take it from me. Put the past behind you and move on. Go for what you want if Theo is The One. The years Thorne and I wasted being stubborn and resentful are my biggest regret." After ten years of misunderstandings and bruised hearts, the couple had found their way back to the true love of their college romance.

"There's no comparison between my relationship with Theo and yours with Thorne. It was like a...like a rosebud that never bloomed."

"It's never too late to bloom. Ever."

"I'm not sure I even believe in such a thing as The One," Amy said. "It's one of those romance novel notions."

"Sue me. I'm still a die-hard romantic. And so are a lot of people." Athena pointed to the Leisure Geezers' table. Charles was stroking Vivienne's thigh, Geraldine was rubbing noses with Pete, and the others were feeding each other morsels of food. "I keep waiting for them to fling their clothes off and go full-bore orgy on the floor."

Amy laughed, a feeble, sad laugh at this vision of enduring love and desire, wondering how much longer it would be until she could go home and cry into the tendrils of her high-sensitivity button fern and Nina's warm fur. And cry some more because a plant and a cat were The Ones.

CHAPTER SIXTEEN

It takes people a long time to learn the difference between talent and genius, especially ambitious young men and women.

—LOUISA MAY ALCOTT, *LITTLE WOMEN*

Amy had never paid close attention to architecture, but she'd come to appreciate the perfectly proportioned rooms of Theo's house and its beautiful woodwork and charming nooks, like the one beneath her bedroom window where Nina liked to curl up. The panel of stained glass above the bathroom window was a daily delight. If the harmony of his home compensated a little for the discord of his childhood, all the better.

She burrowed more deeply into the blankets. A Saturday-afternoon nap on a stormy autumn day was a rare luxury she'd indulge in a little longer. An oak leaf, tossed by the wet wind against the window, looked like a hand waving to her. She waved back. Nina was asleep at the bottom of the bed, sparing her a reproving look.

Amy stretched her legs and wiggled her toes. There was no reason whatsoever to get up and do anything at all. Like wash clothes. Or plan lectures. Or read student essays.

Or call Derek and play the congratulatory ex-girlfriend with a favor to ask. And a burning desire to find out how the hell he had managed to sell his work. For megabucks.

She had memorized the conversation. *Can I borrow the futon? My sister will be visiting, and I don't have an extra bed. Oh, by the way, I'm THRILLED to hear you've sold two paintings. And I was wondering...have you figured out the difference between Manet and Monet by now, YOU TWIT?*

Nina's whiskers twitched as if she'd heard Amy's internal monologue. "Twit," she said out loud for good measure. And grabbed her phone off the nightstand while she'd worked up a head of steam.

Derek answered after six rings. "Hello? Who's this?"

Derek Dickhead Demerest had deleted her from his contact list.

"It's Amy."

There was a pause long enough for her to say *Marsden*. But she didn't.

"Uh-huh. Right. Amy," he said.

She hoped it was his chin she heard him scratching. "Jaycee told me that you sold a couple of paintings. Congratulations."

"Yeah. I'm pretty stoked."

"Which ones did you sell? *Untitled No.* what?"

"Didn't Jaycee tell you about my head series?"

"Head...what?"

"I've taken my art in a new direction." He made a sound that was a cross between a laugh and a grunt. "Thanks to you."

A frisson of pride shot through her, swiftly followed by a frisson of disgust for being flattered that she had been his muse. "Thanks to me? What did *I* do?"

"You drew those mustaches on my mannequin heads. At first,

I was pissed and threw them in the trash. But then I looked at this pile of heads going in different directions, some upside down, some sideways, and I said to myself, *Time to get real people in your paintings, dude.* And then I had one of those—what do you call it? An epiphany? And I thought, people go in different directions, but the mustaches are symbols that we're all the same deep inside."

It was the largest number of consecutive sentences Amy had ever heard Derek utter. He deserved a response. But there didn't seem to be much point in telling him that mannequins were not real people. And that she was not the same as him deep inside.

Deep inside she was an artist who was going to capture the depth and breadth of human emotion in portraits again. Yes, it was time. They'd be true to life, not abstract shapes with mustaches. Just as soon as she decided *who* to paint. And found the spare hours. And—

"Four figures," Derek said.

"You did a composition with four figures?"

"No. That's how much I got paid for the paintings. Uh...no, wait." He counted under his breath. "*Five* figures."

"Each?"

"Yeah."

Amy threw off the blankets, suddenly hot all over. Nina opened one sleepy eye and shut it again. "Actually, the reason I called, Derek—"

"I know why you called. You want to know if I meant it when I said your paintings looked like stuff hanging in hotel rooms."

"Well, no, I...uh...*Did* you mean it?"

"I wouldn't be doing you any favors if I lied."

"Any favors," she repeated.

"Your art is like our relationship. You could take it or leave it. Or like ferns, 'cause you only have to spritz them once in a while."

"Spritz."

"You haven't got the dedication thing going on. It's why I can look at mannequin heads and get inspired. Art's always on my mind."

Amy watched the oak leaf slowly slide down the window and get carried away in a gust. She nearly waved goodbye. "Anything else?"

"Instinct," Derek said. "As in, you don't have any."

She heard a toilet flush. This phone call had officially hit rock bottom.

"You know what, though?" he said over the sound of running water. "You'd make a great artist's model. I'm getting an idea for a new series—bodies with faces all over them. You can be the first body."

Whaddya know? There was a level *below* rock bottom.

From downstairs, Amy heard the front door slam. Theo was coming in or leaving. Either way, she was out of this conversation and headed downstairs to the emergency bag of Cheetos. "Goodbye, Derek."

"But I'm not done talking about my new series."

"But I'm done listening." Not the wittiest repartee, but it would do.

In the kitchen, Theo had beaten her to the emergency Cheetos. In a soaked sweatshirt and his hair sticking up every which way, he resembled a cat having a bath.

"I forgot my jacket on the way out of Brittany's apartment. We had a fight. And then I fixed a flat tire. Mine this time." He lifted the bag. "Stress eating. I'll replace them."

"No biggie. I have a backup bag."

"Shit. I forgot my belt too," he said, hitching up his jeans.

"The argument must have been a doozy."

"She broke up with me. With a lot of screaming. I had no idea she could yell so loud." He looked around anxiously as if he were hearing Brittany's disembodied voice.

Amy reached into the bag for a handful of Cheetos, tempted to lick *his* salty orange fingers and see how *he* liked it.

"It was like she was mad I wasn't as upset as her," he said.

"Bringing women to the point of exasperation. I didn't know this about you, Theo."

"It started because I didn't want to go to a stupid Halloween party with her next week. And then she got on me for being too protective and said I was suffocating her. *I'm a dancer*, she kept repeating. *I have to breathe*. Funny thing is, *I* was going to break up with *her*. Always losing her belongings and...and other stuff she does."

She pointed to his sweatshirt. "It's inside out."

He looked down. "What the hell?"

Handing her the bag, Theo lifted his arms to remove and reverse the sweatshirt.

Brittany was out of her mind. Brittany did not properly appreciate a taut torso and that enticing line of dark hair from belly button to below. It might have had something to do with suffocating and not getting enough oxygen to her brain.

"There should be Lamaze classes for relationships," Amy said. "Learn how to breathe while you're in one."

"That's an absolutely brilliant idea," Theo said, putting the sweatshirt back on. "I might try breathing lessons in my sessions."

"Who does a counselor go to when *he* has a breakup?"

"He suffers in silence because his best friend is sick of hearing about his lousy love life. And he kicks the tires of his car. Don't know what I was doing with Brittany in the first place," he grumbled.

Lousy love life had a nice ring to it.

"She's a dancer!" Amy said, coaxing a dimpled smile from him. "If Brittany's worst criticism is that you're overprotective, that's not so bad."

"Guess not."

"Derek just informed me that I'm not dedicated or inspired enough to be a true artist."

"Why were you talking to him?"

"To borrow his futon for Jo's visit."

He frowned. "Oh yeah. Jo."

"He also told me that I have no instinct."

"Asshole. Don't believe a word he said. You're an artist down to your bones."

Loyal-despite-everything Theo. *He'd* help her bury a body. In this case, Derek's.

Except deep down in her bones, Amy knew the dipshit was right. And she was going to buckle down and prove *him* wrong too.

"I am sorry about Brittany. She was a nice girl," she said. "But you'll find someone else. Someone who's just right for Theo Sinclair. It won't be easy for you, but it'll happen."

"Not easy. That's what Jo..."

She waited an agonizing minute for him to finish the sentence. "What about Jo?"

How did Theo do that with his eyes? Empty them out and fill them to the brim with meaning at the same time?

"She's so positive that it's impossible for me to..." His words trailed off again.

"Go on," Amy whispered.

"I'm 'unsuitable,' according to her. And nothing I'll ever do..." He ran his hands through his hair, staring at the legs of his rain-drenched jeans. "Never mind. I don't know what I'm talking about. Forget it."

Amy couldn't think of a single thing to say. Not while she was in the middle of—what do you call it? An epiphany? The sudden realization that *love* was what Theo and Jo had fought about. Theo was in love with Jo, but Jo wasn't in love with him. The past six years that he and Amy had been estranged, his friendship with Jo—his best buddy—had bloomed into something more. But just as Jo had rejected Laurie in *Little Women*, Jo had made it clear that they weren't suited for each other and never would be.

The truth hit her in the pit of her stomach. Deep down below the place where the old conviction that she and Theo belonged together had settled.

CHAPTER SEVENTEEN

Love covers a multitude of sins.
—MARMEE MARCH, *LITTLE WOMEN*

*T*ying his shoes as he dressed for work, Theo heard a scream. An Amy scream—high-pitched, asking a question, not sure it wanted an answer. He rushed to the kitchen, but she wasn't there. At the slam of the dryer door, he went to the laundry room.

"You okay?" he asked.

Amy pointed to the aquarium tank that he had set up on the counter last night. Judging by her eye roll, she had regained her composure. "Let me guess," she said. "It's a lounge lizard."

"Close," he said, laughing. "It's a leopard gecko. I'm calling him Miles Davis."

"Where on earth, or from what planet, did he come from?"

"The kids down the street found him in the woods. Their mom wouldn't let them keep him, so they brought him to me."

"I don't blame her," she said with a slight shiver. "Those weird eyes. I can't tell which one is looking at me."

"I keep expecting him to talk in a British accent like the gecko in the GEICO commercials."

"If he does, tell him I don't need car insurance anymore. How do you know it's a male anyway?"

"He looks like a Miles."

"It looks like a Martian."

She reopened the dryer door and, emptying her clothes into the laundry basket, hurriedly tucked her underwear beneath blouses and jeans. Theo suddenly remembered showing up at her house covered in mud after a game of touch football with his high school buddies. One did not traipse dirt through the Sinclair home. Ever. Plus, he wanted to see Amy's drawings of his puppy. She lent him her stepfather's clothes while his were in the washing machine. When he retrieved them from the dryer, one of her bras was clinging to his shirt. Jo would have laughed it off, but Amy fled the laundry room, so mortified she made excuses not to see him for days.

Ray poked his head in the doorway and Theo quickly closed the door. "We have to keep this shut or they'll try to get to Miles. And I don't want them snooping around the crickets and mealworms."

Amy lifted the laundry basket. "I'm almost afraid to ask."

Theo pointed to the bins lined up next to the washer. "Geckos need to eat live insects."

"Lovely. Please tell me there isn't a tarantula somewhere in the house too."

"Haven't had one since I was a kid."

"A lizard and live insects. Okay. I can handle it. As long as they don't escape."

"They won't last long if they do."

Amy nodded toward the door. "Can you check if the coast is clear? I have to get going."

He nudged Ray from the doorway and, stepping aside to let her pass, followed her to the kitchen. She was dressed in a suit for work with a buttoned-up expression to match. Ever since he'd broken up with Brittany two weeks ago, Amy often looked like she was on the verge of saying something, then would pull it back. Her smile had faded as quickly as it appeared when he made the joke about GEICO.

He shouldn't read too much into it. Three months in, and their living situation had settled into a smooth routine. Amy ate breakfast with him most mornings and the occasional dinner. They checked with each other if they needed anything at the grocery, Bread and Board, and shared anecdotes about their job. Calm, polite interactions of two adults who'd put their complicated backstory behind them.

When he wasn't licking her fingers. Or thinking about licking—

"Have a good day," she called out as she climbed the stairs to the second floor.

"You too."

Theo walked to his car, reading a text from Brittany about returning one of his jazz CDs. He'd retrieved his jacket and belt with little fanfare. They had agreed to describe their breakup, screaming fit and all, as amicable.

Can't knock a good narrative, he thought as he drove to Happy Haven. He'd decided he'd go along with whatever tale Jo spun when she visited soon. She was the storyteller, after all. And he assumed she was as committed as he was to keeping the details of their argument private. As for reconciling...

He pulled into the parking lot of the counseling clinic. The place he went each day to help people reach a better understanding of themselves and those in their lives. The least he could do was consider making up with Jo. Take the high road.

Let bygones be bygones. Get over every hurtful thing she'd said to him.

Yeah. Right.

～◯～

During Lou and Rose Marconi's session at Happy Haven, Theo was struck again by their uncanny resemblance to each other. White shirts and navy-blue pants tightly hugged their short, lean bodies. Silver spirals coiled from their curly black hair like question marks. He would be afraid of the identical fierce expression in their eyes if they weren't so busy snarling at each other. In Clifford Callaghan's world, the Marconis were anything *but* happy campers.

"You cut the mortadella too thin for Lando again," Lou fumed. "How many times do I have to tell you, Rose? It's not prosciutto. It's mor-ta-dell-a." The Marconis' deli in Rosewood, L and R Deli, supplied the toppings for Lando's pizzas.

"I'll cut mor-ta-dell-a any damn way I please," Rose replied.

"Damn *you.*"

She made the sign of the cross on her chest. "May you go to hell for talking to me like this."

"Constructive language only, please," Theo said.

They waved their hands in the air simultaneously, yelling about other deli products as if he hadn't spoken. "Pecorino Romano can't hold a candle to Parmigiano Reggiano!" Lou shouted. "Get that into your thick head!"

Rose muttered curses involving provolone, and Theo braced himself. Once they entered the volatile world of cheese, there was no telling what might happen.

"If I may offer a suggestion," he began. *Go to Lamaze classes! Learn how to breathe!*

They spun around to face him, eyebrows bristling. He had the distinct impression they had no idea where they were or who he was. "Perhaps to ease the stress in your relationship—"

"Stress? What stress?" Lou barked.

Theo coughed into his hand to keep from convulsing with laughter. "I was thinking you should...uh...Maybe if you tried—"

"Spit it out, young man," Rose commanded.

He cleared his throat and averted his eyes from her glaring ones. "You two are together constantly. At work, at home. If you spent a few hours of the day apart, you'd give yourselves breathing room."

"Work alone in the shop? Are you nuts?" Lou said. "It's too busy."

"You can hire someone to—"

"No, no, no, no, no. We don't trust anyone with our meats."

"Who *can* you trust anymore?" Rose said. "With *anything?*"

"Who's minding the store while you're here?" Theo asked.

Lou stared at him as if he were wearing a clown suit. "Who opens a deli at nine in the morning?"

"I don't know anything about running a delicatessen."

"Nobody does." Lou shook his head mournfully. "It's a lost art."

"Who understands olives these days?" Rose asked with a deep sigh.

The art of deli, olives, Theo jotted down so he'd know where to resume their next session. He'd love to enlighten Lando on the primacy of processed meats in his parents' marriage, but client confidentiality forbade it.

Rose got up and put on her coat. "We only come here, Theo, because Orlando asked us to. We want him to get married."

"Thirty-four years old," Lou said. "What's he waiting for? For us to be dead in our graves before he gives us grandchildren?"

Since the day Stella had mimicked, behind Lando's back, that she would phone him, Theo had waited for her to call. He'd nearly forgotten about it until she finally did a few weeks ago. What they'd discussed, her request for secrecy and his advice that she follow her instinct regarding marriage, worked its way around his conscience as the Marconis grumbled more complaints about their son.

"Do you approve of Lando marrying Stella?" he asked them as they stood in the doorway, ready to leave.

"Compared to the girl his brother, Luca, dates..." Rose said, eyes raised to the ceiling.

"She's got a lip on her, that Stella," Lou said. "I'll give her that much."

Theo was fluent enough in Marconi-speak to interpret *lip* as a positive attribute for Stella to possess. He watched the couple cross the street, huddled in matching tan trench coats against the cold November rain. Lou opened Rose's car door, and she got in. But not before kissing him on the cheek. And he kissing her on the mouth. For not the first time, Theo entertained the notion that their arguments were for show, a piece of theater. Still, he didn't regret his counsel to Stella.

He checked his phone for messages before his next clients arrived. Eugene Farragut had left a voicemail, cancelling their appointment next Tuesday—with Tildy tittering in the background. There was a text from Amy with a brief video of a bald man skulking down a hallway, wearing an overstuffed backpack.

What's your take on this guy? she wrote. She had confided to him that her colleague, Gary Ericson, scared her.

Show no fear. He'll use it to his advantage.

I feel so much better!

And be ready to run like the wind.

Haha. Any more reassuring advice?

Don't delete the video. It's evidence.

Theo was going to add that she should be careful biking in the rain and offer her a ride home but thought better of it. Brittany yelling at him to *Back off already!* was too fresh a memory.

Two cars pulled into the parking lot, matching black Mercedes-Benz sedans driven by Barrett and Olivia Decker, attorneys-at-law. Tidy of hair and dress, they'd arranged their marriage like sushi in a bento box. They had designated specific tasks in the home (she bought the groceries, he picked up the dry cleaning) and in the relationship (she addressed disagreements about their social life, he about their Labradoodle, Hugo). They maintained separate bank accounts and bathrooms where, Theo presumed, Olivia touched up her roots and Barrett meticulously manscaped. If they had a problem, they discussed it rationally, fairly, considerately. They were in therapy to make sure they stayed on course.

They were the perfect couple—and the perfect clients to reassure Theo that he was on the right track with couples counseling. Especially after a Marconi session. Keeping the Deckers on autopilot was the most effective strategy for them. *If it ain't broke, don't fix it*, the saying went. And he had to agree.

CHAPTER EIGHTEEN

Let us be elegant or die.
—LOUISA MAY ALCOTT, *LITTLE WOMEN*

*J*o sprawled on the living room sofa with Nina draped across her legs. "This is, without a doubt, the most boring living room I have ever been in, in my entire life. What look is Theo going for? IKEA showroom meets prison cell?"

"I don't care," Amy said. "I'm upstairs most of the time." Theo hadn't commented yet on the brass umbrella stand she'd placed near the front door. It had been left at the curb of a Victorian-style house with a FOR FREE sign taped to it, and she couldn't resist.

"And he's stuck in a time warp with this menagerie. I'll bet he still wears T-shirts day in, day out, doesn't he?"

"Pretty much. And you should talk about a time warp."

Jo's wardrobe hadn't changed since she was a teenager—plaid shirt, corduroy pants (cargo in the summer), oatmeal woolen socks. Moose was busy chewing on the shoelaces of the worn hiking boots she'd kicked off the minute she came into the house.

"You might have dressed a *little* less casually to conduct the workshops," Amy said.

"Two plane rides, rental car, then the college where the

students look like they just rolled out of bed? Nope. Casual was the only way to go."

"Leave it to Jo to be a walking advertisement for L.L.Bean."

"Leave it to Amy to be a walking advertisement for girly girl." Jo shuddered dramatically. "So many color-coordinated outfits."

"In the words of Louisa May Alcott, *Let us be elegant or die.*"

"Who cares about elegance when you can be original like me? And Theo the First?" Jo blew a kiss in the air as she did whenever she mentioned Theo's grandfather. They had spent many an afternoon playing cutthroat games of Scrabble.

"You are inimitable," Amy agreed. "But—orange pants? You look like you're dressed to hunt."

"*Burnt* orange." Jo lifted a long leg. "Got them on sale. One advantage of growing up poor—I developed a nose for a bargain."

"And a blind eye. No one else would buy them."

"They're comfortable."

"No one else could fit in them."

Jo had inherited their father's tall, rangy build and aquiline features. Amy liked to tease her that, on a good day, she resembled Georgia O'Keeffe, on a bad day, Henry Marsden in drag. Jo's one vanity was her thick, wavy hair, nearly as dark as Theo's. When she was a little girl, Amy would iron her curls, hoping that her hair would drape and flow like her sister's. Until one winter day when she burned the ends. They were all chilled to the bone, waiting for the smell of burnt hair to clear the house before closing the windows again—and waiting for Marmee to please stop comparing the mishap to Jo burning Meg's hair in *Little Women.*

Amy patted her lap for Nina to join her, but she merely twitched her whiskers, licked a paw, and dropped her head back onto Jo's lap. Getting up abruptly from the armchair, Amy knelt at the fireplace and poked at the burning logs. Flames arrowed in a brilliant display of blue and gold as she considered how to approach the subject of the creative writing position.

"You hit celebrity status today, Jo. The students loved you."

Jo grinned. "The trick is to wear ugly pants. And teach what you love."

"And write what you know?"

"Ha! I usually find out what I know *after* I write."

"I've been talking to the dean about adding creative writing courses to our curriculum. I told her about you." Unfortunately, Fiona was at a conference in Los Angeles and didn't meet Jo.

"Me? What for?"

"So you can teach them. Just think: you can move back here, and we can see each other all the time, and—"

"Just think. I love Seattle and have a life there."

"The salary will be higher, and you'll be teaching college-level students."

"I love my *high-school*-level students, thank you very much."

"At least consider it."

Jo stared at the ceiling for a minute. "Okay, I considered it. The answer is no."

"Well, phooey to you." Amy tossed one of the cat's jingle balls across the floor. They all opened drowsy eyes and stretched lazily but didn't chase it.

"Phooey to you too. And don't think I don't know what you're up to, trying to get me and Theo to make up."

"And yet. Here you are."

"Couldn't resist the workshops," Jo grumbled. "And I wanted to see how you two were putting up with each other."

"We put up with each other just fine. C'mon. Admit it. You miss your Teddy."

Jo examined the ends of her hair, whistling.

"If he and I can mend fences," Amy said, "there's no reason you two can't."

"Took you guys long enough. But it doesn't mean you should butt in on our fight."

"You tried to help *us*."

"And you'll have the same result." Jo had initially played referee between Amy and Theo after the exhibit fallout. Exasperated by Theo's refusal to talk to Amy, she gave up. *Sort it out already, for criminy's sake* were her last words on the matter.

"I still think it's worth a try," Amy said.

"Best of luck. I can be a real ball-breaker," Jo said with a rare tone of despondency.

Amy checked her expression for further clues, but Jo had put on what Theo called her "poker face." Her sister was impossible to read when she chose to hide her emotions. Did she mean *heartbreaker* instead of ball-breaker? Was she feeling remorse for breaking Theo's heart? Regret?

Was Theo in love with her? Scaredy-cat Amy was half-afraid of Jo to ask, half-afraid of the answer.

"You haven't told me what you think about my latest story," Jo said.

"Which one?"

"'Igneous.' You didn't like it, did you?"

"Not as much as 'Escarpment' and 'Strata.'" Amy dropped the poker and squeezed herself onto the sofa next to Jo's feet.

"I just realized something. All your titles have something to do with geology."

"Uh-huh." Jo stretched her arms to the ceiling. "I can't wait to go to dinner with Athena tomorrow night. She's an absolute riot."

"Jo. What's the deal with your titles?"

"For a theme? In case I ever publish them as a collection? I'm working on a story I think is good enough for the *New Yorker*. Solid words. Spare, clean sentences."

"What's it about?"

"You know I don't like to discuss my stories ahead of time. Afraid I'll jinx 'em. You doing anything creative these days?"

"Not particularly." She'd put her latest drawings—studies of an elderly woman's face—into a drawer when Jo arrived. Her sister's eye was as sharp as her tongue, and Amy was feeling a bit too fragile lately for cutting criticism. "Dating anyone lately?" she asked her.

"No one special. But then, none of them are."

At the slightest hint a man was "controlling" her, Jo showed him the door. Personally, Amy didn't think the guy who asked Jo to keep an open mind about sushi qualified as bossy. *What is it with him and raw fish?* Jo had complained.

"Maybe you should give someone a *chance* to be special," Amy said.

Jo let out a hoot. "Like you gave your old boyfriend Ramon a chance?"

Ramon, who sported big fur hats as if he were a native of Siberia instead of Staten Island, had always been good for a laugh. And his obsession with fur did have its erotic surprises. But when he insisted Amy wear his grandmother's ratty fox stole—naked—she finally dumped him. The beady eyes still showed up in her bad dreams.

"Brutus is my main man these days," Jo said.

"Oh, for Pete's sake! You're dating a guy named Brutus?"

"He's my bulldog. Though I should have named him Winston. Stick a cigar in his mouth, and he's a dead ringer for Churchill."

They laughed, startling Nina. She jumped off Jo's legs to join the other cats lazing on the floor.

Jo checked the time on her phone. "Whaddya reckon? Will the lord of the manor grace us with his presence tonight?"

"I'm making spaghetti. From a box, not a can. Theo said he wouldn't miss the spectacle for anything."

The front door opened, bringing with it a blast of cold air—and Theo. Moose quit chewing Jo's shoelaces to greet him, followed by Coltrane and Ray. He dropped his jacket to the floor and they rolled on it, purring. Patches of color on his cheekbones and his gleaming blue-green eyes brightened his winter-pale face.

One of Amy's favorite songs from *Camelot* was Lancelot comparing Guinevere to the seasons and explaining why he couldn't leave her in any of them. She had decided ages ago—the day they went sledding in Forest Park and Theo held her in his arms, his breath warm on her cheek—that *winter Theo* would be the one most impossible to leave.

"If it isn't he who talks to the animals," Jo said. "Dr. Dolittle himself."

"If it isn't she who scorches earth," Theo replied. "The dragon lady herself."

"Says the guy who's full of hot air."

"Says the girl who's full of herself."

"Prick."

"Jerk."

"Asswipe."

"Jackass."

"And we're off and running," Amy said.

∼⟲

"What are you? Twelve years old?" Amy chided Jo when Theo stalked off to the kitchen.

"He started it. Calling me a dragon lady."

"I take it back. You're *nine* years old."

Jo sat up and drummed the arm of the sofa with her fingers. "If anybody's full of themselves, it's him."

"It's been a long day. Go upstairs and take a nap. Theo set up an air mattress."

Jo started to rise, but Theo returned, carrying a six-pack of beer. Amy knew what his clenched jaw meant—he wasn't going to let anger get the better of him.

"Just what the doctor ordered," she said.

"Dolittle," Jo snarled.

"Jo," Amy said in a warning voice.

"Might as well get crocked," Jo said.

"I take it that's a *yes* to beer," Theo said, handing them each a can.

They counted to three and cracked them open at the same time. A reflexive Amy, Jo, and Theo ritual, like crossing their eyes when one of them told a bad joke.

"What'd I miss?" he asked, sitting in an armchair. Moose promptly dropped his head in his lap.

"Sisterhood in full bloom," Jo said. "And no, we weren't talking about you."

"Yes, we were," Amy said.

"Whatever," Theo said, thumbing his phone.

Jo swung her foot back and forth, scowling, while Amy filled her in on her latest car disasters.

"I kept seeing billboards of Buccaneer Ben on the drive from the airport," Jo said. "You'd think that absurd eye patch was the law firm's brand. I mean, the guy kicked the bucket years ago."

"It *is* the firm's brand. And Ben wasn't so bad," Amy said to steer the conversation away from the topic of brands and the possibility Jo would mention Banana Brad. He was one "creative" boyfriend she'd rather Theo didn't know about. "I liked him a lot more than Keith Ryan, Marmee's third husband."

"Me too," Jo said.

"You. Liked. Ben," Theo said. "In what universe?"

"I wasn't talking to you."

"You don't have to be rude, Jo," Amy said.

"She can't help herself," Theo said, opening a second can of beer.

"What I meant was, I liked Ben in comparison to Keith," Jo said. "I wanted to throw up every time Keith called Marmee *Peg*. And I cannot *believe* he left his fortune to those ridiculous poodles."

"Mitzi and Bitzi," Theo said.

"Marmee told me that if she had known Keith had excluded her from his will," Amy said, "she would have bonked him on the head every time he called her 'Peg o' my heart.'"

Not that Marmee married rich men for their money. She didn't have a venal bone in her body. But marriage to Ben, who'd healed her grieving widow's heart, had accustomed her to a better "milieu," as she called her improved standard of living. There was no going back once she'd lived in a house a tornado couldn't collapse like an accordion.

Jo grinned. "Husband number three wound up getting bonked but good anyway."

"We shouldn't laugh," Amy said, laughing.

Keith had been an investment banker with a mansion in Newport, Rhode Island, one of his three residences. While entertaining clients on his sailboat, the boom veered out of control and split his skull, widowing Marmee a third time.

Amy swirled the beer in the can, her spirits spiraling downward. Her love life was no less ridiculous than her mother's. As if their blond curls and pretty faces were coupled with a gene for preposterous romance. And preposterous delusions. Like Marmee's *Little Women* fantasy. Like Amy once believing she and Theo were meant for each other.

"Good thing Mrs. M wasn't on the boat that day," Theo said. "Witnessing another husband's bizarre death might have sent her over the edge."

"Get with the program," Jo said. "She's *Mrs. S* these days. And she's been hanging off one edge or another since Dad died."

"The edge of *reality*," Amy said. "It's like she wandered out of *Little Women* into a Tennessee Williams play."

"She's tougher than you think," Jo said. "Don't dismiss the possibility that she tampered with the boom on one of her sailboat rides with Keith. She hurried back to the Midwest when he was barely six feet under."

"A writer's imagination on overload," Theo said. "And she'll always be Mrs. M to me."

"No such thing as too much imagination," Jo retorted. "And who cares what she is to you?"

"Tamper with a boom? Mrs. M needed help operating small appliances."

"Baloney. She—"

"You ought to make it a scene in one of your stories, Jo," Amy interrupted. "What's the latest one called?"

"'Schism.'"

"Geology again. Let me guess. It's about a divorce."

"A marriage of convenience," Jo said with a sidelong glance at Theo. Grimacing, he shifted in the chair like he had a sudden cramp in his leg.

"I'll bet the story's about you two," Amy said too chirpily.

"You'd lose the bet," Jo said.

"It's not *that* crazy an idea. Don't forget the promise you and Theo made that if you were still single in your thirties, you'd go to Las Vegas for a quickie wedding and marry each other." Their presumption was that pretty, pleasing Amy would most certainly *not* be single in her thirties.

"A platonic marriage based on mutual loathing," Theo said.

"*That* would make a great story," Jo said, glaring at him.

He raised his beer can in a mock toast. "Here's to *unsuitable* people no one else wants."

"Here's to *losers* staying single."

"Here's to losing *emotional baggage*, not luggage."

"Here's to Las Vegas," Amy said. *Let us fake enthusiasm or die.* Because this conversation was careening in the wrong direction.

"Shit city," Theo muttered.

"The shittiest," Jo said.

"Tacky."

"Beyond tacky."

"You guys were in Vegas?" Amy asked.

Theo pulled himself up from a slouching position, and Jo ran her fingers through her hair as if checking for knots. The fire crackled like the tension in the air. "Uh-huh," she said.

"Together?"

"Chance meeting," Jo mumbled. "Right, Theo?"

"Yeah. Chance. At Harry Reid International Airport."

"I went to Vegas to research a story," Jo said.

"And I was on my way somewhere else," Theo said.

"Recently?" Amy said.

Theo looked at Jo and shook his head.

"Before or after your argument?"

"What's with the inquisition?" Jo demanded.

"What's with the mystery?"

"None of this is any of your business, Amy."

"None of what? And I smell bullshit about the airport, Jo."

"Smell away."

Jo and Theo, fellow conspirators, sworn to secrecy. They'd shoplifted at a drugstore once, just for the fun of it. If Amy hadn't found the box of Polident and thermometer Jo had carelessly stashed in a drawer, she'd never have known. And then there was the incident of "borrowing" a few of the high school's band instruments, earning them both a week of detention.

God only knew what was up with Las Vegas. But one thing was certain—their instinct to join forces, the old habit of their friendship, was alive and well. Now to bring it all the way home.

"You know what I think?" Amy said. "I think you two did something wild in Vegas. Possibly illegal."

Jo uncrossed and recrossed her legs with a harrumph. Theo pushed Moose's head off his lap and stood up, his hair going every which way.

"Boy, and I thought *I* had a vivid imagination," Jo said.

"Something illegal," Theo said. "Wow."

"As if."

"Ridiculous."

"Whaddya think, Teddy? Has our Amy been sniffing too much varnish?"

"I do believe she has, Jo."

Forces officially joined—and sealed. First goal accomplished.

Amy got off the sofa and smoothed down her girly-girl mauve sweater and gray skinny jeans. "If that's the way you're going to be, fine with me. Now, I'm going into the kitchen to make the damn spaghetti, and you can join me if you want. Or don't."

She glided out of the room like the fifth wheel she was, went into the kitchen, banged a pot or two—but couldn't resist peeking into the living room. And there were Jo and Theo, standing up, cats at their feet. Jo traced the ridge of his nose with her finger. Theo ran a hand gently down the arm she'd broken. They touched foreheads briefly and then stepped away.

If Amy were to paint a portrait of two people forgiving each other, this was what it would look like.

CHAPTER NINETEEN

*I believe we have some power over who
we love. It isn't something that just
happens to a person.*
—AMY MARCH, *LITTLE WOMEN*
(2019 FILM)

Athena's birthday celebration at Benny's Bar came right on time. By December, students were wigging out, and the faculty was fantasizing about island getaways—and Amy was no exception. Rave reviews of Ian Prescott's book on Walt Whitman, assuring him tenure, were the bright spot of the month, until his wife, Kristie, went into premature labor at thirty-four weeks with their second child and he had to take emergency leave. None of the adjuncts would teach his classes, saying it was too late in the semester. The true reason was that Fiona had yet to clear her agenda to address their proposal. Amy couldn't fault them, though her workload tripled and she found herself in front of classrooms discussing poems she hadn't read in years.

"How's it feel?" Eileen had mumbled as she hurried down a corridor, coffee sloshing in her thermos. They barely exchanged words on the days she borrowed her office.

Sitting in a booth at Benny's Bar—which tonight would have to do for an island getaway—Amy had devoured a plate of wings, a thick slab of cake, two beers, and a glass of wine, trying not to feel much of anything. Her fingers pressed to her temples, fighting nausea, she watched Athena mingle with her guests, the As You Like It Café regulars and most of the English Department. Their colleagues had voted to have the party at the bar instead of the café so they could whoop it up and relieve their end-of-semester anxiety with massive infusions of alcohol.

"Great turnout. I'm feeling the love," Athena said when she rejoined Amy at the table. "I wish Jo were here, though. I have a serious girl crush on her." During Jo's visit, they had gotten along like a house on fire. "Plus, I'd love for her to scare the bejesus out of Gary. She's the only one who could."

"I wonder if he'll show up," Amy said.

"That desperate for a man, huh?"

"No. So I'll be on the lookout. I swear, his backpack gets bigger by the day."

"No shit. I give him a wide berth whenever our paths cross."

"Screw it." Amy banged an empty beer bottle on the table. "I'm going to come right out and ask him what's in the fricking backpack."

"Dutch courage, as my dad calls it. You don't tolerate alcohol very well, do you?"

"I'm waiting for the room to stop spinning. Then I'll ask him."

"Gary's not here, you goofball," Athena said, laughing.

Neither was Theo. Athena hadn't formally met him yet, but she'd included him in the email invitation in the spirit of *the more, the merrier*.

Though he and Jo had taken their first steps back to friendship, he had made himself scarce during the rest of her visit, leaving early in the morning, returning late at night. Once Jo returned to Seattle, though, the trio started exchanging group texts again, with Jo calling Theo *Teddy* and *Broody Bear* and Theo joking about resuming their petty crime adventures.

Her first goal behind her, Amy was focused on the second, currently in limbo. The administration hadn't responded to her creative writing curriculum proposal, and Jo maintained she wasn't interested.

"See if I care," Amy muttered.

"Care about what?" Athena asked. "Or are you having a flashback to a fifth-grade playground fight?"

"My whole life's a flashback." Amy rubbed her forehead. For some reason, she expected to find bangs there. "I think I'm wasted."

"You must be. You rubbed against Turner like a cat while everyone was singing 'Happy Birthday' to me."

"I did *what?*"

"You kept nudging his shoulder with your head. It was kind of cute, actually. Blotto. But cute."

"Uh-oh. I hope I didn't agree to go out with him this time."

"He's asked before?"

"Uh-huh. I didn't tell you 'cause you'd be like, *Go for it, girl.*"

"Go for it, girl."

"No way. Workplace issue. Besides, he's not my type."

"You have a type? Besides wackadoodle?"

"Turner is all doodle. No wack."

Athena laughed. "Should I be worried that I know exactly what you mean?"

Amy hiccoughed. "Glad you do. 'Cause I don't."

"I think Turner's motto is *Keep calm and bore my pants off.*"

"My pants are staying on. *And* my skirts. And who in their right mind could stand teaching espistu...epistula..."

"Epistolary novels?"

Amy slapped the table. "Epistullery! The most boring novels ever."

"When's the last time you had sex, Amy Marsden?"

She tried to count back on her fingers to August, but she was seeing double. "When's the last time *you* had sex, Athena Murphy-Kent?"

Athena looked across the room to where Thorne was playing chess with her father, Charles. "A couple of hours ago. In the café broom closet. The hot cider got us all hot and bothered."

"Sounds like we're playing Clue. Who's minding the café while he's here?"

"Robin. And Jaycee's helping him out."

Amy had a newfound respect for Thorne, bordering on idolatry. While at the Murphy-Kent house for Thanksgiving, she'd observed Robin suffer through an episode of acute paranoia. Watching Thorne hold his brother, calm him, and patiently talk him through it was one of the most touching scenes she'd witnessed.

"What did your hubby give you for your birthday," she asked Athena, "besides a romp in the broom closet?"

"These turquoise earrings I'm wearing. My birthstone." Athena fished in her handbag and pulled out a laminated yellow card with a few perforated holes. "My mother gave me thirty-four free yoga sessions at Ricki's studio, Bend Over Backwards. One for every year I've been alive."

"Is the name of the studio Lydia and Ricki's philosophy of exercise or marriage?"

"Both. Want to come with me next time? If I'm going to pass gas in public, I'd rather have a friend nearby."

"To absorb embarrassment?"

"To blame it on."

"As long as you don't blame me if your book on the Brontë family bombs."

"Don't care if it does, as long as I make tenure. And if you can say all those *b* words, you're not drunk enough." Athena lifted their empty wineglasses. "Hair of the dog?"

"What kind of dog?"

"One with a *lot* of hair."

"Okay. Bring me a Newfie."

While Athena was at the bar to order more drinks—after stopping to interrupt her husband's chess game with a long, lingering kiss—Amy rested her head against the booth. It weighed at least two hundred pounds. No wonder her life was stuck in flashback mode. Who could move forward with a...a 'Moose' head?

Athena returned with a tray, holding a carafe and two glasses with tiny purple paper parasols, and put it in the middle of the table. "Guess who showed up?"

Amy swiveled her Moose head so fast, looking for Theo, that her neck hurt. "Where?"

Athena pointed to Ivy standing at the bar with Karl. "I didn't think they'd come. They've been on break number seventy-three. Guess they made up." Though if Ivy's fiery expression was any indication, they were on their way to another argument.

"The delicate maiden and the Neanderthal slash Viking slash construction guy slash...Uh-oh. I ran out of slashes."

Athena filled their glasses. "No Newfies. But here's Benny's infamous Hurricane cocktail. You'll be creating new punctuation marks before the night is over."

Amy's stomach turned after the first sip, but she drank it anyway. Because she had important things to think about. And there was some stuff she didn't like to think about when she was sober. Like sexual desire. Apparently, it was very specific; otherwise, she'd want to jump Karl's bones. 'Cause who wouldn't? He was a tall, golden-blond, muscular stud. But it wasn't likely cats ever wrapped themselves around Karl's legs, or that he smelled like a forest or tasted like...

"I wonder what Theo tastes like."

Crap. She'd said it out loud. Luckily, her speech was as slurred as her brain, and Athena didn't notice. But...wait. Amy *knew* what Theo tasted like. Something fresh like...celery. Or strawberries. What'd she taste like to him? Maybe she'd ask.

"Here's to the worst hangover of my life," Athena said, clinking her glass to Amy's.

"Mine's already...what's the word?" Amy hiccoughed again. "Here."

A group of twentysomething guys strolled by their table, each one glancing down at her and Athena. Amy tried not to blink in case they'd think she was winking at them. Which was not easy because she was also trying to remember how to spell *testosterone.*

"What's your favorite male body part?" Athena asked when they had passed. "Mine's buns."

She was about to tell Athena that she wanted to go home to think about it, this very minute, when the man himself walked toward their booth. He dropped into the seat next to her, and the scent of sandalwood tickled her nose. Nubby hunter-green sweater, wind-tunneled hair, Aegean Sea eyes— Theo personified.

He pointed to the carafe. "Looks like I have some catching up to do."

Amy twirled a purple paper parasol in his face. "Buns up. I mean...bottoms up. No, wait..."

"And it looks like you have slowing down to do."

"Did you just get here, like, just now?"

"About ten minutes ago."

"Where've you been all this time?"

"Circulating."

Theo introduced himself to Athena, she thanked him for coming to her party, and they said other stuff Amy didn't hear because she was reciting the alphabet in her head. She was pretty sure *u* came before *w*.

"I saw you at the café recently with a young woman," Athena was saying to Theo. "It looked like a date."

"It was. That was Gina."

Amy straightened from her slumped position. Who the heck was Gina?

"None of my beeswax, but you didn't seem to be having a good time," Athena said.

"She kept complaining about the Midwest," he said. "When I suggested she give it a chance and go with the flow, she got mad and said I sounded like I was from California. I don't think she meant it as a compliment."

"How could anyone be mean to you?" Amy pulled down the sides of her mouth to make a pout. Because she couldn't feel her lips. "You rescue Geicos. Getsos. Um...geckos."

"And damsels in distress," he said, pushing her glass to the other side of the table.

"Hey, what happened to Miles anyway?"

"Joey Martinelli took him. Two weeks ago. You said, *Bye-bye, Miles Martinelli*. Now, how about I drive you home?"

"How about I...okay."

"Bye-bye, Amy Marsden," Athena said, laughing.

Amy's phone lit up with a text and selfie of Marmee and John at another roadside attraction, this one in Clearfield, Pennsylvania. She put the phone in Theo's face. "Check this out. The Bee Bell...The Bust..."

"The Beer Barrel Belly Buster," he read out loud. "A seventeen-pound cheeseburger with twenty-five slices of cheese and a seventeen-inch bun. The challenge is to eat it in three hours."

"But you're a vegetenarian. Hey. I just remembered. The Alcott family was vegetenarian."

"Yeah. You've told me."

She tried to get Theo into focus but she had gecko eyes, looking in all directions. "I'll bet you wouldn't eat the busty burger if the prize was a million bucks."

He lowered his head and put his mouth to her ear, causing sparks to shoot out of her eyeballs. "You'd win the bet," he whispered.

You're the prize, she almost said. Or maybe she did.

"Here's the thing, Theo."

"There's a thing, Amy?"

She ran her tongue slowly, deliciously up his cheek. "I can't hold my licker."

And with that pronouncement, she keeled over into his lap.

CHAPTER TWENTY

I wish I had no heart, it aches so.
—MEG MARCH, *LITTLE WOMEN*

So this was what death felt like. A head of crashing billiard balls. A mouth of sawdust. A gut of rust.

Amy clutched the sheet beneath her chin, opening first one eye, then the other.

And, oh yeah, eyeballs of flaming cinders.

She was halfway to a poem. Her first. And by the look of things, her last.

She flexed her toes, willing her feet to life. Something walked up her legs, made biscuits on her stomach, and purred like a small motor.

Nina's rough tongue licked her cheek. A tongue licking a cheek was vaguely familiar.

"Hey, girl," she croaked.

Nina stepped daintily over her head and, settling herself on the edge of the mattress, proceeded to wash herself. The fan above the bed whirred, slicing light and then shade on the ceiling. But her bedroom ceiling fan had brown blades, not white. And where was her pile of books on the nightstand?

Amy propped herself on her elbows. Her nightstand was maple with intricate carvings. This one was an IKEA piece with a half-empty bottle of water on it. *Empty* since optimism was not an option when one was half-dead.

A grunt and a sigh, neither of which was coming out of her or Nina.

She wasn't alone in the bedroom, which was not hers.

Theo, sleeping soundly, a thick strand of hair rising from his face with every breath, lay beside her.

She looked beneath the covers. Somehow between total brain shutdown at Benny's Bar and the hangover from Hades, she'd gotten home, out of her clothes, into her cloud pajamas, and onto Theo's bed.

Theo, whose cheek she had licked the night before.

Amy was wide awake now. No caffeine necessary for this girl. She was on full-blown alert. And for a few minutes, while she considered the awful possibilities, she considered the not-so-awful possibility she turn the clock back and be fully conscious this time while they—

"Hey," Theo said softly.

She lay back down and folded her hands across her chest. "You really need to do something about your ceiling. The plaster's peeling off."

"Hmm."

"And it's cold enough in here to hang meat. Comfortable mattress, though."

"Uh-huh."

"Any idea what time it is? Or day?"

He turned onto his side, supporting his head on his hand. His lips were swollen from sleep, his eyes half-closed. Which she preferred to half-open, considering the circumstances. "It's today," he said. "Early today."

"How did I...Where are my clothes?"

"On the chair. I dressed you in the dark."

After *undressing* her down to her underwear. And not for the first time.

"Sir Theo the Damsel Rescuer," she said. Pretty feeble. But her wit was on life support along with the rest of her.

"I'll add it to my resume." He nodded toward the water bottle. "I got you to drink most of it to dull the sharpest edges of the hangover."

"There are degrees of death?" she asked with her sawdust mouth.

He grinned. "You were only halfway there."

"Would you believe me if I said I'll never drink again?"

"Nope. But you're luckier than most. You didn't upchuck and hurl. I stayed with you in case you did."

Amy looked over the side of the bed where an empty trash can waited. Nina stretched into a horseshoe and then sat down again, observing them with unblinking eyes. "Please tell me there weren't any witnesses to my humiliation."

"None that were sober."

"My bike?"

"Athena drove you to the party. Remember?"

"Not really."

Amy massaged her eyebrows. Too many words too early on a day after too much alcohol. And Theo was looking at her with too many eyes. "I must look a fright."

"You scared all the cats except Nina to the living room. Moose never sleeps in here; otherwise, he would have woofed you right out."

Across the room, the glow of an aquarium light caught her

attention. Small, colorful fish swam dreamily past the fake palm trees and in and out of the toy castle. "*Mister Rogers' Neighborhood*," she murmured.

"What'd you say?"

"We used to watch *Mister Rogers' Neighborhood* after school. He would feed the fish at the beginning of every episode."

"Oh yeah. And we'd joke about being too old for it, but turn it on anyway."

"Best cure for teenage angst."

"Yep." Theo threw back the covers, eased off the bed, and opened the blinds. "Back soon. Gotta feed the troops and walk Moose."

Nina followed him out with a prancing gait, and Amy sank into the pillow, watching small cotton balls tumble past the window. The first snowfall of the season never failed to make her feel like a kid again. To rekindle the sense of anticipation childhood was all about. *Maybe today something wonderful will happen. Maybe today I'll get, I'll know, I'll be, I'll . . .*

As soon as she felt younger than a hundred years old, she'd finish the sentence.

She heard Theo put the cats' bowls down on the kitchen floor, the scampering of paws, and a low grunt from Moose before the front door closed behind him and Theo. After about twenty minutes, during which she debated getting up or not, she heard the medicine cabinet squeak open and then shut with a thud.

"I turned the heat up and brought you a couple of Advil," Theo said from the doorway. He wore a thermal undershirt and navy-blue sweatpants, and stubble shadowed his cheeks. He handed her the pills, and she shoved them into her mouth in case *Don't ever shave or comb your hair* spilled out.

"You'll feel better soon," he said.

"Define *soon*."

"Tomorrow. If you're lucky."

"I think my luck went the way of the Hurricane cocktail."

She really should get going. Apologize, say *thanks*, and walk out of the bedroom with as much dignity as hangover face and snarled hair allowed. But Theo and his hunky body and sulky smile were slipping into bed beside her. Amy lay as flat as a paper doll, waiting. It was snowing, and something wonderful could happen.

Somewhere deep in the belly of the house, the furnace roared to life. "This is like the time we camped in my backyard," he said, drawing the blanket around them.

"Except it was summer. And buggy."

"It was Jo's fault the mosquitos ate us alive. She left the tent zipper open."

Amy had heard them buzzing all night, unable to sleep because all she could think was, *Theo is lying next to me. I'm lying next to Theo.*

"I better get up," she said.

"Why?" he murmured sleepily.

Because you're lying next to me. And I may not be able to resist you.

"I have a ton of work to do."

"Give yourself a sick day. Remember those?"

"I remember you and Jo *faking* sick days."

"You were always too chicken to play hooky with us," he said.

"But not too chicken to lie for you. Many times over."

"It *was* nice of you to cover for us. Even when you were mad that we'd gone biking without you or something."

So *many* somethings. Like Jo and Theo going to the movies by themselves, claiming she didn't like horror films anyway. Or talking about people she didn't know and places she hadn't been.

Thick as thieves, Marmee used to describe them. *Those two are a pair.*

So are we, Amy would say to herself. *Or will be someday.*

"Hey, Theo?"

"Hmm?"

"You promised me a snowball fight the first time it snowed."

"You're on," he said, laughing.

"Once my hangover is over, I mean."

"It'll be melted by then."

"*Next* snowfall, then, look out. Oh, and I was wondering."

"Yeah?"

"If I murdered someone, would you help me bury the body?"

They turned onto their sides at the same time. "Should I have slept with one eye open?" he asked, merriment animating his face.

"Don't you anyway? Considering how you piss off your girlfriends?"

"Not *all* of them."

"Well? What's your answer?"

"Why are you asking?"

"Curiosity."

"Curiosity killed the cat," Theo said.

"I'd never hurt the cats."

"In that case . . . sure."

"Speaking of the cats, there's something else I've been wondering," Amy said.

"If Coltrane thinks he's human? The answer is yes."

"Not that. I'm curious why you haven't named any of them after Billie Holiday."

"Haven't found one deserving of the name," he said, plucking at a loose string on the blanket.

Amy twined one of her curls around her finger, tempted to hum a few bars of "Lover Man," the song Billie sang on the radio their memorable night together. Memorable to her, anyway.

"Now that I've got you running scared," she said, "tell me what you and Jo fought about."

"I'm not *that* scared."

"What's the big deal?"

"There isn't any. Just don't want to talk about it."

"I get it. You're scared of *Jo*."

"Maybe." He grinned. "*She'd* help you dispose of a body. And it could very well be mine."

"Okay then, how'd you get the bump on your nose? You used to have, like, the most perfect nose."

"Broke it," he said, lying flat on his back again.

"Playing a sport?"

"No. Accident. Can we talk about something else?"

Amy sat up and stretched. "Actually, I better skedaddle. I've got term papers to read. Being hungover should make for some interesting comments."

Theo drew an arm up behind his head and turned to face her. "You do seem to enjoy your job."

"I do. Very much. But I wouldn't call it my *dream* job."

"Because art is your passion. Always has been."

"There's a huge gap between wannabe and recognized artist." Though if Derek could make the leap, she sure as heck could. "I used to be so single-minded. I have to get that back. I can't let anyone or anything get in the way of my art."

"Like Jo doesn't let anybody get in *her* way."

"Uh-huh." Amy deeply admired her sister's dedication to writing. But she could have done without the comparison at the moment. And what it might mean about Theo's feelings for Jo.

"I used to think that the deal you made with your stepfather was a cop-out," he said. "But when I was getting by on my own with odd jobs, I understood why you did it."

"Now I'm making up for lost time," she said. "I've submitted paintings to an online art show for an objective, professional opinion."

"Good for you, putting yourself out there."

She hadn't intended to tell a single soul but, well, this was Theo.

"Are you putting yourself out in the dating world, since you broke up with Brittany? Besides Gina?"

She hadn't intended to ask, but...

"I'm batting zero," he said. "How about you?"

"Less than zero."

Amy leaned over, her heart thundering in her chest, and kissed him softly on the mouth.

She hadn't intended to, but...

"What's that for?" he asked.

"To keep dateless Amy and Theo tuned up?"

His lips curved in a smile. "I'm not sure a car analogy works for you."

"How about *use it or lose it*?"

"I don't think either of us is in danger of losing it."

But she was—of losing all willpower to resist him.

Because Theo was gazing at her through half-lidded eyes, stroking her cheek, opening his mouth—and she was devouring his hungrily. *Danger*, she thought while his hands roamed her breasts, hips, and legs. As the skin of his muscled back melted beneath her fingers. She sniffed and licked. She couldn't get enough of the feast of him, of his low moans, his lips and warm breath.

This mouth of his.

Maybe something wonderful would happen. Maybe now they—

Except they wouldn't.

He wasn't her Theo—because she wasn't his Amy. If she was, there'd be no holding back, no secrets, no questions. If she was, she'd feel his love down to her cells. He was kissing her because, well, what guy could resist a woman who'd made the first move?

And they'd done this before.

The aquarium pump gurgled. The fish swam back and forth. Around and around. Going nowhere like Amy and Theo had gone nowhere. Thanks to the art exhibit.

Amy gasped as a flash of heat spread through her body. Theo drew away as if she'd burned him. She pushed the covers off herself, and herself off the bed, and stood by the window. Snow spilled from the sky, silently, steadily. It was time to pull out a witty gem from her repartee repertoire. Something along the lines of curiosity and what it was killing this time. But her mind was as muffled as the landscape, and she was wearing silly cloud pajamas.

She steeled herself and faced him. "Sorry. Moment of madness."

If she *were* his, Theo would walk over, fold her in his arms, and ask, while kissing her over and over, what had taken them so long.

"Me too," he said.

"Don't worry. It'll never happen again. I rarely make the same mistake twice."

Because their first time wasn't a mistake. It wasn't.

"Lucky you," Theo said. "Wish I could say the same. What's your secret?"

"Staying in motion works for me." From boyfriend to boyfriend. From fantasy to reality. From one impulsive moment to regret.

Amy walked to the door, one excruciating step at a time. "I really, really, really am never going to drink again."

"You don't want to hear the stupid stuff *I've* done drunk."

Stupid stuff.

Ouch.

"I was only kidding about keeping us tuned up, Theo. I mean, geez."

"You don't have to explain. I know you well enough by now, Amy."

Not well enough at all. Not anymore. As he himself once said, *Nothing lasts forever*.

CHAPTER TWENTY-ONE

Christmas won't be Christmas without
any presents.
—JO MARCH, *LITTLE WOMEN*

Amy stared out the classroom window frosted with ice, listening with half an ear to a student's presentation on a Hemingway short story. A week of winter storms had buried whatever magic and evocation of childhood the first snowfall had brought. Nothing wonderful was going to happen. Today wouldn't be much different than yesterday. Life was a routine of get up, go to work, eat, sleep, repeat.

As for her and Theo, they were so darn mature, and reasonable, and civilized she could spit. So rational she wanted to scream, à la Brittany, when they ate breakfast together. When they laughed at Moose's food-begging tactics. When they reminded each other to lower the thermostat before leaving the house to enter the outside world where everywhere she looked, she saw his blue-green eyes and dark thicket of hair.

That mouth of his.

To add insult to injury, her submissions to the art show had been rejected so quickly she got whiplash. Her best landscape series—a marshland at sunset through four seasons—and not one stinking painting made the cut. Well, some people had to work for a living. Some people didn't have a trust fund, and the luxury to paint all day, and get on their high horse about dedication and instinct.

While the student enthused about Kilimanjaro—whose snows didn't excite her any more than the soot-blackened mounds piled against the sidewalks—Amy snuck a peek at her phone to read Athena's text message.

Don't forget yoga at four. Meet you in the parking lot.

Thanks to Athena, she had managed transportation in the bad weather. If she could make it to spring without caving in and buying a car, she'd consider it a minor triumph. And God knew she needed *something* to feel good about.

As soon as the class ended, Amy grabbed her workout bag and hurried to the parking lot.

"Fricking frick frick," Athena fumed as she maneuvered her cherry-red Mini Cooper around a block of ice on the road. "This is freezing-my-balls-off weather."

"You don't have balls," Amy reminded her.

"I grew a pair when I got married."

"Uh-oh. Trouble in paradise?"

"I am a bit miffed at Mr. Murphy-Kent at the moment." A red woolen scarf was wound elaborately around Athena's head, neck, and mouth, leaving only her eyes and freckled nose visible. She was adorable even when she was mad.

"Aw, what'd he do? Put too many bean sprouts in your sandwich?" Amy asked.

As if Thorne wasn't already the ideal husband, he packed his wife creative, healthy lunches every day, complete with love notes.

"I've been picking the darn sprouts out of my teeth all day," Athena complained. "And he skimped on the mayo."

"First-world problems."

"First-world *breakdown* if he doesn't stop burning the candle at both ends. I keep telling him to let Robin assume more responsibility at the café, but does he listen? No, he does not."

"I thought his brother ran the place just fine whenever he needed a break."

"He does. But Thorne's got a mother-hen thing going on with people he loves. Worries himself into a tizzy that Robin will get overstressed. An anxiety he relieves by baking pies. It gets on my nerves. And my pie-loving butt."

"Hey, don't knock a guy baking for you. It's pretty great."

"I remember you saying Theo liked to cook. He bakes for you too?"

"Not him. Specifically. I meant guys in general."

"Theo's smoking hot for a 'guy in general.' I see why you had a crush on him. Any chance the romance rosebud will bloom?"

"None. At all. I'm just glad we're managing the housemate situation as well as we are. So, what are you going to do about de-stressing Thorne?" Amy didn't trust herself to say anything else about Theo. If Athena smelled even a whiff of their brief encounter, she'd coax every nitty-gritty from her in three minutes flat.

"I'm dragging him to San Francisco to see my brother, Finn, and his partner, Mario, at Christmas whether he wants to go or not."

"He'll thank you for it later."

Athena grinned. "He usually does."

Amy should be so lucky to have Athena's love problems. She huddled in her parka with a shiver of utter loneliness, a sensation she'd been experiencing much too often lately. The slightest thing might set it off. The pulsing jazz rhythms behind Theo's bedroom door. Nina sleeping, oblivious to her. The silent indifference of her plants, including the button fern, as she tended them. The prospect of spending Christmas alone, taking care of Moose and the cats.

Marmee and John would be somewhere on the interstate, Theo was going to Philadelphia to see his mother, and Jo had told her, *Christmas won't be Christmas without my little sister.*

It would be the first time they hadn't traveled to see each other or to meet up with Marmee. Amy could *maybe* see why Jo preferred Seattle to Laurel for the holiday. But why all the mumbo jumbo that neither of them should risk flying in winter weather, and that Jo had a to-do list a mile wide, and . . . whatever.

Athena parked in the lot of Bend Over Backwards, unwound her scarf, and reached across to grab Amy's hand. "Hey, what's wrong? I haven't heard one decent zinger out of your mouth for days. You sure there's nothing going on with Theo?"

"Positive. Why do you ask?"

"I vaguely recall him carrying you dead drunk out of Benny's Bar. Apologies again for the Hurricane cocktails."

"You recall correctly. He was just being a helpful housemate. If I'm preoccupied, it's because I've got a million things to do before I go to New York City after New Year's Day."

Athena sat back, surprised. "First *I'm* hearing about this trip."

First Amy had *thought* of it. But she was so restless she was crawling out of her skin. The urgency to focus on her art was stronger than ever.

"I haven't been there for years," she said. "I'm going to hit every museum and art show I can get into. I owe it to my craft to observe and learn from the best." By which she meant to assess the competition and figure out what Derek had that she didn't. "And I need to establish my artistic goals." By which she meant to change perspective. To take a certain person out of the foreground and put him in the background, for instance.

"Way to go! Follow that dream!" Athena said. "I hope you plan to have fun too."

"Getting away will be fun enough."

"Hmm." Athena crinkled her nose. "I'm smelling man trouble. You'd tell me if you were dating another crackpot, wouldn't you?"

"Since when do I spare you the gruesome details?"

"There isn't a new guy in your life?"

"Nope. Nada. Not a one."

They watched Lydia, Athena's mother, and her partner, Ricki, who owned the yoga studio, enter the building. They were laughing, jostling each other, sharing yet another inside joke.

"Okey dokey," Athena said. "Time to get in touch with our inner chakra or whatever the heck we do in there."

Amy laughed so hard she started crying. And couldn't stop crying, no matter how hard she tried.

⁓◌

Amy turned up the volume on her phone, but her mother's voice sounded as if it were coming from a tunnel. "Marmee? Can you speak up? I can't hear you very well."

"Is this better?" Marmee asked in an exaggerated whisper.

"A little. Where are you calling from?"

"I'm in the can, having a think. Or should I say *the john*, like my husband's name?"

"*Bathroom* will do. Why are you talking in there?"

"It's the only place in this Minnie Winnie thingie I can be alone." She hiccoughed. "*Maintenant, je suis content.*"

"Have you been drinking?" Her mother's tolerance for alcohol was only slightly better than hers.

"*Un peu.*"

"Beer or something stronger?"

"Wine from a box. *C'est terrible*, but it gets me where I'm going."

Amy looked out the window of her study, waiting for her mother's loopy brain to de-loop. The day marked the winter solstice, and it was already dark at five o'clock. The bare trees were ghostly beneath the murky sky. With each passing day, though, spring would inch closer and closer. The prospect should cheer her. "Spring's coming," she said under her breath, trying the idea on for size.

Nope. No cheer.

"Did I ever tell you that I got seven hundred and fifty on the Advanced Placement exam in French?" her mother asked.

"Uh-huh." About seven hundred and fifty times.

"Best score in my class."

"Good for you, Marmee."

"At least my girls put their smarts to good use."

"George Eliot supposedly said, *It's never too late to be what you might have been*," Amy said in response to her mother's rueful sigh.

"What does he know about anything? Men. Always making..."

Amy waited while she arranged her thoughts.

"Pronouncements," Marmee said. "Men are always making pronouncements."

"*She.* George Eliot was a pseudonym for Mary Ann Evans."

"Oh, like Tweety and Big Bird. You can't tell what gender they are."

"If Tweety, my favorite cartoon character, isn't a girl," Amy said, laughing, "I'll eat my *chapeau.*"

"I never thought about it before, but why do you suppose Louisa May Alcott gave Jo a boy's name and Laurie a girl's name?"

"I have no idea."

"Gender-bender names in *Little Women*. I'll be darned. I *am* having a good think."

Amy's laugh turned into a barking cough. "What state are you and John headed to?" she asked to shut off Marmee's flurry of Vicks VapoRub advice, her go-to cure for every ailment. Amy and Jo had spent a good part of their childhood smelling of eucalyptus.

"Somewhere south where it's not as cold, John says. But I like the cold. I think we should...oh my goodness!"

"Marmee? What is it?"

"I know where I want to go. Concord, Massachusetts, to visit Orchard House."

"Again?" A question Amy and Jo had asked in various tones of teenage annoyance as their mother planned yet another road trip to the Alcott family home.

"Hmm, maybe not," Marmee said. "I'm not sure it would interest the illustrious Dr. Smith."

It took Amy a few seconds to realize she was referring to her husband.

"Tell me, Amy. Do you think you'll have a white Christmas in Illinois?"

"It's not in the forecast." *Only a lonely one.* "But it may change." *Not likely.*

Amy doodled sprigs of holly on the notepad on her desk. She should buy Nina a few toys and plan a festive Christmas dinner for one. Attempt a plum pudding, complete with flames, for a Victorian theme. Pretend Tiny Tim from Dickens's *A Christmas Carol* was sitting at the hearth and the Cratchits were the one, big, happy family of Christmas Future. Though maybe she should ditch the flaming plum pudding idea in case she set Theo's house on fire.

"Louisa May Alcott never married," Marmee remarked.

The way things are going, neither will your daughters. But Amy spared her mother this dim prospect—and a demand for an explanation of the non sequitur. Something to do with a not-so-illustrious husband, she guessed.

"Want to know why I've always loved *Little Women*?" Marmee asked her.

"Because it's a delightful, heartwarming novel?" Maybe she *should* have followed Fiona's advice and written about it instead of *Idylls of the King*. Maybe some of that delightful, heartwarming feeling would have rubbed off on her.

"I loved the book because it made me believe that, no matter how hard life was, I could handle it," Marmee said. "I would triumph over adversity like the March family. And leave it to you and Jo to give me that March-sister spirit whenever things got tough."

Yes. They did. But also leave it to Amy and Jo to gripe between themselves that they could do with a little less spirit and a lot more food, clothes, books, and art supplies.

"That reminds me," Marmee said. "I ordered presents for you and Jo online. You should get them soon."

"Thanks so much," Amy said. "When you get back, I'll give you your gift. I already mailed Jo's." Books, as usual. A beautiful volume of Henri Cartier-Bresson's photographs of Paris for Marmee, and a collection of *The Far Side* cartoons for Jo.

"Look at us. Buying presents *before* the holiday," Marmee marveled.

The Marsden family had conquered their shoestring budget by furiously clipping coupons, buying food on the brink of expiration, getting Christmas trees at the eleventh hour—the forlorn trees even Charlie Brown wouldn't want—and buying presents the day after Christmas when everything was half-priced. Their mother and father managed to make it feel like they were playing a game, and Jo would invariably joke that she was going to sell her hair like Jo March.

But the Thanksgiving Eve Amy waited outside the grocery with her dad for the chance of a free turkey, the bitter cold stinging her cheeks, she didn't think being poor was fun at all. It meant living outside of things, looking at the world through a narrow lens. And Amy, the artist, meant to look at the world through as wide a lens as possible. She didn't want to be like Marmee, who had planned to live in Paris every summer after teaching French during the school year. Working in their neighborhood cheese shop, demonstrating the proper pronunciation of Roquefort and Camembert, was as close as her mother ever came to living abroad.

"Pigs," Marmee said out of the blue.

"Are you talking about Great Aunt Sophie's pig farm?" Amy asked, scribbling over the holly she'd drawn.

"Heavens no. *The Three Little Pigs*. It was one of your favorite stories when you were a little girl. You asked me to read it to you all the time."

The illustration of the third little pig's house was what Amy eagerly waited for. Solid, permanent, the kind of house a tornado couldn't huff and puff away.

"I wanted a brick house too and I got it," her mother said. "And three extra husbands in the bargain."

Amy put the pen down, alarmed by a tone in her mother's voice she rarely heard. "Marmee? What's going on?"

"Here I am, married to another wealthy man, and what does he do? He drags me all over creation in a camper with bad suspension and a carpet that stinks of feet. Dead feet. *Les pieds morts. Mort.* Like this marriage."

"Are you and John going through a rough patch?" Amy was tempted to encourage her mother to disconnect from her latest husband—and not just because, statistically speaking, his days were numbered—except she herself wanted so very much to *connect* and wouldn't be convincing.

"I fell in love with your father on the dance floor," Marmee said with a luxuriant sigh. "He swept me right off *mes pieds*."

Watching her parents dance in their narrow kitchen was one of Amy's fondest memories. So elegant and fluid. Rare moments of grace in their hardscrabble lives. Unlike the awkward dance she and Theo had always done. Two steps forward, one behind.

"Life was hard for Henry and me, but I didn't care," Marmee said. "*Non, je ne regrette rien*, as Piaf sang."

Amy doubted there was anyone who could honestly claim they had no regrets in life. Or that there was any child who had to listen to Edith Piaf recordings until she wanted to roll up into a ball and weep.

Marmee snuffled. "I miss my Henry every day. He was my one true love."

"I miss Daddy too." Amy wanted to offer more words of comfort, but a thick sob had gathered in her throat.

"You know what I think, Amy? I think I keep getting married because time stopped when your father stepped off that roof, and I'm hoping the clock will start up again." She lowered her voice to a whisper. "I'm still waiting."

"Oh, I love you to pieces, Marmee. Don't be sad."

"I love you too, Amy dear. And you know what? Once John has seen the next biggest something, I'm going to tell him to turn this camper around and head north."

Her voice was suddenly strong and clear. Purposeful. A couple of tragicomic scenarios flashed before Amy's eyes. Marmee commandeering the Minnie Winnie and dropping her fourth husband off at the side of the road. Marmee leaping from the Minnie Winnie and hitching a ride with a woman who'd take her to LA where she'd launch a career as the next Edith Piaf.

"I like the cold," her mother said as if it were an article of faith. "We're heading north, come hell or high water."

And Amy knew what *she* was going to do. She was going to make that plum pudding and set the sucker on fire, come hell or high water.

CHAPTER TWENTY-TWO

Into each life some rain must fall,
some days must be dark and sad
and dreary.
—"THE RAINY DAY," BY HENRY
WADSWORTH LONGFELLOW, QUOTED BY
LOUISA MAY ALCOTT, *LITTLE WOMEN*

As Theo stood beltless in stocking feet on the dirty floor of Philadelphia International Airport, he realized the indignities of air travel had finally gotten to him. Should he avoid eye contact with the scowling security guard? Or would the guard then assume he was smuggling a nuclear warhead? His eight-ounce bottle of shampoo had been confiscated since he kept forgetting shampoo was a potentially lethal weapon. The obligatory trip to see his mother at Christmas was over, and he was going to hunker down for a while. Indulging his solitary wanderlust was getting old. And he sure as hell didn't need any more T-shirts.

Having boarded the plane without arousing suspicion, he squeezed past a woman holding a baby and wedged into the middle seat. A man in a wrinkled suit, arms and legs splayed in sleep, left him barely enough space to accommodate a Chihuahua. The woman gave him a sympathetic smile. "Happy New Year," Theo whispered.

"You too," she whispered back. "Spend the holidays with family?"

He nodded. "And you?"

"Uh-huh. I couldn't wait to show him off to my folks."

The spit bubble on the infant's mouth burst when she gently kissed his head. Cute little bugger. Theo's mother, Marlene, had surprised him by speaking fondly about the baby, born to a couple in her apartment building, whom she babysat on occasion. As if she missed the years her own son had been raised by nannies. The numerous boards and committees she served on in retirement supplied conversational topics as sports channels did during Theo's infrequent trips to San Diego to see his father, Theodore. He filled in gaps as best he could with reminiscences of happier times when he and his dad had gone camping, and he helped his mom decorate the house for the holidays. At the very least, he didn't have to endure typical parental questions about who he was dating, whether they were serious, and when he was going to settle down.

No one special for him to be serious about. Yet. And their guess was as good as his.

Theo nearly laughed out loud remembering the Marconis' latest session. They'd argued the entire hour about what food to serve at Lando's wedding. If he could have gotten a word in edgewise, he'd have pointed out that Lando wasn't even engaged. *Not engaged? Whose damn fault is it he's not engaged?* they would have yelled. No way would he risk being beaten about the head with a footlong Genoa salami to tell them whose damn fault it was.

The plane rumbled and raced on the tarmac and thrust upward in one sudden, breathless motion. He craned his neck to watch the airport and trees gradually disappear from view. Thousands of feet in the air, mounds of clouds hovered in the infinity of the brilliantly blue sky. Like the clouds on Amy's pajamas, the morning she woke up in his bed. Her body hovering over his. Her achingly soft lips kissing him.

Theo rubbed his thigh to ease a muscle spasm. In this capsule, hurtling through space, pinned to his seat, there was nothing to distract him from his moment of madness—as Amy had so aptly called it. What guy *could* resist her? Playful, funny Amy with heavenly eyes and a lithe body that turned his insides to jelly. Good thing she pulled away before the game went any further. Before they stirred up memories best left in the past.

So *many* memories. So *much* past between them.

He stared at the sky, picturing fish floating by, like those in the aquarium in his bedroom. Hearing Amy remind him how they had watched *Mister Rogers' Neighborhood* together. When Mr. Rogers assured Theo that he liked him just the way he was, she would squeeze his hand. Her sweet smile told him she liked and accepted him just the way he was too. It was the one thing he could always count on.

She'd even have excused him for the inexcusable—throwing a dish at a fellow medical resident during an argument. A shard from the broken plate had nicked the guy's face. A temporary wound, but it scarred Theo permanently. He'd never done anything like that before. Or since. But his worst fear—that he was his parents' son—had been impossible to deny. He'd never confessed the incident to Amy. Her absolution was the last thing he deserved.

Don't be so hard on yourself, he counseled his PTSD client.

Forgive yourself. The veteran was taking positive steps in that direction. But hell if *Theo* would forgive himself.

The pretzels the airline hostess had given him crushed to chalk beneath his teeth. He washed them down with a few swigs of orange juice. The baby squirmed in his sleeping mother's arms when the man by the window emitted a loud snore, but didn't wake up. The stuffy cabin and the exertions of the holiday were making Theo drowsy too.

He woke up as the trees and rooftops of St. Louis came into view, suddenly recalling how Amy loved to sing along with the *Mister Rogers' Neighborhood* theme song. It was always a beautiful day in that neighborhood, where no one was a stranger, just a friend waiting to meet you. To accept you for who you were. In Amy's shining eyes, with her reassuring hand in his, Theo could almost believe there was such a place.

~⌒

Amy paid the Uber driver and wheeled her carry-on into St. Louis Lambert International Airport. With time to kill before her flight to New York City, she might as well kill it with a snack. Or maybe three. After spending the holidays alone in a house full of fretful cats mewling because they missed the Cat Whisperer, not to mention a morose Moose, she deserved treats. "Lots and lots of treats," she muttered, stuffing two snack bags of Doritos and one of potato chips into her handbag.

She'd nixed the plum pudding plan for Christmas Day—along with visions of Tiny Tim—in favor of a Mrs. Smith's apple pie. A slice a day, eaten while she looked at the text Theo had sent of dancing Santas. She'd debated a half hour, an entire thirty minutes of her life, picking the right emoji as a reply. A neutral smiley face was her choice. Because that's what she and Theo were. Neutral and smiley.

She was about to toss her hair over her shoulder—and remembered she didn't have any to toss anymore. After an hour in the styling chair at the Venus de Stylo beauty salon in Troy, a town near Laurel, she now sported a shoulder-length cut, more suitable to the professional woman she was. Though her curls had a mind of their own. Deprived of length, they expanded bushily around her head in rebellion.

Dropping into a seat in the main concourse, she tore into one of the bags of Doritos and stuffed a few in her mouth. She hadn't missed Theo one bit. Not even when she watched the Times Square ball drop on television, squeezing Nina's paw with every second of the countdown to the new year. Frankly, acting carefree to show him that the Make Out Incident was no big deal had been exhausting.

And it wasn't an incident either. Being in bed with Theo, kissing and caressing—she stopped to chomp on a chip— had been more like a...a brief escapade. Transient, best forgotten.

"I almost didn't recognize you with shorter hair."

Theo was standing in front of her, his backpack flung over a shoulder. Crotch at eye level, eyes at sea level, hair regulation windswept.

"Flight from Philadelphia just get in?" she asked, getting up and flipping her nonexistent long hair again.

"Yeah. When's yours leave?"

"Soon."

He glanced at his phone and looked around with a frown.

"Shouldn't you be getting to the boarding area? Security lines have been long."

"I have time. I'm going to hit the ground running in Manhattan and thought I'd better grab a snack now."

"Backup and emergency bags too?" he asked, dimples in full display.

She patted her handbag. "If the plane goes down, I'll spend my last minutes alive in salty, crunchy bliss."

"Whatever you do, don't eat the pretzels." He reached across as if he was about to touch her hair, then changed his mind. A shiver ran through her anyway. "Did the cats get haircuts too?"

"Mohawks. All of them."

"I hope Bessie didn't fuss when you gave her her insulin shots."

"She did, but I fussed right back."

"The vet called to tell me that he found a home for Bill Evans. The couple's picking him up tomorrow."

"I wish I'd known. Hug him goodbye for me." More reticent than Nina, Bill had gradually warmed up to her, winding his cream-colored body around her ankles at breakfast.

"Sure thing," Theo said, checking his phone again.

"Nina was in a pissy mood when I left," Amy said. "You might want to give her extra attention. And keep an eye on the fern I left on the kitchen counter." The poor button fern had been steadily wilting, as if the energy Amy was expending to be carefree had drained it to its roots.

The other travelers were a blur of noise and motion swirling around Amy and Theo. The rhythm of luggage wheels rolling on the linoleum floor, snatches of phone conversations, and announcements on the loudspeakers all conspired to carry her along a flight of fancy. She saw herself walking to the nearest counter, buying a ticket to anywhere, and soaring the skies to a new life where she'd take up with another guy with a weird habit that would drive her up a wall. A man who wasn't the least bit empathetic or hunky or warm and woodsy, and who didn't have eyes she'd gladly drown in.

Theo looked around, biting his lower lip. "Guess I ought to ... *When's* your flight?"

"Sooner than the last time you asked."

"Uh ... I better get going."

She gripped the handle of her carry-on. "Make that two of us."

They did that awkward goodbye dance—one step toward each other, one step away—and laughed that awkward laugh when the situation wasn't really funny.

"See ya."

"See ya."

"Amy," Theo called out as she walked away.

She stopped and turned around. Dismissed another flight of fancy—walking back to him, losing her fingers in that hair, and kissing him into another time zone. In case her plane went down. "Yeah, Theo?"

"Nice hairstyle. It suits you."

"Thanks."

She rode the escalator down, flattery quickly turning to irritation. His compliment had more to do with relief that she was getting on her way than her hair. Something was up with him. It was none of her business, but tough beans, as Athena would say—she was making it her business. And if airport security considered her suspicious for going back *up* the escalator and standing behind a pillar and a potted plant, the heck with them too.

Amy's hunch was confirmed. Theo *was* still there, pacing, texting, scanning the room. Waiting for someone. Someone he didn't want her to know about; otherwise, he'd have explained he was hanging around to meet so-and-so to do such and such, and they were going to—

Jo!

Jo was hurrying toward Theo, an overnight bag weighing down her lean frame, the sides of her open calf-length coat flapping against her legs. Judging by the startled look of a young couple walking by, Amy must have made a weird sound at the sight of them hugging.

In the rare instances when Jo had a stopover in St. Louis on her way to conferences or workshops, she'd contact Amy and they'd get together. What the hell was this about?

She gathered the facts in her mind as best she could. Jo went somewhere for Christmas after all and didn't tell her. She flew in the supposedly dangerous winter skies and arranged to meet Theo. Who'd been so anxious for Amy to board her plane. Because this was clearly not the random encounter that they said they had at the Las Vegas airport. If *that* was even a true story.

She yanked a plastic leaf off the potted plant, then another, as Theo raised his eyebrows at something Jo said. Now *he* was talking, his eyes on the floor, while Jo frowned and scuffed her heel against the tile. He hung on her every word as she replied to what he'd said—then hung his head when she shook hers no. An emphatic no. He stepped back, arms folded across his chest while she talked animatedly, her palms upward as she did whenever she was working out a problem.

Amy cursed under her breath, pulling two more leaves from

the plant. Jo lowered her head shyly as Theo tilted his right, then left, looking closely at her face. They clasped each other's arms in farewell. Theo never took his eyes off Jo as she hurried away and disappeared into the crowd. Amy never took her eyes off Theo as he walked slowly toward the exit.

After a brief session in a bathroom stall tearing toilet paper to shreds, Amy felt almost peaceful going through airport security. She'd decided she was not going to waste another minute trying to interpret the pantomime she'd just witnessed. Once on the plane, she buckled herself into her seat, read an article about the funding of research grants, and chomped, chomped, chomped herself into a salty, crunchy stupor.

The plane wasn't going down, but she was. Back down to the place where she was plucking the petals off the Jo daisy again, chanting, *Theo loves Jo, he loves her not*. The way he'd listened to her every word! The way he'd gazed at her face! While the petal of the Amy daisy always ended with, *He loves me not*.

By the time the Manhattan skyline came into view, her inner debate—tell Jo and Theo what she'd seen or not—was over. Reconciling them had been her concern but, as their recent secret meeting had revealed, nothing else about their relationship was. Jo and Theo, thick as thieves. If they didn't come right out and tell her what they were up to, there was no way on God's green earth she would ask.

⁓

Amy lay in bed with her legs propped on a mountain of pillows, the one luxury the hotel provided. The carpet was threadbare, the bathroom was the size of an airplane toilet, and the window looked out onto a greasy brick wall with rows of pulleys. The room and airfare had cost a small fortune, but this week in "the city that never sleeps" had been well worth it.

She'd walked miles till her feet blistered, absorbing a feast of sensations both physical and mental. In the museums and art shows, the artists' diverse styles and media had invigorated and inspired her. The print hanging above the dresser, which looked a lot like one of the paintings in her marshland sunset series, was no exception.

"*Hotel art*, my ass," Amy said aloud to the empty room.

She had been talking to herself a lot lately. A person was never so alone than when surrounded by thousands of strangers. Alone with thoughts she'd rather not dwell on. Scenes in her head she'd rather not revisit. But did anyway. When her phone chimed, she nearly leaped on it to read the text message.

It's alive!! Athena wrote. The thing in Gary's backpack!!

It's winter break. Where'd you see him?

Had to work in my campus office a few hours. The thing moves, like in Aliens. Right before the creature bursts from a stomach.

Photos?

No. I was too busy running in the opposite direction.

Amy texted Athena the picture Marmee had sent a while ago from Gaffney, South Carolina, of Peachoid, the 135-foot peach-shaped water tower that looked like a giant butt.

Your favorite body part, girlfriend.

Haha! When's your plane land tomorrow?

Around two.

I'll pick you up. You doing okay?

I'm doing great. No ifs, ands, or butts about it.

Ever since Amy's meltdown outside Bend Over Backwards,

Athena had turned into the mother hen she accused Thorne of being. Amy had brushed off the crying jag as a case of PMS and made a point of being relentlessly cheerful in her friend's presence. It wasn't hard. She'd been practicing relentless cheerfulness ever since she'd moved into Theo's house.

Signing off to Athena, Amy caught her reflection in the shiny surface of the blank television screen opposite the bed. For a split second, she didn't recognize herself, forgetting she'd changed her hairstyle.

That day in the Venus de Stylo salon, Eileen, by chance, had been in the styling chair next to hers. They exchanged casual remarks, carefully skirting the subject of their jobs—in Eileen's case, *three* jobs to support herself and her son. But Amy read the cartoon cloud above her head. Someone *else* would have come to the defense of the adjunct professors. Someone caring and considerate and brave, without selfish concern for their own career like Dr. Marsden. The first one finished, Amy had discreetly paid for Eileen's haircut, mumbling something to the stylist about "paying it forward."

"You suck," she said to her reflection in the TV.

She scrolled to a photo on her phone she'd taken earlier on a Midtown street. A vendor selling woolen hats had displayed them on a row of mannequin heads. Bad enough she had been reminded of Derek while looking at the Pollock paintings in the MoMA. Now here were the heads, the inspiration for the series that had launched his career. And one of them wasn't wearing a hat. Jo, she thought of in a flash. Leave it to one-of-a-kind Jo to always go her own way. The sister with whom she'd laughed, cried, and shared every thrill and horror of growing up. How could she be angry at her for meeting Theo in secret? Her lie, that she'd asked their stepfather to fund Jo's tuition, was far worse. And there was always the chance Jo *would* tell her about her rendezvous with Theo.

Amy reached for the sketchpad on the nightstand. Its pages were full of head studies she'd done of herself, Jo, and Theo. But the portrait she was planning of the three of them in the golden years of their friendship struck her as all wrong. It should reflect nothing less than the truth of them now—three adults facing the world on their own terms. One of them by herself.

CHAPTER TWENTY-THREE

I find I don't know anything, and it
mortifies me.
—AMY MARCH, *LITTLE WOMEN*

Amy hurried down the hallway to her office, casting a wistful eye at Fiona's closed door. What she wouldn't give to be in that tropical hothouse, warm and sleepy. But to add to the season's pitiless cold, Fiona had been avoiding her. Sending emails instead of scheduling meetings. Leaving voicemails when she knew Amy was teaching and couldn't answer her phone. She was sure it was avoidance—she'd done the same to Eileen. And Amy had mastered the art of evasion with Theo.

Or was it the other way around with Theo? He spent a lot of time in his study lately, mournful saxophones drifting beneath the crack of the door. Accidental grazing incidents had come to a halt, and her jokes about rutabagas and other assorted odd vegetables fell as flat as the pancakes he piled onto his plate but barely touched.

Broken heart from another Jo rejection? Licking his wounds?

I don't care, she reminded herself. *It's none of my concern.* Especially since Jo hadn't even hinted at her airport meeting with Theo in calls or texts.

I really don't care. Really.

Out of the corner of her eye, Amy noticed movement. It was the dean herself coming down the corridor. She stopped momentarily when she saw Amy, but it was too late for a turnaround. For all her encouragement, perhaps Fiona worried how far Amy's initiative would go. One day Amy was proposing a curriculum, the next she was jockeying for the dean's own position.

"Little does she know I'd rather be painting," she sighed, fumbling with the keys to her office.

She was about to unlock it and go inside, but conscience prevailed. "Fiona," she called out, waving her hand as if she were hailing a taxicab.

The dean looked up and faked just noticing her. "Yes?"

"Do you have time to talk?"

"I suppose so."

Walking toward her, Amy instinctively slumped so as not to tower over the dean. "I'd like to discuss an important issue with you."

"Go on." Fiona didn't tap her foot on the floor impatiently, but she might as well have.

"The adjunct professors submitted a proposal some time ago with a list of..." *Demands* wouldn't do. "Of suggestions regarding health care, salaries, class scheduling—"

"I've read it."

"And?"

"And I am giving it due consideration before presenting it to the administration. It has repercussions for *all* the college departments."

"I understand the need to deliberate. But the economic stresses on the adjuncts are pressing."

Amy had seen Eileen in the Bread and Board parking lot with her son, Tommy, the other day. Pangs of regret and guilt shot straight through her as she watched him load groceries in the trunk for his mother. She doubted his skimpy jeans and tattered sneakers were worn to make a fashion statement.

"The adjuncts do not have PhDs," Fiona said. "They—"

"A few do. Actually."

"They understood the terms of their contracts when they signed."

"They signed because they are dedicated teachers who need the work."

Fiona glanced at her watch. "Anything else?"

Amy threw her shoulders back and lifted her chin. "Yes. I want to add that I would be glad to act as an intermediary between the adjuncts and the administration if one is needed. To be their advocate."

"Is that a fact?"

"Yes. It is."

A smile crept around the corners of Fiona's mouth. "Well, well. Good for you."

Had Amy heard her correctly? No "wee criticisms" or admonitions for how "remiss" she had been? "Does this mean you approve of my...uh..."

"Initiative? Certainly. But you should be aware that I'm between a rock and a hard place with the administration on this adjunct situation. And I have been a wee bit of a coward avoiding you."

Amy was a wee bit inclined to hug the stuffing out of Fiona. "I'm not exactly the world's bravest person. But I believe intervening for the adjunct professors is the right thing to do. And I intend to do it."

"By all means. But I need to sound a note of caution, Amy. If you ask the administration for too much you may get nothing. And you seem to have more invested in the creative writing curriculum. It would certainly be a feather in your professional cap. Whereas helping the adjuncts..."

Her investment in the curriculum was personal, to make up for the wrong she had done Jo. And her sister wasn't exactly champing at the bit, so it could wait. The adjunct professors' situation, though, was more urgent. And here was the important thing—it represented something bigger than Amy Marsden.

"Thank you for your advice, Fiona. I'll inform the administration that the adjunct professors' proposal needs to be addressed and that I will mediate for them. I'll also stress that it takes priority over my curriculum proposal."

"And are you prepared for both items to be rejected?"

"No. Failure is not an option. For either."

"Good. Please keep me posted on developments. And Amy?"

Amy let out the breath she didn't realize she'd been holding in. "Yes?"

"Would you like to step into my office for a few winks?"

"Oh, I...no...uh..."

And just as she was about to say, *Yes, please,* Fiona entered her office, closing the door to the tropical hothouse behind her.

⁓◯

Amy removed her shoes and stood in stocking feet in the hallway after her meeting with Fiona. She had no earthly idea why.

Though when she saw Gary walk menacingly toward her, she was glad she had. Heels were a handicap when you were running for your life.

She counted his steps as he came closer, his shoulders swaying back and forth like a panther, fists clenched, and his gray shirt and pants clinging to his muscled body. For once, the backpack was missing. For once, he wasn't scowling like a villain in a noir crime novel.

"Good morning, Amy. Fine day, is it not?"

"It is. Yes. A fine day." *If subzero weather is your thing.*

His clean-shaven skin stretched tautly over his prominent cheekbones and perfectly shaped bald head. His green eyes reminded her of Nina. Damn if he wasn't attractive. In a hot-prison-guard kind of way.

"Classes going well, Gary?"

"My classes always go well. I read your email about expanding the scope of my courses next fall. You could have discussed it with me in person."

"I've been busy. With meetings and . . . uh . . . other things."

"I'm putting materials together for classes on Norse mythology and sagas. I think you'll be pleased."

Violent stories and epic poems in which most of the characters, the son of the son of so-and-so, wound up headless. It made Ericson sense to her. His trying to please her did not.

"Norse literature is quite brutal. But we must capture the students' attention," he said. "Nothing like axes splitting skulls to penetrate *their* thick skulls, eh?"

She stared at him blankly. Did he just make a joke?

"I'll tie the sagas in with the *Game of Thrones* books to keep their interest," he said. "What do you think?"

Amy thought it was bloody brilliant. "I think the classes will be even more popular than the ones you currently teach."

"I was inspired by your dissertation on the Arthurian legends through history. Fascinating stuff. And quite elegantly executed, considering your comprehensive topic."

Normally, the word *executed* would give her pause. Not this time.

"You...you read my dissertation?" Making him about the fifth person in the universe who had.

"Certainly. As you effectively demonstrated, the Arthurian legends lend themselves to many interpretations and versions. Their suppleness assures that they will endure."

"Suppleness," she repeated.

"The desire to construct heroic figures through human history has always intrigued me. Our need to aspire to something better than our base natures has given civilization its purpose, wouldn't you say?"

Amy couldn't say. She was too stunned to speak.

"Will you be expanding *your* curriculum next fall to include courses on the legends?" he asked.

"They're a tough sell these days."

Gary stiffened his body into its Jo Nesbø villain stance. "Then it's up to you to make the material alive and relevant. Make quests and heroes your brand."

An undignified giggle escaped her, remembering Banana Brad writhing on her bed. And it was one thing to be charmed by headdresses and wimples, but would she actually *wear* them to make students care? Heck no.

He pointed to her stocking feet. "I think runaway professor may be your brand."

"Sometimes," she admitted meekly. Because part of the "wee coward" in her wanted to run from a confrontation with the administration.

"You seek some other quest, perhaps?" He smiled. Gary Ericson never smiled. And shit. His teeth were perfect.

"I'm...I'm a painter. An artist."

"I thought as much when I saw all the Pre-Raphaelite prints in your office." He tipped an imaginary hat on his head in farewell. Or maybe it was a Viking helmet. "As soon as I've had a chance to read your book on King Arthur, I'd like to discuss it with you. I may reference it in my new classes."

"Yes. Of course. Thank you. Yes."

Amy walked back to her office, kicking herself all the way. And considered putting her shoes back on so the kick would hurt, metaphorically *and* literally. For being shortsighted and narrow-minded. For ridiculing Gary and reducing him to a cardboard character. For letting fear get the better of her. She turned to look down the empty hallway. Who else was she wrong about? *What* else? The possibilities were endless.

As for his remark about aspiring to something better than our base natures...wasn't that what she was doing by putting herself on the line for the adjunct professors? By creating the position, albeit postponed, for Jo? Like everyone she knew who was trying to be a better person, meeting each day's challenges with humor, irritation, grace—and sometimes a large thermos of coffee.

"Well, whaddya know?" she said, unlocking her office door— and the problem of making her book on *Idylls of the King* relevant as well.

When it came right down to it, most people tried to live

an honorable life—without the trappings of suits of armor. Or wimples. Without the benefit of magic or sorcery. If the Arthurian legends lent themselves to various interpretations and versions, so could Tennyson's epic poem. She'd reimagine each section as a tale of contemporary people facing modern challenges. Everyday heroes performing unsung deeds of derring-do, which most people often were.

And Sir Theo the Whatever just might appear in it.

CHAPTER TWENTY-FOUR

I make so many beginnings there
never will be an end.
—THEODORE LAURENCE, *LITTLE WOMEN*

*B*arrett and Olivia Decker sat across from Theo in his clinic office. The posture of their slim bodies in matching suits was yardstick straight, their short hair was neatly coifed, and their smiles were pleasant on their fine-boned faces. It was pouring buckets of rain, but somehow they'd made it from their Mercedes-Benz sedans to the door of Happy Haven without a drop of water on them. With five minutes to go before the official start of the session, they didn't speak. Their rule, not Theo's. He refrained from asking what was in the As You Like It Café bag on the floor between their chairs. Identical sandwiches with the crusts surgically removed was a good guess.

Clifford's soggy Hush Puppies squeaked as he tried to get comfortable in the chair across from the couple. The Deckers had signed a consent form permitting Theo's supervisor to observe a session. Theo would have preferred it were videotaped, unsure how the Deckers would interpret Clifford's insincere sincerity, but they said they didn't want any *physical evidence* left behind. Lawyers, right down to the soles of their custom-made shoes.

"Is everyone a happy camper?" Clifford asked.

Theo looked to his model clients for confirmation of their happy camperdom. His composed, cooperative couple who were in therapy to maintain their status quo. The couple who would get him in good graces with the supervisor who had power over his licensure. However, neither Barrett nor Olivia answered Clifford's question. Bad-weather blues, he figured. The sleety rain and gray skies would depress the cheeriest personality.

He doodled spirals along the border of the notebook page that looked curiously like Amy's curls. As tightly wound and controlled as she was these days. Occasionally, he caught her looking at him in a way that made him...itchy. A maddening prickling beneath his skin he couldn't scratch. *Mustn't* scratch.

He followed the end of one of the curls and extended it, longer and longer, like Amy's hair before it was cut. He truly hadn't recognized her that day at the airport—until he was too close to duck away, out of sight.

The Deckers looked at the clock on the wall and coughed. It was precisely ten o'clock and not a second later.

"Shall we begin?" Theo asked.

"I will." Clifford lifted two fingers, their nails bitten to the quick. "Barrett and Olivia, we at Happy Haven strive to help marriages reach their best potential. Care and communicate— those are the key. If you have these two ingredients, you can bake a variety of nutritious treats to feed your relationship."

So, he was going with a baking theme instead of his "best medicine" spiel. All right. Theo could work with that. He checked the Deckers for their reaction. The shift of Barrett's body away from Olivia's was a tad unusual. And he couldn't be sure, but he thought he heard a hiss come out of her pursed lips.

Theo clicked his ballpoint pen, poised above the notepad. "Olivia, why don't you give us a progress report on the chart you created?"

"What chart?"

"Your division of housekeeping chores." He suspected she'd made one for sex too. Tuesday, Barrett was to initiate sex; Thursday, she would.

"Why do you want a report?" she asked in a raspy voice. As if she'd been shouting.

"To...uh...to describe how you tend to your marriage. Maintain its—"

"Useless," Olivia said, abruptly moving her chair a foot away from her husband's and crossing her arms and legs.

"Pardon?" Theo asked, confused by her body language. And by Barrett's finger on his nose. Was he on the verge of excavating a booger—or thumbing his nose at his wife?

"The chart is useless," she said. "Like the loser I married."

"Takes one to know one," Barrett growled.

"Gee. How original," Olivia snarled.

"I aim to please."

"News flash. You don't."

Clifford turned to Theo, eyebrows raised above his staring eyes. This was Theo's cue to intervene. To bake a delectable pastry out of these two suddenly disagreeable ingredients. But he was too stunned to comment. Had he missed something as Barrett and Olivia were autopiloting their marriage?

"Go on," Theo encouraged them after Barrett flipped Olivia the bird, eliciting alarmed whimpers from Clifford.

"Another news flash," Olivia said. "The blue suit you spent a fortune on doesn't do a thing for you, jerk wad."

Barrett bared his teeth. *"None* of your clothes do a thing for *you*, you boring hag."

"Like you're the life of the party, geekhead."

"Like you know anything about *giving* head."

"Aren't you going to say anything, Theo?" Clifford demanded after the Deckers hurled a few more choice insults like *penis breath* and *toe rag* across the room.

The truth was that he was pleasantly surprised by the Deckers' creative invectives. Better than anything he and Jo had come up with when they were mad at each other. She'd agree with him that *twaddle brain* was pure genius.

"Theo!" Clifford expostulated.

Didn't know the Deckers had it in them, Theo wanted to say, but he couldn't risk it.

"I think Barrett and Olivia are reaching a new understanding of their relationship, Clifford. They are coming to grips with their expectations."

Except the only thing the Deckers reached for and gripped was the contents of the As You Like It Café bag. Pies, as it turned out. Baked by Thorne, the café proprietor, they were legendary in Laurel.

"Some counselor you are." Olivia was glaring at Theo, a pie balanced on her right palm as she stood up.

"Excuse me?" he said, trying to ignore the delicious aroma of freshly baked pastry crust.

"You listen and write things down, but you never say anything," she said, pouting.

Barrett rose too, holding a pie in his left hand. "Can't you see how angry we are?"

If it ain't broke, don't fix it was one of his guiding principles.

But apparently something *had* been broken all along with the Deckers that *did* need fixing.

"Well, Theo?" Olivia said.

"I didn't notice any anger," he said. "If anything, you've been extraordinarily polite and civilized with each other."

"Because you expected us to be," Barrett said.

"Like everybody else," Olivia said. "That's why you put us on display for Mr. Callaghan."

"And we're sick of it," he said.

"Yeah. Sick of it," she said. "What if we told you we weren't as compatible as you think we are?"

"Well, Theo?" Barrett said. "Anything to say?"

"I'd say that, if you need to express yourselves more honestly, then by all means—"

And at that, the Deckers let the legendary pies fly at each other, Clifford's baking analogy come to life in all its blueberry and cherry glory. While Clifford, in his sweater vest with baby vomit on the right shoulder and a clump of blueberry on the left, contemplated, no doubt, the incompatibility of Theo Sinclair and the profession of counseling.

~⌒

Theo and Lando walked to the gym parking lot, sweaty from a vigorous workout on the racquetball court. While the weather was mild for late January, the hushed atmosphere and opalescent sky conveyed tension like static electricity. What meteorologists called a "stalled weather pattern." A storm could break any minute—washing Theo's career away with it. Two weeks since the Projectile Pies Incident, as Amy had laughingly called it, and he hadn't heard a word from Clifford besides a terse text that Theo was to get the office cleaned at his own expense.

"Thanks for helping me get the stains out of the carpet at Happy Haven," he said to Lando. "The last thing I need is a visual reminder that I'm a colossal screwup."

"A visual is *exactly* what you need," Lando said, grinning. "Do you know how many likes you'd get on Instagram? Hashtag *slapstick*. Hashtag *piethrowing*. Hashtag *couplescounselfail*."

Fail. As if he weren't discouraged enough.

"All this time, the Deckers have been sitting in front of me, seething, and Clifford comes along with his *care and communicate* lingo, and they let loose."

"You don't think they brought the pies in on purpose?"

"No. They brought them in to keep them warm, then grabbed whatever was handy. Unfortunately, it wasn't the boxes of tissues."

"You really *are* on a losing streak," Lando said. "Gina hightailed it back to Brooklyn. Her answer to your 'go with the flow' was 'girl gotta go.'"

"Good riddance. I can't believe you thought I'd hit it off with someone so abrasive." Any scent *she* wore would be called Skin So Tough.

"Opposites attract," Lando said with a shrug.

"And repel."

Lando might enjoy coming home to his piss-and-vinegar Stella, but Theo preferred a soft landing after a day in the life. Someone to buffer the harsh world—which had become even bleaker with the Decker fiasco. What high hopes and expectations he'd had, believing he could save couples from the abyss that had devoured his parents. But he was going nowhere fast with the Spragues, and he'd gotten the Deckers totally, disastrously wrong.

They got into the '57 Chevy, and Theo drove out of the parking lot situated across the road from the Southern Illinois College campus. The complex of modern brick buildings on what were formerly acres of cornfields looked like a space station. Behind one of the windows of one of the buildings, Amy was working late again, freeing her weekends to paint. Since her art show rejection and trip to New York City, she was, as she put it, "painting like a woman possessed." The single-minded artist she told him she intended to be.

"You know what your problem is?" Lando said. "Your career *and* your love life. 'Cause they're related. If you had a relationship last longer than a few months, you'd be a better couples counselor."

"No shit, Sherlock. I've come to the same conclusion. And I suppose you mean a relationship like yours and Stella's."

"Yeah, like me and Stella. And you can keep your fancy-pants degree. I'm a genius when it comes to love."

"Is Stella aware of this development?"

"Right here," Lando said, pointing to his crotch. "And my girl agrees with me about you."

Theo's heart thumped. "What about me? What'd she say?"

He was bigger than his wiry friend, but he'd never want to tangle with Lando if he was angry. In his defense, Stella had contacted *him*. It wasn't *his* idea to advise her. Fortunately, she had agreed to keep their phone call confidential. But she wasn't the world's most tight-lipped person, to put it mildly.

"Stella thinks you need a woman too," Lando said.

"Any specific woman in mind?" Theo asked, mentally wiping his brow.

"One who doesn't lose her laptop and phone like Brittany. Or call you at two a.m. with panic attacks. What was the deal with that one?"

"Panic attacks *were* the deal."

"And you checking out is *your* deal. So. One more time. Get a lasting relationship so your career will last."

Such an easy formula. Such a hard thing to do.

"Thanks, genius," Theo said.

"And thanks for the lift. Stella had to borrow my car."

"No problem," Theo said, turning the radio on.

Lando tapped his hands on the dashboard to the beat of Ella Fitzgerald singing "Fascinating Rhythm." "It was great to finally meet Amy," he said. "She really is a sweetie, on top of being pretty and smart."

"Yeah, she liked you guys too." The foursome had run into each other by chance at Bread and Board recently. Amy had joked to Theo that since Laurie in *Little Women* was half-Italian, her mother would be sure to connect Lando and Stella to the novel. Mrs. M was a kind soul, and Theo was very fond of her. But growing up, he could have done without all the comparisons to Laurie.

"You and Stella haven't come by the house in ages," Theo said, merging onto the county road. "How come?"

"She's afraid I'll get all estrogen about pets. And if we get one, it'll be a slippery slope from there."

Theo laughed. "*Get all estrogen.* Love it."

"Stella's never more creative than when she's finding excuses not to commit. My Christmas gift to her was a trip to Boulder in April. I figure if I'm willing to meet her halfway on Colorado, she'll meet me halfway on getting married."

"Marriage isn't halfway. It's all-or-nothing once you've taken those vows."

"You keep talking shit like that, you'll never get your license."

"It's not original. I read it on one of the clinic posters." Theo's breath formed small clouds in the cold car as he exhaled his anxiety. "At this point, I'm sure of only one thing—couples need to know how to get through a day without throwing anything at each other."

"Wise words, my man." Lando pointed in the direction of Marconi's Pizza. "Drop me off at the restaurant, will ya? I've got inventory to check on."

Theo peered at the sky as he drove. *Rain or snow, dammit. Do something.* Realizing, as soon as the thought crossed his mind, that this was exactly his sentiment toward Amy lately. Her joking aside, there was a storm cloud behind her every glance and a stalled weather pattern lurking behind her every casual comment. Static electricity in the air between them. If she were Jo, the thundercloud would have burst by now, clearing the air.

He pulled up to the curb of Marconi's Pizza. "I'll let you know the status of my license when Clifford's ready to 'communicate,'" he told Lando. "I may need a job tossing pizza."

Lando got out of the car and came around to his window. "Don't be too hard on yourself. You've had one couple success story."

"Who?"

"My parents. I went to the deli early last week and heard wild animal noises coming out of the supply room."

"Don't tell me."

"Lou and Rose humping away against a case of olive oil. Imported."

"Because God forbid the Marconis should screw their brains out in the vicinity of domestic olive oil," Theo said, laughing.

"I'm scarred for life. I may be your next client at Happy Haven."

"Or my only one," Theo said, closing the window.

"Get a woman!" Lando shouted through the glass.

As Theo pulled away, he noticed a voicemail on his phone.

The Deckers are filing for divorce, Clifford's message said. *I regret to inform you, due to recent events, that your licensure is on hold until you demonstrate effective couples counseling techniques.*

CHAPTER TWENTY-FIVE

I like good strong words that mean something.
—JO MARCH, *LITTLE WOMEN*

Amy felt her way down the stairs in the dark, clutching the blanket around her shivering body. She'd woken to numb toes and a paw-filled mouth—Nina's solution to the freezing bedroom. Cats twined in and out of each other, forming a lump on the living room sofa next to the lump that was Moose. She placed her hand over the floor register, not that she expected heat downstairs either.

Putting her ear against Theo's bedroom door, she held her breath to listen but didn't hear a peep. "Theo," she whispered, spitting out the cat hairs stuck to her tongue. "Theo, wake up."

Nina butted her ankles, emitting high-pitched meows. Coltrane scratched the door from the other side in answer. Amy called Theo's name more loudly. A grunt and then silence again. Turning the knob, she opened the door inch by inch. Coltrane scurried out and he and Nina joined the other cats on the sofa.

She tiptoed to the bed. Theo lay on his back, one arm behind his head, the other by his side. In the dim light, he was a series of geometric shapes—the triangle of nose, the curve of bulging bicep, the rectangle of long legs. The night-light on the wall made her smile. Years ago, he had given her a flashlight to keep under her pillow when she confessed she was afraid of the dark—and admitted he had one too. For the same reason.

She perched on the edge of the mattress. "Hey, Theo."

"Unh."

"I'm freezing my buns off."

"K."

Guess he was used to women describing their buns in the middle of the night. "The cats and Moose have turned into a gigantic fur blob."

"Unk." He sounded like an early version of *Homo sapiens*, before the acquisition of speech.

"They'll force us to submit to their every command."

"Urg," he gurgled like the aquarium pump.

"Theo! The animals are in league against us!"

His eyes fluttered open. "Leak...what?"

"Are you awake?"

"No."

"You sleep like you were bludgeoned over the head with a frying pan."

"Think I was. How come you're in here?"

"I was bored."

He squinted to read the time on the clock. "What?"

"I ran out of books to read," Amy said.

"Hunh?"

"Okay. I wanted to see what you wear to bed."

He lifted the blanket and looked underneath. "Long johns."

"You might want to put on a second pair. I think the furnace is broken."

"Shit."

"And don't panic, but it looks like your left hand is frozen."

He pulled himself to a sitting position, flexing his fingers. "This just isn't my week. Or month."

"It might be our last *day* if we don't get warm. We'll slowly freeze, unable to move, while the cats gnaw our toes."

He pushed the covers aside and dragged himself from the bed. The imprint of his long-johns body on the mattress was waiting for her to curl up in it. "I'll check on the furnace and open the faucets so the pipes don't freeze," he said.

"Good thinking. I'll take care of mine upstairs."

"Then I'll get a fire going. We can sleep in front of the fireplace."

"The furniture has already been colonized."

"I'll blow up the air mattress Jo used."

"It'll be like camping. Without the s'mores," she said, following him out of the bedroom.

He turned to look at her with a half-dimple smile. "Are you always this chipper in the wee small hours of the morning?"

"I'm rising to the occasion." The cold. Theo in long johns. And, lest she forget, Theo possibly in love with Jo. *Let us be chipper or die.*

Amy went back downstairs after opening the bathroom faucets—and brushing her hair, rebrushing her teeth, and changing out of the cloud pajamas, a reminder of the last time she and Theo were horizontal.

Before she saw him and Jo together at the airport.

Theo had covered the inflated mattress with enough blankets

to outfit an expedition to the Arctic—and to put pounds of polyester fiberfill between them. She slipped beneath them and stretched luxuriously. The fire crackled, sending off the aroma of burning oak. Its flames lit the living room with a cozy glow.

"Night-light, huh?" she asked when he had joined her on the air mattress. "Still afraid of the dark?"

"Never was. I just told you that so you wouldn't feel like a wimp."

"Likely story."

"The night-light's so I don't trip over someone in the middle of the night."

"Your girlfriends sleep on the floor?"

He grinned. "I meant the cats. And speaking of tripping, I nearly fell over an ottoman to get to the fireplace. Where'd it come from?"

"The Sheas put it out in the trash this morning. It's in great shape, except for a few tears in the leather, so I rescued it. Like you do animals. Except it won't shed. Or need food."

"You might have asked."

"I'd rather apologize than ask permission."

Theo arched an eyebrow. "You don't sound remotely apologetic."

"Remember the Marsden family motto? *One man's trash is another man's treasure.*" Amy pointed to the brass umbrella stand and a cracked blue ceramic pot she'd also rescued on either side of the front door. "You haven't told me what you think of them."

"I feel like I have to get some umbrellas now. And a plant. That's the problem with possessions. The more you own, the more you have to own." He was staring into the flames as if hypnotized. "I should sleep out here more often. The fire is soothing."

"Anxious about something?"

"The Projectile Pies Incident, as you so cleverly called it," he said with a wry smile.

Her laughter separated the cats long enough for them to look around and twitch their ears before settling into a big ball of fur again. "Couldn't help myself. Was it really that bad?"

"Yep. And it's gotten worse. The couple is filing for divorce, and Clifford has put me on probation. Which means my license is on hold."

"Oh, I am sorry. You're not expected to save every marriage, are you?"

"The real issue is that I didn't recognize their problems. I thought they were the perfect couple."

"Until pies started flying across the room."

"Baked by the husband of your friend Athena, I might remind you."

She nudged him playfully on the arm. "Oh, like it's Thorne's fault."

"Mine. Totally. I didn't pay close enough attention." Theo turned away from the fire to face her. "How's *your* career going?"

"Stalled. I'm trying to intercede for the adjunct professors, but the administration has been resistant, if not hostile. And I've had to put my creative writing curriculum proposal on ice."

"The courses sound like a good idea to me."

"I hope they agree with you. And I'm still trying to recruit Jo to teach them, but she won't budge."

"She probably has good reasons for staying in Seattle," Theo said. Which was the most he'd ever said about the possibility of Jo working at the college and moving back to the Midwest.

"Something to do with love?" Amy dared.

He shot her a look and then lowered his head. "Not Jo. Never."

Why hadn't she thought of it before? Maybe Jo was resisting the college position to keep her distance from lovelorn Theo.

As for distance. Resistance...

Theo was inches away. His eyes were as deep-sea dreamy as ever. The heat of him. That mouth of his.

Her bedroom wasn't *that* cold, was it?

"I wonder if..." Theo smoothed the satin edge of the top blanket. "Do you have something on your mind lately? Besides your job?"

"Nothing besides the usual everything."

"Sounds like double-talk to me."

She shrugged. "Maybe it is. Maybe it isn't."

"Reminds me of another couple I'm worried about. I can't tell you much, just that they talk past each other all the time, like they're in two different conversations."

Amy sat up and crossed her legs. "Never have I ever," she said.

"I don't get it."

"Play 'never have I ever' with the couple. It might focus their attention on each other."

"A drinking game? I might as well kiss my license goodbye."

"No alcohol. Just let them go back and forth and see what they reveal." She tapped her chin. "Never have I ever... walked a dog."

"You've got to be kidding me."

"You know we never had any pets. If it hadn't been for

your menagerie, I would have thought *Lhasa apso* was a medical condition."

"How about walking other people's dogs?"

"Nope. Never."

"Wait . . . you walked Moose when I was in Philly at Christmas."

"Correction—Moose walked me."

At this mention of his name, Moose lifted his head and sniffed the air. Not smelling food, he lowered it again.

"Never have I ever stiffed a waiter or waitress," Theo said. "Even if the service was terrible."

"Me neither."

"I was a bartender. Not getting tips sucks."

"Never have I ever . . ."—Amy was going to say *drunk-dialed anyone*, but it would remind him she'd drunk-*licked* him—"used marijuana."

"I've never taken a selfie."

"I've never cheated on a test."

"Never have I ever eaten food off the floor," Theo said.

"Big deal. Moose beats you to it."

"I said *never*. Life before Moose."

"I'm not ashamed to admit that if a Cheeto fell to the floor, I wouldn't let it go to waste," she said, "no matter how long it's been there."

"Big surprise. Whose turn is it?"

"Mine. Never have I ever . . . skied. Yikes, I've lived a dull life." Though the thrill of flying down a snowy mountain on two sticks would never entice Prudent Amy.

"Never have I ever been to a country ending in *-stan*," Theo said.

"Never have I ever been to another country."

"Too bad. Travel opens eyes. And being in a place where no one understands you, and no one wants to, is a necessary humbling experience."

"I've had plenty of humbling experiences in my own country and language," Amy said. "What do you like most about traveling? The people you meet? The food?"

"Both, for sure. But I like dealing with the unexpected the best. Having to be resourceful."

"Example?"

Theo grinned. "Sneaking a night's sleep in a fisherman's boat when I missed my connection out of Cyprus. Unfortunately, I woke up stinking of sardines."

"Do you travel with anyone?"

"No. Alone. I prefer it. That resourceful thing I was talking about." He yawned. "Long day tomorrow."

"Same here."

"We should go to sleep."

"Guess we should. Are you going to try the 'never have I ever' game?"

"Dunno. I'll play it by ear. I like the blue pot, by the way. Crack and all."

"You're welcome."

"G'night, Amy," he mumbled.

"G'night, Theo."

She listened to the floors creak and the walls sigh. One of the cats was snoring, ticking away the minutes, the half hour, the hour. Theo stirred and rolled over, his back to her. The burning logs snapped, crackled, and popped. She heard him swallow. "You awake?" she whispered.

"Uh-huh."

"I'm thinking about Rice Krispies."

"Rice Krispies?" He sputtered with laughter and turned to face her again. "Where'd *that* come from?"

"Stream of consciousness. Plus, I'm hungry."

"Any idea how to turn the stream off? My mind won't shut down."

Theo was tantalizingly close, a pair of long johns and pink nightgown all that came between their naked bodies. Without them, they'd be skin on skin, her hands grasping his muscled back while he caressed her breasts, his face in her neck and hers in his, breathing in his Theo-ness. Giving herself over to the heat and wet, to his lips kissing her forehead, her cheek—

"Maybe I should take some melatonin," he murmured. "It usually knocks me out. Want one?"

What Amy wanted was to get bonked by the freezer door again. Only this time she'd wake up, and it will all have been a dream, and she wouldn't be a lovesick, sex-starved ninny.

"No thanks," she said. "Sleep meds make me groggy."

"Yeah, me too."

Theo whistled softly, and Coltrane, extricating himself from the pile of cats, jumped off the sofa, padded over, and nestled in the crook of his arm. Nina, sound asleep, didn't follow him.

Amy moved as far away from them as the mattress allowed, legs up to her chest, her fist at her mouth. She watched Theo's chest rise and fall with every breath. Once dawn broke, she hurried upstairs so she wouldn't have to face him on the morning-that-was-not-after.

Never have I ever felt so alone.

CHAPTER TWENTY-SIX

*I want to do something
splendid . . . something heroic or
wonderful that won't be forgotten after
I'm dead.*
—JO MARCH, *LITTLE WOMEN*

*A*my hung her coat, two sweaters, thick woolen scarf, and bike helmet on the coat rack in As You Like It Café. To celebrate Groundhog Day, Thorne was offering free sandwiches and soup to anyone who ventured out in the bitter cold. She'd been doing a lot of venturing herself since the sleepless night in front of the fire with Theo, stepping out into the world some mornings without her caffeine fix and eating meals at the café.

She had come much too close to making a fool of herself—twice—and she couldn't trust herself not to do it again. Like the other day when Theo was bent in concentration over the coffee grinder. His bare neck, his neck that smelled so good, had looked so . . . delicious. She'd tucked in the tag sticking out of his shirt, bringing goose bumps to his skin. And to her own.

But she was done carrying the Theo torch. Absolutely. She had her friends, career, and art. A rich life full of plans and possibilities.

Absolutely.

She surveyed the dining room. As expected on a free lunch day, most of the tables were full, though a small one near the hearth was available. She dropped thankfully into the chair, rubbing her hands to warm them as Ivy approached.

"Hi, Amy. Athena's in the kitchen. She said to tell you she'll be right out."

"Is she helping Thorne make sandwiches?"

"And making out." She slapped a hand to her mouth. "Oops. I shouldn't have said that."

"Don't worry," Amy said, laughing. "I always assume they're canoodling back there."

Ivy drew closer. "I used to have the biggest crush on Thorne," she said in a near whisper.

"Oh yeah?"

"Yeah. But I got over it. Eventually."

And oh, what a long time *eventually* could be when someone had worn a path to your heart.

"Are you performing today?" Amy asked.

"No. Jaycee and Robin are. I'm on waitress duty."

"Karl did a great job repairing the furnace in the house I rent."

"He can fix *anything*." Ivy pointed to him devouring a sandwich at a table with the bachelor farmers. "He left me another note this morning, reminding me...I'm not sure of what. Nearly all the words were misspelled. And when I said he should text and let autocorrect take care of it, he said that was worse because he's never sure if it's the right correction."

"Is it possible he's dyslexic?"

"He's never *said* that he was."

"He may be embarrassed to admit it."

Ivy bit her lower lip. "Gee, I never thought of that. Now I feel terrible."

"Maybe he'll talk about it if you let him know it's not a big deal. Uh...assuming it isn't."

"No! Not at all. The only big deal is not understanding what's going on."

"Couldn't have said it better myself."

"Thanks for the advice, Amy. So, do you want the soup and sandwich or a special order?"

"Which is easier for you?"

"The soup and sandwiches are already made so..."

"I'll have them. But don't rush. I'm not in a hurry."

The kitchen door swung open and Athena appeared, a wide grin on her freshly kissed face. "Why so glum, my chum?" she asked Amy, sitting down.

"Whaddya mean? I'm smiling."

"Not with your eyes. Anything wrong?"

"It's February. Do I need another reason?"

"Being manless might explain it."

"Is that even a word?"

"It should be. What brings you to the café so often these days anyway?"

"Haven't you heard? It's February. If I didn't get out of the house for anything besides work, I'd go stir-crazy."

Ivy brought vegetable soup and grilled cheese sandwiches for them both, dropping them onto the table with a dolorous sigh before slouching away.

"In her case, being manless may not be the worst thing," Athena said.

"This time, I think she's a little mad at herself, not Karl. I'm proud to say I nudged her to a new perspective on him." Having been *kicked* into a new perspective on Gary.

"And *I'm* proud of you going to bat for the adjuncts. Any news?"

"That would be a negative. The administration's bat is a lot bigger." She didn't want to admit how worried she was that her intercession might be jeopardizing her own standing. Curt greetings, unanswered messages, and vague hints from the powers that be that her post as chair was "not set in stone" were making her uneasy.

"How about the job for Jo?" Athena asked.

"Still on the back burner."

An idea flickered across Amy's mind—taking the position for Jo off the stove altogether. She wasn't interested, the administration would probably reject it, and—why bring her closer to Theo?

"Make Gary your wingman," Athena said. "If what you've told me about him is true, he'll have Jo *and* the administration dancing to your tune in no time."

"I'm still in shock that we were so wrong about him. Did I tell you he was *inspired* by my dissertation?"

"Multiple times." Athena snapped her fingers. "Maybe that's what's in his backpack! Bound copies of your dissertation."

"My God, woman. What preposterous ideas you have."

"Check out *this* one—Gary may be the man of your dreams."

"It wouldn't work. He'd expect too much of me. And it's hard enough meeting my own expectations." Like just now, reconsidering the job for Jo so she'd stay in Seattle. Far from Theo. "I'm happy to report, though, that I'm finally making progress on my book on *Idylls of the King*."

"You had a breakthrough?"

"Uh-huh. Something Gary said about the Arthurian legends being supple got me headed in a fresh direction."

"*Supple!*" Athena threw back her head with a hearty laugh. "He's either thinking about assuming a yoga position or assuming another kind of position with you."

"Gary Ericson bending over backward for me," Amy said, grinning. "That'll be the day."

From where they sat on stools at the front bay window, Jaycee and Robin strummed their guitars to the Bob Dylan song Amy's parents had loved, the one about the answer blowing in the wind. Jaycee returned her wave with a beaming smile.

"Couples report," Athena said, sinking her teeth into her sandwich. "Those two are hot and heavy. Thorne's more relaxed since they're together, so he's planned a trip for us during spring break in March. A beach somewhere. The rest is a surprise."

Amy ate a few mouthfuls of soup, picturing the happy pair basking beneath a warm sun while she'd be in her room beneath a blanket, basking in term papers.

"Do you ever get, you know, broody?" Athena asked her.

"Contemplative and moody? All the time." Living with a guy with sea-deep eyes might have had something to do with it.

"Not *Heathcliff* broody. I mean obsessing over having a baby. Calculating how many eggs your ovaries have left while you're making an omelet."

Athena had baby fever lately, babysitting Ian's three-year-old daughter, Zoe, any chance she got.

"I can honestly say I haven't given a thought to my eggs,"

Amy said. "Not only because I rarely make omelets, but there isn't a man in my life to fertilize them."

Athena scrunched her freckled nose. "*Fertilize.* Yuck."

"There are other legacies to leave behind besides genetic material."

"*Material.* Ew."

When Amy was a young girl, she kept a list of quotes from books she liked. A line from *Little Women* was her favorite— *I want to do something splendid . . . something heroic or wonderful that won't be forgotten after I'm dead.* And the "something splendid" she intended to leave behind would be paintings.

Just as soon as she finished the book, helped the adjuncts, set Jo on a new career path (maybe), and—oh, got some sleep.

Athena leaned across the table, her eyes shining. "We've told family, and now I want you to know. Thorne and I have decided to have a baby. Operation Baby Murphy-Kent begins the week we're at the beach. Spring break and my menstrual cycle are in sync."

"Oh, Athena! I'm so happy for you. Congratulations!"

"Thanks. I'm giving up all my bad habits so I'll be as healthy as possible."

Thorne strode across the room and leaned over to kiss his wife on the cheek. "Hi, Amy. How's every little thing?"

"Better, now that I've heard about your baby plans."

"I can't wait to be a dad."

"Best daddy ever," Athena said.

"Heads up, Thena," he said, tapping his watch. "Quentin will arrive any minute."

"Your friend from Seattle?" Amy asked.

"He texted about an hour ago that his plane had landed,"

Thorne said. "We had no idea he was on his way here, but that's Quentin for you."

Athena's face brightened as she waved to a tall, burly man at the entrance of the café. "And here's Falstaff himself."

"Hey, Murph! Yo, Thorne!" Quentin called out, knocking over an empty chair and kicking a woman's handbag clear across the room as he lumbered toward them.

"Way to make an entrance," Athena said, shoulders shaking with laughter.

"Well, shit." Quentin tugged at his mop of auburn curls as he returned the handbag and righted the chair. "Sorry, everybody."

The bachelor farmers grinned and gave him a thumbs-up. If Quentin were wearing overalls and a John Deere cap instead of a fleece jacket, green plaid shirt, and khaki pants, he'd fit right in with them.

"Sit down before you set off any seismographs in the area," Athena said, pulling out a chair. "Quentin, this is Amy Marsden, my boss. Amy, this is Quentin Scott, our college buddy. Currently illustrious criminal defense lawyer. Formerly Thorne's costar in university theater productions."

"Those were the days," Quentin said, dwarfing the seat with his lumberjack body. "What I remember anyway, considering all the beer I drank."

Athena reached across to pat his stomach. "And the tradition continues."

"You know what they say. 'Beer is proof God loves us and wants us to be happy.'" He worked himself out of his jacket and fixed Amy with his light blue eyes. "I've heard all about you, Amy."

"And every word's a lie." She extended her hand and he crushed it in a hearty shake. "Glad to meet you, Quentin."

The well-worn exchange was true in this case. Whenever they hung out together, the Murphy-Kents invariably related a Quentin misadventure to Amy. The latest one concerned a seam of his suit jacket splitting as he delivered the closing arguments in a trial. His beard was scruffy, his clothing disheveled, and his manner rambunctious, but Amy liked him immediately. Intelligence and warmth shone in his face, conveying a generosity of spirit that he was ready to see the best in someone.

Quentin pointed to Amy's hair. "You've got a head of curlicues like me."

"That's exactly how my sister, Jo, describes my curls. As a matter of fact, she lives in Seattle too."

He put his palms flat against his temples and squeezed his eyes shut. "Too many coincidences all at once."

Athena rolled her eyes. "Ever the drama queen. What brings you to your old stomping grounds anyway? On the lam from the authorities?"

"Not this time. I thought I'd check out the possibilities for criminal activity in small-town Laurel."

"Thorne's scones are worth killing for," Amy joked.

"Don't I know it. Truth is, I was on my way to a lecture on igneous rocks. When I saw signs to the airport, I thought, *What the heck? I'll go see Murph and Thorne.*"

"Since when are you into geology?" Thorne said. "You used to call the courses 'Rocks for Jocks.'"

"Since I discovered the joys of rock hunting." Quentin unbuttoned his shirt, revealing a black T-shirt underneath it with

ROCKHOUND printed in bold blue letters above a picture of a pickaxe. "I love that people can't tell if I'm a rock 'n' roll fanatic or a psychotic killer."

"Neither can we," Thorne said, laughing.

"Here's another coincidence," Amy said. "The titles of the stories my sister writes are geology terms."

Quentin stared at the ceiling, opened his mouth as if to say something, and then shut it again.

"How long are you staying?" Thorne asked him. "I'll see what's happening in St. Louis for us to check out."

"I just dropped in to grab one of your famous sandwiches, then I'll be on my way."

"Nonsense," Athena said. "You're bunking in Finn's old bedroom till we're sick of you. Or until the weekend's over, whichever comes first."

"I'll make the cheddar cheese sandwich with apple slices you raved about last time," Thorne told him. "Then we'll head over to Benny's Bar."

"I'm not drinking, so you guys go without me," Athena said. "I'll meet you back at the house."

"Not drinking." Quentin slapped his knee. "Either you got a DUI or you're working on a Mini Murph."

"Plans have been set in motion," Thorne said, winking at Athena. "How's the role of godfather sound to you?"

"Aw, man. I love you guys. That baby's going to be as cute as a button."

Athena grabbed Quentin's hand. "Come on, you big doofus. Tell us why you really flew in all of a sudden. You haven't lost your job, have you?"

"Brace yourself, Murph."

Athena frowned. "Crap. You pissed off a judge."

"Nah, my acting chops are as sharp as ever. They love my courtroom antics."

"What's going on, then?"

"Brace yourself for the cheesiest line this side of Cheez Whiz. I haven't lost anything but my heart."

CHAPTER TWENTY-SEVEN

The sincere wish to be good is half the battle.
—MARMEE MARCH, *LITTLE WOMEN*

After Thorne and Quentin had left the café to go to Benny's Bar, Amy walked her bike with Athena to Athena's car. The Mini Cooper was parked near the apartment building where Amy had lived with Derek. She pointed to a lighted window on the second floor. "The infamous Gallagher love nest," she remarked.

"I hope Thorne and I will be going at it like rabbits when we're their age."

"Right. Like there's even a question."

"Quentin always jokes about us 'making the beast with two backs.' It's a line from *Othello*," Athena said. "What do you think of him?"

What Amy was thinking was that she needed to retrieve something from the back of her mind, an impression stuck there since meeting him. "He's funny, kind, and larger than life. Why were you and Thorne so shocked by the news that he was in love?"

"He's dated a gazillion women, but he's never...how'd he put it?"

"Lost his heart."

"Quentin quotes Shakespeare on nearly every occasion, but he's *never* been poetic about a girlfriend."

"Too bad he doesn't live here. You guys get along so well. And I'd love to capture his vitality in a portrait."

"I can't believe he won't tell us anything about this mystery woman," Athena said. "I'm dying to know who she is."

"Well, hello there," a male voice said.

They turned to see Gary walking toward them, a puppy straining at the leash. His sleek bald head shone beneath the streetlamp.

"Bend over backwards, Amy," Athena whispered.

"Hush up. Stop," Amy said on the verge of laughter.

"I thought you lived in Rosewood, Gary," Athena said, after they exchanged greetings. "Are you dog-sitting?"

"No, she's mine. I moved into this apartment building recently because my other one had a no-pet policy."

Amy knelt to stroke the dog's shiny brown fur. "What's her name?"

"Coco."

"By the size of her paws, it looks like she's going to be big."

"You take your chances when you rescue a mutt puppy. I adopted her through the local vet."

Amy was about to mention Theo's association with the vet's foster program, but she wasn't in the mood to talk about him. Having dropped the Theo torch and everything.

"Good thing I found a place before she got much larger," Gary said. "Carrying her around in a backpack hasn't been easy."

Amy and Athena looked at each other in astonishment, both mouthing the word *backpack*.

"I brought her to campus so the landlord and other tenants wouldn't hear her during the day," he said. "And I snuck her out of my office for potty breaks so the English Department wouldn't catch on either."

"Life on the edge, huh?" Amy joked.

He smiled his perfect-teeth smile. "I might write a Scandinavian noir novel about it, featuring a couple of female professor investigators."

"I used to share an apartment in this building," Amy said to change the subject—and to hide her embarrassment. Athena rummaged in her handbag as if she was looking for something.

"Which unit?" he asked. "I know everyone here, even the eccentric painter, Derek, who keeps to himself."

"Uh...it was...um..."

Gary might find it hard to reconcile the Dr. Marsden who wrote the fascinating dissertation on the Arthurian legends with the Amy who'd lived with a recluse who painted in his underwear. On the other hand, Derek had received glowing reviews recently for his first major exhibition in St. Louis. And along the way had graduated from the weird guy in tighty-whities to what one journalist called *a nonconformist artist*.

"Derek and I lived together for six months. He's become a successful artist, critically and financially," she said, her voice on the very edge of bragging. Athena was quirking her eyebrows as if to say, *Do you hear yourself?*

"I see," Gary said.

"I'm a painter too," Amy reminded him. "Art has been my passion since I was a child."

"Ah yes, your quest. Did you know the college is one of the sponsors of an art exhibit featuring local talent?"

"No. I haven't been keeping up with exhibits." The New York City art show rejection still made her wince.

"It's strictly amateur and open to everyone," Gary said. "But you never know what might come of it."

"When and where?"

"In May. There's still time to register, I imagine. The link is in the Art Department section of the college website. A friend in the department told me it'll be held in a converted barn on the outskirts of Rosewood."

Coco began whining in the middle of Amy's thanks, and Gary said good night. Amy and Athena watched him lift the puppy in his arms and kiss her snout, ears, and paws. After he entered the apartment building, they looked at each other and exploded with laughter.

"A puppy!" Athena exclaimed.

"A fricking *rescue* puppy, no less! And here we thought he was an assassin."

"Are we a pair of morons or what?"

"We are a pair of morons," Amy agreed.

She hadn't only been wrong about Gary. She'd been *spectacularly* wrong, making the odds of her being wrong about other things much higher.

"What was he saying about your 'quest'?" Athena asked as she unlocked the door of the Mini Cooper.

"Part of the conversation we had about my dissertation."

"Methinks, fair lady, he is in love with you."

"I'm not picking up that vibe. At all." Being well acquainted with the *I'm not in love with you* vibe.

"Sure you don't need a ride in this weather?" Athena asked, getting into the car. "You can park your bike at the café, and I'll drive you to pick it up tomorrow."

"No thanks. I'm used to the cold."

"Methinks a trip to the fjords in Norway with Gary is in your future."

"Youthinks wrong."

As Athena slammed the car door shut, a memory opened, the one Amy had been picking at like a hangnail. When Quentin left the café with Thorne, he had turned around, waved to her, and said, *See you around, Amy Mamy.*

Amy wasn't sure what to make of Fiona's request that they meet in the campus's main dining hall. It was where faculty went to dish the dirt, complain, and collude—none of which the dean was likely to do with her.

She walked toward the table where Fiona waited, her stomach tumbling. As a waitress during summers in college, she'd overheard countless couples break up over dinner. A plate of bad clams could push a relationship over the edge, she figured. Until it dawned on her that the dumped was less likely to scream at the dumper or make a scene in a public place.

Amy put her bowl of chicken noodle soup on the table and sat down. Fiona wore a suit as austere as the bun pulled tightly to the back of her head. Pearl earrings and makeup gave a glamorous touch to her executive look. Was she dressing up to give Amy a dressing-down?

"Hello, Fiona."

"Hello, Amy. Only soup for lunch?"

"I ate a big breakfast."

"Brigid makes me waffles every morning, but I'm still ravenous by noon. Pardon me while I devour this bloody burger."

She opened her mouth wide and sank her teeth into the sandwich while Amy pondered her use of the word *bloody*. As the British description for everything from the weather to Brexit? Or was the beef rare? Did the ravenous Fiona want *Amy's* blood for forcing the issue of the adjunct professors after all?

"About the adjuncts," Fiona said.

"Yes?" Amy asked faintly.

"The administration have been stonewalling you, haven't they?"

Amy both shook and nodded her head, unsure how to respond.

"I thought as much, so I decided to intercede in *your* intercession. As you said, it's the right thing to do. And I can't risk losing you as chair."

Amy mumbled her thanks, a wee bit shaken. So she *had* come close to losing her position.

"I'm pleased to say that they've made quite a few concessions. An email will be sent out tomorrow to inform all the parties involved." Fiona flashed her toothy smile. "Good for me, right?"

"Oh yes! Thank you so much, Fiona."

"Thank my bonny Brigid." She bit into the burger again and chewed with her eyes closed.

Waiting for the dean to explain what her partner had to do with the adjunct professors' victory, Amy looked around the room. Thanks to Amy's coaxing and cajoling, Annette Jamison and Bill Parker had ended their long-standing feud over

Shakespeare's identity and were sitting at the same table. Ian was back, eating with a few of his poetry students. He wore the sleep-deprived look of a dad, but with the new baby home from intensive care and thriving, the worried expression was gone. Gary huddled with one of the history professors, an authority on Stalinism with a dubious resume, according to gossip. What were *they* up to?

Don't go down that rabbit hole again, she reminded herself, eating her soup.

"Let me tell you what I admire about Brigid," Fiona said, wiping her mouth with a napkin. "She holds me to a very high standard. When I told her about the adjunct professors' situation and your role in it, she scolded me for being negligent and uncaring."

"You're neither. And you've always been very supportive of me," Amy assured her.

Fiona leaned across the table. "Do you know what you want in this life?"

To never run out of books to read or canvases to paint. Shoes that were sexy *and* comfortable. A forever-firm derrière. World peace. She wasn't asking for much.

"You want a lover who inspires you to be the best version of yourself," Fiona said.

The first person Amy thought of was Theo. He wasn't her lover. And he'd be the first to deny he inspired anyone. But for all her jokes about his being Sir Theo This and That, he was one of the most genuinely thoughtful and generous people she'd ever known. Honorable. And it was this—more than their shared history, those eyes, that mouth of his—that had twined him around her heart forever.

As Fiona filled her in on the finer points of the adjunct professors' new contracts, she wondered if Brigid had also urged her to support Amy's curriculum proposal to the administration. Which would help Amy become the best version of herself. The version in which she made up for the wrong she'd done Jo.

"About my proposal for the creative writing courses. You—" she began.

"I won't mince words. I've decided to step aside from the issue."

There it was, the lunch's bad clam.

"But the courses will enhance the English Department and attract more students," Amy argued. "And you did mention Brigid might benefit from them."

"I love her to death, but she can't write for beans. Hopeless, really. It would be a disservice to encourage her, Amy."

As if Amy had cooked up the whole scheme just for the sake of her "bonny Brigid."

"Thank goodness she's turned her energies elsewhere," Fiona said. "As for your proposal, what I'm trying to say is, the ball's completely in your court. I prefer to stay on the sidelines."

"I understand, Fiona." Having won her point with the adjunct professors, the dean probably didn't want to press her luck.

"I would advise you to set up an interview with your sister, the administration, and a few faculty members from the English Department. She should have a plan in place so they have something to work with. To show what her contribution would be."

A big nothing, if Jo stuck to her guns. Amy was in the hot seat now.

"However, I also advise that you postpone moving forward

for a wee bit," Fiona said. "We don't want to make too many demands at once."

Whew. The hot seat got a wee bit cooler, letting the dishonorable thought creep in again—drop the proposal entirely and keep everything as it was. Jo happy in her high school job, miles from Theo.

"Thanks again for your guidance, Fiona."

The dean reapplied her lipstick until it looked like she'd eaten a bowl of black cherries. "If you don't mind my saying so, Amy, you're looking rather...hungry."

"I'm not. The soup was filling."

Fiona tilted her head as she examined her. "Hmm... something else. I can't put my finger on it."

Six months without sex and counting. Busted. By her boss.

"I'm fine," Amy said. "Really."

She thanked her again for helping the adjunct professors, and Fiona left, leaving her alone with a sex-starved face. If Athena were here, she'd be rolling on the floor, laughing. And positively hysterical if she saw what Amy did next—smiled and waved at Turner Malcolm, who'd just entered the dining hall. And about whom she had instantaneously formed a plan.

It was time to get cracking on a relationship, ideally with a regular guy for a change. It was possible he was out there. Someone she'd get serious with for the first time in her life, now that she was absolutely snuffing out the flame of the Theo torch.

Turner's expression was wary as he walked toward her, uncertain perhaps if he'd interpreted her gesture correctly. Amy encouraged him with a bigger smile and another wave. He was not unattractive. No one could find fault with his trim build, neatly combed hair, intelligent brown eyes, and symmetrical features. Unlike some people with their unkempt hair, moody eyes, and bumpy noses.

"Want to join me?" she asked him.

"No harm in that, I suppose," he said, carefully placing his tray on the table.

Harm? How horny did she look?

"You've eaten already," he observed, sitting down.

"I might get more soup. How are your classes this semester?"

"Splendid. Fanny Burney's *Evelina*, in particular, has provoked many lively discussions." He neatly split his ham sandwich, a considerable feat with a plastic knife. "I think it's fair to say the epistolary novel is still a vibrant form."

Amy repeated the pronunciation of *epistolary* in her head. Since her drunken episode at Benny's Bar, she had yet to say it correctly. "What do you do for fun, Turner?"

"Pardon?"

"Outside of work. What do you like to do?" *Please don't say you make candlesticks or quill pens.*

"I enjoy going to the symphony and dining at fine restaurants." A not-so-subtle reminder that she'd rejected his request for a date to do the exact same thing.

She launched into a discussion of Mozart (about whom she knew zilch) and the merits of farm-to-table cuisine (about which she knew less than zilch) as he systematically worked on his sandwich and fruit cocktail and enlightened her on Baroque music and the art of making sushi.

This could work. Turner Malcolm might be That Guy. Or at the very least, Transitional Guy between Mr. Weirdo and Mr. Wonderful. And he knew how to make sushi. And she, unlike Jo, liked sushi very much.

Amy checked the time on her phone. She had a half hour until her next class to nail this. "I have a suggestion, Turner."

"Suggestion?" His wary expression had returned.

"Let's go ice-skating. There's a fabulous rink at Forest Park in St. Louis, and I've wanted to go before it closes for the season."

She hadn't thought about ice-skating since she'd skated with Ramon in Chicago. They had shrieked with laughter as they careened around the rink, bumping into people who didn't think there was anything funny. Besides Ramon's hat.

"Would it be...Are you asking me to go out on a date?" Turner asked with a puzzled look.

"A *casual* date." Had she insulted him by qualifying it? Did she care? Would Turner let her eat the cherry in his fruit cocktail if she asked for it? Why was she asking herself so many questions?

"I'm confused," he said. "I thought you never dated colleagues."

"I've been rethinking my position on that. As busy as we are, how else can we meet people?"

He smiled, revealing a bottom row of snaggle teeth. The asymmetry was curiously satisfying. "Is this why you snuggled up to me at Benny's Bar?" he asked.

"Uh-huh," she lied.

"I haven't skated for years." He stabbed the cherry with the plastic fork and ate it. "All right. I'm game. I think we can risk it."

As if they were volatile substances instead of geeky professors.

Across the room, someone dropped a tray loaded with dishes,

eliciting whistles, laughs, and jeers. Amy was *not* going to read too much into the symbolism of this. Or the cherry.

"Actually, I don't want anything else to eat," she said, getting up. "Nice talking to you, Turner. Let's make a date for the rink."

CHAPTER TWENTY-EIGHT

Jo had learned that hearts, like
flowers, cannot be rudely handled,
but must open naturally.
—LOUISA MAY ALCOTT, *LITTLE WOMEN*

When the Farraguts called to cancel their sessions "for the time being" while he was preparing breakfast, Theo offered his encouragement and assured them he'd be available whenever they needed him. Considering Tildy's newfound assertiveness and Eugene's amorousness, though, he suspected they wouldn't return. Good for them—and him. The Farraguts' favorable outcome would demonstrate to Clifford he wasn't a complete failure.

As for the other couples he counseled, they were in a neutral state, going neither forward nor backward. With his career at such a critical juncture, he didn't dare jump-start new approaches with any of them. Such as telling couples to quit bitching about the other person and take a good, hard look at *themselves*. In as loud a voice as he dared, like the Marconis.

Using Lou and Rose as examples of his counseling success was an iffy proposition at best. They had spent the last few meetings advising *Theo* how to make a relationship work. Which evidently required screaming and a shared passion—in their case, deli meats.

And then there were the Spragues.

The blender screeched as Theo mixed a vanilla protein smoothie, making the cats flee the kitchen. Getting their marriage on the right track was still his biggest challenge. Burning up the sheets had saved the Farraguts and Marconis from burning the marriage license, but Warren and Cynthia's problem was not as straightforward. They required a subtler approach. He had yet to find a way to get them to see and hear each other, much less recommend sex as a cure for what ailed them. And after the Decker disaster, it was clear his *If it ain't broke, don't fix it* approach was inadequate. What else was he doing wrong?

As Theo drank the smoothie, he noticed the mug, dishes, and silverware Amy had stacked in the sink before she'd rushed off to work. Lately, on the rare occasions she left things behind, the objects, more than her actual presence, were the only signs she lived in the house.

The night that they'd spent in front of the fireplace, she'd changed expressions from sunny to saucy to sad as swiftly as the dancing flames that he hadn't been sure what to think. Rational thought hadn't been possible anyway, not while he was clenching every muscle in his body to keep from reaching for her, holding and kissing her. The few times he'd woken in the night, he'd sensed her restless wakefulness. Not that it meant anything. Put two adults with a healthy sex drive in the same bed, coziness covering them like a warm blanket...

But it was Amy, not just anyone. Her hair gold like the fire, her body as warm. Saying so much while saying nothing.

Only Amy. No one else.

He scratched Moose behind the ears. "Whaddya say, boy? Do you like the lamp Amy rescued and put in the living room? The one shaped like a tulip?"

Moose licked his hand in reply.

"This place looks more like a home since she moved in, that's for sure. Are we happy about that or not?"

The Newfie's heavy tail thumped the floor.

"Yeah, me too."

There were worse ways to start a day than to be grateful for what you had—rather than what you might have had. With one final check that all the food and water bowls were full, Theo went to Happy Haven.

Warren and Cynthia Sprague were as opposite each other in appearance as Lou and Rose Marconi were similar. Today, though, they wore identical looks of consternation. Theo marked the date with an asterisk in his notebook. Could it be the same thoughts were running through their minds for once?

"I thought we'd try something different in our session today," he said. "An experiment, if you will."

"Different?" Warren asked with a leery expression.

Cynthia crossed her arms and legs. "I don't like experiments."

"Have you heard of the 'never have I ever' game?" Theo asked them. "What you would do is—"

"I don't drink either," she said.

"Not the *drinking* version of the game. You and Warren would simply go back and forth, telling each other what you've never done. A way of getting to know each other better."

"We're married. We already know each other," Warren said curtly.

Cynthia shook her head. "I don't like games."

The Spragues were obviously on the same page about one thing—they didn't care for Theo's suggestion. Maybe it wasn't too late to switch careers. Travel tour guide? Veterinary assistant?

"They made us play games in our Children of Divorce support group," Cynthia said.

"Stupid waste of time," Warren grumbled.

"It's where we met," she said.

"Pardon?" Theo said.

"Warren and I met in our Children of Divorce support group."

Theo put the notepad and pen on the coffee table. Clifford had advised him to consider events in couples' pasts to better understand their relationship. Advice he'd dismissed.

Because it hit too close to home.

"I owe you both an apology," he said. "I never asked about your family history."

"Doesn't matter," Warren said. "As my father used to say, *It's not where you came from; it's where you're going.* Though where *he* went, I have no idea. The jerk."

"My dad used to call me Cindy Loo," Cynthia said. "Right up to the day he said, *Toodle-oo, Cindy Loo.*"

"I'm sorry," Theo murmured.

"My mom cried in the laundry room all the time after he left," she went on. "She'd stick her face in the towels, but I still heard her."

"Broken families everywhere," Warren observed.

"We heard about Barrett and Olivia Decker, Theo," Cynthia said solemnly.

"Divorced," Warren said, shaking his head. "The perfect couple."

She fumbled with a button on her blouse. "If it can happen to them, it can happen to anybody."

"He drove by my office the other day," Warren said. "I recognized the Mercedes-Benz."

"My sister is getting a new car," she said.

"The electric bill came yesterday."

"I forgot to bring the cans to the recycling center."

"I may go to the conference in Des Moines in July."

"I have to pick up my dress at the cleaners."

The Spragues' sentences were veering wildly again, but for the first time, Theo was reading between the lines. He heard what the newlyweds *weren't* saying. As children of broken homes, they were terrified of divorce. If they kept talking past each other, they wouldn't hear the other one say, *I don't love you anymore* or *I'm leaving.* They were two scared people looking over the precipice their parents had fallen into.

"Warren, Cynthia, let's try a more creative approach," he said. "It occurs to me that in improvisational jazz, the musicians engage in a conversation—play, listen, respond. I want you to conduct a conversation as if you were jazz musicians, with emphasis on listening to the other person."

Warren placed a hand on each beefy knee. "You want us to be *what?*"

Cynthia blew a stray hair off her forehead. "We told you we don't like to play games, Theo."

"It's not a game; it's an exercise," he explained. "And a very simple one. Let's start out with one of you speaking and the other repeating what was said. And vice versa. See where it takes you."

Warren snorted. "What's the point?"

"The point is to pay close attention to what someone is communicating."

"Or not communicating," Cynthia said softly.

"Good, Cynthia. Nonverbal cues are important too. But let's start with the more basic—"

"Basic? Are we that bad off?" Warren asked gloomily.

"Not bad off at all. You're both here because you want to give your marriage the best possible start. Am I correct?"

The Spragues nodded.

"Your commitment to your marriage is a very positive sign."

"There's an awful lot that could go wrong, though," Cynthia said.

"We should know," Warren said.

"Children of divorce," she said, looking wistfully out the window.

"It is important to acknowledge events in the past," Theo said. "And we will continue to discuss the impact of your parents' divorces on your marriage in future sessions. But as you do so, you need to understand that you are *not* your parents. Their relationship most emphatically is not yours."

Counseling may not have helped the Spragues yet, but it was doing wonders for Theo Sinclair. He wasn't doomed to repeat the pattern of his parents' dysfunctional behavior, or be forever damaged by it, any more than the Spragues were. It had been staring him in the face all this time, like the Deckers' coiled rage toward each other, and he hadn't seen it. Fear had paralyzed

Warren and Cynthia—and he too had been a deer in the head-lights of his own life.

"What if our parents started out like us," Warren said, "and then it all went to shit?"

"Facing your fears is half the battle," Theo said. "The other half is the determination to move forward together with optimism and hope."

If he sounded like one of the posters on the wall, he was perfectly fine with that.

"What should we talk about in the exercise?" Cynthia asked.

"Whatever you want. Anything at all," he said, hoping it wasn't *I can't stand the sight of you* or *I want out of this marriage.*

He listened to them go back and forth, repeating what the other person had said. At first, they talked about the leak in the kitchen sink, the new sofa to be delivered, and then moved on to more personal topics like where Warren wanted to go for vacation, and what book Cynthia was reading. How she needed a hug after a bad day, he some alone time. Theo heard them laugh for the first time ever.

"How are we doing, Theo?" Warren asked.

"You're doing great," he assured them. "You're both going to be just fine."

And maybe, just maybe, so would he.

When his phone vibrated in his pocket, Theo peeked at the text from Lando. What it said made the hairs on the back of his neck stand up.

Stella badly hurt. In hospital. Need you. Pronto!!

As soon as the Sprague session was over, Theo sped to Berryman Hospital. Resting his head against the seat after he parked, he reviewed the nightmarish scenarios he'd imagined as he drove. The mangled bike, Stella's blood on the asphalt, fractured bones protruding through her skin. Broken neck. For Lando's sake, he had to be ready for any of them.

He sucked in a few deep breaths and let them out slowly. It was a cold morning in February—but a hot August in Las Vegas all over again. The swirling red lights of an ambulance at the emergency entrance made his heart pound. The efficient yet urgent movements of hospital personnel in green scrubs were as calming, and frightening, as he remembered.

Theo had pushed the incident to the deep recesses of his mind. But whenever he experienced a near miss while driving or rubbed the ridge on his nose, the accident with Jo on a Nevada highway came rushing back. The car speedometer inching forward as he and Jo accelerated into a screaming match. Both of them at their worst, losing their tempers—and he losing control of the car. The squeal of brakes and the sickening crunch of metal after the car slowed, spun, flipped, and rolled. Their argument ended with them hanging upside down, enveloped in air bags. Luckily, Jo came away from the wreck with nothing worse than a broken arm, he a broken nose. They'd since healed those injuries.

As for the scathing things Jo had said to him in the heat of the moment...

Theo got out of the car and walked through the icy drizzle, determined to hold on to the insights—and hope—that the Sprague session had offered him. Despite Jo's words.

He paused in the vestibule to text Amy.

Stella hurt in bike accident. I'm at Berryman Hospital with Lando.

They were housemates whose lives rarely intersected outside the house. Still, he needed Amy to say everything would be all right. To tell him she'd be there for him if he needed her. Like when they were friends whose lives intersected everywhere.

Smoothing down his hair, Theo passed through the doors leading to the lobby. For all the commotion outside, the hospital was eerily quiet. Everyone seemed to be whispering and walking in foam-soled shoes. As if paying their respects to the dying.

But not Stella. Don't let her be one of them, he silently prayed.

I'm in the lobby, he texted Lando. No matter what happened, he'd be there for his friend completely.

He leaned against the wall, his nerves too jangled to sit. A little boy, his arm in a sling, swung a sneakered foot. His mother's eyes were shut, catching up, probably, on years of missed sleep. A deathly pale woman wearing a pink ball cap clung to the arm of the man sitting beside her. Theo's years as a medical student and resident returned in a flash. Illness, injury, and death were the foes he would have had to face each day as a doctor—and he might have lost the battle more often than won. As a counselor, though, the odds of successful outcomes were more in his favor.

Lando materialized beside him so suddenly Theo jolted. The little boy laughed and his mother shushed him, smiling as she watched the two men hug.

"How's Stella? My God, what happened?"

Lando pushed his curly hair off his forehead. His eyes

were glassy and rimmed with dark circles. "She just got out of surgery. They say she's going to be all right. Broken hip and...and a few other bones. Femur, I think. But she's going to be okay."

The tension released from Theo's body like air from a tire. "Stella was racing in this weather?"

"Fuck me, no." Lando let out a high-pitched laugh. "You're not going to fucking believe this."

When the mother of the little boy raised her eyebrows, Theo led Lando to a chair out of earshot of the others. "What won't I believe?"

"It happened at Spin Cycle," Lando said. "Stella was on a tall ladder, adjusting a bike on a hook, and she lost her balance. When she fell, she pulled the bike down on top of her. Good thing she was wearing a helmet she had tried on or she'd be in worse shape. You know what blows, though? It was such a freak accident she won't listen to me at all now when I warn her about racing."

"At least she won't cycle for a while. You'll get a break from worrying."

"Shit. I'll have to cancel our trip to Colorado. And get somebody to manage Marconi's Pizza while I take care of her."

"Can Stella's parents help out?"

"They're on a Caribbean cruise and won't be back for at least two weeks." Lando grinned. "Just as well. If there's more than one Amoroso in the vicinity, I can't hear myself think."

"I'll manage the restaurant," Theo offered. "Work it around my schedule."

"Running a restaurant doesn't fit into *anyone's* schedule. The hours are brutal."

"How about one of your parents subbing for you? I advised them to spend more time apart. And they *are* experienced in the food industry."

"Intimately. If you remember the olive oil incident. But yeah, that's a good idea."

"If there's anything I can do, say the word."

"Thanks, man." Lando got up, tucking his shirt into his jeans. "I gotta get back to my girl now."

"Give Stella my love."

"Anybody else you want to give your love to?" Lando joked. "It's been a while since Brittany."

"No thanks. But while we're on the subject...I've been wondering...Never mind. This isn't the time or place."

"Hey, you can ask me anything, anytime, anyplace."

"All right. Here goes. You're always telling me to get a woman. Do you think I'm capable of...of a serious relationship?"

"'Cause of all that shit in your past?"

Theo nodded, thinking of all the shit in his *future* if he failed as a counselor.

Lando rested a hand on his shoulder. "Your woman's out there, Theodore. The real question is, are you going to finally let her find you? 'Cause you've been hiding for a long time."

"Playing Yoda instead of General Calrissian, are you?"

"Playing the genius of love that I am."

"Okay. So I 'let her find me.' What then?"

"And then you do everything you can to keep her. Like I do with Stella. As simple as that."

"Easy for you to say."

"Love isn't that hard, *amico mio*," Lando said with a wave goodbye over his shoulder.

In the car, Theo sat listening to the *thwack, thwack, thwack* of the wipers as they cleared ice from the windshield. The sound of a heartbeat—his—coming back to life. And the possibility of love.

His phone chime alerted him to a text message.

Sorry to hear about Stella, Amy wrote. Try not to worry. She's in good hands at Berryman. I'm here if you need me.

And then an earlier text from Jo.

Hamlet dilemma. To go for it or not to go for it.

Yeah. That was the question.

CHAPTER TWENTY-NINE

*I'm happy as I am, and love my
liberty too well to be in a hurry to give
it up for any mortal man.*
—JO MARCH, *LITTLE WOMEN*

This had to be one of the more awkward Amy-Theo episodes she'd experienced. It was definitely up there with passing out dead drunk in his lap.

Theo was driving her to her date with Turner.

"Athena was supposed to take me," Amy explained as he backed out of the driveway. "But Thorne's mom had a medical emergency, and she flew to Florida with him."

"S'okay. I appreciate you helping me pack and deliver healthy meals to Lando and Stella. There's only so much pizza anyone can eat."

"How's she doing?"

"Much better. And the dark circles under Lando's eyes have disappeared. What about the guy you're meeting?"

Amy frowned. "Why on earth are you asking if he has circles under his eyes?"

"I'm not. I'm asking why he didn't pick you up."

"Way to stay on topic."

"One thing led to another in my head. Well?"

"He was in St. Louis all morning visiting his uncle. It didn't make sense for him to come back to Laurel to get me."

"No. It makes good manners," Theo said, merging into traffic.

She could have rescheduled for another day. And yes, she fully acknowledged that *Get it over with* was not the best attitude when one was going on a date. "This is the twenty-first century, Theo."

"Good manners are timeless."

"What I'm saying is, women are perfectly capable of getting to social engagements by themselves."

"Ones with automobiles anyway."

"Does a '57 Chevy qualify as one?"

"I had her overhauled. She's in tip-top shape."

"She?"

"I've named her Lucille. The name B. B. King gave to all his guitars."

"Theo the First would be so proud."

"Indeed, he would."

"I'm definitely getting another car so I won't have to bum rides from people who…" Amy looked around to find something to criticize. "Who listen to strange music on the radio."

"Panpipes from Peru," Theo said. "They're hauntingly beautiful in person. What kind of car are you buying?"

"I haven't decided yet."

"A used army jeep would be your best bet. If it can withstand military operations, it can withstand you."

Amy was tempted to do something absurdly immature, like thumb her nose at him. But number one, he listened to hauntingly beautiful panpipes. Number two, a jeep wasn't a bad idea. And number three, a Theo smile could melt an igloo.

Traffic on the interstate was surprisingly light for a mild, sunny Saturday afternoon. A van full of kids in the next lane kept pace with the '57 Chevy. One of them smashed his face, with his tongue stuck out, against the glass. Amy texted a picture of him to Athena, who couldn't wait for her beach getaway with Thorne because, as she put it, *My eggs will be popping*.

Sure about this madcap baby scheme of yours? Amy typed beneath the photo of the little boy.

"An afternoon date," Theo remarked as he accelerated into the left lane. "You're playing it safe."

"We're keeping it informal."

"Who is he anyway?"

"An English professor. One of my colleagues."

He shot her a disapproving glance. "You're not playing it safe. You're playing with fire."

"You do realize I'm not sixteen anymore and don't need you lecturing me about my dates?"

"Pardon the crude expression, but haven't you heard you shouldn't shit where you eat?"

"Haven't you heard you should keep your nose out of other people's business?"

"Occupational hazard. Though I may not have the occupation much longer."

"Still on probation?" Amy asked, glad to get off the subject of her informal date.

"Yes. Though I've had successful outcomes with most of my clients. Like the boy who's been bullied putting his feet up on the clinic coffee table the other day. Without asking permission."

"That's a big deal?"

"A small victory. It tells me he's more confident and assertive. When he first came to the sessions, he'd huddle in the chair like a frightened rabbit."

"Poor kid."

"Makes it all worth it. Now, if I can just get a handle on couples counseling, I may not have to consider an alternative career."

"Jo always thought you'd have made a great veterinarian," she said with a sidelong glance at him.

"Too late in the game to go to vet school. What's his name anyway?"

Amy grabbed the armrest as he navigated the steep curve of the exit. "You're off topic again."

"I'm on the topic of your hot date," Theo said. "Name?"

"Turner Malcolm." Who was what one might refer to as a *lukewarm* date. If one were bothering to take his temperature.

"Sounds backward to me. Shouldn't it be Malcolm Turner?"

"I'll have you know he's an authority on eighteenth-century literature."

"Authority, huh? There can't be much competition."

"It's an esoteric field."

"Esoteric, not erotic. Got it," he said, turning into the Steinberg Skating Rink parking lot.

This time Amy did thumb her nose at him, meriting a full Theo Sinclair dimple display.

She spotted Turner standing by a silver Volvo and wearing a gray sweatsuit, attention riveted to his phone. As in, not eagerly awaiting her arrival. As in, not dressed for an after-skate activity—besides eating at McDonald's. As in, not likely to incite jealousy in another male for a radius of a hundred miles. Not that arousing such an emotion mattered in the slightest.

She got out of the car and leaned down to thank Theo for the ride. But he wasn't in the driver's seat. He had walked to the trunk and was pulling out a pair of ice skates.

"Haven't skated in ages," he said, looking entirely too cheerful. "This should be fun."

She slammed the car door. "What do you think you're doing?"

"Since I came all the way into the city, I might as well get exercise."

Bending his knees, he bobbed up and down and stretched his arms above his head. She noticed for the first time he was wearing a sleek athletic jogging suit. "Are you for real?" she said.

"You better warm up too or you'll be sore tomorrow."

"*You'll* be sore. From me conking you on the head."

"Don't worry. I won't get in the way of your hot date. You need a ride back anyway, don't you?"

"I thought you learned your lesson about being overprotective from Brittany."

"I'm not being overprotective."

"You're right. You're being obnoxious. Besides, Turner will drive me." Actually, they hadn't discussed it. What if he planned to stay in St. Louis for the night? Or was meeting another woman later, wearing the nicer clothes he'd brought in an overnight bag? It being a casual date and all.

Theo nodded toward Turner. "Is that him?"

For a nanosecond, Amy considered denying Turner's existence. He hadn't even looked up from his phone when she got out of the car. "Yeah," she said.

"Good thing I'm hanging around."

"*Not* sixteen. *Not* needing rescue from a date," she said, stomping one foot like a sixteen-year-old.

"Better get over there, then. He looks like he's dying to see you."

Amy trudged across the lot, ignoring Theo's laughter at his own joke. Her muscles ached already. She should be home, under the comforter with Nina, sleeping until Monday.

"Who's that?" Turner asked, pointing to Theo, who was whistling as he strolled to the rink.

"Theo Sinclair. He's my ride and housemate."

"I feel like I've seen him before."

"He was at Athena's birthday party."

He grinned. "Oh yeah. The party." Where she'd snuggled up to him. Where she'd been carried out over Theo's shoulder.

She was buying a car as soon as possible. If she had one, she could run to it right now, speed home, burrow under the comforter with Nina, and sleep until Wednesday.

They rented skates and joined the crowd on the ice. Grade-school kids zipped around doing figure eights like the annoying and amazing little creatures they were. Turner took a few tentative steps and glides and, after one full circuit of the rink, was all set to go. After multiple stumbles, a near collision with a family of four—and checking and rechecking to see where Theo was—so was Amy. She and Turner skated side by side, chatting about the last things she wanted to chat about—their classes, budget cuts, next year's curriculum.

This was your idea, she reminded herself. *Suck it up.*

She watched Turner's mouth as he talked, picturing herself kissing him. He was intelligent and refreshingly sane. There were clearly no giant fruit costumes or oversized fur hats in his closet. Once he got off the subject of academia, he was not unfunny. The joke about the ballerina walking into a bar was lame, but hey, he was trying.

"Your cheeks are pink from the exercise," Turner remarked when they stopped for a break. "You must stay in good shape from biking everywhere."

Her face and body. *Now* they were getting somewhere.

"Bad weather's a challenge, but I do enjoy cycling," she said.

His eyes were shiny, his perfectly sculpted face aglow with health. Professor Malcolm looked like he'd never read a fusty eighteenth-century novel in his life.

"Are you into health food? Grains and veggies?" she asked. To keep the topic on bodies.

He shrugged. "I eat what I like."

"Have any pets?"

"I'm not an animal person."

Animal person. What exactly did that mean?

After they exhausted the subject of his career goals (just fine where he was) and his taste in music (nothing worth listening to but classical), they returned to the safe subject of academia.

"Have you decided on your fall lineup of classes?" Turner asked.

"I could use a change, so I'm considering a course in medieval literature, my specialty," Amy said. "How about you? I imagine teaching epistolary novels gets old."

Whew. She'd pronounced it correctly.

He frowned. "There's more to eighteenth-century literature than epistolary novels. I offer my students a representative selection of texts."

"Good thing. Those novels aren't exactly exciting, and

students don't appreciate them. Properly," she added lamely as his frown deepened.

"They do when *I* teach them." Turner sniffed the air as if he smelled the melting wax of candles, powdered wigs, and the curious odors of people wearing layers of clothes without the benefit of modern plumbing and deodorant. "The eighteenth is the most sublime century in literature. And, I might add—"

But he was cut short by the sound of clapping from the couple next to them.

"Did you see that?" the woman said. "He did a perfect axel."

"Oh, look. A double axel," the man said.

He was Theo, gliding, twirling, and flowing across the ice as sinuously as a scarf in the wind. When he tilted his body and lifted his left leg parallel to the ground, the entire rink erupted into applause.

"A camel spin," the man said reverentially.

"Our daughter skates," the woman explained to Amy. "We're familiar with the terms."

"And the talent," the man said. "His is exceptional."

"Did you know he skated like a pro?" Turner asked Amy as Theo spun, jumped, and double-axeled his way into more applause.

She shook her head, dumbstruck.

"I pegged him as an ice hockey type," he said.

"He has all his teeth," she managed to get out.

Theo performed a half dozen more applause-worthy moves, then, with a bow, skated to the perimeter, blending in with the crowd.

"Show's over," Turner said.

For the next hour, while skaters as loose-limbed as spaghetti sped by Amy and Turner, her legs got stiffer and heavier. Whenever she spotted Theo, he looked as graceful as her parents floating over the linoleum floor of their mobile home. She had a delightful vision of dancing with him across the kitchen floor, her gown swirling around her legs, one of his hands at her waist, the other—

Her delightful vision was interrupted by Turner asking if they could leave soon.

"Fine with me," she said. Her feet were as rigid as wooden blocks. Her nose and fingertips stung with cold.

"There's a pizza place not far from here," Turner said. "If you want to eat."

So that's what the sweatsuit was about. Pizza. Not exactly the fine restaurant dining he claimed he liked.

"I'd rather go back to Laurel, if you don't mind. I can make us hot chocolate." Turner was going to be her ride back whether he wanted to be or not.

"Sure," he said with more enthusiasm about leaving than he'd shown all afternoon.

After they returned their skates, Amy sank into the seat of his car, weary to the bone. A casual, lukewarm date took a lot more energy than she expected. Fortunately, Turner was as disinclined to talk as she was. He peered into the rearview mirror with a scowl as they approached the WELCOME TO ILLINOIS sign. "I do not believe this," he said.

"What?"

"That Theo guy has been following us."

Amy turned to look out the back window. The '57 Chevy—Lucille—was directly behind them. Theo grinned and waved. She sat on her hands to keep from waving back.

"He's not *following* following us," she said. "He's just heading home too."

"Is he like this with all his housemates?" Turner said.

"What? No. I have no idea. Like what?"

"Driving you to the rink. Watching us the whole time. And now tailgating."

"Watching us?"

"You didn't notice the laser death ray eyes? In between the camel spins?"

Giddiness overtook Amy. She was ready to land an axel or two herself. "I would have expected you to use an eighteenth-century description, like *rapier eyes*."

Turner glanced at her with *You're stranger than I thought* eyes and, putting the radio on, tuned the station to NPR. They spent the rest of the ride pretending they were deeply concerned about the lost traditions of Appalachian cooking.

When they arrived at the house, Theo pulled up next to them in the driveway. Turner let out a long breath as if he'd been pursued by wild dogs. After introducing them, Amy led the way up the porch, followed closely behind by Theo. Reluctantly behind by Turner.

"I'm going to make hot chocolate," she told Theo. "You're welcome to join us."

"Swiss Miss instant or from scratch?"

"What do you think?"

"I'll make it. I've got a tin of Hershey's cocoa."

"Where'd you learn to skate so well?" Turner's question to Theo sounded like an accusation.

"A woman I dated in Syracuse was a figure skater. She taught me some moves."

"You're a natural," Amy said to Theo.

He gazed at her long enough for her to fall into—and swim in—the sea of his eyes. "That I am."

"Skater, I mean," she mumbled.

"That too."

Theo unlocked the door and they stepped into the foyer. Turner threw his head back and sneezed. And sneezed. And sneezed until every cat scurried out of the living room.

"Allergic," he wheezed.

"Well," Theo drawled. "That takes care of that."

CHAPTER THIRTY

Learn to know and value the praise
which is worth having.
—MARMEE MARCH, *LITTLE WOMEN*

Amy took one look out her bedroom window late Sunday morning and fell back onto the pillow with a groan. At the foot of the bed, Nina glowered at her as if the fickle weather—sunny one day, dismal the next—were her fault. There were no degrees of bleakness. Gray was gray, March was fricking March, and sleet was as nasty as its name. The kind of day where the ordinary heroes of her book on *Idylls of the King* decide to screw bravery, let the world go to shit, and go back to sleep. *Little Women*'s theme of triumphing over adversity wouldn't cut it either.

She should get up, get caffeinated, and get going on the portrait of herself, Jo, and Theo that she planned to submit to the college-sponsored art exhibit in May. But her thighs were too sore to get her anywhere. One ice-skating session had reduced her muscles to Jell-O. For all the cycling she did, she expected to be in better shape. Like her date with Turner that had gone in the opposite direction from what she'd envisaged.

"Mr. Cocoa-from-Scratch didn't have to be so smug," she said to Nina.

Nina gave her typical disdainful sniff whenever Amy dared complain about the Cat Whisperer.

After Turner drove away yesterday, presumably never to darken the doorway of the house-from-cat-allergy-hell again, Theo had stayed in his study the rest of the day, doing who knew what. Laughing his brains out, probably. She'd set up the easel, mixed her colors, and painted, painted, painted deep into the night. Unlike *Still Life With ?*, languishing at the back of the closet, the portrait displayed confident brushwork, vivid color, and a fluency she hadn't achieved for a long time.

Careful not to disturb Nina, Amy inched off the bed and went to the bathroom. She mumbled apologies to a stuffed mouse and goldfish that squeaked when she stepped on them, wondering, out of nowhere, if Theo had watched her and Turner with his laser-rapier-whatever eyes because he was jealous.

Yeah. Right. Theo jealous of a guy in sweatpants who was checking a box—*Humor Dr. Marsden; she approves your requisition requests*? Turner could at least have offered to go out for coffee instead of fleeing the house like his hair was in flames. *Should I get the fire extinguisher?* Theo had laughed.

The hot shower washed away the delusion of his jealousy if not her muscle pain. And injured pride. And embarrassment. The first guy she dated since she'd moved in, and Mr. Camel Spin had enough material to spin jokes for the next month.

Once Amy had finished dressing, she followed the delicious aroma of freshly brewed coffee wafting from the kitchen, with Nina at her heels. Theo was at the table, the pieces of another broken something spread in front of him. His dark hair was tucked in the collar of his black turtleneck. And she was not going to reach in and set it free.

"Hiya," he said.

"Hiya." She pointed to the coffeemaker. "For me? Or do you have company?"

"For you. I heard the shower running upstairs. Figured you'd be down soon."

"Thanks. Another favor I owe you, like yesterday's ride," she said, pouring coffee into a mug.

A sly smile slid across his lips so quickly she wasn't sure she'd seen it.

"Where's your buddy?" she asked, sitting in the chair Coltrane preferred.

"In my bedroom. Bessie and Ray were hassling each other again. It got on his nerves." Theo tightened a screw with three twists of the screwdriver. "I never intended to give Coltrane up for adoption, but I decided I'm going to keep Ray and Bessie too."

"I can't imagine this place without them. And Moose?"

"It goes without saying this is his forever home, the big, slobbery baby."

Moose lifted his head from the floor and grunted.

"He said, *Thank you*," Amy said.

"You're welcome, Moose."

"Remember Fred?" she asked.

"How can I forget? He used to lick your face like a lollipop."

A small dog of indeterminate breed, Fred had wandered onto the Sinclair property and was adopted by Theo once his LOST DOG signs went unanswered.

"You were the one who named him," Theo said. "After Mister Rogers."

"That's right. And I'd pretend he was saying things in Mister Rogers's calm voice, like, *It's a beautiful day for a walk. Please won't you give me some kibble?*"

Though Fred the dog's personality was opposite that of the host of *Mister Rogers' Neighborhood*—hyper and intolerant of anyone but them. He met his untimely end chasing a squirrel across a busy street.

"The box you made to bury him in was one of your better power tool moments," she said.

"Your comfort to me was one of your better Amy moments."

"But *I* was the one who was a mess when Fred died."

"I meant all the other times you were there for me. Like when I flunked my trig test, remember?"

"Oh yeah. I went with you to break the news to your parents. We figured they wouldn't pitch too horrible a fit if I was there."

"But they just brushed it off because they both had hated math," he said.

She stirred a teaspoon of sugar into her coffee. "They weren't *all* bad."

"No, they weren't. But it was not knowing when they *would* be that was hard. The truth is, I wouldn't have survived the bumpy years without you."

Amy blinked back the tears threatening to fill her eyes. He was the lonely boy with the unhappy home life all over again. She was the young girl mourning the loss of her dad. Amy and Theo, stitching the seams of their families, making their own family. How it all began.

"That's not to say we didn't have a lot of fun too," Theo said.

"Oh, barrels."

"You were always so funny. And even funnier when you didn't mean to be."

"Is that a backhanded compliment?"

"A front-and-center compliment."

He twined the loose wires on the table around his index finger. "Remember your sketch of the fishing boat? The one you called *Angler Management*? I came across it yesterday."

"You kept it?"

"It was stuck inside a book. I forgot I had it."

"When your parents upset you, I'd tell you to send them fishing on *Angler Management* in your head."

A sad smile came and went across Theo's face. "I sent them on a lot of rides on that boat."

"Did it help?"

"More than you know."

Noticing his phone on the table, Amy grabbed it, shot four photos of him in quick succession, and sent them to her email.

"What was that about?" he asked.

"I need pictures of you for the portrait I'm painting of me, you, and Jo."

"All three of us?"

Should I leave myself out? she was tempted to ask.

"Portrait of a friendship," she said. "Or something like that."

"But why a photo? I'm right here."

"I wanted to capture your Appliance Rescuer face." *Your Appreciate Amy face.* She poked at the snippets of wire he'd unwound from his finger. "What *are* you fixing?"

"A transistor radio. I found it in the car's glove compartment. It's a relic." He snapped it closed. "There. Good as new."

"After skating yesterday, *I* feel like a relic," she said, getting up to add more coffee to the mug.

"You need to repair your muscles. I'll make you a protein smoothie."

"Aha! The secret to your fancy footwork on the ice. And acts of derring-do."

"Derring—what?" he asked, grinning.

"Daring deeds," she said, turning from the coffeemaker right into the just-this-side-of-hunk Theo Sinclair. The little dance they did—he to get to the sink, she to get back in the chair—wasn't the graceful one of her imaginings. Though the accidental grazing of her arm might count as an incident.

"Vanilla or strawberry smoothie?" he asked, washing his hands.

"Neither. I'm afraid of the power protein may unleash in me."

His laughter rang over the sound of rushing water. "Authorities of eighteenth-century literature should be very afraid."

Amy looked out the window. A weak sun had replaced sleet, giving the view of the backyard a watercolor effect. "Turner's safe from me in all circumstances."

"Femme fatale isn't your deal anyway. You'd have to be able to drink alcohol like...Well, you'd have to be able to—"

"Handle my liquor?" And licker.

The night that she was blotto, then in his bed, then in his arms unwound like a skein of yarn across the room. She stared at the floor, trying to rewind it to another topic of conversation. "When were you in Copenhagen?" she asked, pointing to his T-shirt.

"Two years ago."

"I've heard the cost of living is crazy expensive there."

"I paid about fifteen dollars for a sandwich. You'd like it, though. It's the most bike-friendly city in the world."

"On crap-weather days like this, I'm tempted to buy the jeep you recommended." Though, curiously, it didn't feel like a crap-weather day anymore. "I'll name it Thor."

Theo grinned. "See? Funny."

"That time I meant to be."

"I can tell the difference. Need a ride anywhere, by the way? I'm headed out to run errands."

"No thanks. Athena's picking me up later to go shopping."

"Okay. But if you need rides the rest of the week, let me know. More icy rain is in the forecast."

"There you go again," she teased him. "Sir Theo the Protector."

"I'm still working on changing that. It's not easy."

Ray sauntered in, plopped down on the floor, and, closing his good eye, proceeded to wash his face. Half-blind Ray, who, along with diabetic Bessie and massive Moose, had a forever home.

"Don't try too hard to change," Amy said. "The animals wouldn't have you any other way."

He ran a hand through his hair, mussing it up to Theo-level messiness. "And you?" he asked, his voice cracking. "How about you?"

And wouldn't she just love to capture the expression on his face that very instant? In a certain light, with a twist of her mind, he almost looked like Sir Theo Who Loves Amy.

CHAPTER THIRTY-ONE

*I'd rather do everything for myself,
and be perfectly independent.*
—JO MARCH, *LITTLE WOMEN*

Athena slid hangers holding bathing suits across the rack at Macy's with machinelike precision. "Not much selection," she complained. "How am I ever going to find one that says, *Ravish me, the mother of your future child?*"

"Too much responsibility for one bathing suit," Amy said. "Just aim for being irresistible."

Athena held a skimpy red bikini against her voluptuous figure. "How about this?"

"I said irresistible, not incendiary. You and Thorne might never get out of bed."

"That's the general idea. But I wouldn't mind catching a few other admiring glances. Especially since my postbaby body will leave a lot to be desired."

"Never. You'll be knocking them dead when you're eighty." Amy pulled out a sleek black one-piece with a structured bust and high-cut legs. "Found it. Class *and* concupiscence in one sultry package."

"Listen to you with the nerd words. Practicing for another date with Turner?"

"Ice-skating for a couple of hours does not qualify as a date. And I'm not practicing for anything. Except spinsterhood."

"Good for you, though, trying to find someone normal."

"Whatever that means," Amy said.

"Okay—someone conventional."

"Turner's ultra-conventional, and I'm ultra-not interested. And neither is he."

"Don't worry," Athena said. "The man you're going to argue with about the toothpaste cap is out there somewhere, waiting for you."

"Arguing is what marriage is about?" Amy asked.

"Besides yelling *What?* all over the house. And taking emergency trips to Florida."

"Glad Thorne's mom is on the mend."

"So are we."

After trying it on and squealing with joy in the dressing room, Athena bought the bathing suit Amy had picked. The purchase then necessitated a cover-up to wear on the way to the beach, a pair of cute wedge sandals, and an ankle bracelet.

"Not getting anything?" she asked Amy. "Sweaters are thirty percent off."

"No place to go. No one to go there with."

"Anyone else on your dating tryout list?"

"Not a single, unsuspecting soul."

Amy linked her arm in Athena's as they left the store and walked to the parking lot. She was uncomfortably aware that the imbalance of confidences broke the girlfriend code. Athena had confessed her and Thorne's vacillations about having a baby in light of the inheritability of Robin's condition. Meanwhile, Amy kept the vacillations of her relationship with Theo private.

Which was appropriate since most of her relationship with Theo took place in her head anyway. Including her answer to his question—that she wouldn't have him any other way.

"Don't be afraid to get right back on the horse, dating-wise," Athena advised as they got into the Mini Cooper.

"They do say fortune favors the brave."

Athena grinned. "*Jaycee*'s gutsy. She told a guy at the café to keep his hands to himself or she'd glue his fingers to his crotch."

"While cracking her gum?"

"While cracking her gum. You gotta love the millennials."

"*We're* millennials. She's Generation something or other. I've lost track of the letters."

"Today I feel like Generation A for *awesome*." Athena pounded the steering wheel as she merged onto the highway. "I'm going to rock that bathing suit, girlfriend."

Amy fist-pumped the air. "And Thorne's world."

"I'm going to be the best mommy on the planet."

"In the universe."

"Look out, everybody. Here come the Murphy-Kentettes."

Amy swiveled to face her. "How many babies are we talking about?"

"As many as my new bathing suit inspires, on as many beaches as we can lay our sex-exhausted bodies."

The late-afternoon sky was uttering its own rallying cry, having transformed from milky blue to riotous streaks of purple and orange. The branches of bare trees looked as though they might sprout leaves any minute. March was about transitions, a time of longing for spring when everything would come to life again. As ripe for resolution as any New

Year in January. Postponements, negativity, inertia—Amy was done with all that.

She added to the list on her phone's Notes app.

Creative writing curriculum plan—get it in gear.

Jo—get her to interview.

Book and portrait—get a move on.

Dating horse (or pony)—get back on.

She put the phone away and then pulled it out again to add another reminder. Because nothing should stand in the way of giving Jo her chance.

TS—get him out of your head.

They sang along with Athena's Josh Groban CD, every song an anthem to their high spirits. As Athena turned onto the county road, Amy noticed a cabinet propped against a farmhouse's mailbox post. FREE was printed in bold red letters on an adjacent sign.

"Can we stop for a minute?" Amy said. "I want to check this out."

Upon closer inspection, the wooden cabinet was charming. About the size of a small nightstand, it was painted an antique shade of green with a spray of pink-and-violet flowers on each door.

"What would you use it for?" Athena called from the car.

"It'll come in handy for something."

"Maybe it's the *sign* that's free," Athena joked as they drove away with the cabinet in the trunk.

"Too late now. I'll store Nina's stuffed menagerie in it. It grows weekly."

"Not broody, huh? First a cat, then a kid. You'll see."

"First a man," Amy corrected her.

"If all else fails in the male department, you can always use a turkey baster."

"All things considered, that's not a bad idea."

~⌒~

At work, Amy was pleasantly surprised by a lovely card from Eileen, thanking her for the use of her office since she had her own now. She'd expressed her gratitude for the adjunct professors' victory with a beautiful bouquet in a cut-glass vase. Amy had emphasized Fiona's role in the events, but Eileen, sensitive to academic hierarchies, preferred that their advocate be from a lower rank than dean.

One successful intercession to make up for the one she hadn't pursued for Jo with their stepfather. Which she'd remedy by getting Jo to interview and the administration to approve the creative writing curriculum.

Amy looked out her office window, which overlooked a courtyard. Students congregated in small groups, talking, texting, and bouncing in place to stay warm. Raising her arm to adjust the blinds, she caught the attention of Turner walking toward the building. He waved to her with an expression as bland as the afternoon they'd spent together. And then sneezed, as if just looking at her induced his cat allergy.

You'll be married years before us, Jo and Theo used to tease her. *Pretty, pleasing Amy.* Yet here she was, looking down from her ivory tower, alone and lonely. Being married wasn't the point, though perhaps the marital state was Marmee's defense against a perpetual winter of the heart. Loving and being loved, heart and soul—that was all Amy wanted. Besides all the things that she'd mentioned to Fiona. Like a firm derrière.

She snapped the blinds shut, opened them, and then snapped them shut again. A bracing sound to put her in the *You've got this* spirit before calling Jo.

"What's up? How's the weather there?" Amy asked as soon as her sister answered.

"Hunh?"

"What days are you free?"

"Whoa. Hold on," Jo grumbled.

"I waited to call till you were on lunch break. Why do you sound like you're still in bed?"

"I am in bed. Sick day."

"You're never sick. Are you playing hooky?"

"Uh-huh. It's *Silas Marner* week. I'm sick to death of *Silas Marner*. Let the substitute teacher take it on."

"Should I call later?"

"Nah. You already screwed up my sleep-in plans." Jo yawned. "And to answer your questions, nothing's up, it's not raining for a change, and I'm not sure which days I'm...Wait a minute. Free for what?"

"Check your schedule and book a flight out here."

"Shit. Did something happen to Marmee? Did John get crushed to death by the Minnie Winnie while he was changing a tire?"

"What? Geez, Jo. No. They're both fine."

"So why are you being so bossy?"

Amy heard a male voice talking in the background. "Can you turn the TV off? This is important. I need your attention."

"TV? Oh. Okay. Is this about the creative writing job?"

"You bet your booties."

"Chill with the booties already. I've decided to go for it."

"You're kidding! I was just calling to browbeat you into an interview."

"I'll interview, but only on Zoom. I can't spare the time away."

"That shouldn't be a problem. And thanks, Jo. This means a lot."

"Yeah, yeah. What happens next?"

"I'll check with everybody involved and get back to you. What made you change your mind?"

"I don't want you to get into hot water with the dean. And I've been told I can be too stubborn."

"Uh-huh. By me. A million times."

"And other people."

"Like Theo."

"He's not people. He's Teddy. Anyway, it won't kill me. Who knows? Maybe I'll be sold on the idea."

"Wow, that's a switch."

"Miracles happen, little sister. Plus, I'm feeling guilty about things and want to make it up to you."

That sounded familiar.

"I'm almost afraid to ask," Amy said. "What things?" *Meeting Theo at the airport?*

"When we were young. Mostly. Like pilfering the cash you kept in your desk."

"My babysitting money? That I saved for art supplies?"

Jo chuckled. "Pretty seedy, huh?"

"So *that's* where it went. I thought I was counting it wrong."

"Oh, and I hid a stash of cosmetics in your dresser once. In case anyone had seen me steal it, and the cops came to the house."

"You'd let *me* take the rap?"

"You were so sweet and innocent-looking you'd get away with murder."

"You don't even *wear* makeup, Josyphine."

"For the thrill, Amy Mamy. The thrill."

"Leave it to Jo to be a juvenile delinquent."

"Leave it to Amy to be a goody-goody."

Though not so goody-goody that she'd confess the lie about their stepfather. Or admit she'd witnessed Jo's secret meeting with Theo at the airport. Jo might get pissed off and cancel the interview.

"There are other things too, but I forget," Jo said.

"I don't forget you snooping in my closet." And finding Amy's drawings of Theo.

"Didn't you snoop in *my* closet like every self-respecting sister?"

"No! Never."

"I only did all that stuff because you were prettier than me and I wanted attention."

"That's a good one. And pretty or not, you promised to send me a recent photo for the portrait I'm working on."

"Oh, all right," Jo said with a dramatic sigh.

Amy opened the blinds again. The courtyard was empty, the students having dispersed to classes. "I've got to get off to teach a class. One more question. If you're offered the position, are you okay with moving here?"

"That's a hard one. I do fricking love Seattle."

"I mean . . . are you okay living near Theo?"

"The Midwest is a whole lot bigger than Laurel. And Broody Bear."

An answer that told Amy absolutely nothing.

"Anyway," Jo said, "I've got other news. My latest story is getting published in the *New Yorker*."

"That's fantastic! I'm so proud of you!"

"Does it mean you forgive all my bad-girl deeds?"

"You're my favorite bad girl in the world. Which story?"

"The one I mentioned in November. 'Schism' is the title."

"Oh yeah. About a marriage of convenience."

Jo laughed, for no good reason as far as Amy could tell. "What's so funny?" she asked.

"Um...I was just wondering what Marmee will think of the story."

"Is there a geologic term for *her* marriages?"

"*Fault zone* comes to mind." Jo yawned again. "Hey, I'm going back to sleep. Thanks for the call."

"And thanks a million for doing the interview. Love your face. Now send me a photo of it."

"Love yours too. Have I told you how glad I am that you're painting portraits again?"

"Yep. And so am I."

After they hung up, Jo sent a selfie with the text Paint away, Little Raphael, the name the March sisters called Amy in *Little Women*. Jo was looking into the camera with a contemplative expression, her beautiful mane of chestnut hair draped over a bare shoulder. The strange thing was, on the sunny wall behind her, Amy thought she saw the shadow of a man.

CHAPTER THIRTY-TWO

*I could have been a great
many things.*
—*LITTLE WOMEN* (2019 FILM)

$\mathcal{A}$my never took a sick day unless she was at death's door. When she woke with a fever, aching muscles, and sore throat—the flu trifecta—she knew the door had opened a crack. She lay shivering under the comforter, the phone pressed to her ear, eyes shut against the headache pummeling her head.

"I've got your American Essays and Topics in Fiction classes covered," Athena assured her. "Crap. I haven't read Emerson in years."

"A New England transcendentalist will be good for you. Get your mind off sex for a change."

"Can't help it. I just read another novella in the LitWit series. It's called 'Come a Lot.'"

"A takeoff of Guinevere and Lancelot in Camelot?" Amy asked, remembering her former Theo-Lancelot fantasies.

"Add King Arthur and you've got a medieval ménage à trois."

"C. L. Garland is so prolific there must be two of her."

"Uh. Yeah. Maybe. Um, anyway, Ian said he'll teach your Modern Drama class."

Amy was feeling too puny to challenge Athena's usual

Garland evasiveness. "I'll set up online sessions in case this lasts long. I owe you guys one."

"We've already marked you down for babysitting duties, including for my future child," Athena said.

"Wait. A miraculous recovery is coming on."

"Too late. And don't poke a toe out of bed until you've kicked the flu beast. I don't want to catch it while my eggs are dancing."

"What dance would that be?" Amy asked.

"The horizontal mambo. Once I put my bathing suit on, Thorne and I weren't vertical all week."

"Thanks for the laugh. I'm going to get off now and wait for death."

"Dead or not, you're still babysitting for us. Hey, have you or Jo heard anything since her interview?"

"Not yet."

Amy had arranged the Zoom interview with surprising ease and the cooperation of all involved. Jo had passed it with flying colors, impressing Fiona, a few administrative bigwigs, Gary, and Ian with her detailed plan for a creative writing curriculum. She had been serious, incisive, and had even presented a comprehensive report on creative writing departments in small colleges. Watching her, Amy was as proud as punch of her sister, to borrow another Marmee expression. And a smidgen less guilty for having derailed her early career.

"Signing off," Athena said. "I've got to find my old copy of Emerson's essays. Toodle-oo."

"Toodle-oo back. And thank Ian for me."

After Amy called the chair of the Linguistics Department to cancel their meeting, she sank back into the pillow. From her perch on top of the green cabinet, Nina watched her with a tilted head and inquisitive eyes. "I'll get up and let you out in a little while," Amy told her. "Or when my head stops pounding. Whichever comes first."

But Nina loudly expressed her dissatisfaction, leaving her no choice but to brave the walk to the door. She avoided her reflection in the mirror above the dresser, thinking of the legendary Lady of Shallot, who was cursed to regard the world through a mirror. When she dared look at Lancelot directly, "the mirror crack'd from side to side," sealing her doom. Amy's wan, sickly face was enough to shatter glass without any forbidden glances at Lancelot.

Nina scurried down the stairs, and Amy stumbled across the hall to her study where the portrait waited on the easel. Her new routine was to rush home from work, wolf down supper, write a few pages of her book, and lose herself in the swirl of rich autumnal hues on her paint palette—burgundy, hunter green, deep purple, burnt orange, gold. If it weren't the month of March, she'd strip to her undies à la Derek.

In the painting, her figure stood on the left, looking out of the frame, while Jo faced the viewer—and Theo gazed at her. A slash of sun crossed Jo's face while Theo's hair seemed to glow in moonlight. The photos she'd hurriedly taken of him were blurry, inspiring her to paint in an impressionist style. The daubs of color sculpting their faces, necks, and torsos suggested movement. The passage of time. All the years between them.

"Damn good," Amy whispered. "Better than ever."

She returned to the bedroom and crawled into bed. Leaving the door ajar for Nina to get back in, she slept for an hour, or maybe three, when the phone rang, waking her. *Marmee*, the screen said. A dose of unconditional love was just what the doctor ordered.

"Hi, Marmee," Amy croaked.

"You're sick! I can hear it in your voice."

"It's the flu."

"Did you put Vicks VapoRub on your chest?"

"Yeah," Amy lied, wishing she had some in her medicine cabinet.

"Sorry to hear you're not well," John called out.

"You don't have to yell," Marmee told him. "We're on speakerphone."

"This is what's great about being on the road, Amy," John said. "You move on before the germs can get you."

"Unless a waitress in a diner sneezes on your sandwich," her mother said. "Then those germs are coming with you."

"Still complaining about where we ate lunch?" he said.

"And yesterday's dinner. And breakfast the day before. If there are greasy spoons in Paris, I'll eat my hat."

"*Chapeau*," Amy said weakly.

"You're not making sense, Maggie," he said. "How can we go to Paris in a Minnie Winnie?"

Her mother emitted a string of French words Amy knew for a fact were profanities. "Where are you, Marmee?"

"Middletown, Connecticut."

"Home of the world's biggest insurance company?"

"I wish. It's awful. Just awful. A huge jack-in-the-box head on top of a giant silo."

"Reminds me of the Chucky movies." John chuckled. "'Chucky gets lucky.' What a great tagline for a movie *that* was."

"Chucky might get lucky," Marmee grumbled. "Doesn't mean *you* will."

"Now what kind of thing is that to say while your daughter's on the phone?" he said.

"A marriage-tagline kind of thing."

Retorts worthy of Amy. Now that she thought about it, her parents' arguments had been livened by Marmee's snappy comebacks. Her father would shake his head and begrudgingly admit defeat.

"Are you there?" Amy asked after a long phone silence. "Hello? Anybody?"

"*I'm* here," Marmee said. "I moved to the back. I don't need to hear any more commentary from Mr. Know It All. A medical degree doesn't make him an authority on everything. Though you might want to get his advice about your flu."

"It's no big deal. It'll run its course."

"You won't be absent from work for long, will you?"

"I doubt it. In the meantime, other profs are covering my classes."

"Don't get a substitute for your chair position. Someone may try to take it from you."

"Don't worry. I can do administrative work from home."

"Lucky you. Your job must be so satisfying."

"Not as satisfying as painting portraits again."

"Good for you! Now you have the best of both worlds. Whereas I…oh dear. I really don't have *any* worlds. Of my own, I mean."

"It's never too late to follow your dream, Marmee. Yikes. Does that sound lame?"

"*Un peu.*"

"I believe it, though. It's a cliché for a reason. Oh, did Jo tell you she interviewed for a job at the college? I set it up for her."

"She mentioned it."

Substitute *Oh yeah?* and her mother's mild reaction was identical to Theo's. He was probably too busy wrestling with his emotions to comment or ask questions or . . . something.

"I'm so glad everything's coming together for my girls," Marmee went on. "But, Amy dear, do you have someone to take care of you while you're sick?"

To *have* someone. What a quaint and lovely way to describe love. A tear crept from the corner of Amy's eye.

"What am I saying?" her mother exclaimed. "Of course you do. You have Theo."

The tear trickled down Amy's cheek, swiftly followed by another. All she *had* of Theo was the weird sensation lately that he was trying to tell her something with his eyes and with reminiscences of other "Amy moments." She'd completely forgotten about the decorative pillow she'd made for him, embroidered with titles of a few of his favorite jazz songs. It was one of those *It's the thought that counts* gifts, her embroidery skills as lacking as her dexterity with a potter's wheel.

"I wanted to go to Niagara Falls, but John said it was too corny," Marmee was saying. "As if all this gigantic stuff we've been looking at wasn't corny."

"So you dropped the idea to visit Orchard House again?"

"He'd never appreciate it, so why bother?"

Amy heard a cabinet door slam.

"Your *father* would have gone to Niagara Falls if I asked him to."

Amy pulled the comforter up to her chin and closed her eyes. "Tell me again how you and Dad fell in love. I'm in the mood for a romantic story."

"When we met, we were as poor as church mice. He was helping support his family; I was waitressing to pay for college."

"What did he say before every date?" Though Amy knew the story by heart.

"We're going on an adventure, sweet Meg." Marmee's voice held no vision of France, lost chances, or worlds of one's own. "We'd sit in a park and eat a bagged lunch. Or stargaze instead of going to a restaurant or movie."

"Sounds lovely," Amy murmured.

"When he asked me to marry him, I said, *Come what may, I'm yours, Henry.*"

The familiar end to her tale of go-for-broke romance. Which turned into an always-broke marriage.

"Were you worried or scared at all?" Amy asked, her notion of love akin to leaping off a thundering waterfall.

"I'm a Beauregard. You know what my family name means."

"'Always look on the bright side.'"

"It's a cliché for a reason," Marmee said with a touch of mischief in her voice.

Their conversation ended with Marmee humming Edith Piaf's song "La Vie en Rose." Loosely translated, it meant looking at life through rose-colored glasses. Though Amy suspected Marmee had tossed her glasses out the window of the Minnie Winnie somewhere between the giant peach that looked like a butt and the creepy jack-in-the-box.

She drifted back to sleep after her mother's call. When

she woke, she felt pinned to the bed with the weight of her thousand-pound bones.

Sick as a dog...uh, cat. Please take care of Nina until I'm better, she texted Theo.

Within minutes, Amy heard him bound up the stairs. He knocked lightly, then entered.

"Am I glad to see you," he said.

Or maybe *she* said it. She wasn't sure. What with her fever and tears and the sound of rushing water in her ears that might have been Niagara Falls.

CHAPTER THIRTY-THREE

Be worthy, love, and love will come.
—JO MARCH, *LITTLE WOMEN*

$\mathcal{F}$or a vegetarian, you make a darn good chicken soup," Amy told Theo.

"I think the word is *vegetenarian*," he said, reminding her she'd called him that the night she was plastered at Benny's Bar.

"Haha." She lifted her hand and let it drop limply beside her on the living room sofa. "Yikes. Even laughing exhausts me."

He arranged the pieces of the broken blender on the coffee table. "You'll be up and running soon enough. Your fever's gone, and your color's back."

"After five days on this couch, I can't wait to go to work. Weak wrist and all."

"Okay. But I'm driving you to campus. Indefinitely."

"I'll take care of you when *you* get sick," she promised.

"I never do. I've been exposed to everything from traveling. I've got the immune system of a stray dog."

At the word *dog*, Moose looked up from where he lay at the foot of the sofa and woofed a question mark.

"Not you. You'll never be a stray," Theo promised him.

Theo had set up the living room as a sickroom, providing

every creature comfort Amy might wish for. Thick blankets, plush pillows, books, sketch pads, and joy of joys, Vicks VapoRub. The cats, in obedience to their master or some mysterious feline phenomenon, stayed clear of the room. Nina was a silvery shadow slinking between chairs and tables until day's end when she joined her on the sofa to sleep. Moose, though, rarely left her side except to eat or go for a walk.

"Besides resistance to disease, travel does something else for you," Amy said.

"Yeah. It gives me entertaining stories when I'm in bars."

"The one about an ostrich chasing you in South Africa *was* hilarious. But no. Something else."

"Dunno, Amy. A deranged ostrich and a guy practically pissing his pants is about as good as it gets."

"What I mean to say is, you're a moving target when you travel." Like her, always staying in motion.

He unscrewed the base of the blender and examined it. "You should talk. When you showed me the portrait you're working on, the first thing I thought was that you were running out of the painting."

"Maybe I am."

"Oh, okay. Because six more inches to the left, and you'd be out of it completely."

"Anything else?" she asked.

He tousled his already tousled hair. She had captured it perfectly with twisting motions of the paintbrush, thank you very much. Her fingers were practically twitching to hold one again. And run them through that hair.

"Since you're asking, the emotion of the painting doesn't ring true," Theo said. "It's about our friendship, the three of us, but you're so separate. Like you don't belong in the group. You should reconsider the psychology of the composition."

"All right, counselor."

"I meant it as a friend."

Lest she forget they lived in the friend zone.

"I'll take a photo of it and get Jo's opinion," she said. "By the way, there's a good chance she'll get the job at the college."

"So you've told me," he said, looking intently at the blender motor.

Amy waited, but he didn't say anything else. A blender motor, apparently, required one's undivided attention.

"About the portrait," she said in a low voice. "*Your* emotion rings true, doesn't it?"

Theo looked up with a puzzled expression. "Since you mention it, the way you have me looking at Jo...it's like I'm *into* her. Or something."

Something like love.

Maybe she was high on Robitussin. Or Vicks VapoRub fumes. But all of a sudden, Amy knew that it was time to pull the petals off the daisy once and for all.

"Well, aren't you, Theo? Into Jo?"

"What are you talking about?"

Curling her legs beneath her, she wrapped a crocheted afghan around her shoulders. The April afternoon was pleasingly warm but winter's chill might return. "I'm talking about how you two have always been *two peas in a pod*, as Marmee says. How you've always preferred Jo to me."

"Preferred Jo? Because we did stupid pranks as kids?"

"And other things."

He shrugged. "Buddy things."

"Buddies with secrets. Always keeping me out of the loop. Like your argument. Like meeting at the airport, and Jo not even telling me she was coming through St. Louis." Amy poked a finger through one of the holes in the afghan. "I saw you there together the day I left for New York City and you got back from Philadelphia. See? I know more than you think I do."

Theo set the base of the blender down. "You might have told us."

Us.

"I'll bet Jo knows how you got the bump on your nose, doesn't she?"

He nodded.

"You might have told *me* what happened."

"It's too embarrassing."

"I once walked into a glass patio door and fell flat on my back from the impact. My legs were up in the air like a bug."

"True story?"

"Who'd make up something so ridiculous? Come on. Tell me about your nose."

"Would you believe me if I told you *I* walked into a door?"

"Nope. And here I am, out of the loop as usual."

"About the airport. It was Jo's decision not to tell you. She was on her way to meet her boyfriend's parents and—"

"Jo has a new boyfriend?"

"Not exactly new. She told me they'd been together about a year and a half."

The man's voice Amy heard on the phone. The shadow on the wall in Jo's photo.

"And that was the first time you heard about him?" she asked.

"Yes. She wanted my advice about her relationship since we'd be crossing paths at the airport. I was curious if I would read love on her face."

"Miss Poker Face?"

"Poker face or not, if it was true love, Jo wouldn't be able to hide it."

"She did. From me."

"Because you two didn't talk about him. Whenever she said his name, her face lit up, and I knew."

"And they're serious enough for her to meet his parents?"

"That was what she wanted my advice about. How to act around them. I told her to just be herself and be honest about her feelings for their son."

Amy reached down for the comfort of rubbing Moose's head. "I'm surprised she didn't tell me. And hurt. Really hurt. We share all our guy stories."

"Don't be, Amy. She feels awful about it, but she has her reasons. Good reasons. Their relationship concerns other people."

"Oh God, please tell me he's not married."

"No, nothing like that. But I can't say any more. And I'd rather she didn't find out that I told you. I don't like betraying her confidence."

"My lips are sealed. She'll tell me sooner or later."

Her dear Jo, in love for the first time. So vulnerable she didn't dare let her own sister see the crack in her armor. No wonder she didn't want to leave Seattle.

As Amy scratched behind Moose's ears, she replayed the tape of the airport scene in her head. Jo shaking her head vehemently—what was that about?

"Is that all you guys discussed? Her boyfriend?"

Theo rubbed his forehead as if trying to retrieve a memory—or rub one away. "Uh...yeah. Pretty much."

She took a deep breath. "And you're okay with Jo loving someone else?"

"Someone else besides who?"

A blush inflamed Amy's cheeks as she plucked those petals off. "Someone besides you. Since you're in love with her. Or was. Or..."

"Me. In love with Jo. Is this one of your jokes?"

"I...uh...no."

"You're serious?"

"You always...I mean, you and her..."

"I love Jo as a sister. A buddy. But that's it."

Amy wanted to jump off the sofa and do a celebration dance, but it would weird Theo out. And she might step on Moose.

"We wouldn't last a week as a couple. Believe me. I know." He rubbed the ridge of his nose. "Wow. Me in love with Jo. God, Amy."

"Guess Jo's not the only one with imagination," she mumbled.

"You can say that again."

"So why tell *her* about your nose but not me?"

"All right. I will. It happened during the stupid fight we had. Stupid *and* humiliating. Which is why we shut our traps about it."

"I'm a girl who walked into a patio door. Among other catastrophes. I know humiliation."

He flashed her a Theo-dimple smile as he got up to sit beside her. "Can you take another airport story?"

"Which airport this time? The one in Las Vegas?"

"Uh-huh."

"Did you really run into each other by chance?"

"Yeah. She was going to be in Vegas for a couple of days so I decided to stay and check out the city. Long story short, we got into a ferocious argument, I lost control of the rental car, and we were in an accident."

Amy gasped. "Bad enough to . . . to break your nose?"

"And for Jo to break her arm."

"How awful. I hope no other cars were involved."

"No. Just us."

"What in the world were you two arguing about?"

"Seeing all the wedding chapels, we got on the topic of our love lives," he said, mussing his hair. "Jo said I was 'unsuitable.' That no one would marry me with all my 'emotional baggage' as a damaged kid from a dysfunctional family."

"Jo? Jo said that to you?"

"Not at first. It escalated. I said some pretty nasty things to her, and it was like a competition for who could be the bigger jerk. Next thing I know, we're upside-down in the car, encased in air bags. We wanted to spare you the ugliness. And you know the saying: what happens in Vegas, stays in Vegas."

Sunlight was fading from the living room, and in the gathering shadows, Theo's face and body had simplified to planes of gray and black. Amy reached for his hand, seized with a sudden fear he'd vanish. Like the terrible day he'd disappeared into the doorway of his apartment and out of her life where all that lasted forever was her love for him. "But I didn't spare you any ugliness with the portraits," she said in a near whisper. "I placed my ambition above your feelings. Have I told you enough how very sorry I am?"

"More than enough. Rest your mind on that point forever.

As for Jo, her words only confirmed what your portraits had already told me. I *was* damaged. Worse, from what I'd learned studying to be a counselor, I would likely repeat the pattern of my dysfunctional family."

"But you're not your parents, Theo. You're one of the kindest, most generous, and thoughtful people I know. And I—"

"I threw a plate in anger at a colleague once. A shard cut his cheek. I never told you, because I knew you'd talk me into forgiveness like you always did. Make me feel okay about myself. But I didn't want to be let off the hook. Most of all, I didn't want you to keep playing the role of my emotional caretaker."

"But aren't we all caretakers for those we..."

The words would come. She couldn't hold them back any longer.

"I love you, Theo. I've been in love with you my whole life." She beat her hand against her chest. "And I know, deep in my heart, what a good man you are. Will *always* be."

"I'm finally ready to believe I'm worthy of your faith in me." Theo briefly touched his forehead to hers. "And I've been in love with *you* my whole life, Amy. I've carried you inside me through everything. Our childhood bond gave me a sense of belonging like no other. You were my true family."

Theo had loved her all along.

Amy's skin tingled as if shot with a bolt of electricity.

Theo had loved her all along.

He gently lifted a curl from her cheek. "Is there any chance you would have me in your life again?"

To have someone. What a quaint and lovely way to describe love.

Amy held out her arms. "Every chance in the world."

"Will you...Can we...?"

"Yes. The answer is always *yes*."

Theo stood and lifted her from the sofa. Her face in his neck, she swelled with his woodsy scent, absorbing him with every step as he carried her to his bedroom. She stretched her body along his on the bed, their lips nearly touching, a sweet suspension.

"Once I kiss you, it's all over," he whispered.

"Or it's starting."

"I won't want it to end."

"It doesn't have to."

Amy covered Theo's mouth with hers, lights dancing behind her eyelids as he nimbly unbuttoned her top, released her arms, and slid his hand in the waistband of her cloud pajama bottoms, pulling them down, along with her lace bikini panties. She pushed his undershirt above his head and tugged at his sweatpants until he kicked them off. She grasped his arm, his back, his neck as his hands dipped into her every crease and fold.

It was all happening so fast. Years of wanting him collapsed into breathless moments. She saw the seas heave in his eyes as he soaked in every inch of her body. Felt her skin glow as if dusted with the gold powder of butterflies. Their kisses burned her lips while she arched her mound and rubbed against the taut rod of his penis. She stroked its stiff curve and rubbed her thumb over the tip, drawing an animal groan from his throat.

"Not fair," Theo said hoarsely.

"Not fair," Amy whispered back as he smeared her creamy wetness, round and round, up, down, flicking her tender bud till she bucked and groaned and shuddered and spread her thighs to let him in. She heard the tear of the condom's foil before he plunged inside her. Back, forth, slippery, sliding into a burst of ecstasy, coming, until there was nothing left of her or him as they rode wave after rapturous wave.

"What happens next?" Amy asked when their hearts were beating regularly again.

"We do it again. But slower next time."

"Sorry. Couldn't help it."

"Me neither."

"How slow?"

"Slow enough to breathe."

"And not see stars shooting from our eyeballs."

"That too."

"We may have to go a few rounds," Amy said.

"I'm not going anywhere," Theo said. "No more moving target."

All the years of longing and waiting, and here they were, Amy and Theo, at long last.

CHAPTER THIRTY-FOUR

Now and then, in this workaday world, things do happen in the delightful storybook fashion, and what a comfort it is.
—LOUISA MAY ALCOTT, *LITTLE WOMEN*

True to his word, Theo drove Amy to work Monday morning. She didn't protest, though the day was warm and dry enough to cycle. What was a little more pampering when he'd cooked her meals, did her laundry, and had nursed her back to health all week?

He parked at the entrance of the English Department building. "What time should I pick you up, Professor?"

"Not sure. I have a ton of work and emails to catch up on."

"Don't push yourself too hard your first day back."

"Okay." She smoothed down his hair. "How is it you brush this mop, and ten minutes later you look like you went through a wind tunnel?"

"It's a special skill."

"And you have so many."

"Want another demonstration?"

Amy closed her eyes as Theo's hand slipped between her legs and slowly traveled the length of her thigh, her skin warm then hot beneath her skirt, the tights wet as his thumb rubbed her sweet spot, and their tongues entwined, and the windows fogged—

She pulled away, breathing heavily, and looked around. Fortunately, no one was nearby, though if someone were to look out their office window, she'd never live it down. "We better stop or we'll get arrested."

"Campus police," Theo murmured, nuzzling her neck. "Big deal."

"Don't underestimate them. When you deal with stressed-out, partied-out students, you get as tough as nails."

"If you say so." He sat back, looking at her through dreamy eyes. "You know what the best thing about us is?"

"Your tongue on my—"

Theo put his hand over her mouth, grinning. "The *second*-best thing is that we're old friends, but everything we do together feels like it's for the first time."

"If we dismiss the Roommatus Interruptus Incident."

They'd had a good laugh over the time they'd come close to making love and Theo's roommate walked in on them. As for the mystery of who had informed the press of his parents' identity, the ensuing scandal, and their estrangement—all of it was in the past and locked away forever. As if it were a solemn ritual, Amy had watched Theo delete the photos of the exhibit from his phone.

A group of students passed by the car, and one of them waved to her. Amy removed the seat belt and gathered her satchel and books. "Off to face the barbarian hordes and conquer them with pop quizzes and term papers. What do you have going on today?"

"A very full client schedule." Theo brushed a curl off her forehead. "You know what?"

"What do I know?"

"Now that we're together, I feel like...when I sit across from couples in the clinic, I won't be just watching and listening. I'll be *feeling* along with them."

"And what a wonderful couples counselor that makes you."

"I owe it all to you."

"To *us*." Amy pointed to her cheek. "Put 'er here."

He kissed her teardrop freckle. "I have an idea. How about I set up a double date with Lando and Stella? She's doing much better."

"I'd like that. They're really nice. Hey, can I ask a favor?"

"Anything."

"Promise you won't tell Jo I had thought you were in love with her. She'll tease me to the end of my days."

"Mercilessly. Yes, I promise."

"When I tell her about us, can I admit that I know about your argument in Vegas? She'll assume you told me anyway since couples tell each other everything."

"Not every couple."

"The ones in an honest, healthy relationship do."

He looked down with a slight frown. "Honest. Yeah. Sure. Go ahead."

With one final kiss, Amy got out of the car.

"Amy," Theo called out as she walked toward the building.

"Yeah?"

"There's something I have to—" He pulled his head back into the car, his hands gripping the steering wheel.

"What is it, Theo?"

"Nothing. Never mind," he said, driving away.

～◯

After a busy morning teaching and meeting with the Linguistics Department chair, Amy went to her office to eat the egg-salad sandwich Theo had made. She'd begged off lunch with Athena, not ready to share what had happened between her and Theo. She wanted to savor it privately a little longer. But a call to Jo couldn't wait.

After a barrage of big-sister questions to rival an investigative reporter, Jo started singing. "Amy and Theo, sitting in a tree. K-i-s-s-i-n-g. First came love, then came marriage, then came Amy with a baby carriage."

"Isn't that a playground ditty?"

Jo hooted with laughter. "I don't know a ditty from a doohickey."

"I thought you'd be more sarcastic," Amy said. "Or tease me about *mooning* over Theo since forever."

"Sarcasm's getting old, like the rest of me. Sounds like he's been mooning over you too."

"He has. Though *lusting* and *pining* describe us better."

"Guess this means your long history of dating crackpots is officially over."

Amy let out a deep sigh. "Really, what on earth was I thinking?"

"Now that I know you've been goofy in love all this time, I have a theory. You went out with the misfits knowing it wouldn't last, because your heart belonged to Theo."

"That is beyond cheesy."

Jo chuckled. *"It's a cliché for a reason*. Marmee told me you said that the last time you two talked."

"She doesn't sound happy with John. Did you pick up on that too?"

"Uh-huh. I considered texting him to run for his life."

"Jo. For the last time. Our mother is not a black widow."

"I am all-wise and all-seeing," Jo said in her dramatic fortune-teller voice.

"Marmee's been talking about Dad a lot lately. She calls him her one true love."

"They were adorable together. We're lucky our parents had such a loving relationship."

"Unlike Theo," Amy said.

Taking the sandwich from the Tupperware container, she waited for Jo to either confess she'd found *her* one true love or admit to her cruel remarks to Theo during their argument. But she should have known better.

"What are you chewing?" Jo asked.

"Egg salad à la Theo."

"You're making me hungry, and it's not even lunch hour here."

"Jo?"

"Yeah?"

"Theo told me what happened in Las Vegas."

"Did Teddy tell you that he and I . . . Wait. What *exactly* do you know?"

"About the accident. About all the horrible things you said to him."

"Told you I could be a real ball-breaker," Jo grumbled.

"If you mean you hit him below the belt, congratulations. Badly done, Jo."

"He said some pretty mean things to me too."

"You crossed a line, talking about his family."

"Yeah. Mea culpa. But he's the one who flipped the car."

"I can't believe you didn't tell me about it. And then lied that you broke your arm playing pickleball."

"*I* couldn't believe you didn't put two and two together. Broken arm, mad at Theo. Duh. Like the time he and I fell off our bikes racing each other. Anyway, we've made up and said our apologies. We're best buddies again. He even encouraged me to pursue the job."

Buddies with secrets. Theo encouraged Jo to move near him. Both thoughts flitted across Amy's brain, but she swatted them away. She was not going to put two and two together in this case, or get into a tizzy about Jo's unfinished remark, *Did Teddy tell you that he and I . . .*

"Hey, you're going to love this," Jo said. "I wasn't wearing any pants during the Zoom interview."

Amy laughed. "I could tell by the way you kept wiggling."

"My thighs were sticking to the plastic chair, and I was afraid they'd hear me squeak. Last time I pull a stunt like that, Amy Mamy."

"That reminds me. Athena and Thorne's friend came to visit and called me Amy Mamy too."

"He did?"

"Uh . . . I didn't say it was a *he*."

"He. She. Whatever. Amy Mamy isn't exactly original. It falls off the tongue like Joe Schmo."

"Yeah, but it was the way he said it. And looked at me. Like he knew me already."

"Flaky-artist alert," Jo said, between sounds of crunching.

"I'm not flaking out. What are you eating?"

"Pringles. So did you like the guy?"

"What guy?"

"Duh. Athena's friend. Thorne's. Whoever."

"Uh-huh. I was disappointed I didn't get to see him before he left. I would have liked to talk to him some more."

"Why? Was he interesting?"

"He had this larger-than-life thing going on. But the warm-hearted kind, not the egomaniac kind. Wanna hear another coincidence? He lives in Seattle too."

"So not a big deal, as my students say."

"So not *making* it a big deal. You're the one who's asking all these questions about him, Jo Schmo."

"Call me that again and you're toast."

"Empty threat when you live hundreds of miles away."

"Not for much longer. I was going to call you but you beat me to it. I was offered the position at your college, and I've accepted. *And* the administration hinted that they may set up a creative writing department in the not-too-distant future."

"Hot diggity dog!" Amy exclaimed. "I'm so proud of you!"

"Guess I should send you a bunch of balloons or something."

"Don't have to. I'm just happy you decided to move here. But will it be hard leaving friends behind?" *Like the boyfriend you haven't told me about yet? The one Theo said you're in love with?*

"I'll make new ones." Jo bit loudly into another Pringle. "You know me. Easy come, easy go."

The boyfriend might have fallen out of love with Jo, and she was hiding behind her usual bluster. Or, a sadder prospect to Amy, Jo had fallen out of love with *him.*

"Jo? About your *heart or art* philosophy of love. Do you ever think maybe you've got it wrong?"

Jo let out a groan. "All the time, little sister. All the time."

CHAPTER THIRTY-FIVE

*I have ever so many wishes, but the pet
one is to be an artist, and go to Rome,
and do fine pictures, and be the best
artist in the whole world.*
—AMY MARCH, *LITTLE WOMEN*

Taking a break from working on the portrait, Amy examined her face in the mirror above Theo's dresser. Her forehead and the lines bracketing her mouth were creased, and her jaw was stiff with tension. *Let's loosen up and do a waggle dance*, Ralph Wilkinson would say during art class. Amy was always surprised by how much exhilaration *and* anxiety she experienced while painting.

"That's what we artists do," she said to Nina, who was curled up on the bed. "We suffer for our art."

Nina narrowed her eyes and hissed.

"What's your problem?"

She jumped to the floor, fur bristling, and stomped out of the bedroom, tail in the air.

"Sorry," Amy called out. "For whatever."

Apologizing. To a cat. Who'd given her the hairy eyeball. And yesterday, begging forgiveness of the ferns she'd forgotten to water for two weeks. The button fern looked like it was on the verge of tears but was too parched to cry.

With one week to go before the college-sponsored art exhibit, Amy's life resembled Derek's sink, perpetually full of dirty dishes. There were testy emails from Fiona for missing faculty meetings and being "a wee bit tardy" with the budget spreadsheet. Complaints from students for returning their assignments late. Cancelled lunch dates with Athena. Two chapters behind in her book.

And Amy loved every stressed-out minute of it.

She had repainted the portrait, now called *Invisible Strings*, to reflect the new dynamic of the three friends. Theo and Amy sat shoulder to shoulder facing the viewer and the world beyond the canvas with open, expectant expressions, while Jo stood behind them in near profile, gazing out a window.

Amy changed into the T-shirt and jeans she'd let fall to the floor before collapsing onto the bed at dawn. The shirt was a gift from Theo, imprinted with the iconic photo of Billie Holiday singing her soul into a microphone. He'd admitted he never named any of the cats Billie because they'd remind him of Amy's absence from his life.

In the living room, Nina was sitting beside Coltrane on the sofa, watching Bessie watch Ray wrestle with his own tail. The pug named Abigail, soon to leave for her forever home, was pushing a ball across the floor with her snout. All five ignored Amy as she walked to the kitchen where Moose was licking toast crumbs off the floor—but stopped long enough to scowl at her. Moose? Scowling? What was this? Be a Douche to Amy Day?

Theo nodded hello as he listened to someone on the phone. His pale, drawn face was testimony to the long hours he'd donated to a Habitat for Humanity project all month. She should offer to make dinner and fold the pile of clean laundry that grew larger with every wash. Take his hand, lead him back to the bedroom, and express her gratitude for the T-shirt and for saying she painted her soul into a canvas.

Or, after breakfast, get right back to work on the portrait. A person could go crazy thinking about boyfriends, cats, and dogs.

"That was the janitor from Happy Haven," Theo said. "A pipe burst in the reception area, and I'm going over there to help with cleanup."

"Okay." Was *she* being a douche for being relieved she'd have more time to herself to paint?

Amy looked at Theo over the rim of her mug as she drank coffee. Or rather, at the top of his lowered head as he texted on his phone. This past month that they'd been Amy and Theo, he was as caring and attentive as she could wish. Though the cats had been more vocal than he recently. And he wore his *Broody Bear* face more often than not. But a thoughtful lover, whose eyes and hands lingered over her body as if he were memorizing it, was nothing to complain about. Everyone was entitled to their moods.

"Busy day ahead?" Amy asked.

"Not too bad."

"Any word from Clifford about your license?"

"Still on probation," Theo said. "But he's impressed with the progress of the couple who had difficulty communicating. They're doing great."

"I'm so glad. Good for you."

He didn't remark as he usually did that their loving relationship had made him a better counselor. But . . . no biggie.

Through the window, she watched sparrows sparring, their beady eyes fierce with the demands of nature. Eat, mate, build nests, feed their young, try not to be eaten. The clouds were racing across the sky as if they'd heard bad news.

Little had changed in their daily lives since Amy and Theo had entrusted their hearts to each other. Having experienced years of friendship—and estrangement—there were few surprises. Except the biggest one of all she'd never expected—something was missing between them. Something essential.

"Is rain in the forecast?" she asked as a shadow fell over the kitchen.

"Not sure," he said.

"I'm losing the light. Maybe I should move my easel to the living room." She rubbed her forehead. "Wait. That won't work. The porch throws too many shadows."

He got up and stacked plates in the dishwasher. "For a minute there, I thought you were worried the ground would be too wet for our picnic."

He'd planned a romantic sunset picnic in the park with a basket of wine, cheese, crackers, and fruit—and the prospect of putting the lust into the lusty month of May. The picnic that had completely slipped Amy's mind. Along with lust. Her absorption in her art was almost an illness. As soon as the painting was finished, though . . .

"Sorry I've been so absent-minded, Theo. The semester will be over soon, and I'll be more focused."

"S'okay," he said.

Never apologize unless it's absolutely necessary, Fiona had advised her. Fiona, to whom she had promised to deliver a report on faculty projects and upcoming publications. The unfinished draft of her book on *Idylls of the King* would not be one of them.

"Crap," she muttered.

"Thought of something else you forgot to do?" Theo asked.

"A report I should have turned in two days ago." And realizing that it might be *her* fault that something was missing between them.

"Better get to it."

"The picnic. Can we—"

"Postpone till tomorrow? Sure."

"Oh wait. I'm meeting Athena for dinner at the café tomorrow."

"Another time, then." He closed the dishwasher with a loud snap. "If I'm not back by four, can you feed the troops?"

"Uh-huh. And how about we drive into St. Louis and go to the botanical garden one of these days? Or something?"

"Sounds good."

Amy washed the mug, placed it in the cabinet—and couldn't resist the question. "Anything bothering you, Theo?"

"No. Not a thing."

She would have been more convinced if he'd looked at her and smiled when he said it.

~⌒◯

"So I'm slogging through a chapter of my book on the Brontë family, dying to uncork a bottle of wine," Athena was saying over dinner at As You Like It Café, "and I had to remind myself not to be an idiot. I mean, what if Thorne's sperm hit pay dirt?"

Amy brought a forkful of beef stew to her mouth, then

lowered it. "I love you, Athena. But I'd rather not discuss bodily fluids while I'm eating."

"You're the one who once talked about *fertilizing* eggs."

"I didn't go into detail about *how*."

Athena held up her portobello mushroom panini. "This is why I love to eat. As long as I'm putting food *in* my mouth, I don't have to worry about what's coming *out* of it."

"Fiona could use a filter. Or three. She's been commenting on my pheromones. I mean, who uses the word *pheromones* in conversation? And the other day she told me I *glowed*."

"She senses you're getting the big one. As in penis. A word I have no problem inserting into a conversation. Egads. Did I just say *insert*?"

"You did," Amy said, laughing. "Do *you* think I glow?"

"Like a supernova."

And here she was, feeling like a flickering candle.

"It shows in your art," Athena said. "The portrait you're painting is stunning. It's like a dam broke, and all this emotional energy came out in the faces and bursts of color."

"You're not just saying that because we're friends?"

"No, I mean it. Thorne said the same thing. And you know Mr. Keep Calm. He's not the type to gush or exaggerate."

"I'm too close to it—I can't tell. And Theo's no help. He thinks my doodles are masterpieces."

"Anyone can see the man is absolutely besotted when he looks at you."

And wary. Doubtful. If Amy read his glances correctly.

On the stool at the bay window, Ivy was strumming a lively Renaissance song on the mandolin. Her repertoire featured fewer dirges ever since, as she happily reported to Amy, she had coaxed an admission out of Karl that he was dyslexic. *Everything's so much better between us now*, she said. *Honesty is the only way to go in a relationship, don't you agree?*

Amy agreed. Even if honesty was uncomfortable. Unsettling. Like her honest emotion that something wasn't right with Theo. Or them. They were a *them*, weren't they?

She stabbed a cube of beef with the fork and chewed it till her jaws ached. She was *not* going to overthink their relationship. It had led her down too many wrong paths already.

"Am I hearing wedding bells, or will you and Theo delay the toothpaste-cap wars a little longer?" Athena asked.

"Indefinitely. After everything that's happened between us, we're trying not to take anything too seriously. Just enjoying each day as it comes." As good a reason as any to explain Theo's... reserve? Detachment? Preoccupation? There were a lot of synonyms for *emotionally distant*, and Amy didn't like any of them.

"Did Thorne bake any pies today?" Athena asked Robin, who'd stopped by to refill their water glasses. "Lemon meringue? Apple? No, wait. Pecan?"

"Cravings already?" Robin asked, sliding an amused glance at Amy.

"Where've you been, sweetie? I've been eating for two my whole life," Athena said.

"Would you settle for a cranberry or blueberry muffin?"

"I'll settle for both."

"How's Jaycee?" Amy asked him.

"Great. We're meeting up after the café closes." .

"Another love story in full swing," Athena said, watching Robin affectionately as he left to serve another table.

"When I was in a meeting with Gary the other day, I couldn't help giggling," Amy said. "I kept hearing you say he'd bend over backwards for me."

"Let's hope he doesn't. A showdown between him and Theo would get pretty ugly."

"Animal rescuer versus Jo Nesbø fan? I wouldn't put my money on Theo winning."

"Love makes you fierce, girlfriend. Take it from a mama bear in training."

"Actually, Theo wouldn't have to fight. He could just stick a puppy in Gary's face, and it would be all over."

Thorne strode to their table and put a cranberry muffin on each of their plates. "Better eat yours, Amy, before my adorable wife does."

"Gotta keep up my strength to boss you around," Athena said.

"Oh, like I'm not already a pushover."

"About that honey-do list I left on the kitchen table this morning..."

"Honey did," he said as he swooped down for a kiss.

Natural, spontaneous, easygoing dialogue. As hot between the sheets as Amy and Theo were, their conversations lately had been on the order of *You think maybe* and *If you don't mind.* Tentative phrases punctuated by long pauses in which one of them waited to see how the other reacted. Not that it was fair to compare themselves to the Murphy-Kents. Like a lot of couples who'd entered a new phase of their relationship, she and Theo were testing the waters.

Of course. That's what it was. Why hadn't she thought of it before? This time, at least, the waters weren't muddy at all.

The gravel crunched beneath the tires of the '57 Chevy as Theo maneuvered it into a parking space in the lot behind the converted barn. From the open car window, Amy smelled the rain-washed scent of the fluorescent-green grass. Roses and lilacs were on the verge of bursting into colorful splendor. A budding world as full of fresh beginnings that only spring—and an art exhibit—could promise.

She double-checked that her nails held no traces of paint from the portrait of Marmee she'd begun this morning and smoothed her curls. The past few days had been a whirlwind as she put the finishing touches on *Invisible Strings*, got the canvas framed, and submitted it to the exhibit, all the while trying not to get her hopes up. For what, she wasn't sure. Affirmation of her talent? Encouragement? Or something bigger, like a reason to exchange her darn good job for her dream job?

Amy paused before entering the barn, wishing she'd worn slacks instead of her favorite floral dress. Her bare legs made her feel more vulnerable. And despite Athena's conviction that ankle boots gave the wearer all the confidence they needed in this world, Amy's weren't doing a thing for her. The sign above the door, ART FROM ALL, ART FOR ALL, bothered her. And bothered her for bothering her. The sentiment of *from all* was well-meaning—unless you wanted art *from someone special*. And you wanted that someone special to be yourself.

"I can't believe I'm nervous," she said to Theo. "This exhibit is not a big deal."

"Sure it is." He squeezed her hand reassuringly. "You're putting yourself out there again. And it's not every day I wear a tailored white shirt."

"With jeans and a blazer—my favorite guy ensemble. And

no, you are not permitted to say yes to requests to be a male model."

"Are you sure? My career can use a plan B."

She squeezed *his* hand reassuringly in reply.

The cavernous space inside the barn had been made intimate by a series of portable walls arranged like honeycombs, each section devoted to a different art medium—drawing, painting, sculpture, jewelry, and ceramics. They wandered through each—saving painting for last—and mingled with teenagers, young families, and middle-aged couples. Amy recognized faculty from the college and local business owners. Everyone appeared dumbstruck by the impressive talents of their fellow citizens, including that of the matronly cashier at Bread and Board who created intriguing metal sculptures—as in, sexually explicit—using nothing but a blowtorch.

Theo grinned. "I *wondered* why she always compares the avocadoes I buy to testicles."

"Don't get me started on what she says about bananas," Amy said, reluctantly pulling her eyes away from a wooden bowl so impeccably carved it was mesmerizing.

"Ready to find your painting?"

"Let's reserve judgment till we see it on the wall with the other entries."

They entered the painting section, and in the millisecond before she recognized it as hers, Amy knew. As the intricate silver necklace and the sculpture of a mastiff's head were the best of their mediums, so was *Invisible Strings* the best of its kind. Her gift for portraiture was not only undiminished; it exceeded her expectations.

"Beautiful," Theo said reverently. "Stunning."

"It isn't just me? It is that good?"

"You are sublimely gifted, Amy Marsden."

After he took photos of the painting, and of her in front of it, they went to the honeycomb in the middle of the room marked RECEPTION. A table, covered in a white damask cloth, displayed delicate flute glasses, champagne bottles resting in ice buckets, hors d'oeuvres on fine china, cloth napkins, and bouquets of roses.

"Too bad Athena couldn't make it," Amy said. "She would have loved this."

"Morning sickness again?" Theo asked.

"And afternoon and evening sickness. Ever since her positive pregnancy test, she can't keep a thing down."

"Elegant reception, aye?" a familiar voice said.

Amy turned to see the dean standing behind her. Her dark hair circled her head in a braid. Her white peasant-style blouse and flowing blue skirt accentuated her trim figure.

"Fiona! How nice to see you," Amy said.

"We saw your painting, Amy. Simply marvelous!"

"Thank you so much. This exhibit has been inspiring and a great way to connect with the community."

"I suggested that they put fresh flowers on the table." Fiona turned to the woman standing next to her and draped an arm across her shoulder. "My bonny Brigid is the genius behind the rest of it."

"Brigid O'Hara," the woman said in introduction. "Pleasure to meet you, Amy."

She was even tinier than Fiona, impeccably dressed in a navy-blue linen suit. Blond down to her eyebrows, with ice-gray eyes, she might have been her partner's photo negative. And yes, she was as *bonny* as Fiona claimed.

"Thank you so much for making this exhibit possible," Amy said.

"The college has already requested that I manage and promote it again next year," Brigid said.

"Did you just arrive?" Amy asked Fiona. "We've been here a couple of hours, and I haven't seen you."

"We've been flittering in and out of this labyrinth," Fiona said. "Its design is another of Brigid's brilliant ideas."

Amy had no idea Fiona could *flitter*. She was about to introduce Theo to them, but Brigid poked a finger into his chest.

"And who are *you*?" she demanded. Her voice had gone from charming brogue to intimidating bark in two minutes flat.

"Theo Sinclair. Amy and I—"

"Oh. The boyfriend. Not going to get in her way, are you?"

He stepped back, away from her finger. "Excuse me?"

"I asked if you were going to gum up the works."

"I . . . uh . . . no. I don't think so. What works?"

Brigid pulled off her wire-rimmed glasses and, waving a hand as if to dismiss him, focused on Amy. "I'll get right to the point. I'm an art agent, and I'm on the hunt for fresh talent. It's one of the reasons why I arranged this exhibit, to see what it fetches up. I know talent when I see it, and you've got it in spades. You and the guy who did the watercolors of fish. But he's got an ego the size of this barn, so the hell with him."

"Good for you, Amy," Fiona interjected. "I had no idea you were an artist. You've never said a word."

"You never said Brigid was an art agent." Who got right to the point the way a dagger did.

"She does so many things it's hard for me to keep up," Fiona said with a fond glance at her partner.

"I can promise you commissions," Brigid went on as if they hadn't spoken. "Portraits, landscapes—you name it. Have a website? An Instagram account?"

Amy grabbed Theo's hand to steady herself in the whirlwind and shook her head. When Brigid snapped the glasses back onto her face, Amy had the urge to salute her.

"No problem," Brigid said. "I'll set you up. You have ambition, I hope."

"Burning with it." Like Amy March, who wanted to be "the best artist in the whole world."

"Right answer." Brigid produced a business card from her handbag. "Get in touch, and I'll get you going."

Amy and Theo watched in stunned silence as the two women walked away, arm in arm.

"What just happened?" Theo asked.

"I'm about to become a better version of myself," Amy whispered.

"Hey, you look pale. Are you okay?"

"Morning sickness. I do believe I may be giving birth to a career."

CHAPTER THIRTY-SIX

*I've got the key to my castle in the
air, but whether I can unlock the door
remains to be seen.*
—JO MARCH, *LITTLE WOMEN*

Theo slumped to the floor of the racquetball court, wiping the sweat off his face with the bottom of his T-shirt. "You cleaned my clocks," he said to Lando. "How did this happen? I usually kick *your* ass."

Lando pitched a ball across the room with a fierce strike of his racquet. "Stella's healing really well but we've had to ease up on frequency. I'm kind of backed up, if you get what I'm saying."

"You could have warned me I'd be playing with the testosterone terror."

Lando dropped down next to him, his sneakers squeaking the waxed floor. "*Stella's* a terror since she can't cycle. Her favorite entertainment is bossing me around. And eating nearly every hour. Sometimes I hear my mother's voice when she says, *Cut the sandwich in half this time, will ya?* And I turn into my father, yelling, *Cut your own damn sandwich.*"

Theo's laughter bounced off the walls of the court. Stella wasn't far off the mark, worrying they'd turn into Lou and Rose.

Though his counsel to her had been. Fortunately, she never alluded to it. The drama of her accident had put other issues front and center. The best he could hope for was that she'd dismissed his advice and that Lando's dedication had convinced her once and for all that they belonged together. Because the Marconi marriage wasn't perfect, but it worked. And whatever version of them Lando and Stella became, they'd make it work too.

He lifted the T-shirt from his chest and Amy's scent rose off his skin. Her own was so sensitive that if his hand even lightly touched her, goose bumps rippled across her body. *I'm a sea anemone*, she'd joke, fluttering her long, delicate fingers to describe the effect of his caresses. To think she had assumed he was in love with Jo! He still couldn't get over it. He'd observed the sisters for years and was well versed in their personalities and interactions. But he'd been blind, obviously, to so much else.

"Wanna fill me in on what's happening between *your* sheets lately?" Lando said.

"No way. There are limits to the bro code."

"Since when?"

"Since Amy."

Lando put a hand over his heart. "*Amico mio* is in love. As Stella says, it's about damn time."

"Out of curiosity," Theo said—and out of another emotion he'd been wrestling with—"do you tell Stella everything?"

"Let me put it this way. The woman can smell a secret on me like a heavy cologne. My record for keeping one is about thirty minutes."

Theo laughed. "Amy gets a kick out of her, especially when Stella jokes about delivering pizzas on her tricycle."

Though Amy was busy tying up the loose ends of the semester and working on a portrait Brigid had commissioned for her, the two couples had been socializing frequently. Theo was pleased they'd fallen effortlessly into a compatible rapport. He was glad too that they hadn't connected until he and Amy had moved on from their past, the sorrier details of which Lando and Stella were ignorant. It had taken him a few nights out with the Murphy-Kents before he felt completely comfortable with Athena, knowing Amy had confided in her about their personal history.

"I'm glad we all get along," Theo said. "The clients I counsel often complain about how hard it is to find other couple friends."

"You guys are great to play board games with," Lando said. "Mostly because Stella and I always win."

"And we stay awake watching movies while you two are snoring away."

"Some of us work hard for a living."

"Some of us are on probation and may not *have* a living." Theo got up and, extending his hand, pulled Lando to his feet. "Being with Amy makes up for everything, though."

"You're lucky she's cool with your career bump. Stella would be on my case if customers started throwing pizzas like yours throw pies."

"*Two* clients. *One* time. It's not like I host weekly pie-throwing fests."

"Maybe you should. You'd put the clinic on the map for your unconventional methods." Lando grinned. "You could add links to As You Like It Café on the Happy Haven website. It would give Thorne's business a boost."

Theo laughed—at the same time that he cringed at his career being the butt of a joke.

Two women who had signed up to use the racquetball court the next hour entered and waved. "Time to hit the showers," Theo said, waving back at them.

"Make mine a cold one," Lando groused.

"Wanna grab a beer afterward?" Theo asked as they walked to the locker room.

"Can't. My parents are coming over for dinner."

"They stopped attending sessions when they filled in for you at Marconi's Pizza."

"There goes my master plan that they'd turn into a normal couple."

Theo lightly punched Lando's shoulder. "Lou and Rose are normal in their own Lou-and-Rose way. And it was very supportive of them to back you up at the restaurant."

"The bad news is, I'll never hear the end of their big sacrifice and how only one of them could cover their precious deli at a time."

"The good news?"

"As far as I can tell, they haven't done the nasty in the supply room."

Theo's phone lit up, signaling a missed call. Amy's smile and golden curls shone on the home screen.

Lando shook his head and whistled. "Amy Marsden, beautiful, brainy, and, to quote Stella, one badass painter. Ever wonder if she's out of your league? What am I saying? Of course she is."

"Don't you ever get tired of breaking my balls, Orlando?"

"But you're such an easy target, Theodore."

"You're the one who told me that all I needed to be in a serious relationship was to let a woman find me."

"Boy, I can really shovel the bullshit."

"Truckloads."

"I also told you to do everything to keep her."

Theo slammed the locker door. "Amy's not going anywhere."

Or was this something else he was blind about?

Burning with it, she'd said of her ambition—which she'd once chosen in favor of his feelings.

I can't let anyone or anything get in the way of my art, as she also said.

They showered, dressed, and went their separate ways, Lando's comments lurking in the corners of Theo's mind as he drove home. The dark recesses where moody Theo, and his career problems and emotional baggage, let the old fear creep in—that he was all wrong for Amy.

⌀

Stella hobbled on crutches around the apartment she shared with Lando, offering Amy and Theo wine and appetizers, arranging and rearranging pillows on the sofa where they sat.

"Take it easy, my star," Lando said, placing a pizza loaded with peppers, onions, and mushrooms on the trivet on the coffee table. "You're overdoing it."

"You know I can't sit still, my general."

"Look who thinks she's invincible."

"Look who can kiss my *culo*."

Lando reached for a slice of pizza but pulled back. "Too hot."

A mischievous smile lit Stella's elfin face. "That's what you say about *me*."

"*Scorching* is what I say about you."

"Shut up—you love it," she retorted, easing into the recliner.

Theo watched Amy react as she often did to the couple's lively exchanges—with a mixture of amusement and wistfulness. Missing the playfulness of their own banter, he supposed. It was all his fault. His wit was as flat as his spirits lately.

"How much longer will you need crutches?" Amy asked Stella.

"Not much longer. It hasn't been totally bad, though. Especially the part where Lando does the laundry."

"Theo spoiled me rotten when I was sick."

"And what do you call breakfast in bed when you *aren't* sick?" Theo asked.

"A healthy relationship."

"Everybody's a comedian."

"Everybody's a happy camper."

Her eyes sparkled, waiting for more. He kissed the teardrop freckle on her cheek but couldn't think of a thing to say.

"We're pretty lucky our guys like to cook," Stella said to Amy.

"I don't have a choice," Lando said. "You can barely scramble an egg."

"Why bother cooking when there are so many great restaurants? Not that I get out much lately. Hint, hint."

"I'm too exhausted waiting on you."

"If you want a girls' night out," Amy said, "Athena and I can take you to the As You Like It Café or Benny's Bar."

"You're on. If I'm going to be stuck in this Podunk town indefinitely, I might as well make more friends."

"Here you go again," Lando said. "I told you we'll visit Boulder as soon as you ditch the crutches."

"You guys planning any trips together?" Stella asked Amy and Theo.

Amy laughed. "Are you kidding? We can't even plan a picnic."

Theo put a slice of pizza on his plate and hers. "It's cooled off enough to eat. Blow on it first, though."

"Let's go for it," Lando said.

Amy moaned as she ate. "Your pizzas are the best I've eaten in my life."

"My guy is a genius chef," Stella said. "Plus, he's so cute I can't stand it."

"But not cute enough to marry," Lando said.

"And become Lou and Rose? No way."

"Come on, Stella. You don't still think we're gonna turn into them, do you?"

"Don't want to risk it."

"Oh, I get it. You'll race a bike a hundred miles an hour but won't risk getting married."

"We're fine the way we are."

"Did your parents get along better when they were apart all day?" Theo asked Lando.

"They were *more* miserable. Go figure."

"What I figure is they weren't miserable to start with," Theo said.

"Could have fooled me," Stella said with a snort.

"If the couples I've counseled have taught me anything, it's that what you see is not necessarily what's really going on between them. And that there's no one formula for success in marriage."

"Success meaning what?" Lando asked.

"That the couple puts the relationship first. Makes it a priority," Theo said. "I'll say one thing for your parents. Through thick and thin and years of locking horns, they've kept their marriage alive and thriving."

"Wait a minute." Stella kicked the recliner footrest to a closed position. "That's not what you told me."

"I didn't always think this," Theo said. "It's only recently that I—"

"I thought you agreed with me that Lando and I shouldn't get married because we would be just like Lou and Rose. That their marriage stinks, and they should get a divorce."

Oh. Shit.

"What?" Lando shot up from his chair like a coiled spring. "What are you saying, Stella?"

"Chill, babe."

"The hell I will."

"Stella came to me for advice about getting married," Theo said.

"Oh yeah? When was this?" Lando demanded.

"Like, ages ago," Stella said.

"At the time, I believed it was inevitable that relationship patterns repeated themselves," Theo said. "It's conventional wisdom in counseling, though certainly not true in every case."

Amy gave his arm a sympathetic squeeze. Without violating client confidentiality, he had related that his advice to the Spragues—that they were not doomed to repeat their parents' failed marriages—had given him insight into his own concerns about his dysfunctional family.

Lando's wiry frame bristled with anger. "You tell me you don't think you should get involved in our relationship. Meanwhile, you're talking to my girl in secret, telling her we shouldn't get married. You fucking asshole."

"It's not his fault," Stella said. "I wanted his professional opinion."

"Behind my back?"

"Theo's a friend *and* a counselor, so I figured—"

"He's a guy who can't stay with a woman for longer than a month."

Stella darted a glance at Amy. "Yo, babe. Watch what you say."

"It's all right," Amy murmured.

"I'm sorry, Lando," Theo said.

"Deceptive jerk," Lando said.

Amy reached for Theo's hand just as one of the sayings on the Happy Haven posters came to mind.

Three things cannot stay long hidden: the sun, the moon, and the truth.

"Well," Lando said, jutting out his chin, "what do you have to say for yourself?"

"I thought I knew what I was talking about," Theo said. "I believed that I was giving Stella the right advice."

"That I asked for," Stella reminded Lando.

"Can you forgive me?" Theo asked him.

"It depends." Lando folded his arms across his chest. "Stella Maria Amoroso, are you going to quit bullshitting around and marry me already? I'm so crazy about you I can't think straight."

Stella took the bowl of olives from the table and began placing them on top of the pizza. When she was done, they all leaned over to read the word *YES*.

CHAPTER THIRTY-SEVEN

Never get tired of trying, and never think
it is impossible to conquer your fault.
—MARMEE MARCH, *LITTLE WOMEN*

Amy woke as she did most days, with her face buried in Theo's neck and her arm across his broad back. Hip to hip, breath to breath. Whatever separate dream journeys they took in the night, she liked to think that they emerged each day as if they'd traveled together. She loved to watch him sleep. He looked like a god who'd tumbled from the heavens. Who'd never return there, having found sanctuary in her arms. Even in repose, Theo wore a vaguely troubled expression, his brow furrowed as if he were looking for her. "I'm here," she'd whisper. And he'd reach for her hand, fold her in one muscled arm, and hold her tightly.

The night-light, competing with the sunshine behind the blinds, flickered off. She eased away from him and lay on her back, looking around his bedroom. Nina and Coltrane had left to join the others in the living room, including a mutt named Rocky that Lando kept teasing Stella he was going to adopt. Theo's jazz CD collection was scattered all over the floor, and his laundry was tossed in a chair. If his clothes ever made it to the closet, it would be a miracle. As tidy as she was, she found his dishevelment endearing.

Give it time, Athena had joked. *In six months, you'll nag him about leaving his shoes all over the place.*

Amy counted six months in her head, stopping at December. He'd be *winter Theo* then, dedicated to his career, volunteer projects, and foster animals. She'd be in the last stretches of the fall semester and working on as many commissions as Brigid arranged. Sharing the life they wanted to live— with the addition of Jo. Their original friendship configuration restored. Her belief that she and Theo belonged together beautifully realized. Exactly what she'd wanted. Life was good.

Website and Instagram account in place, she had another commission for a portrait of a woman's beloved grandfather. She was especially proud of how she was capturing both the weariness and spirit in Frank's eyes, the spiky gray hairs of his whiskered chin, and the knobby bones of his fingers wrapped around a cane. The semester having ended, she'd have time to give it her full attention. And other people and tasks she'd been neglecting. Including Theo.

She curled into a cashew, absently raking her fingers through his hair. He sometimes seemed like an impressionist painting to her—out of focus, open to interpretation. Maybe she'd create a portrait of him with one of the animals. Coltrane, probably. Alone would be better, though. Then she could concentrate on his expression as he listened to jazz, fixed something, or brooded like Jo's *Broody Bear*.

"Know what day it is?" Theo mumbled sleepily.

"The first day of the rest of my life," she replied, mocking the quote on one of the Happy Haven posters.

He rolled over and rested his head on his hand. "It feels like it's my first day, now that I'm off probation and back on track for my license."

Amy kissed him lightly on the forehead. "It was very thoughtful of your clients to write letters on your behalf. Especially the couples."

"I would have admitted to Clifford that his *care and communicate* philosophy was spot-on, but I was afraid he'd insist I wear sweater vests and Hush Puppies."

"You'd totally rock the Clifford look. Maybe I'll paint a portrait of you wearing your counselor face."

At the sight of the strained tendons of his neck, her own muscles tensed. There it was again, the anxious frown. "What is it, Theo?"

"The thing is...I've been thinking..."

"Yes? About what?"

"What Brigid said the day we met her. About me getting in the way of your art."

"Brigid, the human steamroller? Nothing gets in her way or anyone associated with her."

But her joke did not relax Theo's look of concentration, the one he wore when he was repairing an appliance or solving a problem. She had the distinct impression one of them was missing a part, and the problem was their relationship.

"Back up the train a bit," she said. "How did you get from sweater vests to...what? Stifling my creativity?"

"I wonder whether an offbeat guy...someone more...you know..." He closed his eyes briefly and emitted a sigh. "I don't know what I'm saying."

"I do. You want to add *artist's muse* to your already impressive resume."

"No. I just wonder…uh…if I'm the right one to…uh…"

"The right one to finish a sentence."

Wisecracking Amy was back, a version of herself she hadn't been since Derek. And didn't want to be ever again, now that she and Theo were a couple.

Assuming they were.

She lay watching the ceiling fan go around and around. She hated this. She hated going around and around in an endless circle of doubt. Amy Marsden was confident, talented, and competent. And Amy and Theo were most definitely a couple.

Weren't they?

Theo rubbed his stubbled chin. "We slept in. I better feed everybody."

"Are you serious?"

He yawned. Her heart was beating like crazy and he was yawning.

"You can't drop a comment like that and walk away from it, Theo."

"I was just thinking out loud."

"Thinking you're not right for me."

He got up and left the bedroom, saying something about making breakfast.

Amy listened to the clatter of bowls and the gurgling of the coffeemaker and watched the damn fan go around and around until her percolating anger drove her from the bed, steered her past *Invisible Strings* on the living room wall above the fireplace, and straight to the kitchen.

"You're sloppy, you should have ditched your T-shirts years ago, and you say all the animals are equal, but you give Coltrane preferential treatment," she announced.

"Okay," Theo said, startled.

"That's me, thinking out loud."

Amy marched through the obstacle course that was Moose, Rocky, and the cats and poured herself a mugful of coffee. She ignored Coltrane's indignant stare from where he sat on his favorite chair. Theo's head was lowered over the bowl of granola he was pouring milk into. The Quaker Oats guy on the oatmeal box on the counter, with his Ramon-weird hat, dorky hairdo, and simpering smile, was on the verge of lecturing her. Something along the lines of how she was overreacting and overthinking. Theo was kind and true and caring and moody and reticent and elusive and—

The hell with the Quaker Oats guy.

"Something's not right between us, Theo."

He blinked a few times as if he were mentally changing channels. "I'm not sure what you mean."

"Like no one's ever said this in your counseling sessions?"

"Yes. But they're not us."

"*Us.* Aha! Now we're getting somewhere."

She scraped a chair across the floor, and Moose licked her ankle when she sat down. Bare feet were a distinct disadvantage in an argument. As was an opponent who calmly ate granola while you were gearing up for a fight. Nina, a possible ally, had gone back upstairs as she did most mornings after breakfast. This frustration must have been what Brittany felt when she was mad and Theo had kept his cool.

"Anything you want to say to me, Theo?"

"What is it you expect, Amy?"

"I expect to feel like we're a couple, not housemates who sleep together. For our relationship to be a priority, as you said.

I want us to be AmyandTheo. One word." She shooed Moose away with a light kick.

"I haven't complained when your painting took priority over us. If anything, I've been supportive and encouraging."

"So why say you may not be right for me? I'll tell you why. What you really mean is, *I'm* not right for *you*."

"You're way off the mark."

"Maybe I am. But that's what it feels like."

"It's not like you to be unreasonable, Amy."

"Surprise, surprise, Theo."

"You must be in the mood to pick a fight."

"Oh, and now you're going to ask if I'm getting my period."

Insult roiled in his stormy-sea eyes. "I would *never* do that."

"Would you ever be in the mood for a fight?"

"What's that supposed to mean?"

"Couples argue, Theo, and it's not the end of the world. Sometimes it's healthy."

"This has nothing to do with avoiding conflict because of my parents."

"Huh! You said it; I didn't."

"This is about making a mountain out of a molehill."

"Who are you to say that what I'm feeling is a molehill?"

He ran his hand through his hair and looked up at the ceiling. "All I did was make a few stray comments, and next thing I know, you're telling me I'm sloppy."

"You are."

"Deal with it," Theo said. And he picked up his spoon to resume eating.

Where was a pie when you needed one? They'd call it the

Clearing the Air Once and for All Pie Incident. Moose would clean up the mess.

And then it hit her, looking at Theo's head bent over the bowl of cereal. The vulnerable boy from the dysfunctional family, the man who kept women at arm's length, was backing away from Amy, the serial dater, to protect himself. Amy, whose sister was exiting yet another relationship and whose mother was a serial Mrs. Somebody.

She stirred a spoonful of sugar into the coffee but didn't drink it. Who needed caffeine for a wake-up jolt when a snit fit had done the job? "I know I've been in and out of relationships like a revolving door. But I'm not going anywhere this time, Theo."

He looked at her with a searching expression. A pair of cardinals, attracted to the backyard feeder, flew past the window. It was so quiet she might have heard their fluttering wings.

"I mean it," she said. "Really and truly. And I'm sorry."

"Me too," he said in a low voice. "For everything."

"Being sorry for everything is the same as being sorry for nothing."

A smile lit his face, the first she'd seen in days.

"Poster-worthy?" she asked.

"Yeah. But I have a more important question for you. Am I Amy-worthy?"

She got up, sat in his lap, and wrapped her arms around him. "I'll let you know after makeup sex."

"Our first fight," he said. "If this doesn't officially make us a couple, I don't know what does."

❧

Amy curled in an armchair in the living room, letting lazy Sunday lassitude cover her like a blanket. The cats, including Nina, stretched in the patch of sunlight on the floor, ignoring the birds chirping through the screened window. Her own personal messes were tidied up—Frank's portrait was complete, the first draft of her book was nearly finished, all her chair duties were fulfilled, and life with Theo was delicious again. Nothing like a little bicker and banter to keep the spark between them lit.

She was thankful that his friendship with Lando and the foursome's social life had been restored. Their reconciliation had occurred in fits and starts. *Life is like pizza*, Lando declared after finally accepting Theo's apology, *messy but worth the trouble.*

From behind his study door, Theo's voice was a low rumble as he advised Jo about neighborhoods and moving companies. Unfortunately, none of his houses were available to rent, and Jo didn't want to impose her rambunctious bulldog, Brutus, on them or the Murphy-Kents. Lydia assured her that she'd find her a pet-friendly property, and Gary said he'd keep an eye out for vacancies in his apartment building.

Moose's ears perked up as Theo started speaking in louder, sharper tones. *Pest*, Amy heard him say. Or maybe *presence*. And then *airport*. She definitely heard *airport*.

Jo and Theo squabbling. Yep, it was going to be just like old times.

Nina raised her head, hearing the muffled chime ringtone of Amy's phone, then dropped it to the floor again without opening her eyes. Amy retrieved the phone from beneath the seat cushion where she'd stuffed it to ignore Brigid's latest volley of text messages. Even a "rising star" on the art scene, as Brigid described Amy to potential clients, should be allowed to enjoy a Sunday off. But it was her mother calling.

"Hello, Amy dear."

"Hi, Marmee. It's great to hear from you."

"You'll be seeing me in person soon. I'm heading home."

"Are you and John finished checking out roadside attractions?"

"John and *I* are finished. I'm driving a rental car, all by my lonesome."

"Since when?"

"Since Scarborough, Maine, when I saw Lenny."

Amy straightened herself from her relaxed position. She supposed she should be glad that Marmee was moving on to another husband without the death of the previous one, but it was hard to rustle up the enthusiasm. "Lenny who?"

"Not who. *What.* Lenny the Chocolate Moose. Seventeen hundred pounds of chocolate in the shape of a moose. One look at that ridiculous creature and I thought, *What on earth am I doing with a man who is fascinated by this?*"

"You had an epiphany."

"Two epiphanies. I decided I'm going back to college to finish my degree. I've saved money along the way, and it's time I put it to good use."

"That's wonderful, Marmee!"

"*Oui, c'est magnifique.* I'm going to enroll in your college. Jo's college now too."

"Have you told her yet?" Amy asked.

"It's impossible to get her on the phone. And I don't want to text the news."

"Keep trying. She's busy with the move from Seattle."

"I am so proud of my girls! Two professors in one family."

"Maybe three, if you hang in there."

"If I can stick with a job in a shoe store, I can stick with anything. Did I ever tell you how ugly most people's feet are? Corns, bunions. Ugh."

"I am sorry about you and John."

"Don't be. It's so good to be *Meg* again, not *Maggie* or *Peg* or...or..."

"Madge."

"I'm Meg Beauregard Marsden, and I'm loving it."

"What exactly happened?"

"I told John to head the Minnie Winnie thingie toward home so we could regroup. See who we were when we weren't in motion. If we should stay together or divorce."

Like Amy and Theo, no longer in motion.

"Makes perfect sense to me," Amy said. And if John considered the fate of Marmee's former husbands, it would seem a fair option to him too.

"He said I couldn't divorce him, because I'd never make it on my own. And that, as far as I was concerned, was the coup de grâce."

"Bien sûr."

"Let him look at pig hair balls in Oregon by himself."

"Oh, I completely forgot about the pig hair balls."

"Wish I could." Marmee sighed. "We did have some fun times. And John is, at heart, a good man."

"Just not the man for you."

"No. Not for me."

"How come you're driving and not flying?" Amy asked.

"I went to the airport but for some reason just couldn't get on the plane. It's so confining. So I rented a car. And I discovered that I love being alone on the road. I don't care how much it will cost."

"Don't worry about it. I'll pay for it. You just enjoy yourself."

Her mother giggled. "I feel like Thelma in *Thelma & Louise*. Or Louise. Or both of them. But before they went over the cliff in the Thunderbird."

From Marmee, sainted literary figure, to Thelma and Louise, feminist cinematic heroines. Amy's do-nothing Sunday had suddenly filled with all the possibilities her mother might become. "You're starting a grand adventure. I'm so proud of *you*, Marmee."

"All those husbands. What was I thinking? Trying to duplicate my happiness with your father—that's what."

Amy's memories of her dad—laughing heartily at the dinner table over one of Jo's jokes, sneaking gumdrops to Amy during Sunday church services—were fewer and farther between with each passing year. His image was fading to sepia tones. But then there was Marmee, to whom he was still colorful and vibrant—and always would be. She was the witness to his life. He was The One to her, and she would honor what he meant to all of them.

"And how is Theo?" her mother asked. "Is he your one true love like my Henry?"

"You know he is, Marmee." They had shared a sweet, slightly weepy conversation the day Amy told her that she and Theo were a couple.

"I just *knew* one of my girls would suit him someday," Marmee said. "And goodness knows Theo deserves some happiness in this life."

It had always troubled Amy that Laurie in *Little Women*

transferred his affections from Jo to Amy. How was it possible when someone had laid claim to your heart? And the comparison of Laurie to Derek was disconcerting, to say the least. Girlfriend out, girlfriend in. But for the Marsden sisters to be as interchangeable to Theo as Marmee's husbands were to her was unthinkable.

Amy was about to challenge her mother's comment, but Marmee spoke first.

"Have you had a chance to read Jo's story, Amy?"

"Which one?"

"The one in the *New Yorker*. It's wonderful."

"Jo didn't tell me it had come out yet."

"Me neither. I think because she's so scatterbrained with the move. I subscribe to the magazine and read the latest issue on my laptop this morning."

"I subscribe too. I'll check it out. What's it about?"

"A modern marriage of convenience. She had told me it's based on a true story about a trip she took to Las Vegas."

"True story? You're sure that's what Jo said?"

"I am. But you know your sister. I think she was pulling my leg."

"She does love to tease you," Amy said faintly, all her blood having rushed to her feet. Jo never joked about her writing. Ever.

"I just thought of something," Marmee tittered. "Wouldn't it be funny if one of you was my English professor? Or both of you?"

"Uh...yeah...very funny."

Once Amy had congratulated her mother again for her new life plans, she couldn't get off the phone and upstairs to her study fast enough. Reading the heading of the first page of the *New Yorker* story on her laptop, she wanted to fall onto the floor and twine her body around a chair leg like one of the cats.

Schism by Jo Marsden
To T. S., with love

To Theo Sinclair.
Who had been in Las Vegas with Jo.
For a marriage of convenience.

CHAPTER THIRTY-EIGHT

I will not be the person you settle for
just because you cannot have her.
—AMY MARCH, *LITTLE WOMEN*
(2019 FILM)

*W*hat happens in Vegas does not stay in Vegas. It is a perpetual memory. A recurring dream. A film reel playing over and over in a continual loop. It is Jane and Tom in a rusted rental car beneath a pitiless Nevada sun, inching closer to their drive-thru wedding. Jane and Tom arguing so passionately the car rocks, then bursts out of line, into traffic, into a rollover. It is Jane and Tom singing "All Shook Up" in a hospital ER with an Elvis impersonator with whiskey breath and one rhinestone too many on his white jumpsuit.

And out of the story, into real life, they are sitting on those vinyl hospital chairs, Jane's broken arm in a sling, Tom's broken nose bandaged. The baby-faced couple across from them is oblivious to anything but their interlocking tongues. They don't have a complicated past. They don't worry about the future. They don't discuss marital tax advantages, personal autonomy, or the artist's creative imperative. They are the present tense.

Will Jane accept Tom's proposal and marry him? Does she dare to go into the present tense with him?

Amy cleared "Schism" from the screen and slammed the laptop shut as Marmee's words rang in her ears.

Based on a true story.

One of my girls would suit him.

The joke that had turned into reality—Theo asking Jo to follow through on their promise to marry if they were still single in their thirties.

He'd assured Amy he wasn't in love with Jo, and she believed him. What she couldn't believe was that he'd asked Jo to marry him—a marriage of convenience, but nevertheless, a marriage—and never breathed a word of it to her. Deceptive, Lando had called him. Theo had most likely sworn her own sister to secrecy. But then, he and Jo always did have a special JoandTheo connection.

Or maybe the story was another of Jo's fanciful turns of imagination, like her black widow version of Marmee.

Or maybe...

One of my girls would suit him.

As restless as the clouds scuttling across the sky, Amy had to move her body, exert something other than her mind, which was in a spiral, going nowhere fast. Throwing on a T-shirt, shorts, and sneakers, she went outside, down the steps, and hurried up the walkway as if she were making a getaway. She glanced at the porch where Theo was fitting the screen into the storm door.

"There you are," he called out. "Where are you going?"

"For a walk."

"Wait up. I'll change and go with you."

"I'd rather you didn't."

He put his hand to his ear. "What'd you say?"

"I don't want you to come with me," she said loudly enough to catch the attention of Mr. Shea at his mailbox across the street.

"What's going on, Amy?"

Climbing the porch steps, she squared her shoulders and looked him straight in the eye. "I read Jo's story in the *New Yorker*, dedicated to you. It's about your marriage of convenience in Las Vegas."

"All right." Theo clasped his arms across his chest. "Okay."

"No. It is not *all right*," Amy said through clenched teeth. "There is absolutely nothing *okay* about this either."

"What I'm trying to say is—"

"Don't beat around the bush. Is the story true or not?"

"I haven't read it yet, but I know what it's about."

"It's about you asking Jo to marry you. Yes or no?"

"Yes."

She held on to the porch railing to keep her balance. "And I'm just finding out about this?"

Theo looked past her, squinting, as if he were scanning the horizon. "I couldn't say anything. You know Jo. She's superstitious about discussing her stories before they're published."

So Jo's writing was more important to her than being honest with her sister.

As her ambition had been more important than Theo's feelings about his parents' portraits.

And . . . it *was* the *New Yorker*.

And Jo *did* worry about jinxing her stories.

But still.

Amy paused to breathe. "Jo and her superstitions aside—you asked my sister to marry you. A legal arrangement for tax purposes and whatever. Like...like not being lonely in your old age. But it doesn't matter. What matters is that you were deceptive, Theo. Like you were to Lando, your best friend. And I'm having a hard time getting my head around that."

Sir Theo the Deceiver. Not the honorable man she thought he was after all.

She spun around and practically flew down the porch steps. A cardinal chirped from one of the bushes, a cheerful sound to break her heart and release her tears. Her swift walk became a jog as she moved farther and farther away from Theo's voice crying out, "Wait, Amy! You've got it all wrong."

∼◯

Amy had no idea how long or how far she had jogged. Her chest burned and her palms hurt where her nails had dug into them. As with ice-skating, she discovered muscles she'd forgotten she had. House after house, tree after tree, one mile had become another. She slackened her pace and stopped to relieve the stitch in her side.

Across the street, kids were shooting baskets. Catching sight of her, one of the boys seemed to lose focus and let his ball bounce off the rim. One by one, they all turned to look at the woman with a hand to her galloping heart and what must have been a distraught face. Mistaking her for someone who might be sick or dangerous. As she had been mistaken about Derek's talent and Gary's character.

As she might be mistaken about Theo. It wouldn't be the first time.

You've got it all wrong.

"Dear God, let me be wrong," she prayed.

With what Amy hoped was a friendly wave to the kids, she turned around and began walking back home. The shadows of late afternoon were advancing as she approached the house. Theo was sitting on the top step of the porch, drinking beer. He'd changed his clothes and his hair was wet from a shower.

"Want some?" he asked, holding out the bottle.

Something she might say and do—turn tension and awkwardness into nonchalance.

"No thanks." She climbed the stairs and sat as far away from him as nonchalance allowed. "I'm ready to listen. Tell me what I've gotten wrong this time."

"I don't blame you for feeling deceived."

"I don't really care if you blame me or not. I just want the truth."

Theo swigged beer from the bottle and wiped his mouth with the back of his hand. "What I told you about the argument with Jo in Vegas is the truth. But for the sake of keeping her story confidential, I had to leave out the details."

"And the devil's always in the details."

"As I told you, we ran into each other by chance at the Las Vegas airport. She was there to research a story, either on weddings or Elvis impersonators, she wasn't sure which, and wanted to soak up the atmosphere. I was on a stopover but decided to hang out with her for a couple of days." He took another sip of the beer. "We were checking out wedding chapels, and I *did* ask her to marry me—as a joke. I mean, I was *laughing* when I said it. But Jo didn't find it very funny."

"Really? The situation has Jo humor written all over it."

Theo turned to face her, his blue-green eyes glittering. "I made the mistake of saying we were two losers no one else would want, so why not follow through on our pact? That's when she turned on me, and called me damaged and needy. She said that I had so much emotional baggage I didn't stand a chance of anyone loving me, much less marrying me."

A mess of emotions as smudged as one of her paint palettes surged through Amy. Relief. Sympathy. Sadness over her sister's cruel words.

"Just so you know, I gave Jo shit for saying those terrible things to you," she said.

"Like I said, I gave as good as I got, calling her a man-eater and a ball-breaker. She went ballistic over the word *loser* most of all, though."

"Worst proposal ever."

"No kidding. When we met in the St. Louis airport, she explained that she'd just fallen in love with her boyfriend when we were in Vegas. She was touchy and defensive because she was afraid she'd blow it with him. That she *was* a loser. I'd struck a very tender nerve."

"Too bad she's leaving him behind in Seattle. Or he's letting her go."

"Neither. They're moving here together."

"Really? Oh, I'm so glad!"

"Another of Jo's secrets, but I'm telling you anyway."

"Afraid she'll jinx the relationship, I guess, like the story."

"And she's worried you'll talk about it to someone."

"Geez, it's not like I'm gossip central. I really don't get what's up with her. Is he famous or something?"

"All I know for certain is that other people who live in

Laurel are involved. They prefer waiting till they get here to announce it."

"Jo's not usually a drama queen."

Ever the drama queen, Athena had said to her friend Quentin.

"Love makes fools of us all," Theo said.

"A poster quote?"

"No. I think I read it in a fortune cookie."

Amy reached for his hand and gently kissed his knuckles, bruised from carpentry work. "It's *my* turn to say sorry for everything. For assuming the worst about you."

Theo lowered his head and swung the beer bottle between his legs. "Don't apologize. You don't *know* the worst."

The branches of the river birches drooped low over the walkway. Amy's senses were acutely tuned to the scent of honeysuckle and the slam of a car door three houses down. Theo breathing in, breathing out. The thundering beat of her heart.

"My parents' portraits. It was me, Amy. I'm the one who identified them to the press. I wanted to bring them out in the open and end their charade of a marriage." Theo stopped twirling the bottle and hurled it across the lawn. "And I wanted an excuse to cut you out of my life for good."

CHAPTER THIRTY-NINE

Don't let the sun go down upon your anger. Forgive each other, help each other, and begin again tomorrow.
—MARMEE MARCH, *LITTLE WOMEN*

The dried salt of tears washed from her face, Amy wandered from bedroom to bathroom to study, gathering her belongings. Drawers were open, books scattered on the floor, and suitcases half-filled. She'd accept Athena's previous offer to move in with her and Thorne until she found an apartment. The housing market offered plenty of rental options in June. This time, she wouldn't have to rush into an unknown situation or sign a lease under duress.

Besides Nina and the green cabinet, she was leaving only with what she moved in with. "Trav'lin' Light," like the Billie Holiday song. Robin lived in the converted greenhouse behind the Murphy-Kent home, but a section had been preserved to house Thorne's herb garden. Hopefully, the ferns would be a welcome addition.

She'd told Theo once that she never left anything behind. The things she'd rescued—umbrella stand, ceramic pot, ottoman, lamp—would stay, though. They belonged here, like Moose, Coltrane, Ray, and Bessie.

As for her heart...

Amy stacked canvases against the wall. This wasn't hard at all. But then, the shadow of *goodbye* had been behind every *hello* to Theo, hadn't it? It was in his broody frown and silences. In his deceptions. The promise of her childhood crush and secret love was never meant to be fulfilled any more than Marmee's *Little Women* fantasies were.

She placed a pile of sweaters on top of the dresser. A U-Haul van. She had to rent one right away.

Nina strolled in, and scooping her up in her arms, Amy buried her face in her fur. "I'm sure Athena and Thorne won't mind having you around. You're never any trouble."

When Nina rubbed her head against her chin and purred, she nearly dissolved into tears. But Amy Marsden did not cry over breakups. Ever. She let her down, and Nina settled into her favorite nook beneath the bedroom window.

Dropping onto the bed, Amy stared out the window, at the endless void waiting to swallow her, alone in the universe. Until she found a boyfriend, an archaeologist perhaps, who'd fill their apartment with bones and shards of pottery. They'd argue about the sand and silt he trailed through the rooms, and eventually, she'd send him on his way with a clever riposte or two. Along with her next lover, and the next, he'd become another anecdote.

She and Nina would grow old together, surrounded by a jungle of ferns. She'd cremate Nina when she died and put her ashes in a pot the archaeologist had left behind. When *she* died, the obituary would list her once-promising career as an artist and her out-of-print, long-forgotten books on King Arthur and *Idylls of the King*. No mention would be made of her quiet heroism, how she'd gone through life with the knowledge that Aegean Sea–Eyed Theo, her first love, would be her last. A certainty stamped like a tattoo on her heart.

Amy held her breath at the sound of light taps on the door. It creaked open, and Theo's silhouette filled the doorway. The tension in his body rippled through the space between them. Moving as stealthily as one of the cats, he crossed the room and lay on the bed beside her. His chest rose and fell with hers. The heat of his body radiated, warming her like an embrace. His sandalwood scent was so familiar she might mistake it for her own. A peculiar vision came to her—Sir Theo and Lady Amy, lying side by side, immortalized in sculpture upon a sarcophagus.

"Amy," he whispered.

"I'm asleep."

"Can I talk to you anyway?"

"It's a free country."

"Please listen. I want to explain."

"I'm too busy feeling sorry for myself."

"It's important that you understand. Please let me explain."

"You're repeating yourself." And echoing her plea that awful day he shut her out of his life.

"Because I'm lost," Theo said. "I can't find my way."

"Break out the violins, why don't you?"

"I know you don't mean that."

"Yeah. You're right. I don't."

Minutes passed, maybe an hour, days. Time had no meaning in an endless void.

"I've dreaded losing you since the first time we made love." His voice was a low murmur. Almost soothing. Undeniably sad. "Knowing that you wouldn't stay with me if you knew I'd told the press. That I was responsible for everything else that happened, while the blame was laid on you."

Amy blinked back a tear and turned on her side, away from him. "I could only imagine what your parents thought of me. Losing Theo the First's friendship and good opinion, though, really hurt."

"You didn't. Ever. When I told him what I'd done, he was furious. But he understood my reasons. And he was sure that you, he, and Jo would be friends again..." He sighed. "Someday."

"Why cut me out of your life? We were..."

"Getting closer? Simple. To protect you."

"From needy, damaged Theo and his baggage. Get over yourself already."

"I have. But it's been a long struggle healing and letting the baggage go. As was not telling you. The closer you and I became, the harder it was to withhold the truth. It was wrong, and I knew it. When I met Jo at the St. Louis airport, I admitted everything. In exchange for my advice, I asked for hers. After she read me the riot act, she was adamant that I never tell you."

The emphatic shake of Jo's head *no* that Amy had witnessed during their interaction at the airport.

"For God's sake, why?" she asked, turning to face him again.

"She said that to confess would be self-serving and would ease my conscience at your expense. Living with it would be the penance I deserved."

"I deserved the truth more."

"That's what I said. But Jo reminded me that it was you who'd reunited us all. Telling you would rupture us again, undo everything you'd accomplished. It's been hell, though, especially when you said that couples tell each other everything."

"Couples in a healthy, honest relationship."

"I brought it up with her again. This morning, in fact. She ordered me to shut up about it forever. That we loved each other too much to risk losing our relationship over something that happened years ago. The time is right, though, to tell my parents that I—"

"No. Please don't tell them. Don't disturb whatever peace you've found with them. Promise me."

"But you—"

"It's not about me."

The whir of the ceiling fan and Nina's gentle snoring filled the ensuing silence. Calming enough to lull Amy to sleep, a sleep so deep she'd go back to yesterday, to the day before that. Months. Years. To the time when she and Theo were watching *Mister Rogers' Neighborhood*, hand in hand. When they were on the floor of his apartment, on the verge of becoming AmyandTheo. Before misunderstandings and deceptions set them on parallel courses.

"Why did you do it, Theo? Why did you expose your parents to public shame and scandal?"

"To end the rage and dysfunction once and for all. About a week before the exhibit in Chicago, they'd gotten into an argument so fierce I had to tend to their bruises. When I saw the portraits, it was like kneeling on the floor of their kitchen again, sweeping up broken glass. And the shards from the plate I'd thrown in anger." He ran a hand roughly across his face. "The fallout from the scandal gave me a reason to distance myself from you. The day you came to see me, begging my forgiveness...it just killed me. But I believed, in the long run, your life would be better without me. I'm begging *your* forgiveness now."

"You have it. With all my heart. I forgive you, Theo Sinclair."

"Thank you, Amy Marsden." He looked around the bedroom, strewn with clothes and books. "Letting you go, watching you leave, will be more penance. But I accept it as my due."

She twined a curl around her finger. "Here's the thing, Theo."

"There's a thing, Amy?"

"Jo's *heart or art* equation doesn't work for me. *No art without heart* is *my* motto."

"What are you saying?"

"I'm saying that, if you let me go...well, the art world will lose a very talented painter."

"An *extraordinary* painter," he said, a smile relieving the sadness in his eyes.

"And we don't want that to happen, do we?"

"No. We do not."

Amy held out her arms. "Kiss me, Theo. Kiss me like it's our first kiss."

He touched his lips to her forehead, her cheek, the tender spot beneath her ear. "Are you ready?" he asked, his breath becoming hers. "This kiss may last forever."

"You said once that nothing lasts forever."

"What I meant was, nothing lasts forever but us."

"*Now* you tell me."

～⊙

"You're sitting in your underwear, aren't you, Jo?" Amy said.

"See? This is why I hate Zoom. Wanna just talk on the phone?"

"No. I love watching you squirm in the chair like you've got ants in your pants, as Marmee would say."

Jo whistled. "She's going back to college. I never thought I'd see the day."

"You owe her a call. Like, a hundred calls."

"Soon as I finish packing." Jo pointed to the chaos of boxes, stacks of books, and Styrofoam cups half-filled with coffee behind her. "I found that painting of an owl you gave me in all this mess. The one you copied from May Alcott."

"Oh yeah. It was in Louisa's bedroom. Whaddya think? Should we make another visit to Orchard House with Marmee?"

"I can't plan past the next hour. We promised the landlord we'd scour the place so thoroughly before we left that he wouldn't have to hire professional cleaners. We might have to chain Brutus to a chair so he quits wrecking the place."

"*We?*"

Jo bit her lip. "Oops."

"I'm waiting for an explanation, Josyphine."

"I was using the editorial *we*, Amy Mamy."

"Bullshit. Theo told me you asked for advice about a boyfriend. When you decided to take the job, I assumed you broke up, but he said the guy's moving here with you."

"That Teddyhead shithead! He wasn't supposed to say anything."

"There aren't any secrets between us anymore."

Amy had considered admitting to Jo that she had once thought Theo was in love with her. But not telling her balanced the score of Jo's secrets with Theo. And spared her a lifetime of teasing. She did let her know, though, that Theo had confessed he'd informed the press about his parents' identity.

"I just got off the phone with Gary," Jo said. "I thanked him profusely again for alerting us to the vacancy in his apartment building."

"Apparently, it's the apartment I shared with Derek."

"No shit."

"No shit. He's off to New York City to embrace fame and fortune."

"Dickhead."

But an obviously gifted and successful dickhead. And Amy was perfectly fine with that. As she was with Jo having kept her *New Yorker* story under wraps until it was published. *You know I'm ruthless when it comes to my writing*, Jo had said.

"I have something to tell you, Jo." Amy sat back, putting distance between herself and the laptop screen. And her sister's temper.

"More revelations? Geez, I think my next story will be titled 'The Mother Lode.'"

"Remember when you wanted me to intercede with Ben so he'd help you with the Iowa Writers' Workshop tuition?"

"*Intercede?* I think my exact words were, *Get the rich a-hole to fork over some dough.*"

"I lied to you. I never talked to him about it. I was afraid he'd change his mind about paying *my* tuition. Or reduce it so I'd have to get a work-study job instead of using my free time to paint. I'm so sorry."

"Well, shit." Jo scratched her head, frowning. "You mean I never told you?"

"Told me what?"

"He *did* offer to pay. I figured you'd persuaded him."

"No. I never said a word."

"How about that? Ole Buccaneer Ben wasn't so bad after all."

And neither was Amy. How about that?

"Why didn't you accept his offer, Jo?"

"I realized I didn't want to get stuck in your situation where he'd dictate what I did with my degree. Like, write his legal briefs or something. So, I told him thanks, but no thanks. Shit, if I had known this was on your mind all this time..."

"You want to make it up to me? Who's the boyfriend in Seattle? It's Quentin, isn't it? Quentin Scott, Athena and Thorne's best friend."

"Yeah. How'd you guess?"

"He's too big for you to eat and spit out."

Jo roared with laughter. "Broody Bear *did* call me a man-eater."

"How someone larger than life doesn't distract you from writing is beyond me."

"Quentin *enhances* my writing. And he's two hundred percent supportive. When I was dithering about the creative writing position, he flew to St. Louis to see if he could establish a career in the Midwest." Jo grinned. "He said Laurel was ripe for murder and mayhem."

"Only if you write a murder mystery based here. As for mysteries, why didn't you tell me about Quentin? You really hurt my feelings, Jo."

"Because if you had two glasses of wine, you'd spill the beans to Athena. But mostly because we weren't sure it would work out. The two of us have a horrid track record for relationships. Women always dump him; I always dump men. And with you, Athena, and Thorne in the picture, it would have gotten too complicated if we broke up."

Tears filled Amy's eyes. She blew her nose into a tissue.

"Geez, did I hurt your feelings that badly, girly girl?"

"They're tears of joy. Someone won the heart of my prickly Jo. And I really, really like him."

"We met at a lecture called 'Rock On.' We assumed it was about rock 'n' roll, but it was about geology and rock hunting. There we were, a couple of morons, stuck in a room with a bunch of rock jocks. Funny thing was, we actually got into rock hunting."

"Yeah. I saw his ROCKHOUND T-shirt."

"We do it nearly every weekend. We've collected about ten thousand pounds of rocks, which our new landlord will never find out about."

"Do Athena and Thorne know about you two yet?"

"No. Quentin wants to tell them in person. For the dramatic effect. But the heck with that. If you know, they should too."

"One more question. Do you still believe *Heart or art and nothing in between?*"

"Not since Quentin came *in between*. I've got it all!" Jo's phone alarm went off, and she groaned. "Gotta go. Landlord's coming by to check on damages, and we've got to get some serious superglue action started."

"Just think. Me and Theo, you and Quentin—we'll be stuck together with superglue from now on."

Jo made frantic face and body motions. "Leave it to Amy."

Amy grinned. "Leave it to Jo."

CHAPTER FORTY

*I never knew how much like heaven
this world could be, when two people
love and live for one another!*
—AMY MARCH, *LITTLE WOMEN*

I didn't think all six of us would fit," Amy said, squeezing herself next to Theo in one of the Marconi's Pizza booths.

"Seven," Athena corrected her. "Don't forget my bun in the oven."

Thorne placed his hand on her stomach, beaming. "I can't wait to meet this little one. Nine months is an eternity."

"How are you feeling?" Theo asked Athena.

"Fantastic. Except for having to give up wine. And breakfast and lunch, since the term *morning sickness* doesn't cover the half of it."

Lando placed two freshly baked pizzas on the table with a flourish. "One meat lover's and one veggie extravaganza. Knock yourselves out."

"Yo, Lando," Stella said. "You forgot the pepperoni."

"Don't have any. When my parents weren't working together, the deli fell apart. Their meat orders have been delayed."

She rolled her eyes. "I keep waiting for *them* to fall apart."

"Not gonna happen, babe. They're crazy in love."

"You don't know crazy till you've met my mother and her partner," Athena said. "Not only am I pregnant, but my brother and his partner are adopting a child. We've been exchanging tips on how to handle the grandma-zillas."

"Rule number one," Thorne said with a grin. "Lydia and Ricki are authorities on everything, and if we don't follow their advice—"

"Their *well-meaning* advice," Athena interjected.

"If we don't, our kid will be on the run from the law its entire life," Thorne said.

Theo laughed. "Your friend Quentin would be perfect to serve as defense lawyer."

"And you can help if he or she needs a counselor," Amy said to him. "I'll provide art lessons."

"Congratulate Amy, everybody," Theo said, kissing her cheek. "Fiona granted her request to take a year off to pursue her art career."

Athena raised a slice of pizza in the air. "Dr. Amy Marsden prevails over the mighty Dean Fiona Reilly."

"She didn't have a choice," Amy said, laughing. "Not with Brigid on my side. The best part of it is, I won't have to worry about having my mother as a student. She's enrolled for the fall semester."

"Hold on a sec. Who's going to be the department chair?" Athena asked.

"I recommended Gary, and Fiona approved," Amy said.

Athena smacked the table. "Aha! Don't you see? This was his master plan all along. First, he tried to scare you out of the position. When that didn't work, he encouraged you to follow your 'quest.' And he threw in a puppy to sweeten the deal."

"Let's leave the storytelling to Jo," Amy said, grinning.

"And brace for impact," Thorne said. "Quentin will be arriving with her in four days."

"Long enough for Amy and me to say hello and then good-bye," Theo said. "We'll be leaving for Europe the following week."

Amy and Theo's first trip together—and Amy's lifelong wish to wander the art galleries of London, Paris, and Rome come true.

"What about your job?" Thorne asked Theo.

"My supervisor is taking on my clients while we're gone. His kids are home from school, and he's glad for an excuse to get away from them."

"That'll be me and Thorne someday," Athena said. "Can't wait to see the little stinkers, can't wait to get away from them."

"No worries," Thorne said. "Robin and Jaycee have already volunteered to babysit."

"We're going to house-sit for Theo and Amy and take care of all the pets," Lando said. "It'll be good practice for our bambinos."

Stella lifted herself in her seat, her elfin face on fire. "Babies? Who the heck said anything about babies?"

"Aw, c'mon, Stella. You know you want them."

"I do? Since when?"

"Since I first met you and said to myself, *There goes the mother of my children.*"

She jerked her head toward the front of the restaurant. "She's going, all right. Right out the door."

Amy settled back into the booth, watching them spar and spark and listening to Athena and Thorne debate name choices for their baby. Theo's face glowed beneath the lamplight, shining like their future. He turned to look at her and smiled his deep-dimpled smile. Looked at her through the infinite blue-green sea of his eyes into a world of possibilities. Into them, forever, AmyandTheo.

ACKNOWLEDGMENTS

I can't thank the following people enough. Really. I can't. But here goes.

A warm thank-you from the bottom of my heart to . . .

Erin Niumata and Rachel Ekstrom, my agents at Folio Literary Management, for their enthusiasm, guidance, and vision.

Alex Logan, my editor at Forever, for cultivating my manuscripts into bloom and coordinating the various phases of production with grace, humor, and kindness.

The Forever team for their dynamism and creativity: Tareth Mitch, production editor; Kristin Nappier, copy editor; Estelle Hallick, publicist; and Daniela Medina, art director. A special thanks, once again, to Sarah Congdon for the delightful cover.

Friends and readers for their encouragement, insights, and fellowship.

Bob, Bob Jr., and Eddie for being the men you are—loving, honest, and true.

Louisa May Alcott, whose novel *Little Women* inspired generations of women, young and old, to believe that "nothing is impossible to a determined woman."

ABOUT THE AUTHOR

Annie Sereno holds a BA in anthropology from the University of Pennsylvania as well as master's degrees in library science and British and American literature. Among other libraries, she was privileged to serve Harvard University and the National Geographic Society. When she's not expressing her imagination with pen and paintbrush, Annie gardens, swims, and haunts art museums. In possession of a well-worn passport and memories of all the places she's called home, she shares her life with her husband and two sons. Mildly (okay, seriously) obsessed with birds, Celtic music, and all things Australian, she believes there are no such things as a former librarian, no time to read, or too many shoes. She currently lives with her family in New Jersey.